# SUNDERED SOULS

*The Brotherhood of the Eagle Book 2*

## Tim Hardie

**TJH Publications UK**

*For my parents, Brenda and John, who filled our house
with the books that first fired my imagination*

# MAP OF LASKAR

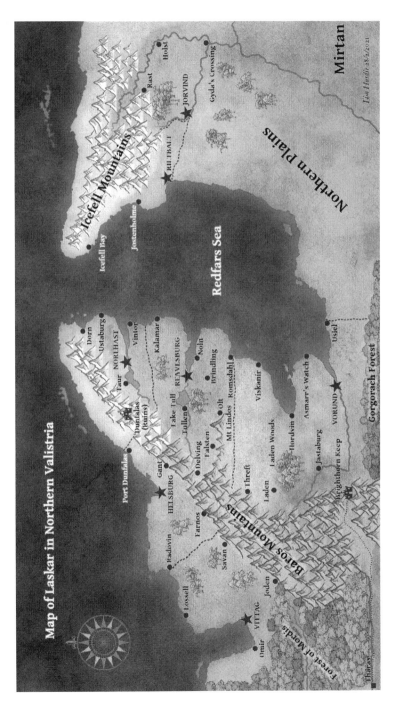

Map of Laskar in Northern Valistria

Icefell Mountains

Mirtan

Northern Plains

Redfars Sea

Baros Mountains

Gorgorach Forest

Forest of Mordis

Holsl
Rast
JORVIND
Gyda's Crossing
RILTBALT
Jostenholme
Icefell Bay
Dorn
Ustaburg
Vintor
Kalamar
Taur NORTHAST
Nolin
Brindling
REAVLSBURG
Fake Tull
Jadken
olt
Komsdahl
Viskanir
Asmarr's Watch
Dunfalas (Ruins)
MT Lindos
VORUND
Usiel
Gant
Delving
Falsten
Threft
Laden Woods
Hordvin
Jastaburg
HELSBURG
Port Dunfalas
Laden
Brighthorn Keep
Radovin
Farnos
Savan
Joden
Lossell
VITTAG
Omir
Tharos

# AUTHOR'S NOTE

Welcome to the second instalment of The Brotherhood of the Eagle series and the adventure set in the disputed lands of Laskar. At the back of this book you'll find a list, summarising the major and minor characters of the story, as well as their houses and their relationship to one another, which you may find useful.

# PROLOGUE

When the sun sets and fires burn low, the bards sometimes tell stories of what lies beyond this life. Everyone knows the avatar Navan is the guardian of the Halls of the Dead. All of us will travel to his halls when our time on Amuran is done, to be reunited with our ancestors and dearest kin. There is no end to Navan's Halls and every soul will be gathered there until Dinas declares that time itself is done. Then the Creator will return, to judge the fate of every soul according to their deeds and the secrets hidden in their hearts. What the bards speak of less is the journey undertaken by every soul who departs Amuran. Navan's Halls are reached by crossing a bridge spanning the river created by time's ceaseless flow. Most souls find the bridge easily, for Navan calls everyone to him and desires that no one should be left behind. However, not everyone is willing to heed his call.

The Warrior trudged through the featureless landscape of the twilight world dividing the realms of the living from the dead. Navan's bridge was always in sight, no matter which way he turned, an elegant structure of living wood, glowing with its own inner luminosity. A steady stream of people walked towards the bridge – men, women, children, sometimes whole families holding hands as they made that final crossing together. The Warrior was surprised to see other races, those forged in secret by Morvanos to wage his doomed war to control Amuran, also making their way towards Navan's Halls. Shuffling ankhalites, covered in tough bony plates, wide-eyed night haunters and powerful winged bashaal were scattered among the humans forming the endless stream of dead souls. He half-hoped to see the fabled dragons or chimera amongst the throng but there was no sign of them. Disappointed, the Warrior reminded himself those races were already dead, long gone from Amuran. No one had seen a dragon or chimera since the War of the Avatars, unless you believed the ancient legend of Sigborn Dragonslayer, of course.

Something held the Warrior back from joining the march towards the bridge. He kept hearing the shouts and screams from the Inner Keep. He'd sworn to protect Asmarr and his family and he'd failed them all. He cried, tormented by his broken oath, and when he wiped away his tears he found his hand covered in blood. Resisting the pull of the bridge, the Warrior walked in the shadow lands. Hungry, thirsty and tired he set one foot in front of the other by sheer force of will, trying to find a way back to Amuran. There had to be a way to right the wrongs of the past. There had to be a way to fulfil his broken oath.

The Warrior crested the summit of a small hill and groaned when he saw the bridge directly in front of him. It radiated a soft yellow light, suffused with warmth and healing. The Warrior knew if he set foot on the bridge it would be a balm to his troubles and soothe away his cares. He would no longer feel the torment of endless hunger and thirst. Instead, he would be reunited with those he loved in Navan's Halls. He hesitated, wondering if they would forgive him for his failure to protect them.

Navan was standing at the entrance to the bridge, dressed in robes of all colours and none. He looked up at the Warrior on the hill and walked towards him. As he drew closer, the Warrior saw that Navan's eyes were bright silver, like a dragon in human form. Whilst Navan's face was smooth and youthful those eyes were old and the Warrior quailed before their gaze.

"What holds you back from crossing the bridge?" Navan asked, his voice rich and melodious. "There is room in my halls for everyone. There is a place ready for you here and your friends await you. You have wandered in the twilight for years.

Do you really want to remain here, trapped between the Realm of Death and the Real? Join me in my halls and your soul will find rest."

"There's no rest for me," the Warrior replied, looking behind him, still trying to find the way back to Amuran.

Navan stared at the Warrior with those silver eyes. It would be so easy to cross the bridge and enter those halls. The Warrior was wrapped in a cloak of weariness and grief. Why not shed those burdens and cross the river? Instead, he stood on the hilltop and waited, tearing his eyes away from the hall and staring into the grey twilight. The clouds hung motionless in the sky above the dreary landscape, the only feature a darker patch of ... cloud? The Warrior wasn't sure what he was looking at. It was like a piece of coiling darkness that rippled and moved, as if alive. As the Warrior stared he thought he heard whispering voices, although he couldn't make out the words.

"You're looking at the Tear," Navan told him. "It's a rent, cutting through the Realm of Death itself. The Tear is so wide it has reached into the other realms."

"What does it mean?" the Warrior asked, unable to stop staring at the living darkness.

"The end of all things."

The Warrior turned and looked at Navan. "*What*? Why don't you stop it?"

Navan shrugged. "This is the time of the mortal races. Those avatars, like myself, who were not banished to the Void reached a pact with the Creator. We withdrew from direct interference in the affairs of Amuran. After the war, the fate of Amuran is in the hands of mortals, not the avatars. Though it grieves me to see what Adalrikr Kinslayer has done, my oath forbids me from trying to prevent it."

That name struck the Warrior like a hammer blow. He felt sick, his vision full of roiling darkness in the chambers deep underground in Vorund Fastness. Adalrikr. The young man he'd sworn to protect. Instead, he'd become the instrument of his destruction.

"If this is Adalrikr's work then my broken oath means I bear some responsibility for this," said the Warrior.

Navan laid a hand on the Warrior's shoulder. "Perhaps. However, you could set all that guilt aside in my halls. Your time on Amuran is done and the future of the world now lies in the hands of others."

"What if I refuse? What if I remain here?" asked the Warrior.

"You would become a shade, trapped halfway between life and death. Why would you choose such a path?"

"To avenge my clan," the Warrior replied, looking up at the Tear. "To fulfil my oath, so I can cross the bridge to your halls with honour rather than shame. You say I can set aside my burdens in the Halls of the Dead. I'm not so sure." When the Warrior turned back to Navan the avatar was looking at him intently, a thoughtful expression on his face.

"The Tear," the Warrior asked. "What can be done? Can this magic be stopped?"

Navan nodded. "If the mortals find a way to defeat Adalrikr it may be possible to close the Tear. *May* be possible."

"Then I should try," the Warrior replied. "Can I return to Amuran as a shade? Can you tell me how to defeat Adalrikr?"

Navan looked up at the Tear and the Warrior followed his gaze. The avatar was silent for so long the Warrior thought he was ignoring his question.

"You can return, if this is what you really want," Navan said at last. "The Tear draws all the realms together and you can follow that path to the Realm of the Real – to Amuran. There you would live a half-life, neither living nor dead, and your presence will be shunned by those you encounter."

"If I can fulfil my oath I'll make the journey. What about my second question? Will you tell me how to defeat Adalrikr?"

Navan's silver eyes glittered and a shadow passed across his face. "Now you ask me to break my own oath. I told you, it is for mortals to decide Amuran's fate. I cannot intervene."

"There must be something you can do," the Warrior pleaded. "How can you stand there and watch all this happen?"

Navan sighed and hesitated before replying. "I can share knowledge, nothing more. Even this will come at a cost. Is this something you're prepared to agree?"

The Warrior licked his lips with a dry tongue. "I'm willing to pay that price if it means I can have my vengeance."

Navan pointed towards the sky. "Look into the Tear. See the realms as they were, as they are and as they will be. Seek out the past and the runes of power."

The Warrior followed Navan's instructions, looking deeper into the darkness. As he watched he saw flashes of the other realms, the Tear running through all of them. The Realms of Dream and Shadow were connected, as were the Real and Navan's Realm of Death. He saw the future of Amuran, the fabric of the world unravelling as it fell in upon itself, millions of souls howling as they were cast into oblivion. He saw the Shadow Realm, inhabited by the banished demons created by Morvanos, imprisoned in darkness so intense it burned his eyes. He saw the Realm of Dream, a broken travesty of the once wondrous place where those with the Sight gathered during the Age of Glory. Reaching into the past, he saw an ancient forge, heat blasting from the furnace. He watched as the seven runes, magic from before the fall, were fashioned in desperate haste by the avatars opposing Morvanos' uprising. They burned with a bright light and the Warrior fought the urge to flee until he had memorised every curve and shape of those symbols of power. The pain grew so intense the Warrior finally had to turn away. His eyes throbbed and he blinked blindly, his face wet with tears, Navan's comforting hand on his shoulder.

"Such knowledge comes at a price," Navan told him. "Return to Amuran and seek out the crippled son of Kolfinnar Marlson. Reveal to him the runes of power and in doing so you will fulfil your oath. Perhaps this will be enough and Amuran may survive the fate you saw."

Far away, Rothgar Kolfinnarson stirred in his bed, disturbed by his strange dream of Navan and the Warrior who refused to enter the Halls of the Dead. When he rose in the morning after his fitful sleep he felt exhausted, more tired than the night before. By the time he'd washed and dressed all memory of the dream had faded from his mind, his thoughts elsewhere as the prospect of war loomed.

# CHAPTER 1

The young man, if I should even call him that, was a pitiable creature; sweat dripped from his brow whilst his eyes darted around, seeking any means of escape. Futile thoughts inside the solid windowless wagon – I'd helped Joldir make this monstrous place, his deft handiwork leaving nothing to chance. The four of us were crowded inside with our prisoner, who sat bound to his chair in the centre of the wagon, manacled and gagged. The stale air stank of sweat and fear, but something else made the small space so oppressive. Every inch of the walls was covered in a dark swirling script, which writhed and moved of its own accord when seen from the corner of your eye. The air shimmered, heavy with an old magic, binding our prisoner far more securely than his solid iron chains.

Petr Hamarrson, the young second-in-command of Johan Jokellsward's company, stepped forward and tugged the gag from the prisoner's mouth, tossing it to the floor. Geirmarr Flint looked unimpressed, the short stocky miner staring down at the shaking man before him. He glanced sideways at Johan, mystified.

"This is what you brought me to see?"

Johan nodded. "This is our real enemy, Geirmarr. You told me the men from Delving wanted to join the Brotherhood and earn your place at my feasting table. All you have to do is take this man's life and pledge yourself to me."

Geirmarr swallowed, looking uncomfortable. Whatever test of strength and loyalty he thought Johan might set, Kalamar's jarl had confounded his expectations. Next to me Petr drew his sword, the prisoner flinching at the ring of steel. The yellow light from the lantern hanging from the roof of the wagon retreated in the wake of a harsh blue glare emanating from the half-dozen runes running up the length of the blade. Even in that strange light I could see Geirmarr's face pale.

"There seems little honour in killing such a man. What was his crime?" asked the elder of Delving, his voice uncertain.

"His crime?" Johan seized the young man's chin, forcing him to look up. "This is a spy sent by Adalrikr Asmarrson, the so-called king of Laskar. A spy, trying to gauge the strength of our forces and discover our plans. You found us more prepared than you expected, no?" Johan spat into the prisoners' face, his own contorted with hatred.

"Please, Johan," the young man begged. "I had no choice –"

"How dare you use our chief's name. You're speaking to Kalamar's jarl," Petr cried, dealing the man a fierce backhand blow with his free hand, which would have upended the chair had it not been fixed to the floor. The prisoner's head snapped back with the force of the impact, blood flowing freely from his broken nose. It ran down his face and over his dirty shirt, a red stain spreading out across his chest as he gasped for breath, shaking with fear.

Even with a broken nose I could see he was a good looking. They all were, since the durath spurned the old, the ugly and the sick. People looked twice now at anyone who was young and handsome. At least I was safe – my misfortunes had some compensations, after all.

"What name do you go by?" I asked, trying to keep my voice calm. The man turned to me, a faint glimmer of hope in his eyes.

"Gerrick ... my lord ..."

"I'm no lord, at least not any more. Thanks to your kind my ancient family home at Ulfkell's Keep now lies in the hands of my enemies. My name is Rothgar Kolfinnarson. You may have heard of me."

Gerrick's eyes widened even further, starting from his head as my words sank in. I made sure my smile remained in place. Hope is powerful motivation for the desperate.

"I don't enjoy seeing this," I continued, glancing around the cramped confines of the wagon and trying to ignore a wave of seasickness as the runes shifted on the walls, giving the impression the floor was tilting. "Believe me, we've barely begun. I've been tortured myself. By the time Tyrfingr Black-eyes finished burning off half the flesh from my body I happily confessed to all manner of crimes I never committed. I told the world I'd conspired in the deaths of my brother, his wife and their son; my own nephew. I did it gladly – anything to make the pain stop. The durath feel pain, don't they?"

Our prisoner nodded, looking like he was about to be sick. Next to me Johan had a hungry look, one I'd seen before when we interrogated durath.

Gerrick's capitulation was sudden and complete, his voice shrill with fear. "Please, you don't need to hurt me. I'll help you. I'm sorry … I'm sorry for your loss –"

"You're sorry?" roared Johan, reaching forward and grabbing Gerrick's bloody shirt. The material split at the seams around his shoulders, several buttons pinging around our feet. "Kalamar Castle, my family's home, is nothing more than a smouldering ruin on the shores of the Redfars Sea. Your people torched our lands, murdered most of my household and you give me your worm-ridden *sorry*?"

"This one's weak," Petr observed. His sword was still glowing blue as he levelled it at Gerrick, giving his face a ghoulish pallor.

"Weak is good," I said, laying a gentle hand on Johan's tense shoulder until he relaxed. "There's no need to break those already broken. This one can help us."

Gerrick nodded eagerly. "I will. I'll help you." Johan shook his head in disgust and released his grip on the man, who slumped back into his seat with a rattle of chains.

"Start by telling us who you are and where you came from," I said.

Gerrick took a deep breath. "This body was a tribute,

brought across the sea from Riltbalt after Gunnsteinn Haddison's clan surrendered to King Adalrikr's army, led by Geilir Goldentooth. After the Calling I found this body to my liking. The young man was too afraid to fight me and I broke his spirit."

I frowned, puzzled. "The Calling?"

"The Calling from the Shadow Realm," Gerrick told me, words spilling from him like water pouring through a broken dam. "The durath were lost in the shadows until Adalrikr built his sacred gateway, where his tributes wait for us. If we are worthy and step out of the shadows into the Real we prove ourselves ready to serve him. Sometimes ... sometimes I wonder if it would not have been better if I'd failed that day. My soul would have been scattered to the four winds but at least I'd now be at peace."

I knew what Johan and Petr were thinking; recalling the stone archway Sandar Tindirson had built in his long hall in Tullen. The one Joldir had destroyed. I kept my face friendly, hiding my eagerness to know more. "Adalrikr's gateway. Are you saying he built this for the durath, as a way to bring others of his kind to him?"

"Yes, King Adalrikr built an opening into the Shadow Realm. I wandered there without hope, lost for over two hundred years, until the Calling. There is no way you can resist when one of the Sundered calls you, you must believe me. I was compelled to serve him, once I had returned to the Real. My king sent me north, posing as just another man answering Johan Jokellsward's call to muster arms, so I could spy upon you. I had no choice in the matter."

"You had the choice about taking an innocent life," muttered Johan darkly, arms folded across his chest.

Gerrick cringed. "You're right, my lord. I was given a chance to live again after so long in the darkness and, to my shame, I took it ... with ... with no thought of the consequences. I'm not proud of my actions and what I've become. You have no idea of the *temptation* King Adalrikr placed before me ... the unadulterated *pleasure* of the flesh." Gerrick's face twisted, his handsome features ugly, grasping, greedy. The transformation was gone in an instant.

"Another of your kind, who went by the name of Sandar Tindirson, said something similar to me once. There was an archway in his long hall, set upon an altar. Are there many of these archways from this Shadow Realm leading to Amuran?"

At my question Gerrick shuddered and looked away. "King Adalrikr was so angry when he learned what Sandar had done. Only the Sundered have the right to call forth their servants but Sandar put himself above his king, gathering his own shadow spirits. He opened his gate so slyly my lord never knew it existed until your warriors destroyed it. His fury that day ... My king is not a man you would ever wish to anger."

"How many of these gates are there?" I pressed. "Sandar's gate was destroyed. Does Adalrikr control the only remaining way into this Shadow Realm?"

"How many?" Gerrick's sweaty brow furrowed as he considered the question. "It is not for a lowly servant to know the secrets of the Sundered."

"You keep talking of the Sundered. I know King Adalrikr is the First of the Sundered and went by the name of Vashtas during the War of the Avatars. Are you telling us the oldest of your race, those who first heeded Morvanos' call, have joined him?"

A short laugh escaped from Gerrick, quickly stifled as blood bubbled up through his shattered nose. "Johan Jokellsward leads his men bravely to war against foes you barely understand. Your ignorance and arrogance will be punished –" Johan's fist connected with Gerrick's face with a crack, whipping his head around. His chin dropped onto his chest, bloody spit mingling with the mess down the front of his torn clothing.

"I'm tired of listening to this nonsense," growled Johan. "Let's do what we came in here to do."

"Wait," I said. "There's more we can learn."

Johan shook his head, flexing his sore hand. "I've already heard enough. This thing will say anything, peddling false secrets it pretends we need to understand. All in the hope we'll listen and keep it alive."

"We're listening to the ravings of a madman, surely," Geirmarr said hesitantly, as if he wanted one of us to laugh and say this had all been some grand joke at his expense. If only that were true.

"You'll find out when you stick him through with this," Johan replied, taking Petr's sword and thrusting the hilt into Geirmarr's hands.

Geirmarr paled. "You really want me to kill him?"

"If you want to join the Brotherhood of the Eagle you must understand this is no easy path and no ordinary foe we face. Are you with us?"

"Right," muttered Geirmarr, starring at Gerrick, breathing hard in his chair. His hand wrapped around the hilt of Petr's sword, testing its weight. "Right then."

Gerrick had recovered enough to raise his head and he looked from Geirmarr to me, eyes pleading as they stared into mine. "Please, you must listen to me. I can still be useful to you. I helped you and answered all your questions and *this* is my reward?"

"I made no promises," I whispered.

"But I *helped* you!" Gerrick screamed moments before Geirmarr drove Petr's sword into his heart with a loud cry.

The blade bit deep, runes glowing and Gerrick grimaced, broken teeth glistening red with blood. Geirmarr grunted and pulled out the sword, the steel etched with five glowing blue runes, the sixth now dark as night. Flame began to lick around the wound in Gerrick's chest and we all took a step backwards, suddenly wishing Joldir had built a bigger wagon. Gerrick screamed as tongues of fire burned around his lips. The fire spread rapidly as we continued to back away, watching as Gerrick's whole body was consumed with roaring flame. As suddenly as the conflagration had started the fire went out and when my eyes adjusted to the darkness Gerrick was gone. There was only a pile of smoking chains on the floor. The blue glow of Petr's sword slowly faded to nothing, the lantern swinging crazily back and forth above us, casting ever shifting shadows on the walls and doing nothing to help my sense of balance in this awful place.

"Welcome to the fight, brother," said Johan, clapping Geirmarr across the back. Geirmarr grunted, shaking his head, and there was a loud clang as Petr's sword hit the floor.

*\*\**

I took a deep breath as I clambered down the steps from the wagon, grateful to be outside in the fresh warm air of the summer evening. Geirmarr was a few feet away, hands on his knees, bent forwards as he retched onto the ground, spitting several times. His younger cousin, Geirmundi, looked on anxiously. When Geirmarr had recovered, Johan and Petr escorted the Flints towards Johan's tent. I paused when I saw Arissa hurrying towards me, her long auburn hair framing her pretty face, which was marred by a deep frown.

"Is it true?" she asked, struggling to catch her breath. She'd obviously run all the way from hospital tent. "Ingirith said there'd been an attempt on Johan's life."

"Hardly. This tale is less than two hours old and already the wild rumours have started. We've apprehended a spy in the camp, that's all." Arissa looked towards the dark wooden wagon behind me and she swallowed. I answered her unspoken question; word would be all around the Brotherhood soon enough. "It was a durath, posing as a westerner from Delving joining Johan's call to arms. He got as far as Johan's tent, tailing Geirmarr, when Joldir's runestones stopped him."

"Thank the gods." Arissa ran a hand through her loose hair, pulling it back and tying it behind her. "Did you ... speak to him?"

I nodded. "The wagon's runes did their job. Once inside he couldn't flee the body he'd stolen, although this one lacked the strength to take another host, even if he'd wanted to. Adalrikr's testing us, probing this new threat from the Reavesburg Clan. He'll learn much merely from the fact his spy does not return."

Arissa pursed her lips. "Perhaps Johan will think twice now about working Joldir to death. He's been repaying him poorly of late."

"That's unfair," I said, my voice rising more than I'd intended, turning the heads of several folk in the camp. I made a conscious effort to lower my tone. "We're at war –"

"Don't talk to me like I'm a child, Rothgar. I've been stitching Johan's wounded men back together ever since we started out from Falsten this spring. More of them might have lived if Joldir had the time to help me ..." She raised a shaking hand to her face, rubbing her green eyes. Tired eyes. Rest was hard to come by and as soon as the men of Delving were ready Johan would have us on the march again. It was unwise to linger too long in one place.

I reached out and took Arissa's hand in mine, squeezing it gently. I felt the anger fall away from her as I enfolded her in my arms, kissing her gently on her forehead.

"I'm expected at the Brothers' Table," I told her. "After that, I'll pay Joldir a visit, I promise."

"Johan's driving him too hard," Arissa replied. "Not everyone possesses the zeal for the Brotherhood burning in Johan's heart. Some people are frightened at where he's leading us. *I'm* frightened."

"You'd be a fool not to be."

\*\*\*

I headed towards the entrance of Johan's large tent in the centre of the camp, walking between two of the runestones I helped Joldir craft, the surface of each densely packed with the same flowing script adorning the walls of the wagon. Two guards stood either side of the open tent flap, one of them nodding in acknowledgement as I stepped inside. Although the summer days were lengthening it was dark and cool within. Johan sat at the head of his feasting table, lit by dozens of candles running its length, surrounded by most of the Brotherhood. My old friend Bandor, Johan's only son, sat in a place of honour at his father's right. He smiled warmly at me as I took my seat halfway down the Brothers' Table, squeezing in between the greybeards Varinn and Old Gunnar.

Towards the head of the feasting table a grey-faced Geirmarr Flint had been rewarded with a place close to Johan, as befitted his status as a noble and elder of Delving. Opposite him sat Sigolf Admundson, Falsten's elder. Whilst Geirmarr was still a relatively young man, broad shouldered from a life spent working Delving's mines, Sigolf was no longer in his prime. Enormously fat, his jowly face was bright red, resembling an apple set on a beer barrel. His thick fingers constantly worried at his short neatly trimmed white beard. Sigolf had been the first to pledge himself and his men to the Brotherhood's cause, swelling Johan's band of thirty warriors and assorted camp followers with two hundred karls and fighting men. Sigolf realised there was no going back after Varinn lynched the small garrison of Adalrikr's men stationed in Falsten. Regardless of his motives, those two hundred proved enough to help Johan Jokellsward rout the occupying Vorund Clan from the much larger mining settlement of Delving five days ago. Geirmarr's force of six-hundred-and-fifty men had been bought for the price of some twenty lives, leaving Johan with a small army at his command. The Brotherhood of the Eagle was growing in strength as the men of western Reavesburg rallied to Johan's call.

"Geirmarr," Sigolf shouted in his deep voice. "You look like you need a drink. Maeva, pour this man an ale."

Across from me I saw Brandr scowl at Sigolf casually ordering his wife to serve drinks. Still, Maeva and the other warriors' wives were better off here, waiting on Johan's table. Ekkill already had many of the young women following the camp in his service. The prospect of them whoring their way through our newest recruits offered a perfect opportunity to further line his purse. I glanced up and down the table and saw

Ekkill and the rest of Ulfarr's crew were absent. Maeva poured ale from a jug into Geirmarr's cup and the man drank greedily, to shouts of encouragement from the rest of the men, led by Sigolf. As he set down his drink Johan stood to address those assembled before him.

"My brothers, we welcome a new face to our table this evening. Flint here has killed one of the shadow spirits, sent by Adalrikr to spy upon us. He has slain our true enemy with his own hand, earning the right to sit at the Brothers' Table. Geir-marr Flint, the Brotherhood of the Eagle drinks a toast to you. The Reavesburg Clan will rise up, thanks to men like you, and together we'll drive Adalrikr Kinslayer from our lands."

"Geirmarr Flint!" shouted Svan opposite me, the big warrior raising his own mug.

"Geirmarr Flint," answered the Brotherhood and I raised my ale with the rest of them, drinking deep. I tried not to think of Gerrick's frightened eyes as he died. It was a death with no honour, like the ones suffered by the men Varinn had hung in Falsten's town square; these days honour mattered little.

I looked at Johan as he stood watching the men toast his newest ally. His frame was lean, face hungry, and there was a sheen of sweat on his brow. A concerned expression briefly passed across Bandor's face as he watched his father. The light from the candles gave Johan's visage a hollowed look, dark shadows gathered around his high cheekbones and eye sockets. Johan had always been a gaunt man but, ever since that first battle with the durath in Tullen two months ago, his zeal to see them defeated consumed him.

Food was served by Maeva, Dalla and Johan's own wife, Damona, to the fifteen men gathered around his table. Aside from the elders of Delving and Falsten a dozen of those men were from Johan's own household of Kalamar. The mighty army that once protected the Reavesburg Clan's northern bor-ders was now reduced to this small band. Then there was me, the only representative from Ulfkell's Keep, the seat of power for the Reavesburg chief for generations until Tyrfingr Blackeyes murdered my brother Jorik on Adalrikr's orders. My hand tightened around my knife at the memory as I ate the roasted beef, a gift from Geirmarr's own herd.

After Tullen had been torched and the durath slain Johan swore his vengeance on all their kind, founding the Brotherhood of the Eagle. Many men followed Johan, believing he would lead them to victory and liberate Reavesburg's lands from the Vorund Clan. However, only a few were invited to join the inner circle of the Brotherhood itself. It included those of us who fought in Tullen, although Johan extended the group to include the remaining men of Kalamar under Varinn's command, who had been guarding the wagons and caravans we'd sent ahead to Falsten. Ulfarr and the five men in his crew, who comprised the rest of the Brotherhood, had questioned Johan's decision at first.

"My men have all earned their place, whether they fought in Tullen or not," Johan told him. "Some might question your presence, Ulfarr. You and your followers were all outlaws until I pardoned you. Some might argue you deserve the gallows for your past crimes, rather than a place at my table as one of my closest advisors." Wisely, Ulfarr chose not to press him further.

Although I was noble born, I felt I had more in common with Ulfarr's men than the warriors of Kalamar, with the exception of Bandor. I missed their presence at the table tonight and leaned close to Old Gunnar to ask him where they were. The old man turned towards me, digging a thick finger into his ear and rummaging around as if this was a cure for his deafness. Few men were better with a bow than Old Gunnar; fewer still were as hard of hearing, forcing me to shout my question at the top of my voice as Varinn chuckled next to me.

"Ulfarr's crew have been sent to scout out the eastern road ahead to Olt," Petr explained.

Sigolf's thick white eyebrows rose as he turned to Johan. "You don't need to send out scouts to learn what lies that way. Olt's a walled town with its own fortress and a garrison of

Adalrikr's warriors hiding inside. A tough nut to crack with less than a thousand men at your command."

"Olt's going to be much more heavily defended than Delving or Falsten," added Geirmarr. "We've still got lads recovering from the wounds they got freeing this town. They'll need a few more days yet, time which will bring more swords to your muster."

Johan shook his head, looking at Flint with his bright blue eyes. "The men answering that call have slowed to a trickle, Geirmarr. A few more stragglers won't make any difference, but staying too long in one place will. Word of the defeat in Delving will reach Tyrfingr Blackeyes and he'll want to take his revenge soon enough. We'll strike camp in the morning and make for Olt before they have time to gather their forces."

Geirmarr pursed his lips, weighing up the options. "We could lose a lot of men taking Olt back from the Vorund Clan."

"Adalrikr's not going to surrender the territory he stole from us without a fight," Johan replied. "Remember what you said when you pledged your men to fight for the Reavesburg Clan. The time to act is now. If we don't our clan will be forgotten in a generation. Do you want your children to grow up serving the durath, the flower of their youth offered up in tribute each year? You've seen how those tributes' souls are sacrificed to devilry."

Petr leaned across the table. "Hrodi Myndillson's able to call on more than a thousand men, who could join us if Olt is freed." As ever, the young man was fervent in his support of Johan.

"Old Hrodi still has those thousand because he was quick to bend the knee when Tyrfingr Blackeyes butchered my family," I observed. Silence fell across the table and all eyes turned to me as I broke a heel of bread, using it to mop up the last of the meat juices from my trencher.

"Always the one to doubt, Kolfinnarson," Svan muttered, the thickset warrior looking at me with disdain. "Maybe the rumours are true and Blackeyes cut off your stones that day in Ulfkell's Keep."

Bandor came to my defence. "I don't remember you standing at our side, Svan, when we fought those skin thieves in Tullen."

"Aye, and Rothgar's made a fair point," added Varinn, the old warrior speaking up for the first time. "You don't get to be Whitebeard's age without being cautious. Who's to say Old Hrodi will welcome the sight of our men marching towards Olt? If he weighs the odds and thinks they lie in the Vorund Clan's favour we could find ourselves fighting *against* his men. After all, he's been barracking Adalrikr's warriors in his town for over a year without a whisper of any opposition."

Johan sat listening to the debate, taking his time, thinking things through. Johan was a dangerous man to fight; a man who strove to end Adalrikr's bid for power in his measured and calculating way. The table fell silent when Johan spoke.

"Hrodi Whitebeard is Gautarr Falrufson's sworn bannerman, the loyalty of their houses entwined for over one-hundred years. Gautarr's still under siege from Adalrikr's army, so the majority of our enemy's forces are surrounding his castle in Romsdahl. We have to break that siege if we're to win this war and Hrodi's house is duty bound to come to Gautarr's aid. You're right, Varinn; a cautious man like Hrodi won't like those odds but Whitebeard's no oath breaker. A week from now we'll have our thousand swords."

The men cheered and pounded the table, though Geirmarr looked thoughtful as he drank. He would have to be made of stone not to have some reservations about the path he was embarking upon. Adalrikr Asmarrson called himself King of Laskar, making us traitors in his eyes. For all Johan's confidence we were taking the biggest risk yet in our short campaign of resistance. Olt was an important town and well-defended, especially now news of the western uprising had spread across Reavesburg. A great deal hung on the true extent of Hrodi's loyalty to Gautarr Falrufson.

# CHAPTER 2

The Brotherhood drifted off into the night, some of them laughing and signing. I smiled watching Sigolf weave his way through the camp, his giant frame supported with some difficulty by Eykr and Ragni. I turned as I felt Johan's hand on my shoulder, Bandor at his side.

"You need to find it in your heart to forgive Hrodi," Johan said. "He had just a score of men with him in Ulfkell's Keep and the fortress was in Blackeyes' hands before anyone rose from their beds. What choice did he have that night, other than to surrender?"

"Brunn Fourwinds didn't surrender," I countered.

"Yes, and Brunn died. His courage was a futile gesture," Johan sighed, his face in shadow. "I share your misgivings, but we need Hrodi Myndillson's men if we're to win this war. We have to secure Olt before Blackeyes sends his forces against us."

"We'll have to face him, sooner or later." Our spies reported Blackeyes held Ulfkell's Keep, the strongest fortress of the Reavesburg Clan until its fall through treachery, with a thousand warriors, whilst Sinarr the Cold One had six thousand men under his command laying siege to Gautarr Falrufson's castle. Both enemy forces had to be destroyed, although either battle looked likely to spell the end for the Brotherhood of the Eagle, with or without Hrodi Whitebeard's aid.

Johan put his arm around my shoulders. "There'll be a reckoning soon enough. Ulfarr's scouting party will be back soon with news of Olt's defences; then we'll know what we're facing and can begin planning our next victory." Johan pressed Geirmarr Flint's sword into my hands, a finely worked piece of steel. "I sent word to Joldir earlier today to ready the forge.

Take this to our artificer and tell him I want it ready by next morning."

***

Word of our imminent departure quickly travelled round the camp. I weaved my way through the canvas town amid sounds of raucous laughter, singing around cook-fires and men sharpening their steel on whetstones. Joldir's tent lay to the edge of the camp surrounded by a circle of runestones, a dull orange glow emanating from the temporary forge erected next to it. Leif was there, the boy's skinny form a black outline as he worked the bellows. Joldir stood next to him wearing a thick leather apron, arms folded across his chest as he supervised his charge. Leif was an orphan from the town of Tullen, its sole survivor after Johan's raid. Ingirith, Rugga's widow, had offered him a home with her two children but Leif preferred the company of Joldir and Arissa. Joldir possessed a knack for collecting waifs and strays and Leif was the latest beneficiary. The boy was also gifted with the Sight. Such was his ability, I suspected that under Joldir's guidance it wouldn't be long before Leif's power rivalled my own.

"Rothgar," Joldir said by way of greeting. I could see why Arissa worried for her adoptive father. Joldir's brown hair was streaked with grey, his face pale and his skin waxy. He had neglected to shave since our arrival at Delving and several days of stubbly growth did little to improve his appearance.

I passed over Geirmarr's sword. "We have a new member of the Brotherhood. Geirmarr Flint took the life of a durath spy earlier today and has pledged his cause and his men to ours."

"And his reward is the forging of a runeblade for this … miner?" Joldir spat sourly into the fire. "Preparing the forge meant I was unable to join the Brothers' Table this evening."

"We missed your presence. Johan appreciates the work of our artificer –"

"Does he? There's space at his table for Ragni, who has scarce any more wits than when he was born, and Old Gunnar,

21

a man as deaf as a stone whose main gift to the world these days is his breathtaking ability to break wind. These are bold men of *Kalamar* after all, so a place at the Brothers' Table is rightfully theirs. I don't recall either of them fighting side by side with us in Tullen, do you?"

I swallowed, wondering how best to approach Joldir in this mood. "Johan knows how valuable you are," I said at last, ignoring his jibe at the elevated status of Kalamar's warriors. "You're his artificer and no one else can forge the runeblades he needs to put an end to the durath. You're one of the most important members of the Brotherhood."

Joldir pursed his lips, a stubborn look on his face. "Johan doesn't like it, though, does he? Look how he tasked you to help me with the runestones and the inscriptions on the wagon. He's made you my apprentice. Perhaps he thinks that one day he can manage without the master."

I shook my head, unable to believe Johan to be as black-hearted as Joldir made out. Johan had always been a trustworthy friend to me, and we were also family by marriage. By marriage and blood.

"He doesn't think that. This is tiredness talking."

Joldir snorted. "Yet I'm the one spending the night in the forge. Runestones are one thing but tonight Johan demands another runeblade, irrespective of the worth of the man wielding it. You don't just make one of those by rote, lad. Forging a magical rune in hot molten metal requires something more. A piece of my soul goes into each one of these, not that Johan cares."

I took my time, controlling my temper, remembering Joldir had given up his home and livelihood to follow Johan. He had his own reasons to hate the durath, reasons he had yet to confide in me. Even so, I knew Johan could only push Joldir's loyalty so far.

"You're right," I said finally. "I'll speak to Johan. In his zeal to see the durath defeated I don't think he understands the toll it's taking on you." I laid a hand on his shoulder and after a moment Joldir placed his on top of mine, his grip firm.

"I'm sorry lad. I'm worn thin, that's all. Geirmarr Flint will have his runeblade come morning. I think the forge is hot enough to begin my work."

"Do you think it will take all night?" I asked, though I already knew the answer. "I was hoping to walk the Path tonight, to see what was happening in Ulfkell's Keep."

Joldir stiffened at my words. "This is no easy task Johan has set. Promise me you won't do anything tonight whilst Leif and I are working here. Remember, Nereth is still out there, watching for you."

"All you ever do is watch *her*," piped up Leif as he continued to work the bellows, the fire now white hot, the heat in the tent almost unbearable. I felt my face redden, knowing it was nothing to do with the forge.

"There was something else I was going to ask," I said, keen to change the topic as Leif smirked. "The durath we captured spoke of the Sundered Souls before Johan had him killed."

Joldir looked at me, his brows furrowed. "What exactly did he tell you?"

"He confirmed much of what we already knew; that Adalrikr is the First of the Sundered Souls. He also told us Adalrikr was gathering his forces to him using something he described as the Calling. It must have something to do with the archways, like the one we destroyed in Tullen, which Gerrick told me Sandar built in defiance of Adalrikr. Gerrick said Adalrikr has constructed another of these gates and is using it to summon the durath to him."

Joldir took a deep breath, rolling his shoulders as he stretched. "There's proof, if we ever needed it, of Adalrikr's ambitions. Make sure you tell Etta what you told me and we'll speak more on the road tomorrow, I promise."

I left Johan and Leif to their work at the forge and walked into the night. Delving nestled at the foot of the northern range of the Baros Mountains on the far side of the valley where we had made camp. Yellow lamplights shone in the darkness beneath a weight of black shadow, the mountains cutting a dark swathe through the night sky. Above their jagged peaks the stars glittered where they were not hidden behind strips of grey moonlit cloud, sent scudding eastwards by the high winds. Fate drew the Brotherhood east, back to Olt and Joldir's former home in Lindos. Drawing us into further conflict with the Vorund Clan and the power of the durath that sat behind them.

# CHAPTER 3

"Well?" Etta peered up from her bed, the old woman fixing me with a piercing stare; one eye milky and clouded, the other dark brown, almost black. An oil lantern hung from the top of the tent, shedding a warm yellow light by which she was reading a bundle of loose papers. A small fire burned low in a pit near her bed, giving off a dull red glow as it died down.

It was growing late and I was relieved Etta was still awake. These days she slept more and more. Bedridden since falling ill at Falsten, Etta never left her tent; increasingly frail and helpless, a shrunken figure wrapped up in thick woollen blankets. Her body might be failing but she wielded considerable influence within Johan's camp; her spies reported to her regularly, her first apprentice Ekkill chief amongst these. When the scouts returned from Olt I was sure Ekkill would be visiting Etta as soon as he had delivered his report to Johan, if not before.

"Don't just stand there," grumbled Etta, setting the papers aside and struggling to sit upright. "Close the flap and keep out the cold, for heaven's sake. The last chill I caught in Falsten nearly killed me. I certainly don't want to catch another!"

I hastened to obey, stepping inside and drawing up a stool next to her bed. When I asked her how she was keeping Etta sighed irritably and waved my pleasantries aside.

"Good as it is to see you, I can tell when you've something on your mind. I'm too old to waste my time on idle talk, so let's hear it."

I gave Etta my report, reflecting how I'd become another of the spies serving her. Etta had trained me well, and I began with the events earlier in the day when Gerrick and been captured. She listened patiently as I explained what had taken place in the wagon and afterwards during Johan's feast.

"We're heading out at first light, so you'll need to get ready," I told her as I finished my tale.

"Here, put these on the fire," Etta replied, passing over the papers she'd been reading. I took them from her thin bony hand and held the corners against the glowing embers. The flames sprang from the pit, eagerly wrapping around the parchment. When they were lit I dropped them into the fire, watching them blacken and curl before turning into white ash, their secrets known only to Etta.

"There, I'm packed," Etta said with a grin.

I smiled, looking around the neatly ordered tent. One chest containing a few clothes and blankets, a small table on which some bowls, cups and other utensils were neatly stacked and a woven basket with spare parchment and writing implements. Meagre possessions for someone who'd spent their life as the advisor to three chiefs of the Reavesburg Clan, first in the time of my grandfather, then my father and most recently my elder brother, Jorik. More than forty years' loyal service had seen her reach her hundredth year. Until she became ill and bedridden in Falsten I'd imagined her to be an eternal force; always at the side of our chief, offering him counsel and wisdom. Now I realised the time when we relied upon Etta's guidance was coming to an end.

"Do you think Gerrick was telling the truth?" I asked.

"You were the one interrogating him. What do *you* think?"

"Johan thought he was playing for time but ... I couldn't say why, exactly, but I believed him."

"And you think killing him was a mistake?"

I frowned. "We can't imprison every skin thief we find in our camp, it's too risky. I would have preferred more time with him, though, to learn more about the durath. I think this one would've talked."

I stared at Etta, who was lying there with a smirk playing at the corners of her mouth. She shivered and wrapped herself more tightly in her blankets. "After two hundred years everything concerning the War of the Avatars is little more than folklore, but there are legends about the rising of the Sundered. When Morvanos first began to plot his rebellion against the Creator he knew he needed an army. He secretly forged new races in darkness, deep within the bowels of Amuran; the bashaal as his messengers and scouts, ankhalites to fight his battles and the shadowy night hunters as spies and assassins. Morvanos also called the original twenty-one Sundered Souls to him, formless spirits able to cast out a person's soul and clothe themselves in their stolen body. The Sundered supplanted many of the rulers and key officials in the human kingdoms. Morvanos was able to use their influence to foster discontent between them in the years leading up to the War, leaving them distracted and unprepared when his army struck."

I nodded and smiled patiently, knowing all this already. Etta's mind wandered more these days and it was not uncommon for a story to be retold. I found it was easier to allow such conversations to take their course, rather than hurry them along. "And these Sundered Souls, Morvanos' original servants, they survived the War?" I asked.

Etta shrugged under her blankets. "Who can say how many of the Sundered survived the War and the centuries that followed? What is clear is that we face a powerful foe in Adalrikr now one of the Sundered has taken him. Adalrikr's spirit possessed the Emperor of Valistria and from that lofty position he did terrible things during the War. That was when he first became known as Vashtas, the Flayer of Souls. History will repeat itself if we don't find a way to stop him gathering the durath to his side."

"If the durath were cast into the Shadow Realm, how did shadow spirits like Adalrikr escape?" I asked. "Surely the Sundered would have been cast into the Shadow Realm along with the rest of the durath?"

Etta cast me a shrewd look. "Now that part of the legend is only found in fragments of text and obscure references. Remember, the Creator only cast the *avatars* into the Void at the end of the War."

I frowned, puzzled. "I'd always assumed the Creator banished the durath as well. Isn't that right?"

"No. If he had, why didn't he banish the other races Morvanos raised in his bid for power? Why not rid Amuran of bashaal, for example? The Creator taught that all life is sacred, and the durath are still living beings. No, it's hardly spoken of but this was one of the dark deeds of Vellandir, carried out as the War ended and the Creator summoned the warring avatars to him to prevent Amuran's destruction."

"I've never heard of this. I thought Vellandir was the avatar of law and justice?"

"Justice depends very much on your perspective," Etta remarked. "Vellandir knew the Creator would banish him and his followers, so he worked one last act of revenge. It was Vellandir who cast the durath into the realm of shadows, an act that probably sealed his own fate. However, in his haste the magic he worked was flawed and the oldest and strongest of their kind managed to resist the spell. The Sundered remained on Amuran and after two hundred years it would appear Adalrikr has finally found a way to bring the durath back into this world."

I pondered on Etta's words, trying to see the durath in the way she was describing. I'd never thought of the shadow spirits being alive, yet as I recalled the look on Gerrick's face I realised she was right.

"So how many could be brought into Amuran through the Calling?" I asked.

"Based on the number of young tributes Adalrikr has demanded from the conquered clans there will be *thousands*. And remember, durath were created from a corruption of the Sight. Adalrikr's gateway would not only draw the durath but also those susceptible in the Real as well." There was a hint of desperation, perhaps even fear, in the old woman's voice. I swallowed and tried not to dwell on the task the Brotherhood was undertaking or the risks I faced, as one blessed by the Sight.

"We need to discuss this further with Johan."

Etta sighed. "I've always liked Johan. He has a thoughtful, measured way about him; a good counterpoint to the more ... direct approach your father and brother both possessed. Lately, though, his visits to my tent have been less frequent. There's a bitterness in him, fuelling his fervour since Kalamar's destruction left him a landless jarl."

"Johan's never really recovered from Rugga's death in Tullen," I mused.

Etta sat forward, her face hard. "None of us could possibly have guessed Sandar had turned the entire town into shadow spirits. Not even Adalrikr knew Sandar was building his own army in secret. All could have been lost that day."

"What it proves is the durath aren't of one mind," I said, pushing the memories of the destruction of Tullen aside. "Not all of them want to serve Adalrikr."

Etta placed her wrinkled hand on mine. "Perceptive as always. Johan thinks he can end this struggle by driving his sword through Adalrikr's heart, yet he understands little of the world he is dealing with. He needs my advice now more than ever before and, when I'm gone, he'll need your counsel too." Etta meant well but her words sharply reminded me of everything Tyrfingr Blackeyes took from me when he broke my body. That's all I'd ever be now – Johan's counsellor.

"I haven't forgotten how to wield a blade," I told her. I stood and drew my short sword in one swift fluid motion. The blade was feather light, beautifully etched Sunian steelwork worth a princely sum, gifted to me so I could control the sword with some of my old skill. I stared at the three runes running along the length of the blade, dragon and chimera locked in battle, each glowing blue. I swallowed and glanced at Etta.

"The durath have already infiltrated the camp," she told me, no hint of surprise in her face. "They will be watching and biding their time, waiting for the right moment to strike. All of Jokellsward's ambitions teeter on the brink. One wrong move, and everything could be lost before we even join battle with the enemy at Olt."

I sheathed my sword, trying to ignore the shake in my hand as it rattled as I drove the point home into my scabbard. "You should reconsider having someone guard your tent." Etta made a disparaging noise as I made for the tent flap. "Arissa will help get you ready tomorrow. You'll be riding in the cart with her when we set out on the road."

"Rothgar, one more thing." I turned back towards Etta. "Johan needs to make use of the Sight. In you, Joldir and Leif he has a powerful tool at his disposal."

I paused. "Reave forswore the magical arts long ago when he founded our clan and Johan holds the same views. It's hard enough to be accepted in the Brotherhood now with everyone already thinking of me of being ... tainted with the dark arts."

Etta looked at me, her lined face stern. "Even though you bear a runeblade, everyone in the Brotherhood knows your days as a warrior are behind you. Johan is never going to win this fight by force of arms alone. He doesn't have the men and his enemies will use magic against him. Adalrikr Kinslayer is no Laskan warrior following the code of his forefathers; he'll use every means at his disposal, fair or foul, to win this war and Johan needs to do the same."

I folded my arms, sceptical. I was tolerated in the Brotherhood rather than accepted. In Laskan society every man aspired to be a warrior who would bring glory to his household through battle. Those who practised the magical arts were shunned and regarded with suspicion.

"There's a reason those with the Sight keep such things a secret," I told Etta.

Etta closed her eyes, breathing in deeply. "There's no

honour in defeat. Johan knows that taste all too well." Etta nodded towards the short sword hanging from my belt. "Bandor gifted you that sword and asked Joldir to carve not one but three runes into the blade. Only Bandor, Johan and Petr have more powerful weapons. If they are willing to use the power of the runeblade, they can be persuaded to embrace the Sight."

# CHAPTER 4

It was pitch black when I returned to my tent. The camp was quiet and still except for the distant sounds of Joldir working at his forge. I wrapped myself up in my bedroll and, despite Joldir's advice, contemplated using the Sight to check on Desta's welfare. I told myself I was gathering intelligence on events in Ulfkell's Keep but Leif and Joldir both knew the truth. Desta had been my first love. It was too late to recapture the past, since Desta was now married to my old friend Haarl and had given birth to their first child earlier in the year. I kept watch on her from time to time, using the eyes of those I could reach through the Sight. It was a comfort knowing she was as safe as anyone could be, living under occupied rule in Ulfkell's Keep.

I was tired and decided Joldir was right. It was safer to use the Sight in unison with him and Leif, rather than venture out alone. That path led to another battle-front, beyond the physical world of the Real. I ignored the temptation, instead holding onto the cherished memory of the time I'd spent with Desta, eventually falling into a deep and dreamless sleep.

*** 

The long column stretched out along the road from Delving; an assorted mixture of carts, wagons, animals and people. The majority were travelling on foot, whilst a few more fortunate individuals, myself included, made the journey towards Olt on horseback. The passage of so many people churned the rutted road into a muddy track, coating feet, hooves and wheels with sucking muck and slowing our progress to a crawl. Although we were protected on all sides by Johan's warriors, in this formation we were still vulnerable to attack.

"We'll be lucky to make ten miles today," I remarked to

Bandor, who was riding alongside me.

"It's slow going. Our men could make faster progress if we weren't dragging half of Falsten and Delving with us."

In addition to the eight hundred warriors who responded to Johan's call to arms, we probably had more than a thousand camp followers. Some of these were essential for Johan's war effort; smiths, fletchers, tanners, carpenters, physicians, servants and cooks all played their part. Even the women Ekkill recruited as whores were an ever-present aspect of any long-standing army. However, there were also the wives and children of many of our fighting men, as well as those too afraid to remain behind in their towns and villages once Johan's army struck camp. For many of them, especially the young and old, making such a long and arduous journey was probably more dangerous than remaining behind. Privately, I wondered if Etta would be with us by the time we reached Olt, still several days ahead at our current pace.

"I'll be happier when Ulfarr and his crew report back with news of the road ahead."

"More members of the Brotherhood would certainly be welcome," Bandor agreed, glancing down and half drawing his sword from its scabbard. I saw the six runes glowing blue, their light faint clear even in the midday sun.

I nodded. "I saw the same myself last night. There are more skin thieves hiding within the camp."

"Can't Joldir find them?" Bandor asked.

"It takes time, skill and more than a little luck. The magic in the painted wagon is strong, but no durath will enter there willingly and we don't have enough runestones to protect every part of the camp. We were fortunate with the last one, yesterday. I can't help wondering if the attempt was so crude it was simply a ruse, designed to make us over-confident."

Bandor pursed his lips. He was of an age with me, eighteen, but just as my broken body put years on me so Bandor's expression belied a life of hardship this past year-

and-a-half. When your father was leading a rebellion against the self-styled King of the North, making you the target for every assassin's blade between here and Reavesburg, life's cares weighed heavy on your shoulders.

I reached over, patting his arm. "And we'll remain vigilant, I promise you. We're prepared for this fight."

"I'm not so sure ..." Bandor glanced around, making certain we were not being overheard. "Amongst the Brotherhood, I'm sure you're right. However, who can vouch for every member of Sigolf Admundson's or Geirmarr Flint's company? Who knows what those men are really thinking, after learning the true nature of their enemy? And if the durath are present here already, then surely it's only a matter of time before the Vorund Clan tracks us down. I'm afraid Tyrfingr Blackeyes is merely biding his time, waiting to choose the ground that favours him in the coming battle."

"Blackeyes' warriors are stretched too thin," I pointed out. "His main forces lie many miles away, besieging Romsdahl, allowing us the opportunity to gain ground in the west. Whilst Falrufson resists Adalrikr's occupation Blackeyes' hold on Ulfkell's Keep isn't as strong as he'd like. A thousand men can defend that stronghold easily. Patrolling the wider lands of Reavesburg is another matter."

Bandor chuckled, running a hand through his red hair. "Who'd have thought we'd owe Gautarr Falrufson such a debt?"

"You'd better get used to thinking better of him. That's your future ... I'm not sure what you'd call him. Future father-in-law? Uncle-in-law?" Bandor was engaged to Freydja, Gautarr's niece, although he had raised her as his own since the death of his brother, Egill.

Bandor laughed, the sound quickly dying. "My father's landless. Gautarr broke off your engagement with Freydja when you were the clan chief's brother. What makes you think he'll honour the promise he made to my father?"

"Your father might be chief soon enough. No, listen to me. Even though Gautarr has more men your father is a natural leader and he ruled Kalamar wisely. Trust me, in the clan moot people will want to follow Johan Jokellsward, not Gautarr Falrufson."

"I see some sense in those honeyed words," Bandor grudgingly agreed. "You remind me more and more of Etta with each passing day." Bandor paused, seeing the dismay on my face and laughed. "I mean that as a compliment, honestly! I mean you help me see things differently. My father thinks the same."

I saw my opportunity. "Speaking of Etta, I need to ask you a favour. There's something I'd like you to raise with your father ..."

***

Etta's tent was crowded that evening; Johan stood at the foot of her bed, alongside Bandor, his blue eyes regarding her intently. I helped Etta sit up, resting her on numerous cushions and pillows although she still looked old and frail. Joldir and Leif stood on the other side of her bed, waiting to hear Johan's decision.

"Well, Etta, you've not lost your ability to surprise me," Johan said finally, after what seemed like an age. "I don't like this proposal. The last time I encountered Sight magic was when Nereth's coven kept Karas Greystorm in thrall in Norlhast. They nearly killed Rothgar and his sister, Nuna."

I glanced at Etta, who nodded at me. I took a deep breath and tried to find the best way to explain things. "Coven is an ... emotive word. Using the Sight as a group is more powerful and effective, as well as being safer than doing so alone. Adalrikr recognised this, using Nereth's coven to control the Norlhast Clan. Make no mistake, your enemy is not from this world. You've already embraced the need for a magic to destroy the skin thieves – every member of the Brotherhood carries a runeblade, forged using Joldir's magic. You've had me and Joldir paint runestones to guard your tent and prepare a warded prison for any durath we capture. So please, think carefully, because Adalrikr will employ the Sight against you and Nereth is not the only spellcaster in his service who can use this gift. If you don't use every weapon at your disposal, you give him the advantage."

Johan looked at me for the longest time. He was one of my late father's oldest friends, those rough features always made soft by his smile. It was a long while since I'd seen that smile; his face taut, his long once fiery hair now thinning, more grey than red. We'd all changed since the fall of the Reavesburg Clan last year.

"This is all I have to offer," I pressed, willing Johan to listen to me. "Blackeyes shattered my body and stole the life I would have had as a warrior and jarl to my brother. When Joldir nursed me back to life from my deathbed the Sight awoke in me. The good fortune of Dinuvillan brought us back together again for a reason. The fact that Leif, who shares the same gift, was rescued by you in Tullen is no coincidence either. The durath spared him because those with the Sight have value. Together we can help you. All I'm asking for is the opportunity to serve you fully, so I can play my part in bringing down Adalrikr and have my vengeance."

Leif spoke up, his voice small as he stared at his feet. "Please listen to him, sir. The Vorund Clan killed my sisters and the durath stole the souls of my parents." He looked up from his boots and fixed his gaze on Johan, who nodded encouragingly. "I can help you with this magic Joldir's been teaching me, but I'd still be here, even if I was just washing pots. You're the only one prepared to stand up to Adalrikr, to face the Vorund Clan and take the fight to them. Everyone else ran away or bent the knee. I can't do that."

"How old are you, boy?" Johan asked kindly; the true voice of my father's friend.

"I've seen seven summers, my lord."

"Young to have suffered so much. Bandor, what do you have to say concerning all this, since you asked me to attend Etta this evening?"

Bandor swallowed. "We're outnumbered, at constant

risk of attack and possess few friends. If there's a chance to use this opportunity, we should take it."

Johan nodded, deep in thought, his brow furrowed. He turned towards me and smiled. "Then we shall use every advantage."

# CHAPTER 5

When Johan asked me to explain the workings of the Sight I was struck by the words that came to mind. Freedom, flight, knowledge, perspective, intimacy, understanding, fear, pain; every word describing life, both in turbulent times and when at peace. The Sight was more than observing events as they unfolded; instead, you experienced other peoples' lives as if it was happening to you. The only limitation was they needed some measure of the Sight themselves so I could make a connection.

Other than Leif, who'd sought me out, I'd only been able to consistently touch the lives of people I knew. My sister, Nuna, was one, now the young bride of Karas Greystorm, the Norlhast chief. Djuri was another – a warrior in my brother's service, he'd bent the knee to Adalrikr after the fall of Ulfkell's Keep and now served in Tyrfingr Blackeyes' army. Leif's inclusion in our Fellowship (the word we chose, as Johan disliked the idea of having a 'coven' in his service) changed all that, as we discovered on the first day we joined together after securing Johan's consent.

Whilst it wasn't the first time we'd followed the Path together, I wondered if the open approval of Johan Jokellsward gave us more freedom and confidence. Perhaps it was Leif's burgeoning skill that gave us greater reach. This time, when Joldir, Leif and I stepped beyond our physical bodies the experience was bewildering. I could sense *all* those within our camp who could be reached through the Sight. There were dozens of them – perhaps as many as a hundred, their mingled voices clamouring loudly for attention.

I ignored the incessant chatter of the camp and sought

out the familiar path to Ulfkell's Keep. We each had a part to play, each according to our natural abilities. Joldir acted as the anchor, holding the three of us together and disguising our presence, calming what he called the wake that marked our passing. In contrast, Leif's ability was akin to raging waters, full of relentless energy that was hard to control and direct. Yet somehow, there seemed to be a bond between me and the young boy, which perhaps explained how and why he had first sought me out when he was imprisoned by the durath in Tullen. I was able to channel his power and bring it into focus, seeking and finding those I could reach with the Sight. Now when I made those links it was effortless rather than exhausting. I began to understand why the loss of her coven had so profoundly affected Nereth, forcing her to use the Sight on her own.

At Ulfkell's Keep Tyrfingr Blackeyes was sitting on Reave's Chair, looking bored as he presided over a feast. The Great Hall was packed, full of raucous laughter and singing, as the Vorund Clan celebrated news of the surrender of the Riltbalt Clan on the eastern coast of the Redfars Sea. It meant they controlled the lands of Reavesburg, Norlhast and Riltbalt. Adalrikr was now able to focus his attentions to the west of the Baros Mountains and the territory held by the Helsburg and Vittag Clans and further east to the Jorvind Clan, whose fortress was set on the banks of the Icefell River.

Djuri was standing guard behind Blackeyes, a significant honour for a Reavesburg warrior. There were many like him who had turned their cloak, following the surrender of most of the clan's surviving elders. Tyrfingr Blackeyes, Jarl of Reavesburg, knew he could never hold the town of Reavesburg and its surrounding lands without the tacit consent of those he ruled. Generous terms were offered to those members of the Reavesburg Clan willing to serve a new master. Djuri didn't pretend to like how matters had turned out, but he was a practical man and there had been a distinct shortage of palatable alternatives not ending in the hangman's noose. Or worse.

Blackeyes' second-in-command, Galin Ironfist, was also in close attendance, as the Reavesburg warriors would never be trusted entirely. Djuri listened as Darri struck up a tune and began to sing a new ballad dedicated to Adalrikr, to riotous approval from those gathered in the hall as they pounded the long table and began to join in. Someone stood up at the back of the hall, shouting drunkenly. Darri played on, raising his voice to try and drown out the racket, until a piece of bread was thrown, hitting him squarely on the head and bringing his ballad to stuttering halt. Djuri felt for the man, once renowned as one of the most skilled bards in Laskar, now reduced to little more than Blackeyes' fool.

Tyrfingr raised his head and looked in the direction of the disturbance. His soft voice carried the length of the Great Hall and stilled the hubbub in an instant. "Bjorr. I was enjoying Darri's song. What was so pressing you had to rudely interrupt him?"

There was a ripple of nervous laughter before the Great Hall fell silent. Bjorr, in whose company Djuri now served, rose unsteadily from his seat.

"Well?" Blackeyes' pressed.

Bjorr coughed and cleared his throat, not enjoying being the centre of attention. He took a breath and placed both hands on the table. "I was just saying, Tyrfingr, how it gets to be frustrating, being stuck inside Ulfkell's Keep. Seems like others are busy taking the spoils, while we're holed up here with nothing to show for our efforts."

Tyrfingr swept his long, black hair out of his eyes and regarded Bjorr. "Are you saying you're displeased, being in my service?"

"What? No, Tyrfingr. No, not at all." Bjorr stood there, fumbling for the right words as Blackeyes continued mercilessly.

"We hold Ulfkell's Keep, the principal fortress of Reavesburg and the Reavesburg Clan's seat of power for generations. They have bent the knee and paid us tribute. You should know, Bjorr, you collected it on my behalf and took your share. Do you feel I wasn't sufficiently generous with you and your men?"

Tyrfingr rose from Reave's Chair and began to walk down the steps of the dais. Djuri glanced at Galin, who nodded, and both men fell into step beside him as he advanced the length of the Great Hall.

Bjorr sobered up fast and put out a placating hand towards his jarl. "Look, chief, there's no need to take things that way. Just the drink talking, that's all. Just saying we've been here a while, whilst others took the spoils when Kalamar fell or when the Riltbalt Clan surrendered."

Tyrfingr was a relatively short man, dwarfed next to Djuri's powerful frame. Bjorr shrank away from him all the same. It was the eyes. Completely black, fathomless and unnatural orbs that betrayed no emotion. It was rumoured Tyrfingr Blackeyes was half-demon and Djuri had certainly never been able to hold that stare for long without flinching.

"It's true, we've been at Ulfkell's Keep for over a year. Men like you are used to raiding, not occupying foreign lands. Sitting here, day after day, it plays on a man's mind. Men of action, forced to wait, can become restless and start to look for life's next adventure. Is that what you want? An adventure?"

Bjorr was no coward, but facing Tyrfingr all his bravado melted away. He licked his lips and swallowed, looking down at his half-finished meal on the table. Tyrfingr's question went unanswered.

"I see." Tyrfingr looked around slowly at his men, all watching him intently. "Perhaps it feels as if we're idly spending our time here, rather than joining our brothers across the Redfars Sea to witness the Riltbalt Clan finally surrender to us after generations of animosity. You need to remember we're no longer raiders. I rule here in the name of Adalrikr Asmarrson, King of the North, and his command is for us to hold Ulfkell's Keep and keep the supply lines open between here and the siege in Romsdahl. Do you object to the task you've been given?

Do you object to the command of your king?"

"No, my lord." Bjorr's voice was little more than a whisper.

"No. You have proved your worth, Bjorr, and you will have the chance to do so again before long. Word has reached me of an uprising in the west, led by Johan the Landless. He's gathering his forces to him and he must be stopped before he reaches Reavesburg."

"You want me to deal with him, I will," Bjorr replied, drawing a murmur of support from his crew.

Tyrfingr nodded. "I see I can count on you." He turned to Djuri, who found himself staring into the dark pools of those eyes, his own reflection deep within. "Djuri, as a native you know these lands better than most. I want you to take half the garrison stationed at Ulfkell's Keep and lead them west to deal with Johan Jokellsward. He can only have a small number of skilled warriors at his command. Bjorr here can act as your second."

Djuri found himself gawking at Blackeyes, drawing a thin smile from the man. Quickly he collected his thoughts. "As you command, my lord."

Tyrfingr returned to Reave's Chair, sitting down and watching languidly as the feasting resumed and Darri struck up his song once more. Djuri took his place at his new master's side and tried to work out exactly what had just happened. His eyes met those of Bjorr, staring at him darkly from his place at the table, his remaining food untouched.

***

"So, Adalrikr is set on seizing Onundr Arisson's lands in Jorvind now Riltbalt has fallen." Johan's face was ashen.

"I warned you of the scale of his ambitions. It comes as no great surprise," commented Etta. Part of the bargain I'd struck involved giving my reports to both Johan and Etta, which meant we gathered in her tent. Varinn and Harvald, both Kalamar's warriors, stood guard outside this evening, whilst Petr and Bandor also accompanied Johan to our meeting.

"Djuri, leading a force against us?" Bandor shook his head. "He was one of Jorik's most loyal warriors. He helped Halfhand train me when I lived at Ulfkell's Keep."

Petr swore. "Now he fights for the Vorund Clan. Whatever he once was to you, Bandor, he's a traitor now, nothing more."

"A traitor leading five hundred men against us," added Etta. "Interesting. Tyrfingr Blackeyes appears unaware of the strength of your forces, Johan. Whatever spies Adalrikr has placed in our camp, word of our true strength has not yet reached him. Better still, Rothgar can follow Djuri's movements and make sure we always stay one step ahead."

Petr looked unconvinced. "It's not just a matter of numbers. Five hundred well-trained warriors who know the territory can move much more quickly than we can. Knowing where they are may not be enough to avoid a confrontation we can ill-afford at the moment. We need Hrodi to join this fight and counter the threat posed by Djuri's men."

Johan's eyes narrowed. "Petr's right. However, we should still reach Olt before Djuri's forces find us, which gives us time."

"Just the small matter of Old Hrodi joining our cause," I remarked. "Petr's quick to call Djuri a traitor, but Hrodi Whitebeard pledged himself to Adalrikr too. We'll need one traitor to turn his cloak again if we're to defeat another."

Etta leaned forwards, her face more alive and animated than I'd seen in months. "All too true. Now you're forewarned, Johan, do you see how you can benefit from the Sight?"

"And what of our scouts? Is there any word from Ulfarr and his men concerning Olt?" Johan asked me.

"I can't use the Sight to see everything that is happening around us," I explained. "Not everyone can be reached that way and it takes time and energy –"

"Rest tonight, then," Johan answered brusquely. "Now, more than ever, I need your eyes added to those of my scouts.

Find us a safe path to Olt so I have the time I need to prepare for the arrival of Djuri's forces."

***

"Already he looks to you," Etta told me as I drew the blankets around her. I'd stayed behind after the others left, helping her to prepare for bed.

"He still doesn't understand the Sight. I've so much to learn myself and he's placing all these demands upon me, as if I can answer his every question."

Etta gave a throaty chuckle. "Better to have a part to play in all of this. I've served this clan for over forty years and I was old when I served your grandfather, Marl. The trouble with living to my age is you have to watch everyone else leave this world. Sometimes I feel ... left behind. I feel *old*, one of those pieces of baggage slowing us down. Petr was right about that."

"It's not like you to be so self-pitying," I chided. "You're the one that pushed me to appeal to Johan and offer my services to him, so don't pretend you don't enjoy pulling the strings. Johan still values your counsel, that's why he was here tonight."

"He values people like Petr Hamarrson more. Petr's an able young man, no doubt, however Johan likes him because he's loyal and never disagrees with him. That's where you can help, challenging Johan's thinking as well as keeping watch on those around him."

"And who do you think I should be watching?"

Etta wrapped the blankets even more tightly around her. "Why do you think I want you to use the Sight? You're the one who's supposed to be telling me."

# CHAPTER 6

Johan's table was uncharacteristically quiet when the Brotherhood ate together the following night. Spirits were low after a day trudging through constant rain, reducing our progress to a crawl. Petr estimated we'd managed to move eight miles closer to Olt, although I heard Varinn confide to Brandr he thought it nearer five. By either measure, it was nowhere near enough.

Sigolf, his white beard stained with grease and fat, bit into a roasted chicken leg, swiftly stripping away the meat. Licking his lips he pointed the bone at Joldir. "So, you're Johan's artificer? We've you to thank for our runeblades and the runestones guarding Johan's tent?" Joldir inclined his head with a thin smile, looking tired. Sigolf raised his cup. "Here's to Joldir of Lindos, then. A man of rare skill and knowledge. No wonder Johan kept you hidden away."

Most members of the Brotherhood raised their cups and drank to Joldir's health, though with little enthusiasm. Svan refused outright, as did his friends Harvald and Faraldr. Sigolf looked surprised and rounded on the men.

"In Falsten it's considered bad manners to refuse to share a toast. Has this man wronged you in some way?"

Svan met Sigolf's gaze. "Your new friend has his uses but … He's not a warrior, nor does he follow our code. In Tullen he let our friends walk into a trap. Perhaps if he'd chosen to share what he knew then Rugga, Ham and Kimbi might still be alive. You said as much yourself, Johan, yet now we're expected to break bread with him."

"I don't recall you objecting to my company, Svan, when I offered you and your wife shelter in Lindos last winter," Joldir replied.

"In Lindos you were Joldir the Healer. Now we've seen ..." Svan shook his head and looked away, drinking deeply.

"Say it." Everyone turned to look at me, surprised at my intervention. "But if you do, Svan, you say it to me as well as Joldir. And think carefully about your words. You weren't even there at Tullen when we fought the durath."

Svan looked at me for a time. "I was going to say I never thought I'd consort with those who practise sorcery and dark magic. You being noble born, Rothgar, and part of Johan's family by marriage I can see he'd have to offer you a place at his table to avoid giving you insult. Can't pretend I liked it but this, this is different."

"How so?" asked Damona, sitting at Johan's side.

"Come, Damona," interjected Dalla, Svan's wife. "Surely you see how this flies in the face of the Laws of Reave. Sharing a table with sorcerers – what they do is *unnatural*."

Damona smiled. "If my husband says it's right, then it's right. Svan carries a runeblade forged by Joldir, his only real defence against the shadow spirits we've sworn to fight."

"One I'm proud to carry too," added Sigolf. The Flints nodded in agreement at his words, Geirmundi now also a member of the Brotherhood as Geirmarr's second. "I may be an old man but after what I saw ... Joldir has given us the tools with which to fight this evil. To disrespect him in this way dishonours the very code you hold so dear."

"I wield my axe in accordance with the warrior's code," replied Svan, his face reddening. "The Brotherhood of the Eagle should still stand for the ways Reave laid down, long ago. A true brotherhood of the warriors of Reavesburg. These days it seems being a warrior counts for little."

Johan stood up, placing his hand on Damona's shoulder. "You're mistaken, my friend. Times have changed. Force of arms can never win this fight. Our foes use magic against us and unless we embrace such things we face certain defeat. It's through the skills of Rothgar and Joldir we know Djuri Turncloak leads a force of five hundred men against us, before he even left Ulfkell's Keep. They've helped defend us, armed us for the struggle that's to come and are to be afforded the honour and respect they deserve."

Johan raised his own cup. "Whole or cripple, warrior or sorcerer, man or woman we are one brotherhood. We have but one cause and our differences will not divide us. All those gathered around my table tonight share my vision to rid the north of this evil. Nothing else matters. A toast, then, to the Brotherhood of the Eagle."

All drank to that, even Svan, Faraldr and Harvald.

***

Arissa greeted both of us with a hug when we reached Joldir's canvas-covered wagon. She could tell something was wrong, and we told her what had taken place that night.

"After everything you've done for them," Arissa said with contempt, wrapped up within thick blankets as we sat there, gathered around the dying flames of her cook fire.

"I was hardly surprised," Joldir told her. "Magic helped break Amuran during the Wars of the Avatars. Generations of rejecting such things are not lightly set aside. I actually admired Svan for being honest and saying what I'm sure many of those within Johan's inner circle really feel. Their position and status within the clan is under threat now there is a new way to rise to power."

"I'm not a sorcerer," Leif said, poking at the fire with a stick and stirring it briefly back into life. "I just see things, that's all."

Joldir smiled and ruffled his hair. "Not tonight, you won't. It's getting late." Leif looked sheepish and poked at the fire again. I could guess why he seemed so guilty.

"You've already used the Sight today, haven't you?" I said. When Leif didn't reply I knew I was right.

"Leif?" Joldir asked, his voice stern.

"I didn't *use* it – not on *purpose* anyways. I was just dozing when Arissa was cooking and I saw … I saw her again. My mother."

"We've been through this, Leif," I said. "The durath took Lina. The woman who was once your mother is gone. I'm sorry, but it's the truth and you need to remember that."

"She's different now," Leif insisted. "She was cruel to me in Tullen. She's different now she's living with Humli – kinder, more like her old self."

Joldir sighed. "It's late. We'll discuss this properly tomorrow and in the evening we'll send our apologies to Johan Jokellsward's Brotherhood. It's time for our small Fellowship to gather and discover the truth of things through the Sight." He gave Leif a meaningful look. "Together."

*\*\**

Humli sat back in his rocking chair, the one his grandfather had made, and took a long, satisfying draw on his pipe, filling his mouth with the pungent smoke. After a moment he breathed out, eyes closed, allowing the smoke to escape through his nose. Sitting in his porch he sensed a familiar presence and opened his eyes. There was his daughter, Desta, the babe wrapped in blankets clutched tightly in her arms, standing at the gate at the end of his small garden, watching him with a smile on her face. Humli broke into one himself and rose stiffly from his chair and waved her forwards, placing a finger to his lips at the same time.

"Lina's sleeping," he told her in a whisper as she approached, before drawing her into a hug. The light was beginning to fade and Humli realised Desta must have walked all this way on her own.

"Where's Haarl?" he asked, taking the proffered basket of food as he did so. Desta's face crumpled at those words and Humli stared at her, unsure what to do. He hugged his daughter again, patting her on the back with his free arm.

"He's gone."

"Gone? Gone where? Gods, he's not *left* you, has he?"

"What?" Desta laughed amid her tears and stood back, wiping her face. "No, of course he hasn't. I mean he's leaving Ulfkell's Keep with Djuri. Oh, Father, I'm worried for him."

Humli hugged his daughter again, making the gentle shushing noise he used to calm her all those years ago when she was just a babe, even though she was now a mother herself. As he did so the door opened and Lina stepped out, pausing when she saw Desta. Desta broke away from her father and walked towards the other woman.

Humli had thought before how alike they were in many ways; both slender of build with dark hair and hazel eyes. He'd pulled Lina from a boat drifting on the River Jelt earlier in the spring, offering her sanctuary. What else could he have done? Lina was with child and had no one in the world she could turn to. It was only in the weeks that followed, after he'd asked Desta for help, that it had dawned on Humli how Lina bore an uncanny resemblance to his long dead wife, and hence to Desta.

Humli wasn't sure what set of dire circumstances had led to him finding Lina, half-dead from exhaustion and thirst, but it was clear she was afraid of the Vorund Clan. He'd never thought of himself as a hero – fishing was all he knew, never changing his daily habits even after he'd been given his freedom by Kolfinnar Marlson. Still, there was something about the young woman. Humli found courage he never knew he possessed, hiding her in his small cottage and away from Blackeyes' reach. She was due to give birth any day now and Humli shared what little he had, so she would be strong enough to provide milk for the baby. He was getting old and found he ate less these days. It was no real hardship, and he liked having someone else around. He hadn't realised how much he'd missed company until Lina arrived. Desta had always been a good daughter, helping out whenever she could after her mother died. But she could earn more as a maid working in Ulfkell's Keep for the lords and ladies there, so Humli agreed to let her go. Her duties kept her working from dawn till dusk, meaning her visits were less frequent than he would have liked. This wasn't like her, though, to arrive unannounced at the end of the day.

"Desta," Lina said by way of greeting, clasping the other woman's hands. "How's your little boy doing?"

Desta smiled. "Well enough. He's growing fast. Carrying him here it seemed twice as far as it did last month"

Lina peered into the bundle of blankets, stroking the boy's cheek with her finger. "He's a strong one, little Finnvidor."

Humli tutted and drew on his pipe again. Haarl had looked up to Finnvidor Einarrson, jarl to Jorik Kolfinnarson and his father before him, and had taken his death hard on the night Ulfkell's Keep fell. He admired Haarl's desire to keep his commander's memory alive. Still, a name like that drew unwelcome attention in these troubled times. As a pretty young woman Desta already had enough of that from the Vorund Clan.

"He certainly is," Desta answered. "And how are you doing? Your time must be close now, surely?"

Lina ran her hands protectively over her stomach. "Yes, it's not long now."

Desta's smile faltered and Humli drew on his pipe to steady his nerves, because he could tell something was wrong. "Desta, my love, what's happened? Where's Haarl?"

Desta told them about the orders Tyrfingr Blackeyes had given Djuri two days ago in the Great Hall. "Djuri's no fool. Bjorr is furious at being made his second, so he needs men close to him that he can trust. He's asked Haarl and Ulf to ride out with him, just in case, but even if all goes as planned and Bjorr follows his orders they're still in danger. Johan Jokellsward won't surrender, I know he won't and if it comes to fighting ... Well, Johan's Company of Shadows are dangerous." Desta's dark eyes were bloodshot and tearful. "Father, I can't go through this alone."

"You won't have to, my love. I'm here and so is Lina. You're safe with us and I'm sure Haarl will be safe too." Although Humli wasn't too sure about that last part it seemed the right thing to say.

"That's what Cook said. She told me she can manage without me – that I can come back when things are back to normal. It's just … Some of Blackeyes' men at the keep won't leave me alone, even though I'm wed to Haarl. With him gone …"

"Then you'll stay with us until he returns," Lina told her. She smiled, holding Desta's hand. "We'll be like sisters."

# CHAPTER 7

"Slow down. Slow down and let me *think*." Etta had been my tutor since I was a boy and her sharp voice still had the ability to bring me up short. "Stop and think about what Desta was saying. With Haarl away she's far safer living outside Reavesburg with her father, away from Blackeyes' men."

"With Lina. Etta, she's one of the durath. She kept Leif imprisoned in a cellar when they were in Tullen and she was one of Sandar's followers. They tried to kill us."

"And has she done Humli any harm? He's only shown her kindness since he rescued her."

"Etta, will you listen to me, please!" I shouted. I caught myself before I said more, aware how my voice would carry beyond the tent. I continued in a lower voice. "She's one of the *durath* and now Desta's living under the same roof as her. What did she mean when she said 'We'll be like sisters'? She's going to do something to Desta, I know it."

"I don't believe that," counselled Etta. "This isn't the same as the situation you faced in Lake Tull. There, Sandar had established a gateway he could use to call the durath to him, so he needed new victims to become hosts for the skin thieves. Lina is completely on her own, without such powers or allies."

"Then what did she mean?"

"Has it occurred to you that perhaps Lina is lonely?"

"Pardon?" I stared at Etta, hardly able to believe I'd heard correctly.

Etta reached out and prodded my forehead with a bony finger. "Think. We know from your interrogation of Gerrick that Sandar was acting outside Adalrikr's orders. Lina was one of Sandar's creations, so she has no idea whether she would find favour with Adalrikr if she were to declare herself openly. And then there is her unborn child to consider."

"Lonely?" I repeated.

"The durath are *people*, just like you and me," Etta replied, a note of irritation creeping into her voice. "People with their usual wants, desires, fears and dreams. And a child. No durath in history has given birth to a child – the very idea is alien to them when they're immortal, moving from host to host. Why is Lina different?"

"She was pregnant when the durath took her? At least, that would be my guess," I answered.

"No – that was my first thought too, but the dates are wrong. The child is due now, which means Lina fell pregnant last autumn and we know she was already one of the durath by then. Once taken, the durath's host ceases to age or develop, yet Lina *allowed* herself to fall pregnant. Perhaps it was an echo of her host's desire to move on with her life after losing both her daughters. Maybe it came from the desires of the shadow spirit itself. Who can say? What I do know is this child is significant, I feel sure of it. And vulnerable too, which might be why Lina is seeking shelter with Desta's family."

"What does this mean? What is the child? Durath or human? Something else?"

"Honestly? I don't know."

"That's little comfort. Desta could still be in danger and there's nothing I can do."

Etta reached out and took my hand, fingers pressing hard. "Help Johan. We can do nothing about events in Ulfkell's Keep unless we ally ourselves with Hrodi and strengthen our forces. That needs to be the focus of your Fellowship."

"We can't mention this to Johan. Lina's child could well be innocent and free of any taint. I'm not sure that's how Johan would see it, though."

Etta frowned. "Keeping secrets from Johan? You're becoming more like me with each passing day."

I pursed my lips, the comparison unwelcome. "I just

want to understand things, that's all. None of us know what Lina's child means and I'd rather discover the truth before taking this to Johan."

Etta let out a sigh, settling back into bed. "I see the sense in that, but tread carefully. You don't want to undermine Johan's trust, not with feelings running high within the Brotherhood. I understand what Desta means to you but in future Johan should be here when you bring your reports, as was agreed. These are difficult times and there's enough to worry about without sowing discord within the camp, whether you mean to or not."

I nodded, realising Etta was right. "He needs to know Djuri's men have already set forth from Ulfkell's Keep. Gods, Etta, at our current pace Djuri's going to be upon us before we reach Olt. The roads between Olt and Reavesburg are more easily travelled and Djuri doesn't have a vast caravan of refugees and camp followers trailing in his wake."

"Difficult choices lie ahead for Johan," Etta told me, her eyes closing as she struggled to stay awake, her strength ebbing away. "You'll need to advise him well in the coming days."

"Me? You mean us, surely?" I asked. Etta made no reply, merely reaching out to clasp my hand as her breathing become shallower. I stayed with her as she drifted off to sleep, her lined face becoming more peaceful as the day's worries and cares were left behind for a time.

***

The absence of a campfire only made the rain more miserable for Ulfarr and his five men, hunched beneath their cloaks in the woods overlooking Olt. I tried to find a way to get closer. Thengill and Ekkill's minds were untouchable, smooth like marble, with no chink through which I could reach them. Ulfarr himself seemed the best prospect, a glimmer there which suggested he might have some untapped ability in the Sight. Try as I might, though, I was unable to establish a connection, so I tried something else that had worked in the past.

The forest teemed with life, all manner of beasts creeping through the undergrowth in search of food or their prey. The vixen I found was a bold one, her head resting on her forepaws as she watched the six men from her vantage point close by. She could smell food; strips of dried meat the men had brought with them. There might be the chance of leftovers and an easy meal, although these men showed no sign of moving on tonight and her belly rumbled. Perhaps she would return after her hunt and see what she could find then. I stilled the vixen. Looking through her eyes I pricked up my ears, flicking them forward to better catch their whispered conversation.

"We should split up," Ekkill was saying. The vixen shivered as she shared my memory of the man debating whether or not he should kill me under a starlit sky. "Johan's company should have been here two days ago."

Ulfarr stirred under his cloak, only the lower half of his face visible; his black beard streaked with grey. "Six is already a small crew if we find ourselves in trouble and splitting up means there'll be fewer eyes to spot it before it finds us. Leaving just three of us here might mean there's no one to give Johan his report when he does finally turn up."

Ekkill laughed mirthlessly. "I've ranged this land on my own more times than I can count. I can look after myself if the rest of you want to stay here."

"Why is it I find myself wondering whether you'd bother to make it back to Johan at all if we let you slip off by yourself?" said Skari One-Eye, Ulfarr's second in his small band of scouts. He gave Ekkill a smile, his maimed face turning the expression into something far more sinister.

"Gold," Ekkill answered. "I'm owed plenty by Etta, which I'll see if this venture is successful."

"Gold is easy enough to come by," Skari replied. "But it helps to be on the winning side when it comes to collecting your dues. Not doubting the side you've chosen, are you?"

Ekkill laughed again. "I'd say that question reveals more about your thoughts than it does about mine, One-Eye –"

He paused as he saw Myr lift his hand and place his finger to his lips, before the mute man indicated with his same finger that someone was approaching from the left. Skari also saw the signal. Sir Patrick and Thengill both tensed and glanced at Ulfarr.

"Are you calling me a traitor?" Skari shouted, jumping up and reaching for his hammer. In an instant all the men were on their feet, weapons drawn. Thengill hefted one of his throwing axes lightly in one hand.

"Easy, Skari," Patrick said. "Ekkill didn't mean anything by it, I'm sure."

There was the distinctive thrum of a bowstring and an arrow missed Ekkill's head by inches. Thengill flicked his wrist, sending his axe whirling into the darkness of the trees beyond the small clearing. Someone cried out in pain as Ekkill nocked an arrow to his own bow and let fly, the shaft passing within a foot of Myr and finding its mark behind him. There was a hoarse scream before another arrow struck Patrick's worn shield, reverberating as he staggered back. Thengill hurled his second throwing axe and downed the archer as the forest around them exploded and armed men burst into the clearing, shouting the Vorund Clan battle cry.

The vixen wanted to flee but I held her there, compelling her to remain my eyes and ears as battle was joined. She slunk to the other edge of the clearing, belly low to the ground and unseen by the men as they fought, the battle swiftly turning against Vorund's warriors. They'd already lost the element of surprise and now found themselves fighting a skilled and battle-hardened crew. Skari smashed the skull of one man with his hammer, causing his companion to trip over his felled comrade. Myr stepped forward and plunged his blade into the prone man.

Patrick's blade moved swiftly, parrying left and right before darting out to find a small gap between his assailant's armour and shield, bringing him down. Thengill had now drawn his two hand-axes and using brute strength drove another warrior backwards with each swing, forcing him to block his blows with sword and shield. The man's strength began to fail, his reactions slowing as Thengill continued to batter his defences, allowing him to hook one of his axes around the man's shield rim and tear it free. As his opponent struggled to regain his balance Thengill stepped in and landed a blow to the chest that dropped him to his knees. The second strike bit through helm and skull and the man was left on the ground, unmoving.

Ulfarr circled slowly around the leader of their foes, the last man standing, biding his time. When the man's back was turned to Ekkill, he let another arrow fly, which at such short range pierced the Vorund warrior's armour easily, the arrow-head bursting from his chest. He looked down in surprise at the wound, coughed and sank to his knees, blood pouring out. Ulfarr raised his sword but there was no need for a killing stroke, as the man coughed again and his head drooped. He remained upright, folded over on his knees against his own shield. Hardly a dignified end, but how many people really died in a dignified way in battle?

"Like I said, six men is a useful number," Ulfarr told Ekkill, staring down at the dead man at his feet.

"Here's the last of them," announced Skari. Myr had hold of a young lad, who had a quiver on his back and the shaft of Ekkill's arrow protruding from his leg. He dropped him onto the ground and the six men surrounded him.

"Please. Please, don't hurt me. I was made to come, I swear it." The boy had a strong Vorund accent and looked about fourteen.

"I see," said Skari. "You were made to sail across the Redfars Sea, were you? You were forced to invade the lands of Reavesburg and drive us from our homes? You had no choice when you took the spoils of victory, too, I suppose?"

The boy looked at his feet and sniffed, holding his calf, beginning to feel the pain of the shaft now the battle was over. "Didn't see much of anything. I just scouted and hunted for my company – the boss took everything from Kalamar and Olt. Told me I was lucky to be fed."

Skari raised an eyebrow above his one good eye. "Sounds like an inspiring leader. Not one you should feel all that loyal to, eh?"

"We were sent out scouting, that's all. And then you stuck an arrow through my leg." The boy nodded accusingly at Ekkill, who shrugged.

"You did try and kill me."

"Anybody else out scouting in these hills?" asked Ulfarr.

"No. No one. At least, not that I know about. My leg hurts," the boy sniffed. "It's bleeding bad and it hurts."

"We can see to that," Ulfarr told him. "First, though, you'll tell me how many men are stationed in Olt." The boy looked furtively at the crew surrounding him and licked his lips, debating whether or not to answer.

"Do you want us to see to that leg or shall we wait awhile?" Ulfarr asked.

"You promise to help me?"

"Of course. But you need to answer my questions first. So, how many men does the Vorund Clan have in Olt?"

"There's three hundred warriors from my clan holding the keep," the boy told them in a small voice. "Led by Hrodmarr Hroarson. He's got Old Hrodi Whitebeard following his orders. That old man's too scared not to do what he's told."

"You heard of this Hrodmarr Hroarson?" Ulfarr asked Thengill.

"I knew him back in Vorund; one of Asmarr's older and more experienced commanders. When Adalrikr made his bid for power and killed Asmarr, Hrodmarr was one of the first to join him. He's no fool, that's for sure. Had a lot of respect for him once, before he turned traitor on my chief."

"That's a pity," Ulfarr muttered. "Would have preferred to have heard you say he's a drunkard and an idiot, so Johan will have no trouble defeating him."

"I don't know anything else," the boy told them, shivering as he held his wounded leg. "Please, can you help me? Can you take it out? It hurts worse than ever."

Ulfarr nodded, patting the boy on the shoulder. He crouched down and slid the knife smoothly between the boy's ribs, right into this heart. The lad's eyes widened as he realised what had happened and he opened his mouth in silent protest, his words lost in a fading whistling sigh. Ulfarr put his arm around the boy's shoulders, holding his weight as he slumped against his chest and lowered him tenderly down onto the ground.

"You killed him!" Sir Patrick cried, looking aghast. "He was only a young boy, Ulfarr."

Skari made an exasperated sound. "Tie him up and he dies. Take him with us and he slows us down and we get caught and killed. Let him go and he's straight off to Olt to tell them about us – and we get caught and killed. Berian knighthood's codes of honour don't apply here, my friend. There was never any other choice with this – don't pretend you don't know that."

"Skari's right," said Ulfarr as he ran his hand over the boy's face, closing his vacant eyes. "It was done before he knew about it. Now we need to move out of here – all of us. We've got what we came for and we need to report back to Johan. Clear the camp and let's get going. I want us to have a good start before this patrol is missed back in Olt."

The battle over, the vixen moved forwards cautiously after the men left, stepping daintily around the bodies. At least she wouldn't go hungry tonight.

# CHAPTER 8

"Rothgar." The voice of a woman, whispered softly outside my tent. I'd been drifting off to sleep until the noise stirred me. I drew back the covers, rising awkwardly, my muscles stiff. "Rothgar?" This time I recognised the voice.

"Damona?" I opened the tent flap, wondering what she wanted. Peering into the gloom I saw Johan's wife was accompanied by her friend Ingirith. There were no guards with them.

"Let me in," Damona whispered. When I hesitated she gave an impatient sigh and nodded towards her friend. "Ingirith will vouch for my virtue – not that I need to stoop so low for my pleasures. Now stop being such a prude and let me in before anyone sees us and we give them a reason for their tongues to wag."

Inside the tent, Damona and Ingirith sat at my feet and I pulled my blankets around me; even on summer nights my thin frame did little to keep the chill at bay. Rubbing sleep from my face I looked at Damona expectantly. "So, what can I do for you? Why the secrecy?"

"I couldn't sleep. Every day we draw nearer Olt, and I fear something terrible is about to happen."

I frowned. "Have you heard something?"

"No," Damona whispered. "No, this is a feeling in my bones. We've ridden our luck at Falsten and Delving. I have misgivings about what we'll find in Olt and the welcome we'll receive from Hrodi Myndillson's house. Johan never liked him – he's too close to Gautarr Falrufson and look how swiftly he bowed to Tyrfingr Blackeyes last year."

"In fairness, Old Hrodi wasn't alone," I argued, unable

to keep a note of bitterness from creeping into my voice. "It was that or run away, something both Gautarr and your husband did when they abandoned Ulfkell's Keep to Blackeyes' men. People were faced with some harsh choices back then, Damona. Johan is trying to offer better terms to redress the balance."

"That's just it. What has my husband got to offer to Hrodi Whitebeard, other than the prospect of fighting the Vorund Clan? You don't get to be Hrodi's age without picking and choosing your battles, and I just don't believe he'll side with us. Do you?" I paused, trying to gather my thoughts and Damona tutted at my indecision.

"The Brotherhood's discussed this already," I said. "Frankly, we need his men and Hrodi is Gautarr's sworn bannerman – he's honour-bound to help Johan lift the siege of Romsdahl."

"How can you know you're right?" Ingirith asked. "My children have already lost their father and I need to bring them to a place of safety, not deliver them into the hands of our enemies. We need more assurance than that."

"We need you to use the Sight to tell us if we're on the right path," added Damona. "I need you to tell me what you know, what you've seen."

Now I understood why they were here. I let out a sigh and wondered how best to explain things. "Listen, I'm no seer. I can't see the future, only what's happening here and now. Even with magic, I'm afraid I can't tell you what Hrodi Whitebeard's going to do."

"Then find out," snapped Damona. "Gods, Rothgar, what could be more important than that?"

"It's not that easy. I have to find the right … vantage point, and it's not something I can dictate or control. I'm able to reach more people now than I could before but the Path is fickle and takes time to explore. I know it's not the answer you want to hear, but it's the truth."

Damona ran her hands through her long blond hair,

which looked white in the scant light of the camp. "You talk of those who ran on the night of your sister's wedding. I was forced to leave my daughter and grandson behind to die that night – my own flesh and blood. I need to be able to protect those close to me I still have left. I need to be able to protect Johan and Bandor and ..."

As she hesitated I guessed at the truth. "You're expecting again, aren't you?"

"No one must know," hissed Ingirith. "Not even Johan. Not yet."

"I'll not breach your trust," I told them. "Nor will I give you false promises I'm unable to keep. All I can say is that I'll help Johan in every way I can."

***

Ulfarr's scouting party returned two days later, while we were still two days out from Olt. Joldir and I were summoned to Johan's tent and found they'd arrived with a visitor. Arnfast introduced himself as an emissary from Olt with a confident air, even though the young man was alone and surrounded by members of the Brotherhood.

"We found him riding by himself on the road," Ulfarr explained to Johan. "Declared himself a messenger from Old Hrodi, seeking an audience with you. He said the message he carried was for you alone."

Johan's gaze turned to Joldir, who nodded. "He passed the test of the runestones. We still have to weigh the truth of his words, however."

Johan regarded Arnfast for a time. "Indeed. Dangerous times to be out on the road alone, even for a member of Hrodi Whitebeard's guard. How did you know where to find us?"

Arnfast smiled. "Word of your deeds has spread, Johan Jokellsward. You've already freed Falsten and Delving from Vorund rule in the west of Reavesburg. It is Hrodi's sincere hope that you are prepared to wrest control of his town from Hrodmarr Hroarson, so he may lend his men to your cause. Hrodi sent me out west to find your army and, discretely, declare his intentions."

"I would rather Hrodi declared his intentions by raising his swords and ousting Hroarson from Olt. Tell me, how many men does Vorund's commander have under him?"

"A little over three hundred," Arnfast replied. That eased tensions a little, Arnfast's answer confirming the information obtained by Ulfarr, which I'd already passed on to Johan. Had he been a Vorund agent, it seemed unlikely he would reveal the true strength of their numbers in Olt. Johan's face betrayed none of this as he tested Arnfast further.

"If the Vorund Clan's numbers are as modest as you describe then Hrodi's own force outnumbers them three to one. Why does he wait for my aid?"

"Because winning such a fight in Olt itself would be costly, both in property and lives, and would achieve little of strategic value. Hroarson holds the town's fortress and the narrow streets make it difficult to marshal our forces effectively to fight him. The town risks being burned to the ground, and Hrodi must think of the welfare of his people first and foremost as their elder. Alone he might win that battle but he cannot hope to prevail against Tyrfingr Blackeyes without aid. Together, with the right strategy, our combined forces could free Olt and be strong enough to break the siege at Romsdahl."

"Hrodi owes a debt to Gautarr after all," acknowledged Johan. "Clearly he's thought this through and I see the sense in what you say. This gives us the opportunity Old Hrodi has been waiting for to free his town. Is there a way we could safely get word to him, in order to agree a time when we could strike at Hroarson's men together? If Hrodi was canny enough to send you here I assume he contrived a plan for you to bring back my answer?"

"Ah …" Arnfast's smooth manner faltered. "Johan, I do apologise. Hrodi Myndillson hasn't sent me here today to receive your orders."

"Is that so?" muttered Thengill, standing just behind Arnfast.

"Johan, whilst I don't doubt the loyalty of your men nor the justness of your cause, I cannot exceed my orders. I'm unable to commit the people of Olt to war when the risks are so great – only Hrodi has such authority."

"Perhaps you can enlighten me, then, on your purpose here," Johan replied, a steely glint to his blue eyes.

Arnfast swallowed as he regained his composure. "Please understand I mean you and your men no offence …"

"Best not give us any then," hissed Skari, drawing a chuckle from several of the warriors listening to Arnfast's speech.

"However," Arnfast continued. "These are hard times for all of us, and it's difficult to know who can be trusted. Hrodi has requested a meeting with you personally, Johan, so he can speak to you face-to-face and hear what you have to say. Only then will he decide what is in the best interests of his people. There is an opportunity for such a meeting to take place, since Hrodi recently left his fortress and went on a hunting trip with his son, grandson and a small group of his most trusted men. If they should happen upon a similarly-sized group of Reavesburg men, say, disguised as if they were headed to Olt for market day then there would be nothing untoward in them breaking bread together."

Petr opened his mouth to speak but Johan forestalled him as he stood up and motioned to Svan and Varinn, who were standing guard nearby. "Take our friend here and see he is given food and a place to rest after his long journey. Make sure he doesn't get lost. Arnfast, I thank you for your message. You've given us much to think upon and I'll let you have my answer before nightfall."

Arnfast smiled broadly and bowed low before leaving with his escort. As their footsteps died away Johan's tent erupted in uproar as everyone began to speak at once.

"… Did you hear the way he spoke?"

"… do they think we're idiots? That's got to be a trap …"

"And a poorly disguised one …"

"… He's seen too much already. We should hang him …"

"I'm known as the Landless Jarl." Johan's voice was soft, cutting through the hubbub nonetheless. "The defiance of my household cost me everything … And no, Petr, don't look like that. I wasn't blaming you for what happened; we all know Adalrikr never had any intention of leaving a single stone of Kalamar Castle standing. Hrodi has worked hard to protect his people and broker a peace with the Vorund Clan and he's not the only one. He's every right to demand this meeting and hear me explain how this isn't all going to end with both our heads on spikes and Olt razed to the ground."

"But you must surely see," I began hesitantly, drawing everyone's gaze. "I mean, Johan, this has to be a trap."

"Have you seen such a thing with the Sight?" asked Petr.

"Gods," cried Skari. "The lad doesn't need the Sight to tell you that. It's plain for any fool to see, which is why I say we hang Whitebeard's messenger, if anyone wants to listen to me."

This time Johan raised his voice, causing everyone to fall silent. "Enough. We need the thousand swords Hrodi can give us and I'm not going to turn aside from those because I'm afraid. There was an attempt on my life in this very camp and I'm sure there'll be another. So Hrodi will get his meeting with me, and then we'll know which clan has his true loyalty, won't we?"

***

Outside, Damona hurriedly walked by with Maeva and Ingirith, glaring at me as if all this had been my fault. Thengill clapped me on the shoulder, a grin on the tall man's bearded face. "Good to see you again, Rothgar. Joldir." He clasped the healer's hand firmly.

"Wish there was more time to hear your news," I told him.

"You have your orders and I have mine," Thengill said. "We can speak properly on the road tomorrow."

"Yes," I answered, unsure how I felt about that venture

and hoping Damona's prediction proved to be wrong.

# CHAPTER 9

I was tempted by Ulfarr's campfire that night. I could hear Patrick and Thengill arguing good-naturedly about the outcome of a game of dice, Skari One Eye's normally harsh laughter softened after several drinks. Fighting alongside Ulfarr's crew in Tullen had broken down the barriers between us. I was listening to the sound of men enjoying a night of relative safety and trying to relax, trying to forget. While I wanted to join them I knew they would be thinking about events I'd witnessed without their permission. I couldn't shake the feeling I'd been spying on them, so instead I took my seat at Joldir's fireside, chatting with Arissa as we ate the last of the day's bread with vegetable soup and some hard-boiled eggs. Leif sat cross-legged at my side, telling me about his day. His work in the forge alongside Joldir hadn't gone unnoticed. Leif was now apprenticed to Curruck, one of the blacksmiths in Johan's army, and by all accounts he was doing well, with a good eye and deft fingers ideal for fine metalwork.

However, Leif's day was far from over as we made ready to join together as a Fellowship, whilst Arissa quietly cleared away the remains of our meal, a frown creasing her brow. Bandor stood guard over us, since we would be vulnerable whilst following the Path. Johan had asked us to discover all we could before his meeting with Hrodi Whitebeard.

***

The little man dabbed daintily at the corners of his mouth with a napkin before mopping perspiration from his bald head. The little *bald* man, thought Nuna as she watched Valdimarr reach across and pour more golden wine into his cup, ignoring her maids Ottama and Katla, who were both in attendance.

The little bald *drunken* man she thought, as Valdimarr's hand shook and he spilled some of the expensive Sunian vintage onto the table.

Nuna was sitting next to her husband, Karas Greystorm, chief of the Norlhast Clan, although under Adalrikr's rule his formal title was jarl. Left ravaged by the blood plague that took the life of his second wife and their two young children, Karas was thin and looked older than his thirty-six years. On their side of the table they were joined by his closest advisors. At over sixty, Albrikt was the eldest, his big frame having long ago run to fat, though his mind remained as sharp as ever. Next to him were his two sons, Sigurd and Kalfr, both warriors. Sigurd had also served as Karas' jarl at Norlhast Keep, before Valdimarr's unwelcome arrival. Next to Nuna sat young Brosa, her personal bodyguard.

Valdimarr had been King Adalrikr's emissary in Norlhast since Karas had surrendered to the Vorund Clan. The little bald drunken man was no warrior, although he was flanked by a half-dozen hulking brutes more than capable of defending him. With the boredom of uneventful occupation, they were probably looking for any excuse to do so. Chief among them was Dromundr, Valdimarr's second, a broad, red-bearded warrior with an ugly face, whose eyes tended to linger on Nuna longer than was seemly. Nuna and those at her husband's court took every care not to offend their so-called honoured guests as they finished their evening meal.

*Please go!* Nuna wished as Valdimarr sat there, drinking from Karas' finest cellars and talking incessantly. Nuna knew she should be listening but his voice only made her more angry. Instead she played with her wedding ring, spinning the band of gold on her finger and watching the play of the torchlights reflected on the surface of the metal. A ribbon of pure gold in which the hall's candles were reflected as a dozen setting suns.

"Nuna," Karas said softly at her side. "Valdimarr was just addressing you, my love."

Nuna started from her thoughts and looked up at Valdimarr's sweaty face, his cheeks flushed with wine. "I'm sorry, my lord, I was distracted."

Valdimarr smiled and waved dismissively. "No matter, young lady. I was just recounting the latest reports received from your former home. It seems there's been a small uprising against Tyrfingr Blackeyes' rule. Perhaps news of such events has already reached you?"

*You're not half as drunk as you pretend.* "My ties to my former clan ended when I wed my husband. Since I made Norlhast my home so much has changed at Ulfkell's Keep. I'm no longer in contact with anyone there."

"Really? It's somewhat surprising that your clan would marry you off and sever all ties with you. How cold."

"As I said, much has changed in Ulfkell's Keep." *After the night Tyrfingr Blackeyes murdered the rest of my family.* "Noble-born ladies are raised to marry for political ends. I have been fortunate to have been matched with someone as kind as Karas." Nuna wrapped her fingers tightly around Karas' hand and felt him return the gentle squeeze. "My home is here, in Norlhast."

"You know nothing, then of this uprising by the Brotherhood of the Eagle? Nothing whatsoever?"

Nuna stared blankly back at Valdimarr. "No, my lord, I do not. A rebellion taking its name from the banner of the Reavesburg Clan, presumably?"

"Indeed." Valdimarr paused, leaning in closer across the table. "They are led by your brother's former jarl, Johan Jokellsward. I imagine you know nothing of this either?"

"I believe the lady has already answered that question," cut in Brosa. There were mutterings on the opposite side of the table. Valdimarr quietened them with a wave of his hand.

"I am sure the lady can answer for herself."

"I can," said Nuna, trying to keep her voice steady as that name brought memories flooding back, of happier times at home when her father had been chief, with Johan as his staunch friend and ally. "Until you told me this I had no idea Johan was even alive, much less that he was leading this uprising against Blackeyes' forces. Surely you cannot believe he poses a threat to Vorund's rule of Reavesburg?"

"None whatsoever," Valdimarr replied, taking a long draught of wine from his cup. "Still, I need not remind you that a rebellion, no matter how hopeless its cause, still represents treason against the King of Laskar. Anyone aiding Johan and his band of outlaws will be treated accordingly."

"Then I wish the Jarl of Reavesburg every success in putting down this uprising," Karas said. "Thank you for informing us of such important news in our neighbouring kingdom."

Valdimarr finished his wine and stood, his warriors rising with him as they made to leave. "There is but the one Kingdom of Laskar now, Karas."

After Valdimarr's men had left the hall Albrikt sat for a time, deep in thought, his fingers running through his thick beard. "Forgive me, my lady, but I must ask you this question. I assume you were telling Valdimarr the truth concerning Johan's brotherhood?"

"Nuna has already answered that question, more than once," Karas told him, glowering.

"And I'm happy to answer, husband, for I know why he asks it. I can assure you I know nothing of this uprising, other than what Valdimarr told us this evening. What I said was true – my only surviving link to Reavesburg is my maid, Katla, who now serves me here in Norlhast Keep. Whatever Valdimarr believes is another matter entirely; clearly he was testing me tonight."

"And I think you have allayed his suspicions," Albrikt told her.

"Who would have believed I would be wishing Johan Jokellsward well?" observed Kalfr, before realising what he had said. "Please forgive me, my lady, I meant no offence. You know better than most I've always supported the alliance between our clans. Please remember until recently Johan was still a bitter enemy of my people. Old habits die hard."

Sigurd sighed. "Whether Johan has our support or not is irrelevant. His stronghold at Kalamar has been destroyed, so it's hard to see how he can prevail against Tyrfingr's men. It was more interesting to take note of what Valdimarr didn't say. There was no mention of Gautarr Falrufson leading or taking part in any rebellion but neither has news reached us of the end of the siege of Romsdahl. Gautarr still commands a sizeable number of warriors, although if he's trapped in his castle I fear Johan's efforts are futile."

"The Brotherhood of the Eagle," Nuna said, more to herself than those at Karas' court. It was the first time she'd heard those words, she was sure of it. *Knew it.* Yet in her mind's eye she could clearly see pennants flying in the wind, the Reavesburg eagle sigil emblazoned upon them. It was almost as if she'd seen them for herself, far away in the land of her birth.

*\*\*\**

Humli rolled over in his bed, trying to get comfortable. He'd need to be up soon to take his boat out whilst it was still dark, if he wanted to be back in time for the fish market at Reavesburg. He loved his grandson Finnvidor, or Finn as they had all taken to calling him, but for someone so small he had a powerful need to howl when he was hungry, which seemed to be all the time. Sleep was hard to come by in his cabin and Humli didn't want to think too much about what it would be like when Lina's child was born. He counted himself fortunate the baby wasn't already here. Lina was huge but the babe seemed more than happy to stay put, although it couldn't be long now. As was her way he heard Lina rise to make water and the noise stirred Desta from her sleep.

"Lina. Lina, is that you?"

"Yes, sister. It's still night, go back to sleep."

"Is Father still here?"

"He's sleeping. Why, what's the matter?"

Humli heard Lina cross the room and sit on the edge of the bed Desta shared with Finn. "What is it, Desta? What's the matter?"

"Oh Lina ..." Humli felt a pang of sympathy as he heard his daughter's stifled sobs and the sound of Lina comforting her. "I've had the same dream for three nights now and I'm not sure I can bear it any longer ..."

"Hush. Who can say what truth there is in dreams? You've not mentioned this before."

Desta sniffed loudly. "I saw him, Lina. I saw Haarl lying dead on the battlefield, surrounded by hundreds of others. There were people crying out in pain, pleading for mercy as they were killed but Haarl was already dead, his eyes ... his eyes open, staring. I've already lost Rothgar. I can't lose Haarl too."

Lina paused for a time. "Rothgar? Do you mean Rothgar *Kolfinnarson*?" Desta gave no answer, just the occasional muffled half-sob. "I'm sorry, it's none of my business – I didn't mean to pry. I just had no idea."

"I was a young maid at Ulfkell's Keep. Do you think I was in any kind of position to turn down the attentions of the chief's brother?"

"Well, that's in the past now," Lina said. "Pay him no mind – he sounds a worthless sort and you have Haarl now. I'm sure he'll be back safe from this venture with Djuri before summer's out, so try not to worry and get some rest while you can."

Humli blinked in the darkness, putting together what he'd heard. All that time he'd been worrying about his daughter under Blackeyes' rule, and now he'd learned a noble from his own clan had been pestering her, perhaps worse. Probably worse. Humli wondered for a time why she hadn't told him before noisily yawning as he rose from his bed, not wanting Desta to know he'd overheard her conversation. Whilst there was nothing he could do about Desta's past or Haarl's fate he could still earn a living and put food on the table.

# CHAPTER 10

Johan pursed his lips, not bothering to hide his disappoint-ment as he listened to my report in Etta's tent the following morning.

"So, on the day I'm due to meet with Old Hrodi and the future of the Brotherhood hangs in the balance, you've brought me news of Nuna Karaswyfe's dinner in Norlhast Keep. It didn't occur to you to try and discover what was happening in Olt or the location of Djuri's men?" Silently, I thanked Joldir for not mentioning Lina, something he'd done reluctantly at my request.

"Father ..." Bandor began before Johan cut him off.

"Don't start apologising for him. What use is their magic to me, when my so-called advisors merely spend their time pursuing their own interests?"

"It's less simple than you make out," Joldir explained, ignoring Johan's glare. "This is still a young Fellowship. The connection between Rothgar and his sister is strong and will continue to be a pull."

"You're too quick to dismiss what Rothgar's told you," added Etta. "Tidings that don't concern what's at the forefront of your mind still have value, if you care to consider them."

Johan shrugged, looking unconvinced. "You mean I should look more closely at what's happening north of our border?"

"Of course," snapped Etta. "You've accused Rothgar of being self-centred but the sun doesn't rise and set at your com-mand, Johan Jokellsward. You need to pay attention to your wider surroundings."

"Events in Olt concern me more than Norlhast."

It felt like Johan was determined to find fault. My mouth was dry, forcing me to clear my throat before speaking again. "The news from Norlhast shows that word of the Brotherhood's deeds has travelled widely. Although Valdimarr played it down, he was sufficiently concerned to question Nuna on the subject. Events are beginning to move, perhaps bringing the Norlhast Clan back into play."

"Hmm, I wouldn't count on that."

I persisted, even if Johan wasn't in the mood to listen. "Karas Greystorm and his people grow increasingly unhappy under Valdimarr's rule. The purpose behind our original alliance could still be rekindled."

"You think so? I never supported that plan," Johan shot Etta a venomous glance. "Personally, I think Karas will remain safe and sound, courting favour with Valdimarr, whilst we fight and bleed for our own land."

Joldir let out a sigh. "Perhaps joining forces with Hrodi and Gautarr will bring him back into this fight. Karas needs to believe you have a realistic chance of victory before risking the lives of his people."

Etta nodded, fussing with her covers as she shifted in bed to make herself more comfortable. "And how go your preparations for the meeting with Hrodi?"

"I've picked the men to accompany me," Johan replied.

"Leaving me with the baggage, women and children," added Bandor, looking unhappy at the prospect.

His father turned to him. "Yes, because that's where I need you and Petr. Hrodi asked to meet me. It makes more sense for the caravan to continue its way south towards Romsdahl, so we can all reach Gautarr's castle as soon as possible. I'll catch up with you once my business with Whitebeard is done."

"Who's accompanying you?" Etta asked.

"Svan, Eykr, Harvald and Brandr, plus Geirmundi Flint," Johan answered. "Ulfarr's crew will scout ahead. Oh, and you too, Rothgar. The rest of the Brotherhood will continue south, under Petr's command."

"Me?" It was the first I'd heard of this, or Bandor for that matter, looking at his expression.

Johan nodded. "I won't lie, this is dangerous and I'm only taking those I can really trust. If things don't go as we hope, I'll need someone to get a message to Petr. You can do that, can't you? Send Joldir a message using the Sight, warning him if things don't go to plan?"

It took me a moment to collect my thoughts – it seemed Johan had faith my abilities after all. "Yes. I can do that," I told him.

"Good." Johan turned to Bandor. "I know you want to come but I need you with Petr. It's important he has someone he can rely on ... and ... someone should be there to protect your mother."

"You're talking like you're not coming back," accused Bandor.

"No, I'm talking like someone who's planning for every eventuality," said Johan. "I'm sure you understand." Bandor looked frustrated as he let the matter drop.

"It's a good plan," Etta added. "Have you thought what Hrodi's demands might be?"

"Well, if he's minded to join us, he'll want to secure the future of his own house. I wondered if he'd want his son, Radholf, elevated to the status of jarl? Then there's the spoils of war. Hrodi's got more gold hidden away than I ever acquired. He'll demand his share and, since his force is the largest, he may ask for more than the elders of Delving and Falsten."

Etta looked thoughtful for a time, again shifting in her bed. "As I recall, Hrodi holds Radholf's son, Alfarr, in particular favour. He dotes on the grandson, so paying the lad a compliment might start things off on the right foot. As for gold, well, you're right. Old Hrodi's well within his rights to demand a sizeable share, perhaps even as large as your own, when you take into account the number of men he might add to your army."

Johan nodded. "He'll be treated fairly. I just hope he deals with us in the same way."

***

Before leaving I made sure Etta managed a little porridge for breakfast. Around us I could hear the sounds of camp being struck, Varinn's voice raised as the old warrior chivvied people to make haste. I noticed that Bandor had stayed behind after his father left, waiting outside.

"Arissa will be along soon," I told Etta as I cleared away the remains of her meal. "You'll ride in her cart with Joldir and Leif."

"Yes, yes. I'll be fine, Rothgar. You need to hurry – Johan's party will be leaving soon. Here," she held out a small loaf. "I don't want this. Take it with you so you've had something to eat, and take care."

"Whose side will Whitebeard take? Honestly, what do you think?"

"Honestly? I really don't know, which is why I want you to take care."

Bandor fell into step with me as I left Etta's tent and headed to gather my own things. "Why do you wait on her hand and foot, like a servant?" he asked. "You're still noble-born."

I was unsure whether he was joking. "What difference does that make? She saved my life, remember. Is this about your father's decision?"

We were once of a height but now Bandor looked down on me, forcing me to straighten my stooped posture, my muscles protesting. When Bandor arrived in Lindos, seeking shelter last winter at Joldir's former home, he'd been gaunt and thin. In recent months, life had been kinder, as he enjoyed an elevated position at his father's side as part of the inner-circle of the Brotherhood. Bandor had filled out, reminding me once again of the strong young man I'd known during our training under my father's late weapons master, Olfridor Halfhand. Once equals in the combat ring, life had taken us on very different paths.

"I ..." he groped for words and stared at me, brows furrowed, running his hands through his bright red hair. "No. No, forget it. I don't know why I said that. And you're right, it's Father's decision."

"Not one I asked him to make," I assured him.

"No, I know that." Bandor swallowed, looking like he was gathering up all his courage. "Rothgar, I wanted to speak to you before you left ..."

"Gods, you've not been listening to your mother, have you?" I asked him, a wry grin on my face.

Bandor looked at me for a moment, before breaking into a laugh. "Oh no, she's been to see you *already*?"

I nodded. "Yes, I've heard what she has to say on the subject of Hrodi Whitebeard."

"The thing is, Rothgar, I've got a feeling ... Listen, I can't say why but I'm worried she might be right. Hrodi's no hero. He bent the knee quick as he could when Tyrfingr took the keep and I don't see that changing. Now Father's leaving me behind, so I can't even protect him if I'm right."

"I'll be there," I assured Bandor, who looked unimpressed.

"Really?" he said with a smirk. I felt a flash of annoyance at the remark, even though it was made in jest. I'd saved Johan's life during the fight against the durath in Tullen, although only Thengill had witnessed the deed.

"*Yes*. You gave me this blade," I patted the rune-etched short sword at my side. "I still remember how to use it."

"Alright, I'm sorry. Listen, one more thing – be careful around Svan. Whilst he's got more sense than to challenge my father again publicly, he's not stopped whispering about you and ... your kind. I've overheard him talking to Harvald and Faraldr. They resent your influence, especially now Father's openly making use of your Fellowship."

I patted Bandor on the shoulder, feeling the strong muscles underneath his cloak. "Thanks for the warning. I'll take care, I promise."

# CHAPTER 11

With Arnfast as our guide we set out on foot from the camp later that morning, with the sun rising above us in a clear blue cloudless sky. As it grew warmer we stowed our cloaks and I was grateful Johan had ordered us to leave our armour behind, the better to give the impression we were a hunting party, rather than a band of warriors.

"We're almost there," Arnfast told us enthusiastically. "Hrodi's hunting lodge is just beyond these woods."

I peered in the direction he was pointing and felt a lump in my throat as I saw Mount Lindos, framed by the dark peaks of the Northern Baros mountain range. I'd lived there for a year, under Joldir's care, and it had become my home. Somewhere a few miles away the caravan would be making its slow journey towards Romsdahl, and Joldir would be looking at that same mountain peak.

"You said we'd be there half-an-hour ago," grumbled Geirmundi, wiping sweat from his forehead as the sun beat down on us.

"Our pace has been a little slower than I expected," Arnfast replied, glancing briefly in my direction. "I'm used to travelling alone as Hrodi's messenger."

"Let's get on with it then," Svan answered, before falling back into quiet conversation with Eykr, Brandr and Harvald. As warriors of Kalamar they enjoyed a close bond with Johan and jealously guarded their influence. While Geirmundi and I were members of the Brotherhood, both of us were excluded and we fell into pace a step or two behind them as Johan led the way with Arnfast.

"Is it true you grew up with Bandor?" Geirmundi asked

me as we neared the woods.

I blew out my cheeks, trying to catch my breath, my body protesting against the extended physical exercise. "Aye. My father was close to Johan and took Bandor in as his ward for six years at Ulfkell's Keep."

"You two close as well, then?"

I nodded. "We've both lost people we care about. It makes you appreciate the friends you have left."

"That's a good way to look on things … after …" Flint looked at me, taking in my broken frame as I laboured for breath. The words died on the young man's lips.

I could have taken offence, yet what was the point? I had enough enemies already and the man from Delving was trying to be friendly. "I've had my share of misfortune at Myshall's hand." I drew in another breath with an effort. "I can still play my part in this war. The way I look at it, one more warrior makes little difference. What Blackeyes did to me had unforeseen consequences, making me into something more … useful."

Flint nodded. "Aye. The Sight. For what it's worth, after what my cousin saw, I think we need your help."

"Some wouldn't agree," I replied, looking in Svan's direction.

"No. Then again, some people don't notice when they start talking straight out their arse," Geirmundi replied with a grin.

*⁕*

"Karl," Arnfast called out. "Good to see you again."

The man outside the entrance to the wooden hunting lodge raised his arm in greeting. "Arnfast. You've brought visitors, I see." As we approached the lodge I noticed other men outside; perhaps ten in all, every one of them armed.

"Hrodi Myndillson inside?" Arnfast asked.

Karl scratched his chin through his wild brown beard, looking Johan up and down. "Who's asking to see him?"

"I believe we're expected," Johan replied.

"That so? What do you think, Jolinn?"

It took me a moment to realise Jolinn, one of the warriors guarding the lodge, was a woman. With close-cropped blonde hair and bright blue eyes she was an imposing figure, dressed in chainmail, a sword with a well-worn grip hanging at her side. At nearly six foot tall, she towered over everyone except Johan. Jolinn had a lean frame and moved with a confident grace as she approached our group.

"Well, I'll be damned. A shieldmaiden," Svan muttered to Harvald, who laughed.

"You have eyes in your head, then," Jolinn quipped, before turning to Karl. "I think we'd better get everyone inside, don't you? The longer we linger the more likely we are to be spotted by Hroarson's men."

Karl nodded as he opened the door and ushered us inside. I glanced briefly at Geirmundi. It was dark within but there was nothing else to do except follow Johan's lead as he strode into the building, flanked by Svan and Brandr. Jolinn followed, closing the door behind her.

It took my eyes a few moments to adjust to the gloom of the lodge, which was lit by a sparse number of torches, doing little to add to the meagre light from small windows set in the walls. The wooden beams and thatched roof were lost in darkness above a small firepit.

"Your visitors have arrived, Hrodi," Jolinn announced and I saw the elder of Olt sitting at the far end of the lodge on a wooden chair. Hrodi rose, a little unsteadily on his bent legs, his long white beard tucked into his belt. He appeared to stumble for a moment and his son took his arm to steady him.

"Who's that?" whispered Geirmundi.

"Radholf Hrodison, Hrodi's last living son and heir," I answered, remembering him from his attendance with his father at clan moots in Ulfkell's Keep.

"Johan Jokellsward," said Hrodi with a smile, holding out his hand as he waved his son away. "So the tales from the western lands speak true, it really is you leading this ... what do you call yourselves again? The Brotherhood?"

"The Brotherhood of the Eagle," Johan supplied as he gripped Hrodi's hand. "For the Reavesburg Clan has risen again and it's time to take back what's ours. Thank you for meeting with us, Hrodi Myndillson. I know this isn't without risk on your part, so we'd best be brief."

"Indeed. I see you're not alone," Hrodi peered at Johan's companions. "I know you, Svan, and you too Harvald. Your other friends, I'm not sure we've been introduced."

"Brandr and Eykr, warriors who guarded Kalamar Castle before its fall," Johan said. "And this is Geirmundi Flint of Delving."

"Ah yes, your cousin Geirmarr is the town elder, I believe. And Rugga? I heard he escaped Ulfkell's Keep. Is he with you or did you leave him in command of your forces?"

Johan sighed, his shoulders dropping. "He fell in battle in the spring. Petr Hamarrson serves as my second nowadays."

Hrodi reached forward, taking Johan's hand in his once more. "I'm sorry, truly. Rugga was a good man. Ingirith and the children must miss him terribly." Johan patted Hrodi gently on the shoulder, holding his hand for a time before letting go. Hrodi looked at me, frowning. "And who is this? You appear to have neglected to introduce me to your final companion, Johan. Step forward, young man, so I can see you better. You look familiar ..."

I could see the recognition in Whitebeard's eyes as I took a limping step forwards. "I'm Rothgar Kolfinnarson. We are, of course, acquainted." Hrodi's eyes went wide and he stared at me in silence.

"Father, are you alright?"

"Yes, of course I am. Don't fuss!" Hrodi waved Radholf away and looked at me intently. "Rothgar. I'd heard your body was stolen away from the crows' cage outside Reavesburg's gates. I thought it was to give you a decent burial – I had no idea you were still alive."

I bowed theatrically, although the effect was spoiled as

my back muscles spasmed, so it took an age to stand straight again. "I'll admit I'm changed somewhat, but I'm very much alive."

"Myshall's bane. That night when Tyrfingr executed Brunn and tortured you," Hrodi's voice shook. "I know they're only words but I've never forgotten that terrible night. I don't know what you did to earn Blackeyes' displeasure – all I can say is it didn't warrant that."

Johan coughed and interrupted Hrodi's speech. "Now we've introduced ourselves, perhaps we could turn to the business in hand?"

"Yes, you're right of course," answered Hrodi. "You know Radholf and I see you've met Jolinn and Arnfast. This is my grandson, Alfarr." A young man stepped out from the shadows, toting a heavy hunting crossbow. "Alfarr recently celebrated his twenty-first year and perhaps, one day, he'll sit on this very seat in my place."

"Grandfather, please. Don't joke about such things. You will be the elder of Olt for many years to come," Alfarr said with a smile, as Radholf scowled at being overlooked by his father.

Hrodi gave a wheezy laugh. "I'm seventy-five. Not sure I can put off the journey to Navan's Halls for much longer. I've seen more years pass by than I have to look forward to, which gives me every right to start thinking of what will come to pass after I'm gone."

"Radholf, Alfarr," Johan bowed to each in turn. "An honour. Now, Hrodi, perhaps we could discuss the reason for my visit."

Hrodi nodded and took his seat, slowly. I could see a muscle playing in Johan's jaw as he grew increasingly impatient but Hrodi was not a man to be rushed. Only when he was seated and comfortable did he continue. "So, you're here today to discuss war with the Vorund Clan?"

"At your invitation," Johan replied.

"Indeed. The Brotherhood of the Eagle has set the western lands aflame, driving out the Vorund scourge. However, that territory was lightly held by Tyrfingr Blackeyes. Olt has a strong garrison and many more warriors hold Ulfkell's Keep. How many have flocked to your banner?"

Johan paused. "Not enough, Hrodi, not enough. Some two thousand follow me at present but less than one thousand of those are fighting men, including the warriors we gained from the muster at Falsten and Delving."

"So few," Hrodi said, and I felt a little of my confidence ebb away at those two words.

"The strength of Kalamar is spent," Johan acknowledged.

"Yet those of us who remain have thwarted Adalrikr's schemes time and again," interjected Brandr, Svan nodding in agreement next to him.

"I don't dispute the deeds of the Brotherhood, yet the truth is Kalamar's warriors number less than twenty, and that includes Ulfarr's crew," said Johan. "Sinarr the Cold One broke our strength when Kalamar fell. This is why we need your swords. You would swell our ranks and give me the forces I need to break the siege at Romsdahl."

Hrodi sighed deeply. "You understand, surely, that Sinarr the Cold One and Joarr the Hammer have six *thousand* men under their command, besieging Romsdahl as we speak?"

"I do, which is why I've come to you. Hrodi, you're Gautarr Falrufson's sworn bannerman. His household has defended your lands against the Vorund Clan since before you were born, and in turn you've sent him men and supplies to bolster our southern border against our enemies. Now is the time to deliver on your ancient promises. If we strike at Sinarr and Joarr together, with Gautarr's warriors at our side, we have the numbers to crush the Vorund army. I assume this is why you called this meeting, so we can plan how to turn this war in our favour."

Hrodi raised his hand and from the shadows I saw figures emerge, in ones and twos, silently surrounding us. I saw

Arnfast move to one side and join them, his hand on the hilt of his sword, whilst Jolinn did the same by the door, our only means of escape. My heart pounded as I remembered a similar scene, when my brother and his family was surrounded and murdered in front of me. My hand fell on my sword as I counted our adversaries, realising we were outnumbered two to one.

*We're in trouble*, I sent the message via the Sight to Johan, many miles away. I didn't stay in contact, bringing myself straight back to the present as Hrodi looked apologetically at Johan from his chair.

"Johan, have you ever met Sinarr?"

"I saw his handiwork. That was enough," Johan growled, looking at the men gathering around him.

"I met him, personally, when he was heading south to Romsdahl. His ships were docked at Reavesburg and I was asked to attend an audience with Tyrfingr Blackeyes, so Olt could contribute additional taxes to the war effort."

"What of it?" muttered Johan.

"Why do you think he bears that name?" Hrodi asked. "If I had any doubts about Adalrikr's right to be called King of the North they were dispelled when I returned to the Great Hall. Sinarr is ... unnatural, Johan. He's less a man, more a ... *creature*, something fell and evil from the legends of old, made flesh and walking here amongst us. When you fled the night of Nuna's wedding you didn't flee far enough. If you had, perhaps you and your family would have survived. You might have found sanctuary beyond the Baros Mountains, in Helsburg or Vittag. By remaining here and continuing this fight, you have condemned them all."

"Is this how much value you set on your oath?" shouted Svan, drawing his axe.

"My oath!" roared Hrodi. "You talk to me of my oath? I swore to serve the clan chief of Reavesburg and he's *dead*. I've sworn a new oath, to the King of Laskar, and I'll be damned if I sign the death warrants for my own family by breaking it to join Johan in a war he can't hope to win."

Another figure emerged from behind Hrodi's chair, a large powerful warrior wearing armour and carrying a heavy shield emblazoned with the sigil of the bear. "Well said, Hrodi Whitebeard. I can see where your loyalties lie. You've chosen well."

Hrodi climbed out of his chair and bowed, stiffly, to the new arrival before turning to Johan. "I'm sorry, Jokellsward, I forgot to make all my introductions. This is Hrodmarr Hroarson, commander of Vorund's forces in Olt."

# CHAPTER 12

"It's an honour to meet you, Johan Jokellsward." Hrodmarr's voice had a rasping quality to it. "It was obliging of you to deliver yourself into our hands. If you'll be good enough to accompany Jolinn, we've some questions to ask you back at the keep." He nodded to Alfarr, who'd levelled his crossbow at Svan. "You can kill the rest."

*Hrodi's betrayed us,* I sent to Joldir, again closing down the link before he could reply so I could remain alert.

Jolinn walked towards Johan and drew her sword. "I'm sorry about this. Please, come with me."

"And what makes you think we'll surrender?" Johan retorted, reaching behind his back towards his two-handed greatsword.

"Surrender?" Jolinn smiled, whirling her blade in a single fluid motion, bringing it to a stop next to Hrodmarr's neck. "I'm talking about coming with me, if you want to live."

Hrodmarr's eyes went wide and Old Hrodi shot out of his chair so fast I could scarce believe it. "What are you doing?" Hrodi cried.

"Doing what you should have done, old man," Jolinn pressed her blade into the skin of Hrodmarr's throat, gently running it over his black stubble. "I'm heeding the banner call of my liege lord, rather than bowing and scraping before this piece of –"

"I can kill them before they leave this room," said Alfarr, still holding his crossbow.

"Damn it, you idiot, let them go," Hrodmarr hissed, eyes fixed on Jolinn's blade.

"What's it to be?" asked Jolinn, never taking her eyes of

Hrodmarr.

The Vorund warrior didn't hesitate. "Let them go."

"With us, then," Jolinn ordered, beckoning Hrodmarr to follow her as Johan's men began to move towards the safety of the door. The warriors of Olt glanced at each other, wondering whose orders they should follow.

"Which of you is with me?" Jolinn called. The door was still blocked by Olt's warriors, including Arnfast, who drew his own sword and looked at the other two men next to him.

"Now!" he shouted. "Kill them."

There was a thrum from Alfarr's crossbow and the bolt took Brandr squarely in the chest. Even if he'd been wearing armour nothing could have stopped the weapon at such deadly close-range. Arnfast brought his blade swinging down towards Jolinn, who reacted just in time to parry the blow, allowing Hrodmarr to roll away, shouting orders to his men.

Johan and Svan also drew their weapons and attacked the two men loyal to Hrodi who were guarding the door. Jolinn and Arnfast duelled fiercely as I drew my own blade and fell into a tight three, protecting Johan's back, with Geirmundi and Harvald. There was confusion within the warriors from Olt as they began fighting amongst themselves. One of Olt's men, carrying a sword and dagger, rushed to join us, making our three a four.

"I'm standing with Jolinn," the man told us. "I'll not see our own clan betrayed."

"A timely choice to join the Brotherhood, friend," said Harvald with relief, wide-eyed as he watched events unfolding around him.

"Sorry *friend*," the man replied, swiftly stabbing his dagger into Harvald's throat. He fell to his knees, choking blood, eyes bulging.

"No," Geirmundi cried as he drove his own sword at the warrior, grunting as his attack was parried. As their blades locked it allowed me the brief movement I needed to drive my short sword through our attacker's ribs. I might have lacked the strength to wield my old longsword but this blade was perfectly weighted and razor sharp. Hrodi's man looked at me with complete surprise, unable to believe he'd been killed by a cripple. He fell onto Harvald's body, who already lay still amid a spreading pool of blood.

"Thanks," Geirmundi gasped as we moved back-to-back. "Any chance we're getting out of here alive?"

I glanced around, watching as Hrodmarr swung his axe and took off the face of one of Olt's warriors who dared to block his path. Johan was still fighting hard with his own opponent, unaware Hrodmarr was advancing towards him. Eykr swung his two-handed sword at Hrodmarr, hitting his shield and forcing him off-balance. Alfarr had managed to reload his crossbow and let loose once more. This time his aim was wayward and the bolt found the head of the man fighting Svan, nailing him to the door in a shower of blood and brains.

Svan roared and smashed open the door. "The way's clear. Let's go."

Together we all scrambled for the exit, pushing people out of the way as we forced our way through.

"Damn it, Hrodi. That door should be locked," Hrodmarr shouted behind us as we burst back out in the bright summer sun, squinting against the glare.

I'd expected to face more opposition as the fighting spilled outside. Instead corpses lay everywhere, stuck by arrows or killed by sword, axe and hammer. Ulfarr and Ekkill stood there, bows drawn and both let loose. Ekkill found Hrodmarr's armoured shoulder, causing him to drop back with a cry, whilst Ulfarr's arrow took Johan's enemy through the chest.

"You stupid bitch," Arnfast growled, again finding his attack turned away by Jolinn as she backed away from the lodge. "You've betrayed us all."

Jolinn stepped forwards, kicking Arnfast's feet out from under him. As he staggered and fell onto one knee she opened him up from thigh to groin with a casual motion, the wound showering bright red blood onto the ground. "No. You've forgotten which clan you belong to, Arnfast." Our former guide screamed as he collapsed, blood pouring incessantly from his leg, soaking his breeches.

The rest of Ulfarr's crew now surrounded us, Thengill shouting a war cry as Myr took off the hand of a Vorund warrior. Forming a loose circle, we slowly began to back away from the hunting lodge. Ekkill and Ulfarr's arrows flew once again through the doorway, producing more yells and screams, while Arnfast moaned weakly on the ground, his blood running less freely now. Only one other warrior from Olt ran with us as we continued our retreat.

"Where are the others, Lars?" Jolinn asked him.

"Our warriors are mustering to the south, although I don't know how many have heeded your call."

"Wait, what about Karl? Where's Karl?"

I saw him now, sprawled by the door with his skull smashed in. Jolinn let out a keening wail.

"I'm sorry," said Ulfarr. "As he unlocked the door so you could escape one of Olt's warriors killed him. There wasn't anything anyone could have done."

"We don't have time to talk about this," barked Johan. "Back to the woods, now."

I glanced back once, checking we weren't being followed. There was no sign of pursuit – only Arnfast dead on the ground, next to Karl's unmoving body.

*⁎⁎*

When I met Joldir using the Sight he was waiting for me in his workshop, the private space in his old house in Lindos. On one side the walls were lined floor to ceiling with small drawers, each carefully labelled. On the other there were shelves containing all manner of strange instruments, glass vials and assorted jars in which various strange objects hung, some suspended in liquids. A well-worn and stained wooden workbench was covered with unfamiliar devices and a large pot steamed over a small oil fire, giving off a pleasant nutmeg odour. I found myself wandering nearer out of curiosity, peering inside. Whatever was in there made my eyes water as Joldir placed a restraining hand on my chest.

"I wouldn't. That preparation is far from finished. We don't want to undo all my hard work putting you back together last year, would we?"

I turned and smiled. "None of this is real, Joldir ..."

My mentor shook his head. "You of all people should know that isn't true. When we create a world using the Sight it's every bit as real to us as if we were in Amuran. Now, to business, whilst this space remains safe. I must say, you certainly know how to alarm someone with as few words as possible. Our fears about Hrodi were justified?"

"I'm afraid so," I said, sitting down in a comfortable rocking chair. It felt good to take the weight off my feet, even if it wasn't there.

"And where are you now?" Joldir asked, sitting in a matching chair next to mine. Identical, in fact. There had only been one in his workshop and I smiled, appreciating his thoughtfulness.

"We're camped a few miles from the hunting lodge, probably a day behind the column making up Johan's army. There's no sign we've been followed, although Ulfarr's set up patrols to be on the safe side."

"What happened? Etta's going to want to know all the details."

I recounted the events of the day as swiftly and concisely as I could, using the skills I'd learnt from Etta to draw out the important facts as I gave my report. Joldir listened intently all the while, only interrupting me when I mentioned the deaths of Brandr and Harvald.

"And their runeblades?"

"Lost. I'm sorry. There wasn't time to recover them in the attack."

Joldir looked thoughtful. "There was no other choice. Adalrikr may suspect my involvement already through Nereth's reports. He'll be left in no doubt if he sees my handiwork. We have to hope Hrodi and Hrodmarr don't recognise the importance of those weapons."

I continued with my tale, describing our escape and relief as darkness fell and we realised we'd evaded our pursuers.

Joldir gave a chuckle, sitting back in his seat. "So, *Jolinn* helped you? I wished I'd seen Hrodi's face."

I nodded, rocking in my comfortable chair. I'd be sorry to leave this place. When the vision ended I'd wake back in the camp, with a night sleeping on the ground under my cloak to look forward to. "That's right, she had her blade a hair's breadth away from slitting Hroarson's throat but the moment slipped away."

Joldir laughed out loud this time, shaking his head. "What's so funny?" I asked him.

"She hasn't told you yet? Jolinn's famous in Olt. She's Hrodi Whitebeard's bastard daughter, born in one of the more reputable brothels in the town."

# CHAPTER 13

Djuri walked into Hrodmarr's well-appointed chambers in Olt's keep, accompanied by Ulf and Bjorr. They were luxurious, the walls covered in thick Berian tapestries and the polished wooden floor with colourful Oomrhani rugs. He guessed they were once Hrodi Whitebeard's rooms, before Hrodmarr's arrival. Djuri expected Old Hrodi to be there too but instead it was a young man, with long dark hair and a haughty manner, who greeted them as he opened the door.

"Hrodi's grandson," Hrodmarr explained, sitting in a comfortable chair by an open window, his arm in a sling. "Alfarr's been most useful to our cause, since Tyrfingr Blackeyes became jarl of Reavesburg. I understand Blackeyes ordered you to intercept Johan, despite being a Reavesburg warrior yourself?"

Djuri nodded. "I saw which way the wind was blowing after Jorik was killed. I know the western lands, so Blackeyes asked me lead the expedition."

Hrodmarr looked at Bjorr with a wolfish grin. "Didn't see fit to put you in charge, then, Bjorr? What's it like to be the Turncloak's second?"

Bjorr shrugged. "Just following orders, same as you. Only we didn't let Johan Jokellsward escape capture, after having him in the palm of our hand."

"And we would have had him, too, if it weren't for my mad aunt," Alfarr complained.

Bjorr chuckled. "I heard she had you at sword point, Hroarson, so she must be quite a lady, this Jolinn. Instead of Johan's head gracing your walls on a spike, four hundred of Olt's warriors have gone over to him following this. Blackeyes

93

isn't going to be happy receiving that report."

"Just goes to show, you don't know who to trust in these times, do you?" Hrodmarr replied sourly, giving Alfarr a pointed look. "Anyway, why have you brought your men into my keep, when you should have taken the fight to Johan? If you'd had the balls to follow Tyrfingr's commands, you might have captured the commander of the Brotherhood of the Eagle before he re-joined his army."

Djuri licked his lips as he thought about his reply, knowing the two Vorund warriors were testing him. They'd be keen to send an unfavourable report back to Tyrfingr, probably regardless of how he performed his mission. His only comfort was the obvious rivalry between the two men, which might distract them long enough to get the job done. Alternatively, they might simply get in his way; only time would tell.

"Think we made the only sensible decision," he said, trying to sound self-assured. "My scouts report Johan's force is much larger than we were led to believe when we set out from Ulfkell's Keep. Even knowing the lay of the land it's hard to turn that to your advantage when you're outnumbered two to one, and those odds have only worsened now Jolinn's joined forces with them."

Hrodmarr looked unconvinced. "So, Turncloak, what do you suggest?"

"Regroup and take on fresh supplies here," Djuri replied, ignoring the jibe. "Then we take six hundred men from Olt and head south together, in pursuit of this Brotherhood. If we send riders to outpace Johan we can work together with Sinarr, choose our ground and trap Johan's army. This battle needs to be decisive – striking too soon with too few men just risks giving Johan another victory, one that will only add to his growing reputation."

"You're asking me to take *all* of my men, after what just happened?" Hrodmarr asked with a frown.

"No, I'm just asking you for a hundred, the rest can come from Olt's warriors. Those who remained loyal to you, rather than heeding Jolinn's call. They should be men we can rely on."

Hrodmarr thought on that for a time. "You'll have your six hundred. Pick yours carefully this time, Alfarr. Men we can absolutely trust to fight alongside us when the time comes. I don't want any more surprises. Your father and grandfather can ride out with us too, in order to set an example to your people about who they follow nowadays."

Alfarr bowed low as he left Hrodmarr's chamber. "I'll make the preparations immediately. We'll be ready to ride out the day after tomorrow."

***

"I don't like the way he keeps talking to you," Ulf muttered as he walked with Djuri back towards the barracks. Djuri turned to his friend, who was young, like most of those who'd gone over to Blackeyes' banner after Ulfkell's Keep fell. At thirty-one, Djuri was one of the oldest and most experienced of Reavesburg's warriors and the one they looked to for leadership. It was not a position he'd craved or sought, but Tyrfingr Blackeyes had recognised that quality in Djuri before he'd fully appreciated it himself. Giving him this command was a way to test that further and find out where Djuri's loyalties really lay.

"What, 'Turncloak'? I guess it's a name I've earned, wouldn't you say?"

"Just saying, the way Hrodmarr and Bjorr talk to you doesn't show any respect."

Djuri shrugged. "After this is over I might have earned a new name for myself, and Turncloak will be long forgotten."

Ulf looked sceptical. "Those two will never let you forget it, or any of us for that matter. We're still Reavesburg warriors, Djuri, and the Vorund Clan won't give us equal status with them, no matter what happens at the end of this battle with Johan."

"You think we picked the wrong side?"

Ulf paused, head down as they walked through Olt's cobbled streets. Djuri watched the townsfolk, his own people, giving them a wide berth, their eyes fearful. Things were different now and they'd never go back to how they were before.

"I was angry," Ulf said at last. "I was angry with Johan and Gautarr and all the rest of those cowards when they just … ran away, that night when Blackeyes attacked. They left us behind, rather than standing and helping us fight. The way I see it, Blackeyes was more merciful than any of us had a right to expect, giving us the chance to live when this so-called hero Johan left us there to die. Adalrikr's already conquered the Norlhast and Riltbalt clans, with Reavesburg's resistance weakening. If he's going to rule as King of the North then I'd rather serve him. Not saying I'm entirely proud of it, but I don't intend switching sides again – no one would trust me then."

"I came to much the same conclusion," agreed Djuri, clapping Ulf on the back, though it was with a heavy heart. "Now, ready the men. You heard Alfarr, we're leaving in two days' time, so make sure you and Haarl have organised all our supplies and provisions by then."

"What about you?" Ulf asked.

"Got other business to attend to. Don't worry, I'll be back before too long."

***

Djuri drew up the hood of his cloak as he walked alone through Olt's streets, even though it was a warm summer's day. His feet followed the familiar paths of his childhood, bringing him to the house without really thinking about it. Olt's merchant quarter had always been a bustling, noisy place, almost like a village in its own right, where everyone knew everyone else's business. Djuri fully expected to meet people he recognised. However, the streets were almost empty here and he passed just one woman, head down, carrying an enormous bundle of laundry in a basket over her shoulder. They walked past each other without a word.

He stood for a time looking at his parents' house from across the road, remembering his father's face the day he told him Finnvidor Einarrson, Kolfinnar's jarl, had picked him from all those in training. He'd been selected to join the clan chief's guard in Ulfkell's Keep and would be trained by Olfridor Half-hand, veteran of more battles than he could count and newly appointed by Kolfinnar as the chief's weapons master. His father had looked at him with a mixture of sadness and pride. They'd both known Djuri would never follow in his father's footsteps and join the family wool merchant business. He'd been too wild for that and, as he grew taller and stronger, it seemed inevitable he would serve Hrodi Myndillson as one of his warriors. It was all Djuri had ever wanted.

"Einarrson's obviously seen something special in you, lad," his father told him, hugging him tight. "Won't lie and pretend I don't want to lose you but I understand this is a chance you've got to take. It'll bring honour to our family and you'll be serving Kolfinnar Marlson himself, in his own keep. It's a real honour."

Djuri had looked up at him, surprised to see his father was crying. "I won't forget my schooling, Father. You taught me my letters and I'll write to you as often as I can, I promise."

His father smiled at that, wiping the tears from his face. "I'll look forward to that, Son. I really will. I want to know everything that happens." Djuri was only eleven but it had been the proudest day of his life as he hugged his father once more.

Standing there now the family home was quiet, the windows shuttered even though the shop would normally have been busy serving customers at this time of day. Djuri took a moment to collect himself, walked across the road and knocked firmly on the door. There was no answer and he found it was unlocked. He gently pushed it open and walked inside.

With the shutters closed the shop was only dimly lit by thin shafts of sunlight that found their way through the gaps in the windows. The house was deserted, shop counter thick with dust, the shelves normally piled high with dyed woollen cloth all empty. Djuri looked again at the door and noticed the lock had been broken. Someone had forced their way inside and taken everything of value.

With a sense of dread he walked through the shop and into the back of the building to his father's study, each footstep echoing dully in the deserted house. He found his father's writing desk in the corner where it had always been, again covered in dust from long disuse, although his father's chair was missing. As Djuri peered closer in the gloom he could see someone had forced open every drawer, probably with an axe, leaving deep gouge marks. The once beautiful dark polished oak was splintered and split, the desk drawers hanging open or lying scattered about the room on the floor.

Djuri had remembered his promise to his father, writing to him at least once every month from Ulfkell's Keep. He could see those letters now, written in his own hand, scattered all over the floor, some still bundled together with faded ribbon. He stooped to pick one up and was surprised to see it was dated just one year after he'd begun training with Halfhand, his flowing script still distinctive, although nowhere near as neat and tidy as it was today. It took Djuri a moment to realise his father had kept every single one.

Djuri closed the shop door behind him and as he stepped outside he pulled back his cloak to let the sun fall on his face. There was no one here to see him. His father had been a dutiful correspondent, always replying within a week. Since Tyrfingr Blackeyes' army arrived last year and moved inland Djuri had not received a single letter. He'd written several times, letting his father know he was safe after Blackeyes released him from prison. At first he assumed his family had disowned him for bending the knee to the Vorund Clan. When yet another letter went unanswered as winter came Djuri grew worried and by the spring he'd ceased writing them altogether. When he asked the merchants and traders who travelled to Reavesburg from Olt if there was any news about his family their answers were always vague. No one was going to tell a traitor like Djuri Turncloak anything useful, and in the end he stopped asking questions, fearing his interest might draw unwelcome attention to his family. He needn't have worried.

"They've gone, Djuri." The voice made him start and it took him a moment to realise it was Birna, Olt's resident healer and physician. She was now a stout, middle-aged lady but Djuri still recognised her, despite the lines on her face and her hair being more grey than brown.

"It *is* Djuri, isn't it?" Birna asked, moving closer to look at him.

"Aye, Birna, it is. It's good to see you again."

"Is that so?" Birna replied, her eyes narrowed. "Saw you ride in here under Blackeyes' banner. Seems things have changed quite a bit since you left your parents' home. What are you doing back here? Hoping to get a warmer welcome than you received from your new friends?"

Djuri held up a placating hand. "I've not come here for a fight. I just wanted to know whether my parents and brothers were safe. I've not heard anything from them in over a year, so this might be my last chance to find out how they are and where they've gone ..." He paused, unsure of what to say. "Well, we're heading out soon to bring Johan down and there's no guarantee who's coming back from that fight."

Birna folded her arms across her chest and carefully studied Djuri. It was only after she sighed and began to speak he realised he'd been holding his breath as she made up her mind.

"When Old Hrodi returned to Olt, with hundreds of Vorund's warriors at his back, folk panicked. There'd been rumours already, of course, a few days before, and a steady trickle of people had already packed and headed west, making for the passage over the mountains. Your father didn't believe it, though, and was all for staying put until Hrodmarr Hroarson's men were seen marching down the road towards the town. Place was in uproar before Hrodi reached the gates, with some getting ready for a fight and others all for surrendering. It was Alfarr who ordered the gates open, when he saw his father and grandfather's banners flying next to Hroarson's. We knew then the rumours were true and by nightfall Old Hrodi confirmed our worst fears, putting Hroarson into the finest rooms of our keep like an honoured guest."

Birna's face wrinkled in disgust. "Hrodi had a thousand swords to call on that day. We could've sent Hroarson back to Blackeyes with his tail tucked between his legs. However, he's our elder and so the people did what they were told. While plenty were glad to avoid the fight, I'll tell you, there's just as many, if not more, that agree with what Jolinn did. That girl has more warrior spirit in her than Radholf or Hrodi, and that's the truth."

"Keep your voice down," Djuri urged. "You can speak openly with me, but remember what you're saying is treason. If one of Hroarson's men hears you say these things, they'll hang you."

Birna stared hard at Djuri, her face defiant. "Gods, your father would be so proud. I'm glad he left."

"Left? Left where?"

"West, like everyone else, trying to get away from the reach of our noble 'King of the North'. Gates were kept open for trade and there were plenty of folks in the weeks that followed who left Olt and never returned. Your family were amongst them, abandoning this place for good and trying to make a new life for themselves."

"And you've not heard from them since?"

Birna shook her heard. "Not sure I'd tell you even if I had but no, there's been no news. My guess is your father would have struck out for the mountain pass and made for Vittag. He did a lot of trade with the White Widow's merchants. Might be he thought he could set up business there and start over, although I don't know for certain. The roads have been pretty dangerous since Blackeyes' men were sent out to collect the king's taxes, as I'm sure you know."

Djuri reached out, trying to take Birna's hand. She glared and stepped away. "I just wanted to thank you, that's all.

You've helped me more than I deserve –"

"Don't look for any more favours from me. When the time comes, I hope the Brotherhood puts your head on a spike, alongside every other traitor fighting for Adalrikr Kinslayer. I'm glad your father isn't here to see what you've become – it would break his heart."

Birna turned on her heel and walked away down the street, without a backwards glance. Djuri watched until she turned a corner and disappeared from view. He drew up his hood and headed towards the barracks to find Ulf and Haarl, knowing he would never return to this house.

# CHAPTER 14

Johan sat at the head of his feasting table, one hand slackly holding his cup, the remains of his half-eaten meal long since cleared away. Damona was next to him, holding his free hand. Most of the Brotherhood had departed some time ago. Ragni and Yngvarr stood guard outside, while I sat at the Brothers' Table, with Bandor and Thengill.

"Alfarr's betrayal was the worst," Johan told Damona, not for the first time that evening. "He was one of our own and he didn't even hesitate when he killed Brandr. He actually seemed to enjoy it. Our own clan turned on us. Our own clan ..."

Damona squeezed her husband's hand. "Johan, things are different now. The Brotherhood staying strong is more important than the clan and those old loyalties."

Johan looked outraged. "Of course the clan matters. The Reavesburg Clan is what we're fighting for."

Damona shook her head. "No, the Brotherhood is more than that, far more. We're all that stands against the shadow spirits and Adalrikr's rise, and that's the only side that counts for anything. Reavesburg's own warriors march against us, alongside the Vorund Clan. The time is coming when kin will be forced to kill kin." Her eyes flicked to me. "A pity Rothgar couldn't have seen what I always knew was in Old Hrodi's treacherous heart. Otherwise Harvald and Brandr might still be alive."

I let the remark pass, not wishing to rouse Johan's temper by arguing with Damona. Bandor, though, was quick to leap to my defence. "Mother, you know that isn't fair. Hrodi Whitebeard must bear full responsibility for breaking his bannerman's oaths. He and no one else."

"Enough," snapped Johan, rising from his seat, his face flushed. "Enough, all of you. I met Hrodi knowing the risks, as did those who came with me. If anyone's responsible for their loss, it's me." He shook his head and swayed on his feet. Damona rose and gently put her arm around his waist, smoothing Johan's long hair with her hand and moving it away from his lined face.

"No, my love, that's not true. You don't have to bear everyone's burdens."

"No? Who else put us on the path to war?"

"That's a fool's way to think of things," Thengill told him, picking up his cup and draining it. "Your wife's the one talking sense. We're all here because of one man, Adalrikr Kinslayer, and no other. Brandr and Harvald joined the Brotherhood because their home was destroyed by this so-called King of the North. They'd every right to seek their vengeance, stand by you and, if it came to it, die for you. With their deaths you've gained four hundred swords under Jolinn Hrodidottir's banner. That's the business we're in, the business of war. Now we need you to be strong, because people are looking up to you, Jokellsward. They're looking to you to lead us into battle and get us through this."

Johan stared at Thengill for a long time and I wondered if he'd gone too far, until Johan's shoulders shook and he laughed, quietly at first before growing louder. "I'm sorry. The drink is doing more than its fair share of the talking tonight. Who am I to argue with my brother?" Johan clapped his hands down on Thengill's shoulders, still laughing. "And sitting before me is proof of the changed world we live in; Asmarr's own guard from the clan of the bear, fighting alongside us. And I'm glad of it, Thengill. I'm glad you're with the Brotherhood and not fighting for Adalrikr. If I had fifty of you, we'd already have swept Sinarr aside and be standing on the walls of Romsdahl."

"You only need me for that," Thengill told him with a smile. Johan swayed again and this time it was Thengill who helped keep him upright. I rose from the table, sensing it was long past time to retire for the night. I looked at Bandor as he put his arm around his father's shoulders, gently leading him away.

"I'll see he gets to bed," he told me as I took my leave. It was late and I was tired, my head pounding not just from drink but also from my more frequent forays with the Sight.

Outside it was a clear night, a swathe of stars shining bright above us. I paused, stretching my stiff back, and heard the faint sound of sobbing nearby; Maeva mourning her husband's death. I could hear Ingirith's soothing tones as she comforted the younger woman, Rugga's widow sharing her pain.

"Poor woman," Thengill said, listening with me for a moment before we started walking back to our own tents. "I've always said marriage isn't for a warrior. At least Ingirith has her son and daughter, whereas Brandr's left Maeva both childless and a widow. Life's short, and no mistake."

"All the more reason to seize the moment, surely?"

"You think? If a moment's all you're interested in then perhaps you should speak to Ekkill. He seems to have more girls working for him every week." Thengill turned to look at me. "There's no shame in that, you know; more honest in some ways, I reckon. Man like me, I can't promise I'll be here next week, let alone next year. That's no way for a woman to live, bound to a man and all the while wondering if she'll ever see him again. They could … Well, Ekkill could arrange for you … too …" Thengill paused as I fixed him with a fierce stare, before breaking into a smile.

"What do you mean? How could any woman fail to be drawn to this?" I jested, with a flourish, exaggerating my limp and hunching forwards.

Thengill chuckled. "I'm really sorry, I meant no offence."

"None, taken. I left someone behind, back in Ulfkell's Keep."

Thengill nodded. "Think she's still waiting for you?

Does she even know you're alive?"

I shrugged. "No, but it doesn't matter. I'm just not looking to find anyone else, not right now."

"You're eighteen years old, Rothgar. A man your age shouldn't feel so tied down – you didn't marry this girl or get a child on her, did you?"

"No, of course not. But you forget, as a noble I was betrothed by the age of ten."

"What?" Thengill spluttered. "Who to?"

"Freydja Egilldottir, Gautarr Falrufson's niece and ward since his brother's death."

"That I didn't know," Thengill admitted. "So if we free Romsdahl are you going to ask Gautarr for her hand in marriage?"

I laughed. "It's more complicated than that. Our engagement was broken long ago, and Freydja is now promised to Bandor."

Thengill shook his head. "Not sure I'll ever understand how the noble-born conduct their affairs. I don't envy Bandor the notion of having Gautarr as his father-in-law. Perhaps you've had a lucky escape. The fellow did try and kill you, after all, if there's any truth in that wild story."

"Oh yes. I was a warrior once ..." I tried to keep my voice light but all of a sudden my throat tightened and my breath caught in my chest. "Now ... I'm Johan's pet cripple –" I'd meant to say it as a joke, only for my emotions to betray me.

Thengill frowned. "Now listen here. Can none of you Reavesburg men hold your drink without getting maudlin? You're one of Johan's closest confidants and Etta's natural successor, any fool can see that. Why else do you think Svan and his friends try and do you down every chance they get?"

We reached a fork in the road between the rows of tents. Mine lay to the left, next to Joldir's wagon, whilst Ulfarr's crew were camped out some way distant to the right. Thengill smiled and took my hand in his big, strong fist.

"Take care of yourself. I'd come with you, to say hello to

Joldir and … and Arissa … but …"

"It's late," I told him, my composure restored and a smile playing on my lips. "She'll long be abed."

Thengill nodded. "Aye, of course. Another time, though, I'll break bread with you all, like we used to back in Lindos under Joldir's roof."

I patted Thengill's thick muscular arm. "Take care yourself. You're leaving tomorrow morning with Ulfarr's crew?"

"At dawn. Can't have those riders you saw Djuri Turncloak send out reaching Sinarr, can we? Reckon they'll be easy to take down, especially since, thanks to you, we know the route they'll be taking. I'll be back before long."

"I'll hold you to that," I told him, surprised at the lump in my throat as we parted company.

***

Ulfarr's crew slipped away at dawn, just as Thengill had said, heading north as the rest of the Brotherhood continued its journey south towards Romsdahl. Djuri's army would be two days behind us, perhaps less, and they would move more swiftly than the assorted mass of humanity, animals and baggage following Johan Jokellsward. There had been debate amongst the Brotherhood about whether to split our forces to counter this threat. Sigolf Admundson offered to lead a rearguard action, pitting his forces against Djuri in order to give Johan more time to reach Romsdahl. Others, including Varinn and Yngvarr, counselled splitting the Brotherhood and taking different paths, forcing Djuri to choose which route to follow.

In the end, Johan made his decision. "Djuri isn't planning to attack us," he reasoned. "His role is to make retreat difficult and herd us towards Sinarr's forces. Dividing our own smaller army only risks inviting an attack, Sigolf, rather than preventing it – though your offer's a brave one. No, the Brotherhood stays together."

"You understand the risks to our families and wives with such tactics?" asked Svan, his arm wrapped protectively around Dalla's waist. "There's nowhere for them to retreat if we remain together."

"We're safer together," Johan reasoned. "With Reavesburg under occupation there are no safe havens, not unless we liberate Romsdahl."

Petr nodded in agreement. "We'll need outriders and patrols to protect the caravan as it heads south. If you're right then Djuri will hold his distance."

"And perhaps we can buy some time, if we intercept Djuri's messengers," added Jolinn. Though not yet a full member of the Brotherhood, no one had dared suggest she'd not earned her place at Johan's table. "Are you sure Ulfarr and his men are up to the task? Our lives depend upon it."

"That's why I sent them," Johan replied. "You saw how they handled themselves in Olt."

Progress was slow, but at least we were not hampered by the weather as the hot summer sun shone down upon us. The constant riding and camping each day was taking its toll on me, so I gratefully rested my aching back and buttocks by accepting Joldir's offer to sit alongside him in his wagon. However, within an hour I discovered this mode of transport merely caused me to suffer agony through the cramping of a different set of wasted muscles. To gain some relief I climbed into the back of the wagon, which was covered by canvas and provided somewhere for Etta to rest when we were travelling.

Arissa smiled at me as I entered. Much to my surprise I found Etta was awake, wrapped in blankets and lying in a small cot. It must have shown on my face.

"No, lad, I'm not dead. Not yet, anyway. That said, I might die of *boredom* any day now; I can feel it creeping up on me. This is what happens when you neglect your friends."

"I've not come here to quarrel," I told her, sitting down gingerly amongst all Joldir's supplies.

"No, and I'm not looking to take offence at the insults to my company," added Arissa in mock outrage. The old woman cackled, proving there was life in her yet.

"Well?" Etta asked, her eyes wide. "Has Johan come up

with a battle plan?"

"He wants to use the Fellowship first," I explained. "We've not received news from Gautarr directly, so we plan to use the Sight to try and scout out the enemy positions."

Etta waved me to draw closer. "Gautarr's part in this is vital. He and his bannermen must join the fight at precisely the right moment to ensure victory."

"That's more difficult," I admitted. "Sinarr has Romsdahl surrounded."

Etta smiled brightly. "I see I still have my uses. Listen carefully to what I'm about to tell you, because this is what *I'd* do in Johan's position."

# CHAPTER 15

The caravan continued its journey towards Romsdahl, now less than a week away at our current pace. After a couple of days' rest in Joldir's cart I resumed riding again, spending the time talking to Bandor, reminiscing about growing up together in Ulfkell's Keep. It was a welcome distraction from the challenges awaiting us in Romsdahl. During one brief stop I watched Leif playing with Egill, Ingirith's eight-year-old boy, and smiled as the two of them chased each other around the carts and wagons. Knowing what Leif had already been through in his short life made the scene more precious. Here was a chance for a small piece of normality – a snatched moment of childhood amid the chaos and uncertainty of the coming war.

"Is Leif Joldir's boy?" Jolinn asked, making me start. I'd not heard her approach until she was standing right beside me along with her second, Lars, the young warrior who'd fought with us at Olt. He looked like he only had a few years on me.

"No, he's not, although Joldir cares for him. Leif was left homeless after the destruction of Tullen, so Joldir took him in." It was a shortened version of the truth.

Jolinn looked at me with those hard blue eyes. "Yes, the first strike by the Brotherhood of the Eagle as Johan Jokellsward's uprising began. A strange tale, though. Perhaps you can explain it to me – you were there, weren't you?" I nodded, wondering where this was leading, as Jolinn continued. "What I can't understand is why Johan torched a town belonging to the people he was supposed to be liberating. He mustered his forces in Falsten and Delving and tried to do the same in Olt, so what did Tullen do that warranted its complete destruction and the death of its people? I knew Sandar, although my father tried to keep me out of the way. Very handsome, bright and able. I would have thought he was a man Johan could use, so what happened? Is there a darker side to Johan, one that shows itself if people don't join his cause?"

Whatever else Jolinn might be, she was no fool. I chose my words carefully. "Sandar attacked us when we came to Tullen and we were forced to defend ourselves. I'd be wary of bringing up the subject around Johan if I were you – it's where Rugga died, and the two of them were very close. Sandar was a traitor and Johan dealt with him as such."

"Much like the rest of my family, then. You're not really giving me any reason to imagine Johan will treat them more mercifully, are you?"

I shrugged and held out my hands. "I'm sorry, what do you want me to say?"

"Lad's right," added Lars. "We've already found ourselves fighting against those we grew up with, and it'll only get worse. This Djuri was one of Ulfkell's Keep's warriors, wasn't he? Whole world's gone mad."

"I know that, Lars. We've picked our side, just as my father, half-brother and nephew have picked theirs. What I'm asking, though, is whether Olt will suffer the same fate as Tullen? Will Johan burn it to the ground for defying him? If that's what's in his mind, then we might have the beginnings of a disagreement about that particular approach, because I didn't sacrifice Karl to save Johan, only to watch as he sets light to my home town. Johan may play the hero, but a lot of innocent people must have died that day in Tullen. I won't let it happen in Olt."

I remembered the horror we felt when we realised all the Tullen townsfolk had been consumed by the shadow spirits; watching in terror when they showed their true form, more animal than human, rising up to fight against us. However, there was no way Jolinn and Lars would believe the truth of such a tale. Even if they went through the same ritual initiation as Geirmarr I wasn't sure Jolinn would change her mind about Olt. "As you say, people make their choice. The folk of Tullen sided against us as one and tried to kill us all. There wasn't anything we could do other than defend ourselves. Things just got … out of hand."

"Out of hand? Is that how you put it?" Lars shook his head. "Like I say, this world's gone mad."

Jolinn also looked unconvinced. "I know there are things people are holding back. Things people aren't telling me concerning the Brotherhood." She towered over me and now she took a step closer, her face inches from mine. "I'm asking you nicely, Rothgar. I don't have to be this polite."

I raised my eyebrows. "Where's the honour in hitting a cripple?"

"Hmm. I saw you defend yourself in Olt. You move pretty quick for a cripple and you've some skill with that blade. Is it true Olfridor Halfhand was your weapons master?"

I nodded. "I know how to look after myself, not that I've got any desire to test myself against you."

"No. After all, where's the honour in striking a woman?" Jolinn replied archly.

Lars laughed. "There's plenty in Olt that aren't so sure on that score."

Jolinn scowled. "Very funny. Remind me again why I made you my second?"

"Look," I said. "I can see why you have so many questions and you'll have your answers in time. However, Johan doesn't know you, so whilst you might have saved his life you still need to earn his trust."

"I've heard there's some sort of initiation rite to become a full member of the Brotherhood," Jolinn pressed. "If fat old Sigolf, with less than two hundred swords from Falsten, has been granted that honour then why is it being withheld from me when I've got twice that number under my command? Doesn't he think I'm ready? Look at what I've already sacrificed to join his cause."

I sighed and held out my hands. "Look, I can't speak for Johan. Perhaps this is something you should be taking up with him, rather than with me?"

Jolinn snorted. "Don't worry, I intend to. l don't like being kept in the dark." She turned on her heel and headed off, Lars walking in step beside her.

Bandor walked up to me as I watched the pair leaving. "What was that all about?"

"Let's just say Jolinn has a lot of unanswered questions about the Brotherhood. I'm not sure how much she'll like the answers."

***

We knew Djuri's army was tracking us but they never showed themselves. Four days after their departure Ulfarr's crew returned, bringing with them five extra horses, each carrying the bound body of a man.

"Didn't want to leave any sign behind," Ulfarr was saying to Petr as I rode up to the group. "As far as Djuri is concerned, we need him to believe his men made it through to Romsdahl. Of course, when he doesn't get any reply he'll probably guess what happened."

"Are they alive?" I asked, though from the way they were tied and slung over their horses it seemed unlikely.

"Tried to capture them, but they fought hard," Skari said, nodding in Myr's direction. The big man's face was swollen and bruised, one eye half-closed. I could see Sir Patrick had a bandage round his leg as well and the rest of them had various cuts and bruises. Only Ekkill seemed to have come through the encounter unscathed. The man regarded me coolly as I looked at him, his face inscrutable as always.

"These men were loyal to Blackeyes," Thengill explained. "They fought to the death and took any secrets to the grave. No sign of any written orders either, not that I expected to find something so useful. Djuri's no fool."

"No, he's not," I replied. "I came here to see if you wanted me to interrogate them, Petr. Clearly that's unnecessary."

Johan's second shook his head. "No, but Johan wants to see you about something else."

***

Johan was riding at the head of the column and seemed pleased when Ulfarr gave his report. "Well done. Get some rest today, because I want you out there again tomorrow. I want you to circle out wide and help Petr to cover both our advance and rear guard. Sinarr will have scouts in the area and Djuri may send out a second set of messengers as well, just as a precaution. Are you all fit to travel or do you need Petr to find you some additional men?"

"I'm fine, sir," Patrick told him. Myr nodded as well, patting his sword.

"My men will be ready," Ulfarr told him. "No sign of Djuri making a move?"

"None," Petr replied. "It makes me nervous. So far, our approach has been far too easy."

"Petr, see that these men are well fed and rested," Johan ordered. "Rothgar, a word, if you will."

Petr followed Johan's orders, looking nonplussed at being given such a menial duties. Thengill clapped me on the shoulder as he rode away with Ulfarr and the rest of his company. "I'll see you later."

I watched them disappear into the slow-moving column as Johan leaned in close to speak to me. "Romsdahl draws near and I need more information. Joldir counselled me to give you some rest. Now the time has come when I need the Fellowship to play its part once more."

I nodded. "We're ready." My headache had faded in recent days and at night I'd felt the faint insistent pull drawing me towards the Path once more.

"Good. I'll order an early halt to the march today, so you can make your preparations while everyone gets some rest. There may be precious few days left when we'll be able to choose to do that. And Rothgar, whatever you learn, you bring to me and Etta at once, you understand?"

# CHAPTER 16

Randall stared at the farmhouse and the large ruined barn off to the left, which had been converted into Sinarr the Cold One's headquarters. Joarr had been furious at being demoted when Sinarr took command of Vorund's forces in the autumn of last year. He wasn't brave or foolish enough, though, to take issue with The Cold One. Instead, Adalrikr's jarl moved out and found new quarters, leaving Sinarr to take possession of the building.

Whilst Joarr favoured life's comforts, Sinarr had no interest in such things and the windows of the building remained permanently shuttered. They were closed and dark through winter, as the army hunkered down, shivering, outside Romsdahl's walls. They stayed shut throughout spring, when the heavy snows melted and green grass shoots emerged. They remained shuttered now, in the warmth of summer. No noise came from the farmhouse these days – no songs or laughter, no sounds of feasting and drinking. Joarr's warriors had commented darkly on all this, gathered round their cook fires as they nursed their wounded pride at their leader's treatment. For Randall it was different – he was used to such things. He'd served under Sinarr since Asmarr's death eight years ago and nothing could surprise him. Randall shifted his weight from one foot to the other as he continued to stand guard. At fifty-four, he was one of the oldest men in Sinarr's army and this past year of sleeping under canvas had taken its toll. His knees were stiff and his feet never warm, even now in the summer months. He rubbed the small of his back and stretched, trying not to think about such things. This was army life; a lot of waiting around, all the while enduring various hardships and terrible food, with the occasional moment when you were forced to fight for your life thrown in.

Waiting was all they'd done since reaching Romsdahl, the great southern fortress of the Reavesburg Clan. Kalamar fell swiftly in the end, although it had presented a different challenge. Johan Jokellsward's castle was smaller for one thing, although when Sinarr's ships first landed Randall recalled it seemed a daunting prospect. The tactics were the same as those they were now employing here: blockade the docks with their fleet, surround the castle and attempt to starve out its occupants. By the autumn, with supplies running low, Jokellsward's men were weakening. Randall expected Sinarr to order the building of siege engines and launch an attack to end the stalemate before winter. Instead, a lone ship from Vorund slid through the dark waters of the Redfars Sea one night and landed at their own makeshift docks. It brought not more men, weapons, equipment or food, as Randall had expected. All it contained were a dozen barrels stacked neatly together and covered by two layers of oilskins to protect them from the salt water.

"King Adalrikr himself has given the order to deliver these to Sinarr the Cold One," the captain explained when Randall greeted him at the dockside.

"What is it?" asked Randall, suspiciously eyeing the cargo.

"Fire powder from Samarakand," the captain told him. "Don't drop it when you carry it off my ship and, whatever you do, don't keep it near a naked flame."

Randall had watched in amazement the following night when the mysterious blasting powder erupted into a fireball so bright he had to turn aside – the after-image burned onto his eyes. As the thunderous roar of the explosion faded he saw giant stones raining down from the sky, huge chunks of rock torn free from the breach made in the castle walls. Even before the deadly shower of stone had finished one of the towers began to list to one side, the screams of its occupants carried all the way to Randall by the wind. He watched in shock as it tore itself free from what was left of the walls, bringing much of them down as it hurtled to the ground with a roar, vanishing into a cloud of dust and debris. Then a second tower began to slide slowly down, the base bulging out as the ancient masonry gave way and spewed its foundations out over the ground. The tower gathered pace as it slid downwards before pausing for a moment, teetering on the fragments of stone still supporting its weight, before it twisted and crashed inwards through Kalamar Castle, wreaking more destruction with its passage.

There was stunned silence in the ranks of Sinarr's army as they stared at the ruined remains of the Reavesburg Clan's northern fortress. Then, with a huge shout, they surged forwards through the enormous breach in the walls, engulfing and overwhelming the remaining defenders in a tide of unthinking and remorseless destruction. By dawn it was all over, the charred smell thick in the air as Kalamar burned fiercely, the plume of smoke visible for miles around. By the time Sinarr's army began to head south the remaining three towers of Kalamar Castle had also been brought down, on The Cold One's orders. Not one stone was left standing, Johan Jokellsward's seat of power reduced to rubble.

Romsdahl was a small city, surrounded by a thick curtain wall, its castle built upon a steep motte in the centre. It was an altogether more formidable prospect than Kalamar. When Randall had landed with the rest of Sinarr's army it was clear Joarr and Gautarr's forces had reached a stalemate, as each tried to outwait the other. Randall had expected Sinarr to deploy similar tactics to shorten the siege but Romsdahl was a more important strategic site, one Adalrikr wanted to capture intact. Instead the Vorund Clan besieged Gautarr through the rest of the year, waiting beyond the walls through the harsh winter that cost them more than five hundred lives, as men fell prey to the cold. Waiting as spring and then summer came, with various wooden buildings, an inner and outer palisade and fortified towers being built as the siege took on a more permanent aspect. Waiting while they sent the message to Gautarr and the city of Romsdahl that Sinarr's army was going nowhere.

Imagining Romsdahl's supplies must be almost exhausted, by the spring Randall expected negotiations for their surrender to begin. Yet Gautarr sent no emissary suing for peace; the eagle flag of the Reavesburg Clan continued to fly from the castle walls, defying Sinarr each day. The men grew impatient, until Joarr argued the time had come to build siege engines and begin an assault on Gautarr's stronghold. Sinarr refused to consider such a plan and, increasingly, talk in the Vorund camp was that they might have to face another winter staring at Romsdahl's thick walls.

"What do you think this means?" Kurt asked Randall, the younger warrior pointing down the road from the farmhouse. Randall screwed his eyes shut against the glare of the sun and saw Joarr the Hammer, accompanied by a score of warriors, advancing towards them.

At their head was the distinctive short figure of Joarr. Almost as broad as he was tall and tremendously strong, Joarr was a fearsome adversary when fighting with his two-handed warhammer, *Foebreaker*. Although over forty his hair was still blond, with no trace of grey, his thick beard his pride and joy. Many made the mistake when first meeting Joarr of not seeing past his jovial appearance. Randall knew better.

"Joarr," he called out. "Don't recall Sinarr sending word that he wanted to see you."

"I don't need any such invitation, Randall. We're both Adalrikr's jarls," Joarr replied, as he marched towards the farmhouse.

Worry settled in the pit of Randall's stomach as he tried once more. "Not sure now's the time to go demanding an audience, if it's all the same with you."

"Really?" Joarr replied, stopping in front of Randall and Kurt. The rest of Randall's guard gathered behind him, facing

Joarr's men.

"Not looking to argue with you, Joarr," Randall persisted. "Sinarr told me he didn't want to be disturbed when I took up my post this morning."

Joarr took a deep breath and let it out slowly, hands on his hips. He turned to Hasteinn, his right-hand man, and in a stage whisper said "Did you hear that? Sinarr's been holed up here so long people are wondering if he's still in command of this army. Getting this sort of reception hardly helps quell those rumours."

Hasteinn, a strong dark-haired warrior with a sour aspect, folded his arms across his chest and looked hard into Randall's eyes. "Reckon you've every right to speak to the boss, jarl to jarl."

Randall sighed, placing a hand on Kurt's arm before he could remonstrate. "I can't stop you from going in there. I just wanted to give you fair warning of the kind of mood he's in, that's all."

Joarr nodded to his men, who were busy telling him to speak to Sinarr now. Randall could see something in the jarl's eyes, though. There was a brief flicker of fear on his face as Joarr approached the door. Hasteinn made to move past until Kurt laid a hand gently on his chest and shook his head.

"No. Only Joarr and Randall go any further."

"It's alright, Hasteinn," Joarr told him. "Wait here for me."

Randall took a lantern off a hook and lit the wick before entering the dim building with Joarr. The faint light revealed a long-disused kitchen, the fireplace cold and dark, the farmhouse silent save for the noise of their booted feet on the stone floor. Randall led them to the doorway leading to the back of the house, breath fogging in the lantern light.

"Randall, I thought I made it clear I was not to be disturbed. Why have you disobeyed my order?" Sinarr's voice came from the back room, husky and raw.

Standing at the doorway Randall's light struggled to

penetrate the gloom, the far wall remaining shrouded in shadow. He could just make out a dark shape, sitting cross-legged on the other side of the room, so he spoke in that direction. "You have a visitor, my lord. It's Joarr the Hammer, here to see you."

"Joarr?" The shape in the shadows moved again, uncoiling and loping into the meagre light with frightening speed. Randall took a step back in alarm, accidently jostling Joarr in his haste.

Sinarr was a large man, well over six feet tall, with thick arms and legs like tree trunks. He was naked except for a loincloth, the tattoo of a black bear standing out on his well-muscled chest. Eight years ago, when Adalrikr led the uprising to become chief, Sinarr was the first to join his cause. He'd been a handsome young man back then, always courted by the ladies and admired by the other Vorund warriors for his strength and skill. In the aftermath of the rebellion Adalrikr named Sinarr, Tyrfingr and Joarr as his first jarls, dividing his forces between the three of them.

At first Randall had been pleased to find himself assigned to Sinarr's army but, in the years that followed, Sinarr began to change. His sleek long dark hair started to fall out in clumps, until what little was left hung limply from his head like a dozen rat's tails. His teeth turned brown and his hazel eyes misted over, becoming red and bloodshot. Slowly Sinarr's tanned skin took on a duller aspect and began to mottle, until eventually there were streaks of dark blue and purple running across his whole body in long veins of colour, stark against his now pale flesh.

"Well, Joarr, what brings you here ... uninvited?" Sinarr said, looking both men up and down with an appraising glance. His lips moved slowly, forming the words awkwardly. Sinarr's breath was foul and Randall gagged as the putrid stench rolled over him. The temperature dropped as Sinarr drew near, radiating waves of coldness over both men, leaching the warmth from their bodies.

Joarr coughed into his hand, taking another step back. "Sinarr … There's things you need to know. The men in the camp are growing restless, with supplies running short and no end to this siege in sight."

"That's why I have you, Joarr. To attend to the little things and keep my campaign running smoothly. I don't expect you to bring such petty problems to me."

Joarr folded his arms and met Sinarr's stare, swallowing hard. Randall had to admire the man's courage. "With respect, these aren't petty matters I'd leave in the hands of my seconds. We've had desertions – another ship slipped away from the blockade during the night."

"What's one ship to me, when I have a fleet in the Redfars Sea?"

"That makes five now," Joarr persisted, wincing as Sinarr's foul breath washed over him. "The fleet's down to thirty-five ships, with four of those still being repaired after the damage they suffered last winter. There's also been two outbreaks of disease; the bloody flux has struck in both the northern and southern sides of the camp. At least fifty men have died and maybe two hundred more are ill, with the numbers increasing every day."

Sinarr blinked once, deliberately, almost as if he had to remember how to perform such an action. His eyelids closed and opened again with a leathery, audible *snap*, his eyes lost in a web of red veins. "Then take those who are ill or show any signs of disease and move them into the hospital, away from the barracks."

"Hasteinn's already seen to that. The point is the men are growing more anxious about how long this siege is going to last, especially with conditions worsening like this. Myshall's bane, *I'm* getting anxious. It's mid-summer and still we've made no move against Gautarr. The men don't want to spend another winter dying from the cold outside Romsdahl. Last winter Gautarr's warriors watched from the walls and taunted us. *Taunted us*, as we buried our own in the frozen ground."

"I remember," Sinarr told him. There was a long pause as the three men stared at each other before Sinarr turned and walked back into the room. "Come with me, both of you. You should see this."

They followed Sinarr, Randall holding up his lantern to pierce the gloom. The room was cold and dank, with an unwholesome odour that caught in the back of his throat, making him cough. Sinarr sat down, cross-legged, in front of a silver basin full of water.

"Gather round," Sinarr ordered. As Randall drew closer he could feel the chill radiating from Sinarr as he took a seat with Joarr. The three of them looked into the water in the basin, which was smooth and dark, swallowing the light from its surroundings, reflecting nothing back.

"I've spent many days in the darkness, studying these waters," Sinarr told them. "They've shown me the Landless Jarl draws near. With his defeat, victory over the Reavesburg Clan will be assured."

"Johan Jokellsward finally shows his hand?" said Randall.

"We've heard the reports of his uprising in the west. Now he marches for Romsdahl, where we have been lying in wait for this very moment."

"I thought we were here to fight Gautarr Falrufson," interjected Joarr, looking confused.

Sinarr looked at the jarl, shaking his head. "We've merely been preventing his participation in the war. It's the Landless Jarl that King Adalrikr wishes to see destroyed, along with his allies. Afterwards, Falrufson will surrender and hand us the keys to Romsdahl, allowing us to take the city intact."

"This battle you've seen coming," Joarr asked carefully. "You've seen that we win, right?"

"I've seen its importance and how the outcome will shape the future of Laskar," Sinarr replied. "Which is why we must be ready, and not waste our strength in a futile effort to try and break Romsdahl's walls. Jokellsward will be here soon and then you will know the answer to your question, Joarr the Hammer."

Once they were back outside, Randall squinted in the welcome light of the sun, deeply breathing in the fresh air as he tried to get rid of the revolting odour from the farmhouse. "What did you make of that?" he asked Joarr. "I did try and warn you."

Joarr coughed, his face grey. "Since when does Johan Landless pose such a threat? Some weakly held towns in the west heed his call and now this is all Adalrikr's interested in?"

"Couple of scouting parties haven't made it back these past two weeks," Randall said thoughtfully. "Figured they'd deserted, but if Sinarr's right it could be Johan's accounted for them. Perhaps he's closer than we know."

"Perhaps," Joarr mused. "If you're right then we should increase the number of patrols. Only assign men you can really trust – I don't want to give them any excuse to desert, especially if the Landless Jarl is as close as Sinarr believes."

Randall nodded and went to carry out Joarr's orders himself, glad to have the excuse to leave the farmhouse.

# CHAPTER 17

Nuna stood on the dockside, watching with a crowd of excited onlookers as the ship headed towards the quay. Waves broke over the distinctive shape of a whale being towed tail-first by the vessel.

Brosa leaned in close to be heard over the chatter. "That's the largest beast I've seen them catch this year. Good news for the families of those sailors – there's enough food and oil there to keep them in coin and fed through to the end of next winter."

Nuna nodded, drawing her cloak more tightly about her against the strong northerly breeze blowing in off the sea. A warm day in Norlhast still took some getting used to, even in summer. Her maids Katla and Ottama stood nearby. Katla was shivering but Ottama, a Norlhast native, looked comfortable. After the ship docked Nuna watched, fascinated, as the huge animal was hauled out of the water using a giant wooden crane and laid out on the purpose-built stone quayside. A number of the crew emerged from the ship, carrying long-handled knives, whilst more men on the docks headed towards the carcass carrying barrels on their shoulders and calling out greetings to the new arrivals.

"This might not be so pleasant to watch, my lady," Brosa said. "Perhaps you would like to retire to the keep?"

"Nonsense," Nuna replied brusquely. "How am I to learn the ways of my people unless I see them for myself?"

"Really, my lady?" asked Katla, the colour already drained from her face and her lips blue.

Nuna gave her maid an exasperated look. "Yes, *really*. Tell me again, Brosa what was that word you used before, for dismembering a whale carcass?"

"Flensing, my lady. The flensing knives are used to cut off long strips of blubber – there, you see – just like so. These men will spend the rest of the day rendering the animal, ensuring not a thing is wasted."

"Oh my," Katla gasped, leaning on Ottama, who was watching her with amusement.

Standing downwind from the operation the pungent smell of fish soon became overpowering as the men flensed each piece of blubber from the whale with practised ease. Nuna watched with interest as the pieces of meat were placed into barrels and carried away, the great sea creature slowly vanishing as the men worked. Perhaps the smell was disagreeing with her, though, as she felt a pulse of pain behind her right eye. Glancing behind her, Nuna saw Ottama also looked discomforted and she caught Brosa's attention.

"I think it would be a kindness to my maids if we headed back now. I've seen enough for one day."

"Of course, my lady," Brosa replied, offering her his arm as he began to escort her back towards Norlhast Keep. They had only gone a few steps when the pain in her head intensified. Nuna stumbled and would have fallen if Brosa hadn't been there.

"My lady?" Brosa asked, looking concerned.

"Brosa, Ottama's been taken ill too," Katla called. Nuna glanced over and saw that her maid was clutching her head as she sat on the ground. Already a crowd of onlookers was starting to gather.

"Help me home, Brosa. Quickly," Nuna told him.

Her skull felt like it was going to split apart and she was hit by a wave of nausea. Nuna fought against the urge to retch, squinting in the bright afternoon sun as she kept walking. She was the Lady of Norlhast Keep and it was important to maintain her dignity in front of her people. With an effort she set one foot in front of the other as the pain behind her eyes continued to build. Katla followed, supporting Ottama as they made their way back to the gates of the keep.

***

Norlhast vanished and it took me a moment to realise I was lying face down on the ground; I could taste the earth in my mouth and somewhere I could hear Leif screaming. When I tried to rise my head pulsed with pain, my limbs lifeless and unresponsive.

"Keep back." Arissa's voice came from some way off, shrill with fear. Leif was still screaming nearby. "Joldir. Rothgar. Wake up!"

I tried again to raise my head, the pain beginning to subside. My arms felt weak as water and shook as I put my weight on them. With an immense effort I managed to rise onto all fours. Something had broken into our Fellowship, ripping us away from the Path. Leif was curled into a ball, screaming continuously with his hands wrapped around his head, as if trying to prevent it from exploding. Joldir lay unconscious next to him within our protective circle of runestones, each of which were blazing red hot, like coals on the fire. Light arced from one stone to another, revealing the normally invisible web of magical energy protecting us from the durath. Beyond the circle the members of the Brotherhood stood transfixed, frozen in time. Bandor's sword was half-drawn from its scabbard, his teeth bared in an animal snarl. Nearby, Eykr and Yngvarr were similarly affected. I could see the runes etched onto Bandor's blade shining bright blue – confirming what I already knew. The durath had come for us and were standing on the edge of our circle, pressing in on all sides, testing Joldir's runes for any sign of weakness. A dozen of them in all and one or two faces were familiar – people I'd seen about the camp in the last couple of months. Had they been durath all this time or had their souls only recently been snatched away by the skin thieves? Now all pretence at disguise was forgotten, their movements had acquired a bestial quality, snarling and spitting as the runes thwarted their attacks, hands curled into claws that scratched and pawed at the glowing barrier standing between us.

There was one who was different. A young man with short curly blond hair and a smirk playing on his lips was staring straight at me. He stood tall and proud, hands clasped behind his back and licked his lips. His cheeks were flushed, his eyes bright and an unwholesome desire radiated from him. I was flesh, flesh this one wanted to possess and consume. I shut my eyes, head still pounding from being wrenched so violently from the Path, and brought up my defences as Joldir had taught me. I knew I was dealing with one of the Sundered – this one had no fear of leaving the body he now possessed nor the life and death struggle required to take on a new form. He'd done it before, countless times, and no one had ever been able to defy him.

"Master, please hurry. We can't reach them and more men with runeblades will be coming." The woman spoke in a high girlish voice full of fear and frustration, her eyes rolling wildly.

"Help us, master. We want to live on …"

"We want to feast, feast on their flesh …"

"Help. The Brotherhood's under attack." Arissa was running towards us, closer now, her knife a glowing blue blur. The blond man held up his hand and it was as if Arissa had run straight into an invisible wall, bringing her to a crashing halt and leaving her gasping and winded on the ground.

There was a sound from beyond the circle, a scraping of metal as Bandor's sword slid another inch from its scabbard. The blond durath's eyes flicked to one side, a small frown momentarily creasing his smooth forehead, and the movement ceased. Bandor fought against the magic controlling him to no avail, a sheen of sweat across his face, the tendons in his neck taut. Arissa's shouts and Leif's screams had raised the alarm and I could hear cries and commotion rising up from the camp. The leader of the durath heard it too and he turned to look at me once more, eyes boring deep into mine. He took a breath and stepped inside the circle. The runes flared into life, brilliant white against the glowing red stones, halting the durath's progress. Teeth bared as tendrils of light criss-crossed over his body like a net, the shadow spirit tried to force his way through.

"Master. They're coming."

"Kill them," the blond man snarled, his eyes never leaving me as he took another halting step into the circle.

*Move*, I told myself as my attacker advanced, the runes glowing brighter as they tried to repel the incursion. I could feel the durath trying to control me as he had the other members of the Brotherhood. Fortunately, inside the circle his magic was weaker and I felt something in his spell give, his hold on the Brotherhood unravelling as its effect on me faded. Shrieks and yelling came from outside and fear clutched at my heart as the painted protective inscriptions started to peel away from the runestones, curling like autumn leaves. I watched in horror as one shrivelled and boiled off the stone, turning into ash as it was carried away on the wind. The durath laughed, sensing victory as my defences weakened and he advanced another step closer.

*Move!* My legs shook as I found my feet, the ground feeling like it was swaying beneath me. I drew my short sword, the three dragon and chimera runes a dazzling blue along the blade, humming with magic so loudly they drowned out the sounds beyond the circle. Beyond the runes battle was joined with the other durath as the Brotherhood's warriors tried to save me. The Sundered continued to press through the web of protective magic, another of the runestones splitting open with a sharp crack.

"The Cripple dares to face me with his toy blade. Only your profound ignorance gives you the courage to challenge me," laughed the blond durath, his voice full of scorn. "I've lived lifetime upon lifetime as one of the Sundered. My king commands your death, along with the rest of your troublesome Fellowship. His will is not to be denied."

I raised my sword with shaking hands. "We'll see about

that."

The durath threw back his head and laughed. Up close, I saw his clothes were singed while his handsome face showed signs of strain, his eyes half-shut against the glare. With a cry born of desperation and fear I stepped in close, setting my weight behind my blade and driving it towards the durath. Entangled within the runestones' protective shield his reactions were slow. The durath barely moved as the sword point bit through cloth and skin. With a roar I pushed again, driving the blade into his guts. The Sundered grunted in surprise, looking down at the wound. There was no rush of blood from what should have been a mortal blow and I knew something was wrong. The hilt of my sword began to grow hot as I tried, unsuccessfully, to release my hold on the weapon.

"You're the broken plaything of King Adalrikr," the skin thief hissed in my face, his own twisted in pain as he reached out with smoking hands and took a firm hold of my head. "The game ends now."

I tried unsuccessfully to break his grip with my free hand as his fingers pressed into my skull. I shrieked as the bones in my head ground together and my right hand, still refusing to release my sword, burned like fire. Slowly he forced my head upwards until I was looking into the eyes of my enemy; old eyes, eyes that had lived for so long and seen such terrible things.

"Your life's over," the durath told me. "King Adalrikr will reward me beyond measure for –"

There was a swishing noise and a blur of blue. The man's blond curls were matted with dark red blood that oozed down his face. The durath opened his mouth, gasped, and dropped me to my knees. He reached back with shaking fingers to inspect the ruin of his head, drew back his hand, dripping in his own blood and stared at it.

"No."

He blinked and gasped again while the blood continued to flow. I pulled my sword out of his body and dropped it to the ground, my fingers and the palm of my hand red raw and blistered.

"No ..."

The blood became a river, pouring onto the ground in a great torrent as the life of the Sundered ended. His body folded in on itself like a discarded wineskin and took on a leathery aspect, shrivelling before us as the remaining runestones blazed brightly and destroyed the last vestiges of the durath's host.

"I spent years of my life etching fifty runes into that staff," Joldir panted, sinking to his knees. "Never thought ... Never thought I'd need to use them ... all ... against one of the Sundered Souls."

I was too tired to thank him. Instead I pulled Joldir into an embrace, resting my splitting head on his shoulder, each of us supporting the other's weight as the sounds of battle raged around us.

# CHAPTER 18

I winced as Varinn finished tying the bandage around my right hand, gently turning it over as he inspected his work with a grunt of satisfaction. The old warrior's hands were thick and calloused, fingers slightly bent with age, so I'd been surprised by his gentle touch as he applied the salve to my burns.

"Stitched up enough folk in my time to know this trade all too well," he told me, his smile softening his scarred face.

"Thank you." I nursed my wounded hand, gingerly flexing it and wincing as pain lanced up my arm.

Varinn tutted and shook his head. "You need to rest and let that ointment do its work. Leave it well alone and make sure you apply fresh salve and clean bandages every day for the next week."

Joldir entered the hospital tent, looking like he'd aged ten years, his face grey and pinched. "Arissa's still unconscious," he told me as he examined my hand. "Thankfully I don't think she's suffered any permanent harm. Leif's calmer now – I've left him with Ingirith and it might be best if he stays the night with her and the children. There's still work to be done and Johan wants answers. He's called a meeting of the Brotherhood and he's asking to see us."

Varinn patted Joldir on the shoulder as he took his leave, heading off to tend Eykr, who had broken his leg during the battle. We'd been lucky to escape so lightly, with the Brotherhood descending upon the weaker durath and destroying them without any other serious injuries. Once the Sundered had turned his full attention to breaking through the rune circle his hold on Bandor and the rest of our guards had been released, allowing them to join the fight with Ulfarr and his men. We'd lost people all the same. A dozen folk had been consumed by the durath, people who'd once been friends, wives, husbands or parents to members of our camp. Whilst a runeblade would destroy a skin thief it could never restore the soul of the person whose life had been taken. Those lives had been casually thrown away, their only purpose to delay the Brotherhood for long enough to allow their leader to destroy our Fellowship. A plan which almost succeeded.

I passed the runestones guarding the entrance to Johan's tent on shaky legs, accompanied by Joldir. Inside, with the exception of Varinn and Eykr, the entire Brotherhood was assembled. Jolinn stood with Lars, watching me from the far side of the tent. Her arms were folded and I couldn't meet her penetrating blue-eyed stare for long. Johan walked over and hugged us both, before sitting at the head of the Brothers' Table. As I took my seat and food was served my stomach roiled, my head pounding once more. I set aside the bread, meat and spiced fruits, leaving them untouched.

"You should try and eat something," Joldir told me quietly.

"You eat something, then," I retorted, repulsed by the very thought.

Joldir picked up some dried fruit and looked at it for the longest time before setting it back down on his plate. "You might have a point."

"Word of the attack has spread throughout the entire camp," Johan announced. "After what people witnessed the true nature of our cause can no longer be kept a secret. Perhaps it's for the best. People have demanded an explanation concerning what took place."

"He means me," Jolinn supplied.

"Indeed, and you're entitled to an answer. No one here knows more regarding the durath than Joldir of Lindos. I want you to listen carefully to what he has to say and think about what this means for you and your men."

Jolinn looked directly at Joldir. "I saw a dozen people,

one of them a warrior in my own company, become something ... inhuman. When they died they turned into rivers of blood. What evil magic was this and why were they so hell-bent on killing you and Rothgar?"

Jolinn and Lars listened carefully as Joldir told them King Adalrikr's true nature. Lars shook his head when Joldir explained how the gift of the Sight made us particular targets. Jolinn, however, looked thoughtful, watching the rest of our company carefully as Joldir continued to tell his story. She saw nods as folk agreed with a particular point or recalled an event they had been involved in. No one in this battle-hardened group scoffed at the story, each instead affirming with deadly seriousness their intention to see this through to the end.

After Joldir had finished Jolinn joined the Brothers' Table and was quiet for a time. She raised her cup and drank deeply before speaking. "That tale would've been hard to believe, if I hadn't seen those things. I've saw the runestones encircling your tent, Johan, thinking they were nothing more than superstitious symbols, until today. Now, I'm wondering why every member of this camp doesn't have the same protections?"

Joldir sighed. "Forging a rune in metal or even painting it onto stone is ... exacting. Part of me goes into creating each one, and I need time to recover. There are over two thousand people in this camp and it's simply impossible to create enough runestones to protect them all."

Jolinn looked at Joldir, resting her chin on her hands, eyes boring into him. "That's a concern. Without our artificer it sounds like we'd be helpless against these shadow spirits."

"I've been teaching Rothgar what I know," Joldir replied. "However, it takes years to learn the skills required."

"One day I'll be able to play more of a part," I added.

"Hmm. You stood your ground well enough today," Jolinn said, giving me an appraising glance. "You didn't back down when that creature tried to cross your circle and you fought well when my old man tried to hand you over to Hrodmarr. You're full of surprises, Rothgar Kolfinnarson."

"So are the durath," interrupted Ulfarr. "Is this the first of many attacks we're going to face? And why didn't Rothgar's weapon kill that monster? I don't know about anyone else but I slept easier after Joldir inscribed those runes onto my sword. Was that a waste of time, if they don't work against the Sundered?"

"And how long have these shadow spirits been among us?" asked Damona, her face strained. "Have we been breaking bread with our enemies this whole time? How can we fight these creatures when we don't know who to trust?"

Sigolf Admundson banged his hand on the table and let out a cry of exasperation. "Surely there must be some way to prevent this? A test everyone who joins the army must pass? Isn't it as simple as making everyone crossing a circle of runestones?"

"I thought the same, Sigolf," Johan answered. "However, with thousands following us such a task would be huge. Faced with certain capture we would simply force the durath to leave one host and take another – most likely someone who had already passed the test. This is why we've hidden a number of runestones throughout the camp, trying to trap those durath who might be in our midst. It's how we caught the one calling itself Gerrick when he tried to enter my tent, before they learned that lesson. If they don't venture far from their camp fires they can evade such measures, as long as they choose to remain hidden."

"Until now," Jolinn said.

Joldir nodded. "Until now, when the Sundered exerted a force of will so strong over their lesser brethren they were willing to sacrifice themselves. I suspect the Sundered called all the shadow spirits in our camp to his side before mounting this attack. In a way I take heart, because what we saw today proves our foes fear us and we've forced them into action, perhaps before they were fully prepared. We've dealt a serious blow to Adalrikr today and destroyed one of his most valued servants."

"You haven't answered his question," pressed Skari One-Eye, sitting next to Ulfarr. "Even one of these Sundered Souls nearly killed you – probably would have done if you hadn't woken when you did. So, how do we kill them?"

"A weapon possessing the power required to kill a Sundered Soul takes a great deal of time to create. It was my main focus when I first moved to Lindos, all those years ago. I'm sorry – there are no short-cuts." Joldir spread his hands apologetically at the discontented murmurs round the table.

"Are you telling me we have your staff, and that's it?" asked Ulfarr.

"Thengill's axes as well," Joldir said, glancing at the warrior. "I learned valuable lessons by the time Thengill joined me and completed the work in twelve months. Fewer runes applied more precisely, the spacing and alignment between them maximising their power and impact."

"So, when the time comes to deal with Adalrikr either your staff or Thengill's axes must be used to do the deed?" Johan asked.

"Exactly."

Jolinn whispered something to Lars, before rising to address the Brotherhood. "The way I see it we have the tools we need to finish the job we started, which is all that really matters. Johan, I thought you were mad to try and fight Adalrikr's army but I still joined your cause. Nothing I've seen or heard today makes me think I made the wrong decision, and my father's certainly not going to welcome me home with open arms. There's no going back, not now, so I'm with you."

Everyone pounded the table at Jolinn's words, the noise making my head throb. Johan stood and raised his cup in a toast. "To Jolinn and Lars, the newest members of the Brotherhood of the Eagle."

Skari leaned across to Ulfarr. "Can a woman be a member of a brotherhood?"

Ulfarr raised his eyebrows. "If you want to take issue

with it, then be my guest."

"After the way she cut Arnfast open?  Nope, I think on reflection I might let that matter slide," said Skari, lifting his cup and taking a long draught as he watched Jolinn intently.

# CHAPTER 19

I left the celebrations early with Joldir, the cool evening air soothing the throbbing pain in my skull. Johan walked alongside us, four guards led by Svan a few watchful steps behind.

"Being wrenched so violently from the Path has its effects," Joldir told me as we walked away from the noise emanating from Johan's tent. "It may take a little while before your balance is fully restored, so you should refrain from using the Sight for a time. In fact, with your defences weakened, you might benefit from taking further measures."

"Meaning?" asked Johan.

Joldir produced a small stoppered vial from his pocket, offering it to me. "Ataraxia will provide both relief and protection from … unwanted intrusions. I'm sure Leif is sleeping more soundly at Ingirith's under its effects."

I shook my head, instantly regretting the movement as pain pulsed behind my eyes. "No. Last time it took me months to recover my abilities. I don't want to touch that stuff."

Johan spoke up, not bothering to conceal his anger. "You didn't think to consult me? Is my Fellowship no longer able to function until the effects have worn off?"

Joldir looked unapologetic. "I'm trying to protect the Fellowship, and after what happened here today we're lucky we still have one. It may take us a few days before we can use the Sight again but that's preferable to the alternative."

"I'm still not drinking your potion," I told Joldir.

"We'll discuss this later."

The three of us approached Etta's tent, pitched in its customary place near Joldir's wagon. Arissa was outside, checking the guy ropes were secure, and she greeted us with a strained smile as we reached her. The bruises on her face were obvious, even in the faint light from the campfires.

"You're back. I was beginning to worry."

"My fault," explained Johan. "I called the Brotherhood together and now I'm imposing on your family's time just a little longer. I wish to consult with someone older and wiser."

"Then stop yapping outside. At my time of life I sleep half the day as it is, so I'd rather not waste my waking hours listening to your prattling."

"Clearly *not* possessed by one of the durath," muttered Joldir, giving Arissa a smile as we entered.

Etta's tent looked the same as ever with its sparse furnishings, the space almost entirely taken up with the mountain of thick woollen blankets piled high on Etta's bed to keep her warm. As I looked at Etta's frail form her harsh words lost their edge – she looked tired.

"It would have been more considerate to have conducted this visit earlier in the day," Etta told us as we took our seats on stools round her bed.

Johan spread out his hands apologetically. "We're here now – better late than never. I suppose you've already heard the stories about what took place."

Etta nodded. "My spies are ever dutiful and attentive. However, I would still hear the full tale from you, Rothgar. Once again, you were at the centre of events."

I picked up a couple of logs and put them on the brazier, watching as the flames quickly took hold, smoke rising up and escaping through the vent in the tent roof. At this time of year most people were warm enough sleeping under canvas, lighting their cook fires outside. However, Etta always felt the cold and I knew we would be talking late into the night. I gave my report as the brazier burned fiercely and spread its warmth.

Etta listened quietly to my tale, though her eyes glittered with some of their old sparkle when I reached the part where the Sundered Soul was destroyed. "So, the rumours *were* true. And there can be no doubt?"

"The killing stroke required the energy of all fifty runes on my staff," Joldir said. "I think that's evidence enough."

"Did you learn his name?"

I shook my head. "There wasn't time for introductions. Joldir's right, it was one of the Sundered. I ... felt it, *knew* it when he crossed into the circle. There was something in the way the other durath behaved. They were bound to him, forced to do his bidding even as it cost them their lives."

Etta sighed deeply, taking my hand in hers. "You did well. Adalrikr has made his first bold move, sacrificing one of his closest allies in a gamble that failed. He wanted to blind you, Johan, before the coming battle. Sinarr the Cold One's no longer concerned about conquering Romsdahl – his entire focus is breaking the Brotherhood. That must not come to pass."

"It won't," Johan said grimly. "Still, today they came far too close, and such an open move has started rumours I'm unable to quell. There's fear in the camp tonight – I need victory in Romsdahl to give the people heart. It's time to put your plan into action and send a delegation to reach out to Gautarr and ensure things are in place before my army arrives. Are you sure this secret route to Romsdahl is still open? We can ill-afford to leave the advance party trapped with Sinarr's forces camped outside the walls."

"Yes, I'm perfectly sure – my sources are reliable. How many more days will it take for the army to reach Romsdahl?"

"At our current rate two weeks, longer if Djuri decides to attack rather than merely tracking us."

Etta looked at me. "Are you able to travel? How's your hand?"

"Better," I lied, ignoring the throb competing with my dull headache. "I'm ready."

"Ekkill knows the route but don't let him forget Ulfarr's in command," Etta told me, a note of concern creeping into her voice. "I don't doubt his loyalty ... but ..."

I raised an eyebrow. "Ekkill's a devious untrustworthy

spy?"

"Well, he was my first apprentice. I taught him everything I know," answered Etta with a chuckle.

***

Outside, Johan pulled me into a firm embrace. "Everything hangs on this. Take care, and travel swiftly and safely."

"I know and I will. I won't fail you."

Johan nodded. "You both need to rest. Joldir, tomorrow we remain at camp here so you can light the forge. Jolinn and Lars need to carry their own runeblades by sunset. Rothgar, that gives you a day to make your final preparations. I'm going to ask Bandor to accompany you too."

"I thought you'd want him by your side," I replied, surprised.

"Bandor remains betrothed to Freydja, which I hope still counts for something. We need to exploit every opening and opportunity. You'll be Gautarr's guests and whilst you live under his roof it will be his duty to protect you."

"Hrodi Myndillson easily forgot his duties as host." I was unsure why I said those words, regretting them instantly. In the darkness Johan's face was impossible to read, but when he answered I heard the catch in his throat.

"I know. If Gautarr doesn't ride out to fight then Bandor will be safer in Romsdahl, even if he's held prisoner. I owe ... I owe Damona that much, at least ..." Johan turned away, rubbing his hand over his face.

"My lord?" Svan stepped forward, concerned. Johan waved him away and he retreated into the shadows.

Johan's voice was steadier as he continued in an undertone. "I've already lost my daughter – Damona still cries herself to sleep most nights. Now I've committed us to war, one we can't hope to win unless you can persuade my bitterest rival to come to my aid. If I can keep my son safe and use his betrothal to bring Gautarr to my side then I'll be satisfied. You've been schooled well and have a natural talent for diplomacy. Bandor has similar gifts and will be able to help. You see the sense in what I am saying?"

"I think Gautarr may favour Skari One Eye's ideas concerning diplomacy."

Johan laughed. "Why do you think I'm sending him too?"

Svan stepped forward hesitantly once more. "My lord. The hour grows late and after today's events you should retire to the safety of your runestones. It does not do to linger in the darkness."

Johan nodded. "I must go. Tomorrow night we will feast around the Brothers' Table one final time before we go our separate ways. I trust you will both afford me the honour of your company?" We said our goodbyes and watched as Svan and his men escorted Johan back to his tent.

"What was that about?" asked Arissa as she stepped down from her wagon and approached us, her cloak around her shoulders to ward off the cold. The sky was clear, the moon bright while ribbons of stars glittered in the darkness.

"Share a cup of wine with us," Joldir said to me, putting his arm around my shoulders. "It would be good to spend time together tonight, as we used to back in Lindos."

"Now I'm worried," Arissa said, looking at each of us in turn. "What's happened?"

"We can talk more freely inside," Joldir told her. "Rothgar's going to leave us for a short time."

\*\*\*

Nuna sat in her bed under the covers, knees drawn up tight under her chin. There was a soft knock at the door of her chambers and a moment later Katla let her husband inside. She closed the door and left the two of them alone.

"How are you feeling?" Karas asked, sitting down gently on the bed.

Nuna shivered. "Better than before, thank you."

Karas took her hand and gave it a squeeze. "I was worried. When I heard you and Ottama had both fallen ill my imagination ran wild ... I thought perhaps you'd been poisoned for standing up to Valdimarr. I've lost two wives – I couldn't bear such loss a third time."

"I'm fine," Nuna reassured her husband. "Whatever it was has passed. If I sleep well tonight I'm sure I'll be restored by tomorrow. How's Ottama?"

"She's sleeping in her chambers and Albrikt is tending her. He's baffled as to what might have been the cause. He wanted to speak with you, but I told him it could wait until the morrow."

Nuna smiled. "Tomorrow would be better. Perhaps it was just the sight and smell of the whale being rendered – who can say?"

Karas chuckled. "We're a *whaling* clan, my dear. If that was the cause then perhaps I married the wrong woman."

Nuna reached out and put her arms around Karas. "I'm sorry if your southern wife has proved to be a disappointment."

"Far from it, my love," Karas told her, putting his hand under Nuna's chin and drawing her close as he kissed her.

***

Humli groaned and turned over in his cot, pain dancing behind his eyes. He should be rising whilst it was still dark to bring in the day's catch. He didn't think there was much chance of that happening today, not with him feeling like this.

Lina's babe stirred and began to whimper and Humli heard his mother try and shush the child. "Quiet, little one. Let's not wake your grandpa – he's sleeping."

*Grandpa?* Humli smiled in surprise. He'd thought the word made him sound old when Desta first told him she was expecting. Now Lina was in their lives and, like it or not, she seemed to be making her home with him and his family. When her time came Lina had given birth easily to a strong, healthy boy with a thick head of dark hair, just like his mother. Humli had never felt prouder of his daughter than when he watched Desta help deliver the baby, dealing with things assuredly and keeping Lina calm. It was what she told him after-

142

wards that gave him cause for thought.

"This isn't the first child she's carried, I certain of it. She already knew *exactly* what to do and the stretch marks on her body looked old to me. Little things like that."

Humli frowned, turning those words over in his mind. "She's never mentioned any other children. If you're right, what happened to them? Where are they?"

"Left behind? Worse?" Desta said in a low voice. "Who knows? She's never confided such things to me or even spoken about who the father is. Maybe she doesn't want to think about it – I know I wouldn't if anything ever happened to Finn."

Lina's son began feeding contentedly, and Humli tried to sleep again. He felt weak and drained, even though he hadn't left his bed since being taken ill on the porch whilst sitting in his favourite chair. One moment he'd been enjoying watching the afternoon sun creep across the sky as he puffed on his pipe – the next he was lying on the floor, the pain blinding him, feeling like someone had driven a spike through his skull.

He would be better tomorrow, he told himself. One day's catch mattered little, especially with the coin Desta saved from Haarl's wages. Even so, he *needed* to be better tomorrow – now he had two daughters and two grandsons to feed.

# CHAPTER 20

I woke stiff and sore, curled up on the wooden bench in Joldir's wagon. Someone was calling outside and as I rubbed the sleep from my eyes Arissa untied the opening of the tarpaulin.

"Arissa." Thengill's deep voice. "I'm sorry to call so early, Ulfarr's sent me to … Myshall's bane – your face looks terrible."

"Morning, Thengill. Don't worry, this is just what I look like before I put my make up on."

"I don't think so," Thengill answered, not appreciating the joke. "Came to see you yesterday at the hospital tent only Varinn turned me away – said you were sleeping. Didn't realise you'd hurt yourself so bad."

"It looks worse than it is."

"And it could've been a whole lot worse. What were you thinking, trying to fight the durath on your own? Promise me … Just promise that you won't …"

"That I won't *what*?" Arissa's voice was clipped and I began to wish there was another way out of the wagon.

"Well … act so stupid." I closed my eyes and waited until it was all over.

"Stupid?" Arissa cried. "What was I supposed to do? Joldir, Rothgar and Leif needed help and *you* weren't around, were you?"

"What? They were being guarded by three members of the Brotherhood –"

"And where were the rest of you?" Arissa's voice continued to rise. "Getting drunk in Johan's tent? Making merry with one of Ekkill's whores?"

Thengill spluttered in shock. "No. No, of course not. I

144

was sparring with Patrick if you must know ..."

"*Really*?" Arissa folded her arms and turned her back on Thengill, glaring in my direction. "Rothgar, get up. Thengill's come to collect you."

The pair of us walked through the camp as it slowly stirred into life, mist hanging in the air.

"You handled that well."

"Shut up," growled Thengill.

"Don't worry. I've seen Arissa angrier than that. I'd settle for getting the silent treatment. She can simmer whilst we're travelling to Romsdahl and she'll be in a better mood by the time you get back."

"I didn't mean to insult her." Thengill sounded genuinely confused and I was unable to stifle a laugh.

"Really? So why did those words come out of your mouth?"

"Shut. Up."

After a few minutes we reached Joldir's forge at the edge of camp. Inside Leif was working the bellows and the fire glowed brightly, the heat inside the tent already oppressive.

"Leif," I called out. "I didn't expect to see you here this morning."

The boy turned to me and I was shocked by the dark rings under his eyes. He smiled brightly enough and when I reached out gently with the Sight I felt nothing – ataraxia had closed his mind to me.

"Felt better and Joldir needed help with the forge, so Ingirith let me go," he answered, wiping his hands on a small leather apron. "I told her I'd rather keep busy."

"And he's been a welcome pair of extra hands," added Joldir. "Keep that fire hot, Leif. We're nearly ready to start working the metal." I glanced over to the bench, where I saw two swords wrapped in oiled cloth on the workbench, recognising the worn hilt of Jolinn's blade.

I leaned in close to Joldir. "There's something you should know." I quickly explained in an undertone Leif now had a brother. Joldir didn't try to hide his displeasure that I'd used the Sight against his advice.

"Etta will want to know of this ..." Joldir paused as Leif approached, sweat dripping from his face. Joldir looked at the white-hot coals of the forge. "We're ready," he announced. "Take care and have a safe journey, both of you. Use the Path sparingly and only if you need to send me a message. They've tried to destroy our Fellowship once already, and Nereth is always watching. It's only a matter of time before she shows her hand."

\*\*\*

After my detour to see Joldir, Thengill brought me to Ulfarr's tent. The older warrior was sitting outside, eating hot steaming porridge with a wooden spoon. He nodded as we approached.

"Have you broken your fast?" he asked. I shook my head and he gestured to the pot next to the fire. Thengill and I each helped ourselves to a bowl and sat with Ulfarr, hungrily eating the hot sweetened oats.

"That's good," I said, wiping my mouth.

"The secret is adding a little honey to the pot – I think the stuff tastes foul otherwise," Ulfarr told me. "Enjoy it while you can. There'll be no campfires after we leave and no hot food until we reach Romsdahl."

"Sounds delightful, though I'm guessing you didn't send for me to show me the secrets of making good porridge."

Ulfarr nodded and set his bowl aside, smiling as Thengill scraped the pot and helped himself to another serving. "No, you're right. We have our orders to set out before the end of today and I wanted to make sure you're fit enough to travel. You were only attacked yesterday and I remember what you were like when we made the journey to Tullen." Ulfarr sighed, looking apologetic. "We'll have to move fast. Djuri and Sinarr have both sent out their scouts and we'll need to stay one step ahead of them. If you fall ill and slow us down then I'll have a difficult decision on my hands."

146

"Are you asking me to bow out?"

"No. If I'm being honest I'd rather have you at my side when dealing with someone as slippery as Gautarr. What I need to know is that you can make the journey to Romsdahl and keep up the pace. We'll be more difficult to spot travelling on foot but that'll make the going harder and you've been used to riding at a steady pace with the main convoy." Ulfarr fixed me with a penetrating gaze. "I don't want Skari to be right about this, so be honest with me – are you able to do this?"

I nodded. "I'm stronger now. My head and hand both hurt but that doesn't stop me putting one foot in front of the other."

"If he's wrong, I'll carry him," Thengill announced, smacking his lips as he devoured the last of his breakfast. I raised my eyebrows and he looked at me and laughed. "What? I've already got Arissa mad at me – imagine what she'd be like if I didn't bring you back safe and sound."

*** 

My preparations for the journey were nearly complete, everything stowed neatly in my pack. When I visited the hospital in the afternoon I found Arissa working alongside Varinn. She ran to me and wrapped me in her arms, giving me a hug.

"Take care. Remember to look after yourself – here, take this." She pressed the jar of salve into my good hand. "Apply it once a day and the skin will heal."

My hand was aching and stiff as I let Arissa apply the treatment herself before I left for Johan's feast. My palm had blistered and a few of them had burst, although the oozing liquid was clear, which Arissa told me was a good sign. I took a breath as Arissa gently applied the ointment, waiting for the stinging sensation to pass.

"Thanks. Take care yourself and don't let Etta boss you around too much."

Arissa smiled. "I can look after myself – it's you I'm worried about."

"I'll be fine," I joked. "After all, I'm heading to the strongest holdfast still under the control of the Reavesburg Clan. Where could be safer?"

***

I took my leave at Johan's feast early, with Jolinn and Lars admiring their new runeblades amid cries of welcome from their brothers round the table. The intricate dragon and chimera symbol stood out on their weapons, black against the bright steel. Whatever the durath might be plotting, they were doing it far away from the Brotherhood.

Sefa, one of Ekkill's girls, gave me a furtive glance as she slipped out of Etta's tent, hurrying away without a word. When I ducked inside I found Etta sitting up in bed, looking brighter than she had in some time.

"Are you spying on your own spies now?"

Etta wagged her finger at me in mock admonishment. "What Sefa and I were discussing is none of your concern. You'll have to do better than that if you want to prise any secrets from me."

I took a seat next to her. "That wasn't one of my better efforts, I'll admit, but time is short; we're leaving at dusk." Ulfarr's plan made sense, helping to mask our departure being noticed by the Vorund Clan. However, enough people knew about our mission to make me wonder how far our secret had already spread within the camp.

"And yet I feel this is more than a social visit to an old lady."

"There's something you should know. I've told Joldir ..." I trailed off, seeing that Etta was smiling, her wrinkles a web of shadows on her face. "You already know about Lina."

"Why else would you have come here alone, unless it concerned the secret you believe Johan isn't ready to learn? And I'm afraid Leif's ears are sharper than you imagine, even in a noisy blacksmith's forge. He's bright, that one, and you should have taken greater care, knowing the interest he still has in his 'mother'. One successful battle with the Sundered Souls and you've grown careless. Still, what Leif heard and what you saw are two different things – so tell me what you know and then we can dwell on the meaning behind this."

Etta leaned forwards after I had given my report, looking at me shrewdly. "So, what do you think?"

"What do I think? You're supposed to be our expert on the durath."

"Even so, tell me what you saw, learned and felt from this latest encounter."

I paused and reflected for a moment. "That my connection to those I can reach with the Sight is strong; they were affected by the attack almost as much as I was. It wasn't just Humli and Nuna. Ottama was struck down too, and I've never touched her with the Sight."

"I thought that was interesting; a new piece of information I hadn't expected to find. Perhaps the beginnings of a second Fellowship in Norlhast?"

I stared at Etta, horrified. "You're not going to bring my sister further into this – she's in enough danger as it is. I don't want to make her more of a target for Nereth."

"And yet despite the risks you still used the Sight last night, without the protection of your Fellowship?"

"Joldir was right," I accepted grudgingly. "After the attack my control slipped and I strayed onto the Path. It won't happen again."

Etta passed me a small leather pouch. "Which brings me to this."

I pulled on the drawstrings and took out the small glass vial inside. I carefully unstoppered the bottle and smelled cinnamon. Annoyed, I pushed the cork firmly back into place.

"I said it won't happen again."

Etta tutted. "You're happy to take a healer's advice to treat the wound on your hand, yet choose to leave your mind unguarded against Adalrikr's agents? If you want to protect Nuna from Nereth's threat then first look to your own safety. You may think your defences are strong enough, but what if you're wrong? Joldir won't be there to help you. You'll be on your own and it's best to be prepared."

With as much good grace as I could muster, I returned the vial to the bag and stowed it within a pocket of my cloak. I glanced up find Etta looking at me.

"What else did you learn last night?"

"We haven't discussed the meaning of Lina's child." I leaned back on the stool, running my hand through my hair and trying to sort out the jumble of feelings racing around my mind. "I thought Desta was in danger when Lina arrived. Now … I'm not so sure. Perhaps you're right, and Lina is looking to start a new life. Yet I can't shake what I saw yesterday … and earlier this year, back in Tullen … When the skin thieves showed their true form they were more like animals. Lina was so cruel to Leif after she was taken, so it's hard to accept everything has changed just because she's now a mother again."

"I know what the durath can do all too well, boy. In this case, though, you're right, we don't really understand what we're dealing with and where Lina's loyalties lie. I need to find a way to get closer to events back in Ulfkell's Keep, so we can act if we have to."

"In that case we need to stop the army marching south."

"Now you're being selfish," Etta chided. "The best way to help Desta is to defeat Adalrikr's army and cut off support to Blackeyes' forces in Ulfkell's Keep. You know this – don't pretend that you don't. The time to act is now, playing the longer game – this is kings, not a game of dice. Already there is talk against Johan and a handful of desertions from his army as people grow afraid. We need to show them that we can still defeat such a foe."

I nodded. "So, that's what Sefa was telling you before."

Etta smiled. "You see, you can work things out if you apply yourself. Men can be particularly unguarded in the words they whisper to their lovers late at night amongst the pillows. Sefa knows what's of interest to me, such as the current mutterings against Johan in some quarters of the camp. However, that's for me to worry about. Just make sure you reach Romsdahl safely and get Gautarr back into this fight."

# CHAPTER 21

Djuri blinked in the sunlight, allowing a wave of nausea to pass as he rocked in the saddle to match the steady pace of his courser. The previous day's persistent headache had eased to a dull ache, until the sun rose higher in the sky and it returned with a vengeance. Djuri stared straight ahead, resigned to another monotonous day of slow riding and constant quarrelling. The trail of mud, trampled vegetation and tracks left in Johan's wake was easy to follow. Djuri's army of over a thousand men churned that path into a muddy river as their horses and infantry marched behind them. Catching Johan would have been easy, but Djuri's orders were to hold his position until they reached Romsdahl, where Sinarr was waiting to crush Johan Landless. Djuri knew it was the right strategy, even if it meant making slow progress each day; most of it spent making camp and then striking it the next morning. If Old Hrodi's guess was right then another two weeks of this stretched before them.

"You feeling alright?" Haarl asked, riding alongside.

"Damn headache's back," Djuri grunted, taking a deep breath and trying to sit a little straighter.

"The way that lot bicker it's a wonder you haven't had one every day since we left Olt," Haarl observed, looking towards Hrodmarr and Hrodi at the front of their column of riders.

Djuri laughed, regretting it instantly as his head throbbed. Haarl had a point. Old Hrodi Myndillson might have bent the knee but that didn't make his relationship with Hrodmarr Hroarson easy. Hrodi had ruled Olt for longer than anyone could remember, outliving most of those who thought they would succeed him, including three of his own sons. That counted for nothing as far as Hrodmarr was concerned, not now the Vorund Clan occupied Olt and Hrodi's line were his vassals.

It didn't help that along with Hrodi and Hrodmarr's constant verbal sparring Djuri also had to endure the antics of Hrodi's son and grandson. He couldn't decide which was worse: Alfarr's insincere fawning over his grandfather or the mutual dislike that existed between Radholf and Hrodi. Rather than presenting a united front the warriors of Olt were divided into three factions, with groups loyal to different generations of Myndillson's house. Djuri wasn't surprised Jolinn had been able to call so many men to her own banner, even though she had no legitimate claim to rule Olt. It was another complication, making him wonder how steady Hrodi's forces would prove to be in battle if they faced Jolinn in the field. He sighed, knowing there was little point worrying about it now – it wasn't helping his head and what would be would be. Djuri squinted into the sunlight and rode on.

***

"Rothgar?" I blinked and shook my head, turning to Bandor. "I'm sorry, what did you say?"

Bandor frowned, looking concerned. "Skari was talking to you."

I glanced at Ulfarr's second, who scowled and shook his head. "We're a scouting party, heading deep into enemy territory. That means keeping your wits about you and looking out for trouble, not daydreaming."

I held up my hand by way of an apology. "I'm sorry, it won't happen again."

Skari spat onto the ground and gave Ulfarr a venomous look. "Told you. On a trip like this he's a liability, even if the Princeling is Johan's new favourite." He stalked off in the direction of a small stand of trees and bushes.

Bandor looked ready to speak up in my defence before I put a hand on his arm. "Leave it. Please."

"We're stopping for a short rest," Ulfarr explained.

"Myr, you keep watch."

I sat down and rubbed my face, a hollow feeling in my gut. The Sight breaking into my dreams was one thing but happening during my waking hours was something else. I was unable to remember *anything* after breaking fast with Ulfarr's crew that morning, which frightened me. I reached into my pack and pulled out the pouch containing Etta's cinnamon draught, for the first time relieved I had it in my possession.

Bandor sat next to me. "*Are* you alright?" he asked in an undertone.

I paused, unsure what to say. "Ever since the attack by the Sundered the Sight has been … harder to control."

Bandor frowned. "We're you even with us before?"

"I was … away," Bandor's frown deepened at that. "Only for a short time," I protested.

"Away? What does *that* mean?"

"Don't fuss," I said irritably. "I can deal with this."

Bandor looked sceptical. "I think I preferred it on the march to Lake Tull when you were coughing your guts out. This is … Well, I don't like it."

"I just need to work harder at maintaining my control, that's all."

"If this continues to be a problem, you need to share it with me," Bandor replied. "I can't help you if I don't know what's going on."

"It's not a problem," I lied, pushing the unopened pouch back into my pack.

***

The eight of us headed south towards Romsdahl, moving through green rolling hills interspersed with patches of woodland. The mid-afternoon sun was hot and sweat was soon trickling down my back, the straps of my pack rubbing my shoulders. Ekkill led the way, moving with practised ease and often ranging some distance ahead to check our way was clear. Patrick tended to take the role of rear guard, at times falling back to ensure we were not being followed. As a consequence we walked together as the day wore on and I found the pace being set becoming more of a challenge.

"Bearing up?" Patrick asked as he jogged up to where I was walking. Bandor was now a fair way in front of me, his red hair easily recognisable.

I nodded. "I'm doing alright. Walking *and* talking might be too much, though. You may have to carry the conversation."

Patrick smiled. I liked the Berian, though how he'd come to be in such company mystified me. Ulfarr had a level head and could be reasoned with, but he and his crew were seasoned warriors with no qualms about killing. Patrick lived by a different code and as I got to know him better the story that he was a fallen Berian knight rang true. Feeling bold, I asked him outright if the rumour was correct.

"You want to know if there really was a Sir Patrick Wild in Beria?" he asked, his face darkening momentarily.

"I meant no offence. A story can help a long journey pass by, that's all. It's your tale to share, as and when you choose."

We wended our way through the long grass and thickets of gorse in full flower in silence and I wondered if I'd gone too far with my question. When Patrick did answer his voice was slow and thoughtful.

"What is the truth of such things?" he asked, tapping the battered steel breastplate he wore. "Did I rob this piece of steel or has it been in my family for generations? Does that matter when I was a self-confessed outlaw until last year? Can those deeds be washed away by Johan Jokellsward's pardon and admission into his Brotherhood?"

"I don't think Johan claims to have the power to forgive sins – that's a matter for the Creator."

Patrick laughed quietly. He was the wrong side of thirty and looked older, although that smile took away some of those years. "Just as well such things lie in the hands of the One God – I made plenty of mistakes in my old life, back in Beria."

"We've all done things we regret."

"I broke my code as a knight," confessed Patrick. "We swore allegiance to the king of Beria and to protect the kingdom's citizens. I'll never forget that procession along the streets of Silvergate towards the palace, people waving flags and cheering. Proudest day of my life. A bright new kingdom, raised up from the ashes of the War of the Avatars and we were its guardians."

"So that would make you, what exactly? The knights are respected warriors in Beria, aren't they?"

"Yes. It gave me the right to give orders in the regular army and a knight commander is roughly equivalent to what you would call a jarl in Laskar. The problem was that as a knight you're in a privileged position – you hear and see things others don't. Things that, after a time, make you question the value of your oath."

"Such as?" I asked.

"The king of Beria is weak – little more than a figurehead, servile to the dukes of Tharas and Medan, who in turn are in hock to the Merchants Guild. The real king of Beria is gold, and people will stoop at nothing as they chase after wealth and power."

"Isn't that true for most kings and kingdoms? The games of politics and the pursuit of wealth are played out everywhere, even here in the wild lands of Reavesburg."

Patrick gave a bitter chuckle. "Let's just say I was young and naïve and it cost me. I was manipulated whilst stationed at Brighthorn Keep and found myself drawn into a conspiracy to put my commander on the throne in place of the rightful king. We were betrayed, the plot was uncovered and I was forced to flee for my life. So in a sense, what I said was true. After breaking the law and my oath I no longer had any right to my sword, shield and armour. When I ran and took them with me, theft was added to my crime of treason. I was an outlaw long before I ever set foot in Laskar and ran into Ulfarr's crew."

Patrick's face relaxed as he turned and smiled, making

me wonder how long he'd kept this secret. His past mattered little to me – the man in front of me now was more important and I told Patrick the same.

"Like I said, I've made my mistakes and all I can do is try and be better. In Johan I've found a fine man – a leader I follow gladly. That's what I tell myself every day since joining the Brotherhood, that he's the right man to follow. While I can't undo the past, I can choose to change and follow the right path. Johan's given me the chance to do that and he's earned my loyalty. I think Ulfarr feels the same way, too."

"And Skari?"

"Hah. Skari's loyal to Ulfarr, so where he goes Skari follows. Those two go back a long way, over a dozen years, and there's a bond there; closer to brothers than anything else. Don't ask me to explain it – they're very different men, but perhaps when you've shared and survived so much together such things are inevitable. In the same way, you've grown closer to Bandor through your trials together and earned Thengill's respect; not something lightly given.

"Of course, it doesn't always work out that way. Skari never wanted Olaf to join our band and showed him nothing but contempt until he died. Ekkill's a difficult character too – he seems happy being the outsider."

"He's ... a strange one," I said, breathing hard as I struggled to keep up. "He's got skills but making friends ... That's not one of them."

Patrick nodded. "He doesn't need to be my friend. He just needs to lead us safely to Romsdahl."

\*\*\*

Our camp was a miserable affair without a fire. Out of habit the six of us sat together in a circle whilst Patrick and Skari took the first patrol. Only a day out on our journey we could at least enjoy fresh bread and passed a skin of wine around between us, talking and laughing in low tones. I saw Bandor staring at Myr, watching as the mute warrior soaked his bread in the wine, the better able to eat it without a tongue. Myr glanced up suddenly, catching Bandor's gaze. He closed his gaping mouth and turned away, embarrassed. My eyes met Myr's and he raised an eyebrow at me, shaking his bald head before going back to his food.

"Let's run through this again," said Ulfarr, looking at me. "Johan's decided to send you as his emissary to Gautarr, even though the last time you met he tried to kill you in an unsuccessful bid to become clan chief? After he'd attempted to murder your brother, to be exact."

"Actually the last time we met was at Nuna's wedding, when half the guests were massacred by the Vorund Clan. It was the time before when he tried to kill me."

"Hmm. Not exactly ... What's the word I'm looking for?"

"Auspicious," supplied Ekkill with a smirk. "It doesn't bode well for their next meeting," he explained to Thengill, who was sitting next to him looking confused.

"Perhaps not," I replied. "But after his defeat Gautarr swore fealty to my brother and he has more reason than most to hate the Vorund Clan. Joarr the Hammer killed his elder brother, Egill."

"And Tyrfingr Blackeyes murdered his other brother, Olfridor," added Bandor. I was still getting used to that fact. I'd been close to Olfridor and had learned only recently before his death that he was related to Gautarr.

"Old Hrodi had no love for the Vorund Clan and he wasn't too bothered about breaking his oath," muttered Thengill.

"It's a risk," I admitted. "The trouble is we're short on friends. Like it or not we need Gautarr and Bandor's pledge to Freydja means they're honour-bound to admit us and treat us as their guests."

Ekkill laughed and took a swig from the wineskin. "I can't wait to see Gautarr's face when you turn up, Rothgar, and tell him Johan Jokellsward has commanded him to ride out to battle. It'll be a moment to savour."

"And if he says no, what then?" asked Thengill.

"Then Johan had best run for the hills, because Sinarr the Cold One will destroy him otherwise," Ekkill answered. Seeing Bandor's expression he held out his hand. "I'm just speaking the honest truth, lad. People talk about what a great man Johan is but he's playing some very long odds here to try and win this ... Well, let's call it what it is – the holy war he's started."

Bandor looked ready to strike Ekkill and again I placed a hand on his arm, waiting until I felt him relax. Ekkill might have been older but his wiry frame was lean, fit and strong. If it came to a fight I had no doubt who would win, even though Bandor was a skilful warrior and appeared the stronger and quicker of the two.

"There's truth in your words, though you might have chosen them more carefully," Ulfarr interjected, his voice calm. "If Gautarr says no, what then? The eight of us riding out of Romsdahl's gates will hardly strike fear into Sinarr's heart, if he has one."

"Father can't retreat," Bandor said, staring hard at Ekkill. "Djuri's forces block the way back to the Baros Mountains, leaving him with little option other than to fight Sinarr, with or without Gautarr's support. You make him sound like a fool, Ekkill, but my father understands the risks perfectly well. It's clear to me why he's sent us on this mission, and I suspect you know the reason too, even if you feign ignorance ..."

"That means pretend," Ekkill told Thengill.

"... whilst you play your petty little games with us. We're the second chance to fight the durath. Father chose to split the Brotherhood deliberately. Rothgar has the Sight, we bear eight runeblades and Thengill's axes are two of only three weapons powerful enough to slay Adalrikr. If my father is defeated whilst Gautarr watches from the safety of his walls then I know what I must do – what we must all do."

Ekkill shook his head, a smirk playing on his lips. "If you're about to say that the eight of us should march into

Vorund Fastness and kill Adalrikr by ourselves then you're out of your mind. If your father is dead I don't get paid for that foolhardy venture, and neither does anyone else in this crew. I'm interested in loosening his purse-strings, not dying for his memory because he's had some half-mad revelation about his purpose on Amuran."

"If you say one more word about my father –"

"Enough," said Ulfarr. His voice was low and calm, steel behind it. "Ekkill, walk away and take Skari's place on watch. Now." Still smiling, Ekkill stood and took a long draught from the wineskin before tossing it to Thengill.

"What was all that about?" asked Skari as he took Ekkill's place and began unwrapping some dried meats and cheese.

"Tell you later," Ulfarr said, his tone making clear the subject was closed.

"I knew what feigned meant, by the way," Thengill said, to a ripple of laughter round the rest of us in the circle.

"And auspicious?" I asked.

"No idea."

# CHAPTER 22

I was afraid. My body lay in the hill country of southern Reavesburg, sleeping under my cloak next to Bandor as Ekkill and Patrick kept watch. My mind, however, was somewhere else entirely. In that other world it was daylight, the sky bright blue with the occasional white cloud drifting by on the faint breeze. I found myself looking out across the waters of a sea, standing on the black sands of the shore. In the distance I could see a town, an assortment of fishing vessels tied to a long wooden jetty. Without thinking I walked towards it, feet sinking into the soft wet sand and leaving a trail of footprints behind me. The town was built of stone, its smooth cobbled streets bustling with people; merchants and traders, fishermen and farmers all bringing their wares to market. They spoke a language I didn't know yet somehow understood and I realised I was in Tivir, which lay on the shores of the Sea of Mirtan.

Despite having only ever seen the Kingdom of Mirtan on maps in my father's chambers, I knew where I was heading. I wended my way through the narrow streets away from the noisy market square and into a quieter district of Tivir. The houses here were grander, brick built on two or three storeys with well-appointed gardens enclosed within low stone walls. I opened the black wrought-iron gate and stepped onto the path leading to one of the larger houses, ivy creeping up the frontage and softening its grey stone walls. As I got closer I realised the windows were made of glass, comprising dozens of small panes set in lead.

I turned the handle and pushed open the white-painted wooden door, stepping into the hallway. A servant was standing there, dressed in a fine waistcoat and a spotless white linen shirt, his hands behind his back and his eyes staring directly at me – through me. I walked down the hallway unchallenged and, following the faint sound of voices, I entered a drawing room, bathed in light as the sun streamed through windows that stood from floor to ceiling. The room contained more luxurious furniture than I would have found in the whole of Ulfkell's Keep and I found myself rubbing my hands on my shirt, anxious not to touch anything and soil it. The wooden table was polished to such a sheen that it perfectly reflected the windows and the garden beyond. Glass fronted cabinets contained crystal ornaments and glassware glittered in the light, scattering it like a thousand luminous gems. The room had four occupants. A young dark-haired girl sat between two people who could only be her parents, so striking was the resemblance between them. Opposite them sat an older man, perhaps fifty, with wild grey windswept hair that stood out at various angles. My eyes were drawn to the ring on his left hand, silver serpents entwined around a blood-red ruby.

"Please, you must understand," the girl's father was saying. "I know this is a great honour, of course. We've always supported our rulers in the Chapters of Seroch and been generous with our taxes."

"Generous?" asked the visitor. "Taxes are due or they are not, surely?"

"Ah. Yes, that wasn't quite the word, I suppose … What I meant to say is we're your loyal supporters, here in Tivir. Most loyal, and willing to be *more* generous in the support we provide in the future."

The grey-haired man sat straight-backed in the chair and fixed the girl's father with a stern gaze. "Generous in every way other this, it would appear."

The girl's mother began to cry and she held her daughter's hand tightly, looking fiercely at their guest. "She's our only daughter – our only child. You must understand, what you're asking … It's too much, Ramill. Please, don't ask us to do this."

Ramill sat unmoving, staring at the girl sitting between her parents. "And what do you say, Nereth? It's clear that your parents love you very much. Tell me, what do you think?"

*Nereth*. My insides turned to ice as the girl lifted her head and I saw those instantly recognisable fine, delicate features, softened in childhood. When her dark eyes met those of Ramill there could be no doubt in my mind whose memories I was seeing. I knew I should leave, *wanted* to leave but I remained rooted to the spot. Nereth licked her red lips and gently disentangled her hand from her mother's, who was watching her daughter with eyes glistening with fresh tears.

"I'm different. I've known that all my life."

Ramill nodded. "I know. Can you explain how you're different from your friends?"

"I see things, the lives of other people as they happen. I saw when Jon fell down the well at the Hallen's farm and he was there, just as I said. There were other things too, like when I was with Grandma when she died, even though my parents wouldn't let me actually *be* with her." She gave her mother an accusing look, making her turn away, her cheeks flushed.

"Yes, I heard about the incident at Hallen Farm. In fact, it was what brought me here. Tell me, what do you know of the Chapters of Seroch?"

Nereth's eye's brightened. "They're in the capital city of Mirtan, where those who are special ... those who have gifts like me, go to study and become mages."

"Indeed. But it's much more than that: Mirtan is ruled by its Three Chapters, the most powerful place of magical knowledge and learning in the whole realm of Valistria. To study magic and to harness it to your will, that's the key to knowledge and power." Ramill smiled and produced a small box from a pocket of his coat. "Have you seen or heard of one of these?" he asked, opening the box to reveal a silver necklace into which was set a bright green emerald.

Nereth peered into the box with interest. "No. What is

it?"

"It is called a heartstone, and through it I can see more clearly what skills you possess. If I may?" Nereth nodded and bent her head, allowing Ramill to slip the necklace around her neck as her parents watched anxiously. "It reveals powers which you are aware of and discerns those that still lie hidden, for now. The heartstone sees into a person and can tell whether they have the strength to wield the power they possess."

"And if they do not?" asked Nereth's mother.

Ramill glared at her. "Only the strong survive."

"I am strong," Nereth declared, holding the jewel in her hand and turning the emerald so it caught the light and sparkled.

Ramill smiled, erasing all trace of his dark expression. "I can see that. Here, pass me the jewel and sit back, this will take but a moment." Silently, he took the emerald between his finger and thumb as a jeweller might, peering deep into the heart of the stone. Softly he murmured some words, just on the edge of my hearing and I stepped forwards to see better.

There was a faint light in the centre of the stone, like a dancing flame, which grew and filled the jewel as it became brighter. Nereth's mother put her hand to her mouth, the other now clutching her husband's whilst the child stared straight at the emerald, her face rapt as different colours swirled and shifted inside. The jewel winked out suddenly, making the room appear dark and small, the sunlight pouring through the windows a feeble trickle. Ramill took the necklace and carefully placed it back into the box with a self-satisfied air.

"It appears my journey here was worthwhile. You have the gift of the Sight, that much is clear, and there is more, much more. I know Serena, the head of my own Chapter, will be very interested in meeting you, Nereth. You have a great deal of potential."

Nereth smiled. "I'd like to meet her."

"Darling," her father began. "You're only nine years old and although this sounds very exciting this is something we need to discuss. Seroch lies hundreds of miles away, far beyond the Sea of Mirtan. You're not yet ready to leave home."

Ramill stood and glowered at Nereth's father. "Enough! There is nothing to discuss. You're being unfair to your daughter, acting as if there's a choice when Mirtan's laws leave no room for debate. Leaving her here means she's a danger, both to herself and those closest to her if she's unable to control her growing power. Her future lies in Seroch in one of the Three Chapters, where she will be instructed properly and given a chance to realise her full potential. You should be proud of her and what this day represents, not trying to hold her back and keep her here. She is no longer a banker's daughter – she is a future mage of Mirtan, and she is coming with me. Today."

Ramill held out his hand as Nereth's father stood up to protest and her mother began to weep. "Come child. You will look back on this day with pride." Nereth reached out and Ramill gently took hold of her delicate fingers.

The room changed, its occupants vanishing whilst the furniture disappeared under white dust sheets and the sun tracked across the sky with unnatural speed. Nereth stood before me, now the woman I remembered from her time as Karas Greystorm's advisor, before I helped oust her from power.

"Rothgar," she purred. "It's good to see you once again – the Crow Man has kept you hidden for so long but today is different. You're all alone. Why is that?"

With some difficulty I found my voice. "I believe in keeping my enemies close. Knowing and understanding them shows me how they can be defeated."

Nereth swept her long black hair out of her eyes and arched an eyebrow. "*Really?* You'll have to do better than that. This is my memory and this is the world I have created around it. I called you to me, as I have every night, and this time you came. You seem … how shall I put it? Less *grounded* than usual, less in control. Where is the Crow Man?"

"He's ..." I stopped, biting off the rest the words Nereth was drawing from me.

"Where is the Crow Man?"

"I'm telling you nothing," I replied. Last time I'd faced Nereth in one of her dreamscapes I'd been strong enough to push back. Now it was all I could do to bring up the defences around my mind and block Nereth out. My headache was returning, the pressure building with each passing minute.

Nereth paused, looked at me and smiled. "He's not coming, is he? Has Adalrikr broken your little Fellowship, I wonder?" Her smile widened as she saw my expression. "I hope he has, so you can understand the pain I felt when you took my sisters from me, breaking those bonds forever. They were my real family, and your part in their deaths is something I can never forgive."

All at once the pressure vanished and I staggered, as if someone had lifted a great weight from my shoulders. Nereth walked around the room, running her hand over the shrouded furniture until she came to the windows and looked out across the garden.

"You are right about the importance of understanding your enemies; I understand you all too well. Your weakness is your love for your sister, Nuna. I was able to set my birth family aside, so I could grow into the person I was destined to be and set out on the path to learning the truth."

"And what is the truth?" I asked.

"That Adalrikr is our king and he will usher in a new era, one that shall sweep away the Fallen Age and restore us to glory."

"And you actually believe that?" I replied, unable to keep the note of scorn from my voice.

Nereth's dark eyes narrowed. "You will too, in the end, once you've been defeated and everything has been taken from you. Once you watch your sister die at my hand."

\*\*\*

"Wake up Princeling, you're on watch." Skari thumped me

hard and I started awake with my heart pounding, blood rushing in my ears. I gasped and tried to breathe, my throat tight, and coughed loudly. Nearby I heard Thengill groan in his sleep and roll over.

"Gods, you're not going to die on the first night, are you?" Skari asked, his shadow looming over me, black against the stars.

I coughed again and sat up, heart still racing. "No ... Sorry to ... disappoint. Just ... a bad dream, that's all."

Also due on watch, Bandor sat up next to me and leant in close. "*Are* you alright?" he whispered.

"Yes," I answered, as with shaking fingers I drew out Etta's pouch and took a sip from the vial of liquid inside.

# CHAPTER 23

"What do you think it meant?" Bandor asked me in hushed tones as we walked together the following morning. I'd confided in him about the events of last night, glad to have someone I could trust to share the burden.

"She threatened Nuna and I've no idea where she is or how she's going to carry out her plan. I've only seen her in the dreamscape world since her escape from Norlhast. I just feel ... powerless. Even with Joldir's help I couldn't get a warning to Nuna using the Sight and what can I tell her? Karas has already assigned Brosa to protect her and she's one of the most closely guarded people in Norlhast Keep." I kicked a stone lying in my path, watching it bounce away into a tussock of brown grass.

"For what it's worth, I think you did the right thing, taking Etta's potion," Bandor told me. "No more ill-effects?"

"None." I'd only taken a tiny dose and it had proved effective. My worry was how long it would blunt my abilities, after bad experiences with ataraxia in the past.

The scenery was slowly changing, as we left the sparse woodland behind and crossed open moors. I could tell Ulfarr felt exposed with so little cover but there was nothing we could do if we were to reach Romsdahl quickly enough to have the time to coordinate Johan's attack. The landscape stretched on before us, the rolling hills interspersed with grey lichen covered gritstones. The giant stones looked like they'd been cast upon the ground by the gods, standing out starkly and breaking up the monotony of our journey. We rested at one of these landmarks, the jumble of cracked stones providing some shelter from the wind, which was strong today. I gratefully dropped to the ground, wiping sweat from my face and taking a drink from my waterskin. Ekkill scrambled up one of the rocks, using the vantage point to scan the surrounding land.

"Anything?" called Ulfarr.

"Not a soul out here," Ekkill replied, hunkering down on the rock and taking some food out from his pack.

I relaxed a little and took off my boots to give my feet a rub. Skari wrinkled his nose.

"Proof a prince's feet smell every bit as bad as those of a commoner."

"Another thing we share," I replied, flexing my toes.

"Hah. Funny."

"He's being kind, Skari," added Thengill. "Never known anyone's feet reek the way yours do." Ulfarr's crew laughed at that and Skari scowled, eating the rest of his meal in silence.

"You shouldn't let him talk to you in that way," hissed Bandor.

"It's not worth it. Skari's not got a good word to say about anybody, so why should I get special treatment? Don't let it bother you; you'll just encourage him."

"Hmm." Bandor looked unconvinced but said no more.

*** 

By nightfall my headache was gone and I had to admit Etta may have been right. However, I'd be unable to relax until I knew whether I could use the Path again, so after applying salve to the burns on my hand I reached out once more.

*Joldir?* I waited, desperate to hear a response.

*I'm here, Rothgar. Are you safe?*

*Yes, and you?*

*All is well. Join with me tomorrow night. I can prepare a safe place for us to meet.* With that Joldir vanished. In those brief moments of contact I'd sensed bone-weary tiredness in him and remembered that when I left he was forging more runeblades; a demanding enough task at the best of times, never mind immediately after the attack on our Fellowship. Johan needed to take better care of my friend and I resolved to speak to him when all this was over.

Though my body ached I was pleased my skills had returned and my defences felt strong. Emboldened by the ease with which I had reached Joldir I ventured forth again, this time turning my attention to the way ahead.

***

Randall took shallow breaths as he sat across from Sinarr, a silver scrying basin between them, the still water within black as ink. The stench was even worse than last time, almost overpowering him. It was like sharing a room with a fly-blown corpse. The floor was ice-cold too, making his buttocks ache and he began to wish he hadn't sat cross-legged to mirror Sinarr's pose. It had felt like the right thing to do but now his knees were screaming at him to change position. With an effort, Randall pushed such things from his mind, concentrating on the waters.

"Do you see?" asked Sinarr in his rasping voice.

Randall peered closer at the basin, where the water remained flat and black. He coughed and shook his head. "I see nothing, just the dark waters."

He blinked as those waters rippled and, for a moment, thought he saw colours swirling in the centre.

"Patience. Look closer. Look deeper."

Randall took a breath, gagged a little and coughed again.

"Be still. Put all else from your mind. Look closer. Look deeper. See with your mind."

The dark water was gone, replaced by the image of an army camped out on the edge of the moors.

"The Landless Jarl draws closer to his doom," Sinarr told him. "She is there at his side, still guiding him but she weakens."

"She?"

"Etta, the crone. The constant advisor to the line of Marl during their rule of Reavesburg. When the time comes and Johan has been defeated, you must find the old woman and bring her to me, alive. Adalrikr wishes to see her in person."

Randall nodded. "I'll see that it's done."

The waters rippled and the scene changed, showing a small group of scouts camped out in the moors. Sinarr hissed and stirred the waters with a thick finger, the nail black. The image wavered and then resolved once more, centring on a young dark-haired man sitting wrapped in his cloak, eyes closed. Then the scene dissolved, vanishing in a jumble of images that flashed by faster than Randall could see. On the edge of his hearing he thought he heard shouts and screams, the clash of sword on sword then the basin became dark and still once more.

"What did you see?"

Randall told him and Sinarr rose and carried the basin carefully to an alcove in the room. Randall gratefully took that as a cue to stand, wincing as the blood flowed into his tingling feet.

"You have a good eye," Sinarr said, reaching out and putting on a cloak, which he fastened about his neck. "Not all can read what the scrying pool tells them. Come, walk with me."

Sinarr pushed open the door to his headquarters, causing the guards stationed outside to shrink back as the pair of them strode off into the encampment. Randall looked up and saw the battlements of Romsdahl lit by torches. He could hear singing in the distance coming from Romsdahl Castle, perhaps a feast of some kind. The sound annoyed Randall – Gautarr's men defied them every day and now he was forced to listen to their revelry, whilst disease continued to spread through their camp. Over one hundred dead now, with five hundred laid low in the hospital and not all of them would live to see the morning. Randall hated this camp, watching the Vorund Clan become weaker as Gautarr's men stayed safe behind their walls.

"Something troubles you," Sinarr said as they walked past the palisade wall.

"Just sick of it. All this waiting."

"Soon it will be over. Soon the battle we have been waiting for will be fought and victory will be ours, if the men hold true."

"Not everyone has your confidence," Randall admitted. "Two nights ago another ship slipped away and deserted the blockade. People's patience is wearing thin and no one wants to spend another winter here."

"Those ones are weak. We have no need of them," Sinarr replied.

"We need *some* of them," Randall persisted. "Our army shrinks at the very time you're predicting battle. That's not something I'd be happy with."

Sinarr laughed, an unsettling sound, like sandpaper rasping on wood. "I like you, Randall. You're an honest man, which is a rare thing. You give me good counsel and you're not afraid to speak your mind. Would that I had a thousand like you."

"You'd have a thousand men with aching backs and stiff knees."

Sinarr laughed again. "Just so, but youth and beauty are not everything. Look at me."

Randall stared at Sinarr, taking in his mottled pallor and the stink of his flesh, obvious even in the fresh night air. Unsure what to say, Randall remained silent.

Sinarr grinned, his long brown teeth visible in the torchlight as they climbed the steps leading up to the battlements of a wooden watch tower rising up from the palisade. Warriors saw them approach and parted to let them through without a word. Sinarr leaned out between the battlements, looking over towards Romsdahl and the coastline beyond.

"What do you see?" Sinarr asked him.

Randall squinted and looked out, trying to see something unusual. "Just Romsdahl. It's a familiar sight – we've been staring at those walls for over a year."

"Look beyond Romsdahl to the coastline. You see those cliffs?"

Randall nodded. "Aye. What of them?"

"That is where the Cripple is heading, the one who serves Johan Landless. I showed him to you in the scrying pool, him and his seven companions. Johan sends them to Gautarr and there's a secret way to reach him, hidden somewhere on those cliffs."

"The Cripple?" Randall asked, trying to picture the image Sinarr had shown him of the young man resting against the rock. "Who is he?"

"The Crone's pawn – Rothgar, the surviving son of Kolfinnar who now serves the Landless Jarl. He brings a storm with him, shadows cloak his shoulders and doom follows his footsteps."

Randall frowned, not sure what to make of any of that. "Trouble, then?"

"Most assuredly. I want you to take some men, men you can trust. Make for those cliffs, catch the Cripple and bring him to me. You can kill the rest."

"That's a lot of cliff to cover. We've heard rumours before of caves reaching deep underground but we've never found the entrance to anything like that. They could be heading anywhere."

Sinarr rounded on Randall; a swift, sinuous motion that placed his face inches away. Randall stepped backwards and his hand strayed involuntarily towards the hilt of his sword. Sinarr's eyes followed the movement before flicking back, fixing him with a stare from his clouded, bloodshot eyes.

"Do not test my patience and make light of this. You will watch that cliff face. You will find the Cripple. You will bring him to me, unharmed. Nothing is more important than this, Randall, so tell me, is my faith in you misplaced? Should I choose another for this task?"

Randall slowly and deliberately moved his hand away from his sword, breathing steadily and trying to control the shake in his legs as he stared at Sinarr. "No. It will be done, just as you ask."

# CHAPTER 24

The air smelled fresh, the carpet of pine needles soft underfoot as I walked next to Joldir. Leif ran ahead of us, weaving in and out of the tall conifers, laughing loudly.

"How did Ulfarr take the news?" Joldir asked me, smiling as he watched Leif's antics.

"Not much throws Ulfarr. Skari started cursing as soon as I'd finished. Ulfarr just nodded and said it was better to know a trap has been set, rather than walk blindly into one."

"Ulfarr's right," Joldir said. "Ekkill might be slippery but if there's a way through to Romsdahl he'll find it. As you say, you're forewarned now, which gives you the advantage over Randall. It's Sinarr's keen interest in you that disturbs me more; he was watching your movements as closely as those of Johan, which means ... Well, if I'm honest, I'm not sure what it means."

I shrugged. First the attack on our Fellowship, now Sinarr had ordered my capture – I wasn't enjoying being the centre of attention and it was obvious my use of the Sight was no longer a secret from the Vorund Clan. "I'd rather not find out," I replied. "I never thought I'd say this, but I think I'll be glad to see Gautarr after all this time."

Leif ran back to us and skidded to a halt, sending up a shower of pine needles. "I don't believe it. How can none of this be real?" He spread his arms wide and gestured at the forest, which looked solid enough. I could hear birds chattering nearby and a soft gust of wind pulled at my cloak, caressed my face.

Joldir smiled indulgently. "While the Path offers insight into another person's soul the gift can also be used to create worlds, somewhere secret that only those in your own Fellowship can find. Somewhere where you can gather together, safely."

"It all looks real to me," Leif said, shaking his head and staring around in astonishment. He whooped and scampered off once more, chasing a squirrel.

"That's the idea," Joldir called out to Leif's retreating back.

"Are you sure this place is hidden?" I asked Joldir, not for the first time. He raised an eyebrow at me for bringing up the subject once more. "I mean, I found Nereth almost without trying."

"I made sure this place is hidden from all except our Fellowship. As for your encounter with Nereth, I can't say why she was exploring her childhood memories but you have to remember she's actively looking for you. Whilst you're not part of her Fellowship the principle of allowing certain people access is the same. She probably left the door slightly ajar, tempting you to walk through." Joldir sighed and I knew what was coming next. "You need to be more careful."

Although I bridled at the reprimand, I knew deep down it was one I deserved. "There's no need to lecture – I took your cinnamon draught as soon as it happened."

"It would have been better if you had taken my advice when I first suggested it – then you wouldn't have been in that situation. What would you have done if Skari hadn't woken you? You're letting Nereth toy with you and every mistake like this places you in danger. Please, Rothgar, surely you must see this?"

"I know. It won't happen again, I promise. So, was it real, what I saw?" I asked, keen to change the subject. "There was something different about that last encounter … It was, I don't know how to put this exactly. More personal, I suppose."

Joldir looked thoughtful. "It's another aspect of the Sight, which is useful at times. You can bring your memories to life and observe them from a different perspective, giving you fresh insight into those events. But I don't need the Sight to know what you saw that day was one of Nereth's childhood memories. Ramill was my tutor when I was studying with the Mages of Mirtan and he told me that same story when he brought Nereth back with him to Seroch. He was so impressed with her composure and what he'd seen with the heartstone. Nereth's future seemed so bright, with all three of the Chapters vying for her, although she remained loyal to Ramill, back then at least. Looking back now, I'd say she had a deeper bond with him than her own parents, although that wasn't uncommon. In Mirtan you're raised to aspire to join the Three Chapters – it's a great honour."

"This Ramill, is he still close to Nereth?"

"Not any more. He's dead," Joldir told me flatly. "It was a very long time ago."

I knew this wasn't the time to pursue this particular subject – Joldir was a private man and rarely spoke about his past. I forced down dozens of questions bubbling up in my mind and steered the conversation back to Johan's preparations for war. Joldir told me how Damona fretted over Bandor, arguing with Johan over his decision to send their son away. Etta was coping with the journey, stoically travelling with Joldir in his wagon.

"Make sure you tell Arissa that everything's fine and we're all safe. Maybe best not to mention Sinarr's laying a trap for us, though."

"Hmm. I think ... Wait – where's Leif?"

My stomach lurched and I glanced around wildly, looking for any sign of the boy.

"That little ... He's slipped away from us, though I'm pretty certain I know where he is."

***

"I'm just saying I find it strange," Desta was saying to Lina. "From the moment he was born I thought of him as my little Finnvidor, that was just who he was. The idea of him not having a name, well, it just seems so hard to imagine."

"Names mean things," Lina explained as she nursed her child on her lap. "I want to get to know my son and choose the right name for him. There's plenty of time."

"That's just maddening. I need to know, now," Desta cried in exasperation. Lina just smiled and shook her head.

Humli smiled too, pleased to see his daughter sounding brighter and happier than she'd been in a long time. He dipped the oars and steered his small boat towards his cottage on the riverbank, calling out a greeting to the two women. Desta looked up from her basket weaving and waved. There was no sign of Finn; Humli guessed he must be sleeping inside.

Desta helped her father out of the boat and assisted him with the moorings, chattering all the while of inconsequential things. Humli's heart swelled with pleasure as he produced the basket and saw the excited look on her face, reminding him so much of when she was a little girl. Desta stopped mid-sentence.

"Hah. Thought that would get your attention. Had a good catch and made a little extra coin down in the market, so I thought I'd treat my girl and grandson."

Desta smiled, her face aglow, as he opened the lid of the basket and pulled out a small cloth-wrapped bundle. Before he had even finished opening them the smell wafting up gave away the surprise. "Honey cakes," Desta said, licking her lips as she stared hungrily at them.

Humli chuckled. "I didn't forget Finn," he added. "I know the lad's not weaned yet, but in time he'll be wanting to play with toys and I couldn't resist these." He produced two small wooden horses, brightly painted yellow and red. "One for Finn and one for Lina's new baby. They're too small to play with them now but when I saw these on the stall I had to buy them – no knowing when there would be something like that for sale again."

Lina walked across, holding her infant son close. "Humli, you're too good to us." Something in the way that she spoke gave Humli pause for thought. Her expression was hard to read and Humli wondered if he'd done something wrong. In a moment it was gone, replaced by a warm smile as she bent over and kissed his forehead.

"Just don't go spoiling the boy," Lina told him. "You know I can't repay your kindness."

"Pay it no mind," Humli said. "After what you've been through and the help you've given around the smallholding it's the least I can do. Can't give a gift to one child and not the other, can I? There's pheasant pie and a leg of ham in there too. Thought you ladies needed to make sure you ate well so you're strong enough to care for those boys."

"Thank you," Desta said, hugging her father. "Here, let me put this in the pantry."

I took a deep breath as I watched Desta walk inside and, with an effort, I stepped away from Humli as he entered his cottage. I sat down next to the unseen boy crouching by the riverbank and put a hand on his shoulder. Leif didn't shy away from me, leaning in closer and resting his head against my chest.

Joldir knelt down next to us. "Leif, what are you doing out here on your own? It's dangerous to walk the Path without us by your side."

Leif looked at me, face stricken. The carefree boy of a few moments ago gone, replaced by a frightened child, who'd seen more in his seven years than many of the warriors in Johan's army. "There are times when I feel ... forgotten. She never even looked for me and now she's doting on that ... nameless baby boy. She never speaks of me or my sisters."

"That belongs to another time. We've been through this before. Lina isn't your mother, you know that." I spoke gently because the unspoken truth behind my words was hard. *Your mother is dead.*

Leif shook his head. "She was mean to me in Tullen. Locked me in that cellar once my dad was gone. She never had a kind word to say, only telling me there was power in my blood and she wanted me for something. Why did she talk to me like that and then love this new baby like it's her firstborn child?"

I hugged him tighter, blinking back tears for Leif's lost childhood as my thoughts mingled with memories of Ulfkell's Keep. I cleared my throat. "Listen. You need to stop coming here and torturing yourself. This isn't your mother; she's gone now. I'm sorry ..."

Leif stared straight back at me. "Stop coming back? Like you do with *her*? Desta's married to someone else and you still watch her – I know you do. That's not right, so don't tell me what I can and can't do."

There was a gust of wind and a shadow passed over the three of us. Joldir looked up, staring into the sky, watching a falcon wheeling high above. Although the bird was distant the shadow it cast darkened the riverbank and chilled the air.

Joldir looked at Leif, his brow furrowed. "Nereth watches these ways, as always. She senses we're here. We have to go, now."

Leif got to his feet without a word, wiping his eyes with the back of his hand. I wanted to say something that would make all of this better. The words refused to come.

"I'll look after him, I promise," Joldir told me before he and Leif vanished. As the wind grew stronger I also stepped away from the Path, Humli's cottage dissolving before my eyes.

# CHAPTER 25

"He's back with us," said Thengill, his voice distant. I blinked and sat up straighter, drawing in the smell of the grass, heather and gorse of the moorlands north of Romsdahl.

"I don't like it," Skari muttered. "It's not natural."

"No, but it's useful," said Ulfarr.

"Any news?" Thengill asked.

Skari looked unhappy when I'd finished telling them of my meeting with Joldir. "What about this trap Sinarr's set for us? You didn't think to find out more about that?"

"We were interrupted," I explained, telling Ulfarr's crew about Nereth's unwelcome appearance, although I avoided mention of Humli, Desta and Lina.

"So, this witch from Norlhast continues to pursue you?" asked Patrick.

"The Path has its dangers. You don't need to worry – she didn't find me."

"Perhaps not," said Skari. "But Sinarr's looking for you and we've been sat in the open ground for more than an hour waiting for you to come back to us. I'll say it again, I don't like this one bit. We need to make for Romsdahl as fast as we can, not stop to talk to your friend in Johan's camp about things that have precious little use to us out here."

"My father needed to know about Sinarr's ability to scry and that he's being watched too," interjected Bandor. "It's not all about us."

"Listen, what happens to us out here is a damn sight more important to me than your father."

"Enough," said Ulfarr, staring hard at Skari who glared at his chief before falling silent. "Like everyone else I want to know what Randall's doing, but we've lingered too long already. Let's get our gear together and move out. Sinarr's army's still several days away, so I don't think it's likely Randall's going to show up any time soon. Let's get moving and find out more tonight."

***

The others had eaten whilst I was using the Sight, so I munched on some stale bread and hard cheese as we walked. Ekkill was a skilful hunter and would have been able to keep our bellies full with game. However, this close to Romsdahl, Ulfarr wouldn't allow us to light a cook fire and there wasn't time to dry the meat in the sun. Our rations would have to last until we reached Gautarr's halls.

As usual, Ekkill ranged ahead to make sure our path was safe. Myr was our rear-guard, the bald warrior's eyes watchful as he scanned the horizon and made sure we weren't being followed. Ulfarr walked alongside me, setting a steady pace I'd be unable to match for more than an hour.

"You'll have to forgive some of my crew. This use of magic isn't something they're used to and it doesn't help when they're told that some big bastard with bad breath is using the dark arts to watch their every move. It's not good for the nerves."

"If you want to know the truth, I think …" I paused, unsure whether it would be useful to continue.

"What? What do you think?"

I took a deep breath. "Sinarr's dead. He may move and talk and give the orders in the Vorund camp, but there's no life behind those eyes. I've seen him through Randall and he knows the same, although I don't think he can admit it to himself."

Ulfarr shook his head. "So, the Vorund Clan's army is commanded by the undead. You remember me saying how my nerves were getting frayed? Well, that kind of talk doesn't help. How is that even possible?"

I wiped sweat from my brow and swallowed down the

last of my cheese. "Nothing is normal any more, Ulfarr. I share my life now with ... what is it? Six other people, and I don't think twice about it. What does that make me?"

"As I said before, useful, but the road in front of us is what I care about. I'll worry about how we kill something that's already dead when the time comes. Right now, what I want to know is how to get to Romsdahl without being killed. So, tell me, is that something you can help us with?"

\*\*\*

The sun was setting, the sky ablaze with red shafts of light amid the glowing pink clouds, reflected in the waters of the Redfars Sea. Randall watched the sun slowly sink into the waters as he sat on the clifftops before turning his attention back to the shore far below. The tide was out, revealing a jumble of jagged black rocks that reared out of the white sands. The coastline here was full of caves, some a few feet deep, others leading much further inland. Randall had already heard rumours that some of these caves opened out into a network of tunnels which led to Romsdahl. The question was, which cave? Kurt was out there too, further north, doubling their chances of catching this Rothgar Kolfinnarson that Sinarr was so anxious to find. Randall didn't expect to stumble upon the secret entrance to Romsdahl that had remained hidden for the past two centuries – he didn't need to. He only had to find Johan's scouting party. Once they'd been left awhile with Sinarr's torturers the route to Romsdahl would be revealed soon enough.

He hawked and spat over the edge of the cliff, listening to his crew quarrelling in low voices behind him. This was dull work, though it felt good to be away from the disease-infested army, breathing in the fresh salt-tanged sea air. Gulls wheeled over the water, their mournful cries carrying far. Romsdahl's fortified walls lay just a couple of miles south of their camp, rose-tinted in the sun's fading rays. They looked as impregnable as ever as darkness fell.

\*\*\*

Nuna rubbed her eyes and tried for the hundredth time to make herself comfortable in bed. She straightened the covers, wrestling with the heavy bedspread that bore the Norlhast Clan whale sigil. She must have fallen asleep, although the vision of the cliff face and castle, illuminated by the setting sun, had seemed so real. She groaned, sitting up and rubbing her temples. Her headaches had slowly eased since being taken ill at the quayside, although they were never far away. It left her with a short temper, which her husband bore the brunt of when no one else was around. Karas would be getting ready for bed in his own chambers and Nuna rolled over on her side, trying to relax.

The knock at the door made her start. She waited a moment, deciding whether to feign sleep or allow herself to be disturbed, in which case she'd probably be awake for half the night. The knocking sounded again, louder and more insistent.

"Come."

The door was opened by Vrand, who was guarding her chambers that evening. "I'm sorry to disturb you, my lady. Your maid Ottama was most insistent."

Ottama appeared furtively in the doorway. "I hope I didn't wake you, my lady?"

Nuna shook her head. "No, it's fine. Thank you, Vrand, you can let her in."

Ottama scurried inside as Vrand closed the door behind her. Nuna noticed she was still dressed in her maid's attire despite the hour and wondered just how much sleep Ottama enjoyed. The girl was up before dawn to help her dress and always had chores to finish when she took her leave each evening.

"Forgive me, lady. I know the hour is late but there's something I must speak to you about. The trouble is, I hardly know where to begin."

Nuna sat up in bed and patted the covers, indicating Nuna to take a seat. The serving girl stepped forwards and hesitantly sat down, her fingers knotted together in worry.

"What is it, Ottama?"

"It was the whale, my lady. When you were taken ill at the docks, that was when I knew."

"What are you speaking of? What did you know?"

Ottama looked up and Nuna was struck by how fierce the girl's stare was. Despite her high status she sat back a little, drawing the covers more tightly around her.

"My lady, what I am about to tell you, what you *need* to know, is a secret not everyone would understand or ... be tolerant of." Ottama dropped her voice to whisper. "I am speaking of magic."

Nuna resisted the urge to laugh – that was the last thing she'd expected Ottama to say. "Magic? Are you saying someone attacked us with *magic* down at the docks?"

Ottama shook her head. "I don't think so. It was something else, my lady; an encounter with another realm altogether. A powerful surge, one that touched you. And me."

"Explain your meaning more plainly, please," Nuna pressed, an odd sensation in her gut. Was the girl raving? Her earnest expression suggested otherwise.

"When I was small my mother told me a story, one I've never forgotten. When our clans first moved north to settle this land we turned our back on the works of magic, which had been the cause of so much ruin, pain and suffering. My mother told me such thinking is folly, for when the avatars forged the world and brought forth life in the seas and the lands it was through magic. Magic is found in the very bones of Amuran, it touches everything and weaves its way through every living thing." Ottama laughed, her brown eyes sparkling. "The idea you can turn your back on magic is as foolish as saying you no longer want to breathe the air itself. The Laskan clans may have rejected magic but it followed them all the same as they set up their new homes and built their first ships. There have always been those with gifts – people who were different, through no fault of their own, just blind chance. They were shunned by our people but that wasn't right or fair. My mother had certain gifts and as I grew older I learned I had them too. And so do you."

Nuna shook her head, trying to make sense of what she had just heard. "What are you saying, Ottama? That because I had a headache that means I'm ... What, a *witch*? My husband only escaped the coven's enchantments last year. They would have had him live out the rest of his days in their thrall as a feeble broken man. I hardly think he'll welcome the news that I'm one as well."

Ottama's eyes flashed and there was anger there, a fierce passion contrasting sharply with her normally demure and deferential nature. It was gone in an instant but Nuna knew what she'd seen. When Ottama spoke, however, her voice was measured, calm and controlled.

"Witch is the name ignorant people use, when they want to mock something they don't understand. It's a word that speaks of their fear."

Nuna raised an eyebrow. "Are you saying I'm ignorant?"

Ottama did not break her gaze, staring intently at Nuna. "What other word can there be for your situation, my lady, when you are completely unaware of your gifts?"

Nuna drew in a breath, taken aback at the boldness of her maid. She had made a great deal of effort to become close with Ottama, trying to build bridges between their peoples by setting an example for all to see. Now she wondered if she understood this girl at all.

"And you've come here tonight to enlighten me?"

"You have the Sight, my lady, there can be no other explanation. A gift you share with me."

# CHAPTER 26

Bandor slapped me on the back, smiling broadly. "We did it. Well done."

I shrugged, trying to appear nonchalant despite a glowing sense of pride. Tapping into Randall's thoughts over the past few days had been enough to steer us on a safe path between him and Kurt's scouts further north. Despite Skari's scepticism I'd been proved right, which was timely as the journey was taking its toll on my stamina. We would have arrived two days ago if my pace had been faster, a point Skari made on numerous occasions. However, when Patrick and Ulfarr spoke up in my defence, pointing out our original path would have led us right into Randall's hands, I felt I'd earned my place in Ulfarr's crew.

"Useful? Aye, I'd be a fool to deny *that*," Skari admitted. "Don't mean I think it's natural or have to like it." He adjusted the strap on his back holding his warhammer and set off along the base of the cliff with Ekkill at his side.

Ekkill reached the mouth of the cave, urgently waving us forward before disappearing into the shadows. I glanced up at the cliff face, checking there was no one watching us, a sudden sense of dread that my confidence had been misplaced. Thengill saw me watching and nodded. "The way's clear. Let's get on with it."

I patted him on the arm and set off with Bandor across the sharp stones jutting out from the sand on the shoreline, heading towards the gap in the rocks. I knew the cave was there – I'd just seen Ekkill standing in front of it, but now it was black on black and I was afraid that if I looked away I would never be able to find the spot again. My fingertips lightly brushed the stone face of the cliff before I half-stumbled as the wall suddenly fell away from my left.

"This way," hissed Bandor, stepping into the shadows. After a moment's hesitation I followed him into the darkness.

Ekkill led us further inside and around a corner. Only then, away from any prying eyes out at sea and in the faintest light reflecting off the jagged black stone walls of the cave, did Ekkill and Patrick unwrap the bundles they'd been carrying. Sparks flew from Ekkill's flint and one by one we lit the torches. When I raised mine, I found the roof was hidden from sight, vanishing into the shadows above the smoky light of the torch's flames.

"Stay close to me and watch your step," Ekkill told us. "These paths are treacherous and you don't want to be left on your own down here, so keep up."

Without a word Thengill took up a position at the rear of our group, next to me, whilst Ulfarr moved up to the front where Ekkill was standing.

"Let's make sure we set a pace everyone can manage," Ulfarr said quietly. "No sense throwing caution aside for the final part of our journey. I'd rather we all got there in one piece."

"I'll take it steady, chief, don't you worry," replied Ekkill with a wolfish smile, glancing in my direction.

***

The temperature dropped as we moved deeper into the network of tunnels, the rock beneath our feet worn smooth by running water. Bandor lost his footing on the slick stones, stumbling over and dropping his torch into the underground stream. It went out with a hiss. Skari swore and shook his head as Patrick helped Bandor to his feet again.

"You alright?"

Bandor winced in pain, rubbing his knee. "I'll live. Don't suppose this is going to light again now."

"It'll dry out," Patrick answered with a smile. "Good job I brought a couple of spares."

"Get that lit and hurry up," hissed Ekkill. "Tide's going to turn soon."

Ulfarr touched Ekkill lightly on the arm, leaning in close though his words still carried. "Tide? Is there something you should have mentioned to us?"

"Didn't see much point. This is the only way in and there's no problem, as long as we reach the lake before high tide."

"And if we don't?"

"Tunnels at this level flood. Don't look so worried, all of you. We've plenty of time, as long as we don't waste it." Ekkill gave Bandor a withering look before leading us off once more.

Time soon lost all meaning as we headed further into the cave network. The water level began to rise and before long my boots were soaked and my feet ice-cold, making it hard to keep my balance. I wasn't the only one suffering, as Skari and Bandor both slipped a number of times.

Occasionally we reached a fork in the tunnels but Ekkill never hesitated, confidently guiding us through the maze. Eventually, the path formed a ledge above the running water, until we were looking out over a deep gorge. More underwater rivers must have joined together at this point, because the roar of the water flowing unseen below our feet was deafening. Ekkill held up his hand and passed Ulfarr his torch.

"This is the most difficult part of the route," he told us, unbundling a coil of thin rope from his pack. He moved down our line, tying the rope around each of us with swift precise motions.

Bandor rubbed at his feet, trying to get the circulation going and I bent down to do the same. I could barely feel the stone floor, my toes numb and cold as I flexed them. We exchanged a worried glance. We might all be tied together, but no one wanted to be the person to test Ekkill's knots.

Once he was satisfied Ekkill took the lead once more, matching his pace to the shuffling line of men behind him. Slowly the ledge began to narrow and I was grateful our torches were not bright enough to reveal exactly how deep the gorge was. The roof also began to drop, jagged cracks running through the overhanging stone, forcing us to crouch and duck. Behind me I heard a thud followed by Thengill's cussing.

"Use the handhold here, your feet here and here," instructed Ekkill as the ledge narrowed to just a few inches. Each of us copied the man in front, holding our torches out to the left, setting our right hand into a crack in the rock as we bridged the gap. Arissa's salve had helped mend the burn on my palm but I still felt the pink new flesh pull tight as I put my weight on the handhold and sought out firm footing with my feet. I released my grip with a rush of relief, curling my hand into a fist until the pain subsided.

All the while I waited grimly for a tug on the rope signifying someone losing their footing, sighing with relief once all of us managed the short climb without incident. I grimaced as I scrambled up the ledge before taking a turn to the right, stumbling slightly as we entered a wide cavern. The floor here was level and we were standing by the side of a lake, mirror glass smooth, which stretched off into the darkness.

"You can all relax," Ekkill said as he untied us, coiling the rope back up and placing it in his pack. "That was the most difficult part of the journey. We're also above the high tide line."

Ulfarr stretched his back and took a drink from his waterskin. "How much further?"

"Not far. An hour or so and then we reach the bowels of Romsdahl. I suggest we stop here for a short break and then press on."

I stepped up to the water, torch held out in front of me. I peered into the gloom, unable to see the far wall. I saw myself reflected in the lake, an indistinct figure holding a torch aloft.

"Don't disturb the water," Ekkill called out softly.

"Why?" I asked, gingerly stepping back.

Ekkill flashed me a smile, white teeth gleaming in the dark. "Trust me, you don't want to find out." Unsure if his was jesting, I followed his advice.

Some of our torches guttered out as we rested, so we lit fresh ones before continuing our journey. Summer had no meaning down here and I shivered, pulling my cloak tightly about me as we walked through the cavern and into a tunnel on the far side. Again, the tunnels divided regularly, Ekkill leading us confidently and always knowing which way to take. By now it was obvious that without him we would be hopelessly lost – an uncomfortable thought. The going was easier and less damp, allowing my feet a chance to dry out. My toes tingled at first as the feeling returned, before being replaced by the sensation of sharp pins being driven into my flesh. I winced with every step and bit my lip to keep quiet. The last thing I needed was to give Skari an excuse to goad me. A few minutes later he accidently kicked a jutting stone and yelped so loudly I couldn't help but laugh.

"How much further in this accursed place?" Skari snarled.

His voice died as a shape was revealed in the torchlight, propped up on the walls of the tunnel. As we approached it became clear it was a body, skeletal remains wrapped in the rotting remnant of a tattered cloak.

"Like I said, you don't want to get lost down here," Ekkill muttered, his voice muffled in the confines of the narrow cave. We all filed past without a word except Patrick, who whispered a prayer as the body of the poor soul was swallowed by the blackness.

I had no idea if Ekkill's estimate of an hour was accurate or not but after a while the stone walls were replaced by bricks and the tunnel began to head upwards. I thought I could detect a change in the air as well, a freshness brought by a slight breeze. The others sensed it too and we all quickened our pace. The brick-built tunnel continued to rise until we reached a locked wrought-iron gate. Beyond the gate I was able to see there was another short tunnel, again brick-built, with a light at the far end.

"Tell me you have the key," Skari muttered, scowling at the locked gate.

Ekkill sighed, picked up a rock and began banging on the metal, the deafening din reverberating in the narrow tunnel mingling with his shouts.

"What are you doing?" cried Ulfarr.

Ekkill paused and turned to him. "They could hardly send me out into the wilds, at risk of capture, with the key to the secret passage leading to the castle. Trust me, they'll let me in."

At the other end of the tunnel I heard the sounds of people shouting and the scrape of another metal gate being opened.

"Looks like they heard me," Ekkill said with a grin.

A few moments later I saw a number of heavily armed men running down the tunnel towards us, bearing torches. Their leader held his out as he approached in order to get a good look at us. After more than a week on the road we weren't a very wholesome sight and his torch lingered over Skari's scarred face for several moments. Finally the torch swung back towards Ekkill.

"Tomas, is that you?" asked Ekkill.

Tomas scowled and looked hard at our crew. He was a young man with a short close-cropped beard. "I know that voice. Ekkill?"

"Indeed it is, Tomas. Good to see you again after all this time," Ekkill said, grinning broadly. I'd never seen Ekkill using charm before and it was unnerving. I exchanged a look with Bandor, who raised his eyebrows.

"Is that a fact?" Tomas replied. A couple of the men behind him joined in a short humourless laugh, which died in the tunnel all too quickly. I stared at the iron gate, thinking it looked very solid.

"You two know each other, then?" asked Ulfarr. "Think you could maybe unlock this gate and let us through? It's been a long journey and we need to see Gautarr Falrufson urgently."

"Is that a fact?" Tomas repeated. "It's unfortunate you came here with him." He stared hard at Ekkill, who raised his hands apologetically.

"Tomas, come on, now. No one *forced* you to lay down that wager. I was as surprised as you were when those cards were played. I mean, those odds, those were long, long odds but sometimes that's what happens in a game of chance –"

"When you have a *special* deck of cards, it seems that those odds can shorten. Dramatically."

Ekkill shrugged and glanced at Ulfarr, who glared back. All of us looked again at the gate and thought of the maze of tunnels behind us. Ekkill leaned in close, resting his arms on the gate and smiled again at Tomas, who glowered back.

"Tomas, listen to me. A man in my profession needs to have a certain *persona* ..."

"A what?"

"Er, appear in a particular way. Act in a certain manner. I cheated you, I admit it. It was nothing personal – I just needed to show everyone I was quicker, sharper, more *cunning* than they were."

"You cheated me?"

"Yes, and now is your chance to gain the upper hand."

Tomas grinned. "That's right. I can leave you locked up behind that gate."

"No. You can play a key part in helping me complete this mission and share in the bounty as a result. You don't want to be the one who delayed the urgent message we're carrying for your chief. When he hears what we have to say you can be sure we'll be well rewarded. I'll split my share with you – far more than the coppers you lost playing cards with me."

"It was silver, as I recall," Tomas growled.

"Silver? *Really?* That *was* unlucky. Fortunately for you, the value of our message isn't weighed in silver. We're talking *gold.*"

"Why should I believe you, of all people?" Tomas asked, looking torn between exploiting his advantage over Ekkill and passing up an opportunity that might never come round again.

Ekkill waved at Tomas to come closer. He did so, reluctantly. "Because, my friend, if I'm lying you can throw us into the dungeons. Once you've opened this gate and locked it behind us, where are we going to go? We can hardly flee the city when Sinarr's army is camped outside, can we?"

# CHAPTER 27

The tunnels led into the cellars of Romsdahl Castle itself, Tomas watching us warily, pausing only to lock each door behind us as we passed through. Eventually we were left waiting with a number of guards while Tomas spoke to another warrior, a blond man I vaguely recognised. It was Haki, one of Gautarr's favoured men, who had been present when I duelled with his chief for the right to lead our clan. All a long time ago. If Haki knew who I was he kept it well-hidden when he addressed us.

"Tomas has explained who you are, why you're here and how you arrived. If you're spies, you're not very good at your trade. Gautarr will decide what to do with you, so come with me and we'll make sure you're presentable."

We followed Haki and Tomas up some more steps and down a corridor with windows that looked out onto Romsdahl. Looking down at the stone houses beyond the castle's defensive wall I was surprised at its size – there was wealth here and as we walked through his stronghold Gautarr's long-standing claims to be clan chief began to make more sense. Romsdahl, the powerful southern bulwark against our enemies, was twice the size of Reavesburg. Never before had it been so tested and yet here the Reavesburg Clan still endured and defied Adalrikr.

Each of us was shown to a small guest chamber on the same corridor. Haki apologetically produced a key and locked us inside, a move which Skari objected to loudly as the door was slammed in his face. As the door to my own chamber swung shut I took a breath, trying to relax. Outside I could hear Tomas and Haki discussing our arrival with the rest of their men in low tones.

*We're safe in Romsdahl,* I sent to Joldir.

His response was instant. *All of you?*

*Yes. Gautarr's men are still sizing us up but I think it will be fine. We're about to meet him.*

*Good. We'll talk more later – we're only about five days away from you. Djuri's army continues to track us, although they've made no move against us so far.*

*Take care,* I replied, but Joldir was already gone.

I shivered as I splashed some cold water on my face, alone in my chamber. I dismissed Gautarr's servant when he arrived with a change of clothes and lit a fire in the hearth. I didn't want to endure the stares of a stranger as they took in the scars than ran across my body. Stripped to the waist, I washed quickly, reflecting that there was a message here. Gautarr was showing us every courtesy as a host, lavishing fresh water and fine fabrics on us even whilst he lay besieged by Sinarr's army.

Gautarr's servant had made a good guess at my size. I set aside my damp boots and travel-stained clothes, dressing myself in a pair of finely spun woollen breeches and a blue-dyed linen shirt. I savoured the fact the clothing was fresh and clean as I arranged my old clothes in front of the fire to dry. I buckled up my belt and felt the familiar comforting weight of my short sword at my side. My belly rumbled and I wondered what time it was. It was a strange feeling, waiting for Gautarr's summons. On the road danger had been ever-present. Now whilst we were safe, under the protection of our allies, doubts began to surface as I paced the floor. There was no denying the history between our families was difficult. Gautarr's desire to rule had led him to try and murder my brother, so Jorik had not just defeated Gautarr in their duel to decide who would be chief. Jorik had humiliated him, making him swear fealty to our family as he knelt there before him, bloodied and beaten. Gautarr had never openly defied Jorik during my brother's short rule but he had broken my engagement with his niece,

Freydja, soon afterwards, pledging her hand to Bandor instead. The more I remembered the past the more I began to realise how my return would stir powerful memories for Gautarr. Our audience needed to be handled with great care.

One link to my past was missing; when not occupied with using the Sight to track Randall's movements I had unsuccessfully reached out to my sister over the past few days. Somehow Nuna was hiding herself from me, perhaps under Ottama's guidance. Sigurd's serving maid, who I'd overlooked completely, possessed a valuable gift. Only Nuna had seen something in this girl when she'd been drawn towards her and now I knew why. There was more to it than that, though. If Ottama had been hidden from me it meant she had some measure of skill and training to prevent me accessing her thoughts. That was what bothered me more than anything else – who was Ottama and what was she telling Nuna? I needed to know.

Haki knocked and opened the door. "Come with me." It was not a request.

I pushed all thoughts of Nuna aside as I walked with the others down more corridors and up a winding spiral staircase. The doors to Gautarr's feasting hall were solid oak, the Reavesburg eagle embossed in black iron, interwoven into the reinforced metal bands on its surface. Haki pushed them open, revealing a well-lit hall illuminated by tall glass windows. I let out an involuntary gasp when I saw them, trying to imagine the cost. The Great Hall at Ulfkell's Keep was small, dingy and mean in comparison. We walked the length of the hall towards a group of figures at the far side, past luxurious tapestries hanging from floor to ceiling depicting various scenes from our clan's history as well as myth. I saw an image of Vellandir, avatar of justice, Garradon at his side, rallying the forces of light to his banner as he battled Morvanos' great army during the War of the Avatars. In the background I could see Dinas and Navan with the remaining avatars who did not take part in the war, their pleas for peace ignored as battle was joined. Rannoch reached out, trying to prevent the lands from splitting asunder whilst Bruar knelt, head in his hands, as he saw the fell weapons wrought with his metal-working skills. Whilst the avatars who refused to join the battle escaped the Creator's wrath and banishment to the Void, if they still walked upon Amuran they did so in secret. Whilst many a sailor offered a prayer to Nanquido, wishing for calm seas, or Culdaff, desiring good weather and favourable winds, I doubted they heard such supplications.

Nearby was an earlier scene from legend, depicting another struggle between light and darkness. Altandu's contest with Ceren ended with the sun appearing in the sky during the day and the moon at night. These were the first signs of discord between the avatars that, eons later, led to war. One of Darri's poems came to mind, as I recalled his description of Altandu's tears softening the darkness Ceren wreathed Amuran in at night, scattering the sky with glittering stars. The colours were vivid and fresh despite the brightness of the room, which meant the wall hangings were brand new. As I walked down the polished oak floor and passed by each tapestry and window I was forced to re-evaluate my estimate of Gautarr Falrufson's fortune. No wonder Sinarr the Cold One wanted to capture Romsdahl and its wealth intact.

I swallowed as we approached the welcoming committee. Gautarr looked no different, a great bear of a man, grizzled with grey though still powerful, his eyes narrowing when they fixed on me. Next to him stood his slender wife, Jora, her arm entwined with her husband's. She had once been a great beauty and even now retained her poise and confidence, unbowed by the years. They were flanked by Ragnar, their dark-haired and serious-minded son, and Gautarr's younger nephew, Throm. The two looked so similar they were often mistaken for brothers. I felt my breath catch as I saw Throm's sister, Freydja, standing behind them, dark-haired and slim like her aunt. I glanced at Bandor, who was looking at her with a strained expression, meeting her for the first time since Ulf-kell's Keep fell. It struck me that in different times Freydja and

Bandor would already have been wed.

"So, it's true," Gautarr said quietly, taking a step towards us. There were a dozen warriors in the hall and, as one, they moved with him, protecting their chief.

Jora nodded. "Johan sends Rothgar Kolfinnarson and his son, Bandor, to plead for our aid. I see Etta's spy, Ekkill, skulking there with them too."

"I see someone else I recognise," Gautarr said, jabbing his finger at Thengill. "I know you."

Thengill looked up, hands resting easily on the handles of his axes. "Maybe we've met – I couldn't say." The men stood with Gautarr stiffened at those words, marking his Vorund accent. One of them, a bull-necked man with a wide face and short black hair, snarled and drew his sword. In a moment, Ulfarr, Skari and Myr stepped forwards, interposing themselves between Thengill and Gautarr's men.

"Domarr. Put your blade away," shouted Gautarr, holding up his hand. "The rest of you, stand down."

"We're all on the same side here," Ulfarr said, slowly moving his hand away from the hilt of his sword. "I can vouch for Thengill. He's no friend of Sinarr and has fought with us many times as part of my crew. If Johan didn't trust him he wouldn't be here."

Gautarr folded his arms and stared at Ulfarr. "That's a nice speech but I don't set much store by Johan's judgement, a man who's treated with his enemies and is now fighting a war he can't win. You're all members of the Reavesburg Clan and earned the right to bear arms in my hall. As for you, Thengill, you should never have come. You've seen the secret passages leading to my castle, something we've kept hidden from our enemies for centuries. Such things shouldn't be trusted to a man who betrays his own clan. There's no honour in that. You've no right to stand in my hall after taking up arms against me. I remember your face on the field, fighting in Asmarr's guard. You had a reputation, Thengill, as one of his most loyal men, destined to be one of his jarls. You were even close to

Sinarr back then, as I recall. I may not have the letters and learning of some but I never forget a face." Gautarr gestured to his men with a rueful smile. "Disarm him and take him to the cells."

Without hesitation Thengill raised his hands, allowing Tomas to take his weapons. "You weren't there that night," he said quietly as Tomas bound him. "My brothers raised arms against me. The Vorund Clan was lost the night Asmarr died and Sinarr was one of the men who turned against him and sided with Adalrikr."

"In other words, you failed to protect your chief and fled," said Gautarr with a mocking smile. "Better to have died than become what you are today. Take him away."

Bandor gave me a worried glance as I shook my head. "There's nothing we can do, not here. Not now," I told him in a hushed tone. We watched, helpless, as Thengill was led away by Tomas, vanishing from view as the doors of the hall closed behind him.

Haki had taken Thengill's axes and passed one of them to Gautarr, who ran his fingers over the flat of the blade, lingering over the chimera and dragon runes. The symbols were dark and black – at least durath had not penetrated as far as Gautarr's inner circle.

"So," Gautarr said after a moment, still staring at the runes. "Johan sent you to me for a reason. Let's hear what he has to say."

# CHAPTER 28

Gautarr ordered tables to be put up in the hall and for food to be served. We all fell upon the bread, pastries, pork and fish with little ceremony, greedily drinking the ale brought to us by Gautarr's servants and marvelling that, after a year-long siege, he could show such generosity. As we ate we answered Gautarr's and Jora's questions. Ragnar looked unimpressed when we finished our tale.

"As we thought, Johan brings too few men. Once again, it falls to Romsdahl to bleed while the rest of Reavesburg cannot muster enough warriors to fight for their own homeland. Indeed, some have already turned their backs on that cause. Old Hrodi now rides with our enemies, rather than to our aid."

"You've no right to speak so disrespectfully about my father," Bandor growled, setting down his cup. "He's been fighting the Vorund Clan for a year, while you've been hiding here, safe behind your walls. You should admire his courage, not mock him."

Ragnar shrugged. "I'm stating facts, nothing more. If it hadn't been for us weathering this siege you'd have no safe refuge where you can eat and drink in comfort. We *chose* to come back here after the fall of Ulfkell's Keep, to protect our friends and families. We took advantage of the secret passages to return to our home and, by using them now, we can keep ourselves fed and watered. We've long planned for such difficult times, which is why Sinarr still sits outside our gates. We've endured, unlike others. Your father and Rothgar brokered an alliance with Norlhast that lasted not a single day after Ulfkell's Keep fell. Our foolish young chief was too short-sighted to see the danger he placed us in when he provoked the wrath of the Vorund Clan. It's the failure of Reavesburg's leaders that have left us in this position."

"Now you insult me and the leadership of my brother as well," I said quietly, looking at Ragnar from across the table. He met my gaze defiantly.

"Enough," said Jora. "We did not welcome you into our home to trade insults."

"Begging your pardon, my lady, you didn't welcome Thengill in at all," Ulfarr remarked, mopping up gravy with a piece of bread. Ragnar opened his mouth to protest, but Ulfarr spoke first. "I'm stating *facts*, nothing more. It's nice to be sat here wearing fine, clean clothes and eating good food but Thengill's one of my crew and I'd like to know what you plan to do with him."

"We've more pressing concerns," answered Ragnar.

"I want your word that he'll be kept safe," I said, drawing a surprised look from Gautarr's household. "Thengill's protected me and saved my life. Johan sent him here because things have changed and you'll need his help in the coming battle."

Gautarr laughed. "What battle? We can outlast Sinarr's army in here for another two years if we have to. I've heard nothing to persuade me that we can win and break this siege by riding out to join Johan. He has too few men – we could lose everything if we follow the plan you're proposing and end up giving Sinarr the keys to the city as well."

Ekkill made an exasperated sound and shook his head. "You have, what, some two thousand men here defending the city and the castle? I don't see your second, Audwin Strongshield, amongst us. Where is he? Further north, mustering more men? I don't believe you were planning to sit here for another two years – you were getting ready to break the siege yourselves this summer and you're worried now Johan is here, fearing he'll get the credit if you join forces with him. You need to think – he has over a thousand warriors under his command. If Audwin is ready to march he only needs a thousand more answering the call to join his banner and the numbers are more or less equal. In fact, I think you'd be disappointed if he hadn't raised at least two thousand swords from the northern lands, which if I'm right gives us a chance."

Gautarr's face darkened as Ekkill spoke; the man had never been able to disguise his feelings. "You seem remarkably well-informed."

Ekkill shrugged. "I'm paid as a spy and informer, so I'll take that as a compliment. I'm right about Audwin?"

"Audwin has already ridden south with two thousand warriors," Jora said. "He is awaiting our signal to attack and we can't wait much longer, or we risk his forces being discovered. It's true that with Johan's help our numbers would be close to those of Sinarr, but it's not a decisive advantage. Either way, we are outnumbered and the battle could easily turn against us."

Ulfarr frowned. "That just shows you need Johan's aid and his arrival is timely. More than that – a gift, one that's fallen into your lap. Why are we even debating this?"

"Because you don't want Johan's help," I said, addressing Gautarr. "You've made your plans and spent a year getting ready for this moment, and now Johan makes an appearance. Johan, the man who's always supported my family's claim to rule, never yours. It would be very convenient if Johan's army was crushed between Sinarr and Djuri's forces, removing your rival and weakening the Vorund Clan. Then Audwin could emerge from hiding and you could ride out from Romsdahl and strike at Sinarr. If you're victorious you'd have no rivals and a chance to become chief, if you could take Ulfkell's Keep back from Tyrfingr Blackeyes."

"You always were bold," muttered Gautarr. "Tyrfingr didn't cut off your balls then, when he tortured you. Perhaps you're right – Johan Jokellsward's always sided against my family and thinks he's better than us. Now he's looking to unite Reavesburg, so what should I do? Bend the knee to him like I did for your brother, when my army can muster four men for every one of his? I don't think he's worthy of that honour."

Bandor was on his feet, his protest interrupted as Patrick and Ulfarr each took hold of his shoulders and shoved him back into his seat with a thump. I quickly spoke over Bandor, before he had chance to argue.

"Adalrikr has declared himself King of the North. He has no respect for the clans or the bloodlines of their ruling families, nor any care for our petty feuds. He seeks to bring us all under his heel and we can only prevent that by uniting against him. You need an experienced warrior like Johan fighting at your side. Otherwise, even if you succeed and break this siege without him, you'll find that in a year from now more ships flying the banner of the bear will be landing on your shores. They'll be commanded by men from Vorund but they'll also bring warriors from the other clans that have been defeated and sworn fealty to Adalrikr; men from Norlhast and Riltbalt. Perhaps by then Jorvind, Helsburg and Vittag will also have surrendered, further bolstering his forces. You can't afford to remain isolated, not if you want your household to survive."

A number of people began to speak at once before Gautarr held up his hand and the hall fell silent. "I would speak with Kolfinnar's son. Privately."

***

Haki and his men left with Ulfarr's crew, Bandor shooting me an anxious glance as the doors to the hall were closed. I was left alone with Gautarr and Jora. Curiously, Gautarr had also asked the thick-set warrior called Domarr to remain behind, something which obviously surprised him as much as me. Ragnar stalked from the feasting hall, angry at being excluded. Throm looked at me curiously as he left, his sister Freydja holding his arm.

I watched Domarr from the other side of the table, trying to remember anything of note about the man; he was dark-haired with a square jaw, probably in his mid-thirties. He had been there during the duel when I fought Gautarr to assert

Jorik's right to rule. If we'd met again since then, I couldn't recall. And yet, as I looked at him more closely he seemed familiar. Domarr caught my eye and scowled, folding his arms. Jora stood and walked to one of the tall windows, which looked out onto the inner wall of Romsdahl Castle. She hugged her thin frame and sighed before addressing me.

"You think a great deal of Johan, don't you, Rothgar?"

I nodded. "He's a good man, and one the men follow willingly. He can't do this alone – he needs your help as much as you need him to free Romsdahl."

Jora's eyes narrowed. "That's some of it, I'm sure, but there's more here, isn't there? Show me your sword."

I stood up, surprised by the request and drew out my blade. Gautarr walked across and picked up my sword with casual ease. It resembled little more than a dagger in his big fist. He scrutinised the runes along its surface, exchanging a look with his wife.

"The same symbol?" Jora asked. Gautarr nodded, handing the weapon back to me.

"Ekkill is not the only spy in Reavesburg, though he may be the most arrogant," Jora said, returning to her seat and picking up her glass of wine. "We heard strange rumours concerning Johan's army and those closest to him – those forming the Brotherhood. I understand you're a member of this group."

I paused, knowing that simply blurting out the truth would make me appear a madman. However, it was clear that Jora already knew something – the question was how much?

"The Brotherhood consists of Johan's closest confidants."

Crow's feet crinkled around Jora's narrowed eyes as she stared at me. "Don't play us for the fool. There have been rumours that Adalrikr is using magic to defeat his enemies and Johan has discovered the means to stop it. Is this true?"

"Such talk seems ... outlandish."

"As outlandish as Kalamar Castle being obliterated?" growled Gautarr. The head of Romsdahl's house stood up and stared down at me. "This is my home. This is my family we're talking about. If you know something that would help me protect them and hold it back ..."

I sighed and took another sip of ale, trying to give myself time to think. "Such things are not my secret to tell. That is part of the oath we swear when joining the Brotherhood."

"So, you admit that it's real, this Brotherhood?" Jora demanded.

I nodded. "Of course. In the past year I've seen things ..." I sighed, shaking my head. "Where to begin? The world is a very different place from what I imagined, that much is true."

"That's it? That's all you're willing to tell us?" Gautarr said.

Jora placed a hand on his arm, shushing him. "Don't interrupt. Let him say what he *can* tell us."

"You'll never defeat the army outside your walls unless Sinarr is destroyed," I explained. "You've surely heard the tales concerning Sinarr the Cold One, and we have learned every one of them is true. There is something unnatural about him – dark magic used by Adalrikr, that makes him a powerful foe. Johan has discovered a way to break the magic protecting him, but he can only get near Sinarr with your help."

Domarr drank the last of his ale and put his mug down with a loud bang on the table. "How convenient. So, Johan is the *only* man able to kill Sinarr, thus taking all credit for the deed, and we're supposed to help him do this? Chief, surely you can see this is nonsense. Why did you want me to stay and listen to such talk?"

Gautarr looked angrily at Domarr. "Why? Because he was there. In Ulfkell's Keep the night my brother was killed – your father."

Domarr stared at him and in that instant I saw the truth – my old weapons master Olfridor Halfhand as a younger man. The likeness was so remarkable I was astonished I'd not seen it before. Olfridor and my father had been close when I was growing up. I had only recently learned how Olfridor's family ties had been broken years ago, when he refused to support Gautarr's claim to rule the Reavesburg Clan.

"He sired me – that's all," Domarr replied. "What does it matter?"

Gautarr's face became thunderous. "I raised you better than this. It doesn't matter you were born a bastard, he was your father and that counts for something. The Vorund Clan have taken both my brothers from me and I'd like to know the truth about what happened the night Olfridor died. It's a tale you deserve to hear as well." Domarr's face flushed and he did not argue further against his uncle.

Gautarr sat back down and turned to me, breathing deeply. "I don't know what to think about you. You've come here today making demands you've no right to make, in the company of spies and our enemies, talking of magic and a secret brotherhood – one from which I might add that I am excluded. Do you really expect me to put my life, the life of my only surviving son and those of my nephews, at risk on such flimsy terms, trusting that you'll share your secrets with me later?" Gautarr shook his head. "If I'm to join this fight then it's not to heed Johan's call to arms but to avenge my family, so tell me something I can understand. Tell me about what really happened the night Ulfkell's Keep was taken and I had to run for my life. Tell me what happened to Olfridor and who killed him."

# CHAPTER 29

Reliving the shock and subsequent horror of the ambush in the Great Hall left me drained. Gautarr listened silently to my tale, bowing his head when I described Tyrfingr Blackeyes murdering Jorik's family one by one before his eyes. How Olfridor had died trying to protect us. Jora's hand was shaking as she covered her mouth during my description of Tyrfingr torturing me into confessing to the murder of my family, treating me as a criminal and leaving me to die a traitor's death.

"Yet you survived," Gautarr said, looking at me appraisingly. "He took your strength, broke your body and tarnished your reputation. Now here you are, in my hall, having lived to tell the tale." Gautarr rose and began to pace, whilst Domarr watched, a frown creasing his forehead. Gautarr looked agitated as he turned to me. "I often think something changed within our family, after Egill died. He was the eldest brother and born to be the head of our house – I could see that. Everyone could see that, which is why Olfridor never had any designs to lead, even though he was next in line. You know the man who killed Egill? Joarr the Hammer." A shadow passed over Gautarr's face. "He's outside my gates, grown rich and powerful as one of Adalrikr's jarls, while my brother's body rots in the crypt beneath this castle. Throm and Freydja lost their father during that battle but Joarr did more than that, he broke their mother's spirit too. Tora was never a strong woman and when Egill was killed in battle ... well, she lost all reason ..."

"Uncle, why are you telling him all this?" demanded Domarr. "This is private, and nothing to do with him."

"Because it concerns your father as well," Jora told him

impatiently, eyes flashing. "Listen to what your uncle is saying, please."

Gautarr composed himself. "Olfridor tried to help her and look out for the children, while I was too consumed with anger to care. I blamed your father for Egill's death, telling myself and anyone who'd listen that if Kolfinnar had sent us more men we wouldn't have been outnumbered that day and forced to flee. That it was Kolfinnar's fault Joarr caught and fought my brother. I demanded a clan moot and laid down my challenge to lead the clan, even though I'd lost the vote to Kolfinnar eight years earlier. Even Egill supported your father back then, saying he was the right man to lead us, but I was too young and brash to care.

"Olfridor argued against calling a second moot when he returned to Romsdahl for Egill's burial. He'd been your father's second since the start of his rule, part of a pact we made to seal the ties between us after he became chief. Those two were close after that, perhaps even closer once Olfridor was maimed and Kolfinnar stood by him and made him his weapons master."

Gautarr drank deeply, ale dripping into his beard. His wife poured him another cup as he continued his tale. "Olfridor told me straight. Egill was killed by a man nearly thirty years younger than him, just coming into his prime as our brother's skills with a blade were beginning to fade. 'See this?' he said, showing me his three-fingered hand. 'It's a reminder to me every day that nothing stays the same and age catches up with all of us, sooner or later. Might was well blame Dinas himself and tell him to turn back the river of time.'

"I didn't listen – didn't want to. So, I called my clan moot and said some things about Kolfinnar that weren't so clever and lost the vote, only Old Hrodi supporting me. Always my loyal bannerman, until now. Olfridor had words with me afterwards but I didn't take back what I said about your father, even when he asked me to for his sake. We argued and he stayed loyal to Kolfinnar – after all, Kolfinnar had only ever been loyal and stood by him. There were sharp words between us, and those were the last ones we shared. Later I heard Olfridor never again spoke of me being his brother – didn't even like the subject being raised. In time I found myself thinking the same way, and that was the way things stayed for the next fourteen years, until I learned of his death."

"He made his choice," Jora said, laying a comforting hand on her husband's.

"Aye, and I made mine. Tora's death hardened Olfridor's heart against me further – a year later she took her own life, unable to live without Egill. She cast herself into the sea off the cliffs outside Romsdahl, the waters returning her to us three days later. Olfridor came back for her funeral, making clear to everyone he thought I should have taken better care of my sister-in-law. He left shortly afterwards, without even speaking to me. I tried to make amends, raising Throm and Freydja as my own. Freydja became the daughter Jora and I never got to see grow up, after my little Svena was taken from us. My sons got on well with Throm, even though he was much younger. A few years later, I learned of Olfridor's bastard son, born to one of the whores in the lower city. I took Domarr in too, teaching him the skills he needed to be a warrior and giving him a place at my table. Whatever you might think, I tried to do the right thing by my family. Olfridor certainly wasn't perfect."

Domarr raised an eyebrow at those words, saying nothing, drinking again from his cup. I'd lost count of the amount of ale the young man had drunk since we'd begun this conversation. He sat there listening as Gautarr continued.

"Whatever the reasons, rights and wrongs, all that matters is I wasn't there when the Vorund Clan butchered Olfridor and I lost my middle brother. I couldn't even give him a proper burial; Tyrfingr Blackeyes made a pyre with the bodies of the defeated, my brother's bones naught but ash, scattered outside the walls of Reavesburg."

"You tell a sad tale," I observed. "But you're neglecting the less favourable parts of your story. For example, you've conveniently forgotten your part in ambushing my brother at sea on his first raid into Vorund lands. You tried to kill him before our father even passed into Navan's Halls, an act that set you further apart from your brother, as I'm sure you've guessed."

Jora stared at me indignantly. "My husband did what he had to do, even if you can't see it. This was about the survival of our clan and who was the right person to lead us with Vorund threatening our borders. Kolfinnar was weak – dying in fact, and Jorik as his heir was a young man with a hot temper and little wits. You know I'm right. You were younger still, and neither of you had the experience or the support to rule and protect our clan. That's why you lost the vote in the moot. That wasn't enough, though, was it? You were so proud, clinging on to the pretensions of your dynasty, of Marl's line and denying my husband's right to rule. And with that decision, the opportunity for the best man to lead our clan slipped away, leading us to where we are today."

I was taken aback by Jora's words. "We'll never agree on who should have been chief, but you're talking about ... murdering my brother being the right course of action. You seem proud of your part in this."

"I admitted this already, before all the elders at the clan moot," snarled Gautarr, waving his hand dismissively. "You really think I was *proud* of what I did? No, of course not. It was for the good of the clan, to try and secure our future." He glanced at his wife, who gave a small nod of support.

I stared back at Gautarr, weighing his words, still sceptical about what I was hearing. He drank again from his cup, draining it and setting it down, shaking his head when Jora made to refill it once more. His eyes met mine, his stare unflinching.

"The Vorund Clan wasn't content with taking both my brothers. My eldest son, Hroarr, drowned at seventeen in a storm off Vorund's coast, leading his first raid against our enemy. It was the fates and Nanquido's ill-will that broke apart his ship and took his life, but he was seeking vengeance for his uncle and his kin, so I hold the Vorund Clan responsible. Ragnar has risen to the task of being my heir – I'm proud of the boy. He bears the heavy burden well."

"Why are you telling me all this?" I asked. Gautarr had never shown me anything but contempt. Finding him so open was both disturbing and unexpected.

Gautarr looked genuinely surprise at my question. "Why? Because I want you to understand what and who I'm fighting for. The Vorund Clan has taken much from me, just as you've suffered at their hands. I've been blessed as well, seen Ragnar marry Asta and live to see my grandchildren born. But I'm no fool and I know that soon the time will come for Ragnar to lead my house. I'm old – this is my fifty-fifth summer and Olfridor's words come back to me more and more often these days."

My heart began to pound. "Are you telling me you'll give the order to attack when Johan arrives?"

Gautarr's eyes glittered. "I'll not pass up this chance. Johan's welcome to take Sinarr's head but understand this; Joarr is mine. As for what happens after, well, I'm not pledging allegiance to Johan's cause beyond clearing out the scourge surrounding my city walls."

"In that case, let Myshall and Dinuvillan decide the outcome," I replied. "If the battle is won and both of you are still standing, the question of who is called chief of the Reavesburg Clan can be decided then."

Gautarr's teeth flashed through his beard as he grinned at me. "Arkon is the avatar of war, so I'll trust the outcome to him rather than the Fates. Him and my axe."

"One last thing," I began.

Gautarr grunted. "I've just agreed to fight in Johan's battle. Be careful what you ask for, in case I change my mind."

"You've judged Thengill harshly. He has many reasons to fight in the coming battle and he's a fearsome warrior. Please –"

Gautarr shook his head and interrupted me. "Don't try my patience – I've made my decision and I won't change my mind. He'll stay in the dungeons. I've already promised no harm will come to him, at least not until after the battle. Let the next chief of the Reavesburg Clan decide his fate."

I sat back in my chair, frustrated, as I let the matter drop. There was too much to lose by antagonising Gautarr and Thengill was safe, for now at least. Instead I nodded in agreement.

"If that's your decision, so be it."

We talked further into the night, as the sky outside darkened and servants entered to light torches in the feasting hall. Gautarr explained how the beacons could be lit in the watch towers to send a message to Audwin's forces to the north, to ensure he attacked on the appointed day. Johan's plan was to strike without delay upon his arrival, and unless he was hindered on the road battle would be joined in just five days. Things were drawing to a close, one way or the other.

Domarr was obviously growing bored of listening to such details. He rose from the table and excused himself. "Olfridor may have treated you as one of his favourites," he told me as he left. "Don't think that counts for much with me. He chose to spend his time in Kolfinnar's service rather than raising his own son, so I know where my loyalties lie."

# CHAPTER 30

Ulfarr and the rest of his crew crowded into my chamber when I returned that evening, eager to learn what had happened.

"Looks like I'll be bringing good news back with me to Johan," Ekkill said with a smile, before looking pointedly at me. "Although I'm sure it won't come as a surprise." As the only one who knew the secret underground passageways, it had been agreed Ekkill would report back to Johan on Gautarr's agreement to fight alongside the Brotherhood. Trying to explain we could send word by magic would only have made us either a laughing stock or raised suspicion among Romsdahl's more superstitious warriors. That discussion was for another day, although as Ekkill had intimated, I'd already reached out to Joldir with the Sight to advise him of our success.

"Have you paid Tomas back yet and made good on your promise?" asked Patrick. A number of the men laughed and Ekkill's smile grew wider, white teeth flashing.

"Think I'll be leaving before dawn."

Ulfarr laid a hand on my shoulder. "You did well. Just a nudge in the right direction and now we have the men we need."

"Assuming Audwin Strongshield turns up," remarked Ekkill.

Ulfarr ignored the jibe. "Johan's orders were to keep you safe, which is why I need you to listen to what I'm going to say. When Johan's army reaches Romsdahl and battle is joined you stay here, in the castle."

I chuckled. "I'm no fool, Ulfarr. I know I'll be little use on the battlefield."

Bandor looked worried. "I don't think you'll be safe

alone with Gautarr. He has a long memory and he won't forget the wrongs your family have done to him, just as he's held onto all that bitterness against the Vorund Clan."

Ulfarr scratched his greying beard and let out a long sigh. "We swore an oath and our brothers will need us in a few days' time. I won't to speak for any of you, but I'll be taking my place in Gautarr's ranks when the gates are opened. Gautarr and Johan need every able-bodied man fighting out on the field, not guarding Rothgar."

I looked around the room and saw Ulfarr's crew nod in agreement with him, as I knew they would. Bandor did so less enthusiastically, meeting my gaze as he did so. Soon afterwards people left, tiredness from the journey finally catching up with them, the lure of sleep in a warm comfortable bed for the first time in months too strong to resist. Bandor lingered, taking a seat as I closed the door behind Ulfarr. I sat opposite him and asked what was on his mind.

"Only that this is dangerous, and I don't trust Gautarr. I feel ... helpless."

"Careful, that's your future father-in-law you're talking about."

Bandor shot me a venomous look. "Don't joke about such things. My father's the Landless Jarl, remember? I doubt Gautarr has any intention of seeing me marry his precious niece any more than he did you."

"You like her, though?" Bandor blushed, saying nothing. "Who wouldn't?" I told him. "She's an attractive young woman – she just has an over-protective uncle."

Bandor laughed, the sound reminding me of happier times. "That's one way to put it. Gods, I don't know what to think any more. We're so close now. I'm excited and yet there's this fear, gnawing at my guts at the same time."

"I know. I feel the same way, wishing these next few days would pass by and at the same time terrified of what's going to happen when the fateful day arrives."

"And if we win? Gautarr's not going to accept my

father's leadership, that's obvious from what he said tonight. Can you really see the Brotherhood surviving under Gautarr's rule?" The thought filled me with dread – not the answer Bandor needed to hear.

"Johan's army may be smaller but it represents most of the minor houses of Reavesburg. Gautarr's main bannerman has turned traitor, leaving him with few supporters across the wider clan. Don't be too quick to think he'll get his own way."

Bandor frowned, looking unconvinced. "I remember similar words before the clan moot we lost supporting Jorik's claim to be chief. Regardless of what the elders might say, Gautarr's numbers mean he can dictate what he wants to do and who he wants to serve."

I arranged a smile on my face and placed a hand on Bandor's arm. "Let's face one problem at a time. We've found a way through worse odds."

Bandor looked at me, still sceptical, knowing there was little more to be said. We embraced and retired for the night. Or at least Bandor did. I still had work to do as I gave my full report to Joldir, Leif sleeping soundly with Arissa in the wagon.

Afterwards, we didn't need Leif to join our Fellowship that night as we reached out together to find those we were looking for.

*** 

Djuri pushed open the tent flap and stepped out into the night, blinking as his eyes adjusted to the dim lights of the campfires, bats flitting between the tents as they chased their prey. The canvas did little to muffle the sound of Alfarr and Radholf arguing. Alfarr was growing impatient and wanted to strike out at Johan's army, harry his supplies and kill his scouts. It wasn't the first time such tactics had been discussed, and Djuri suspected Alfarr's motivation was partly to undermine him in front of Hrodmarr. Whilst Alfarr had accepted Djuri's decision with little grace, since then he'd complained about every other aspect of army life.

Djuri wended his way through the camp, which was

quiet as most people were asleep, taking what rest they could before the march resumed in the morning. There had been no word back from Sinarr, so Djuri had to assume either his scouts or Sinarr's messengers had been intercepted by Johan's men. In the absence of any other orders they prepared for battle outside Romsdahl's walls. He would be glad when it was all over. He passed Haarl, standing guard with a number of warriors from Reavesburg and chatted to him for a few minutes.

"Quiet night," Haarl told him with a smile, only half his face visible in the torchlight.

"Don't wish for any other kind," Djuri replied, slapping him on the back before continuing his walk.

The camp was well-ordered, those on watch at their posts alert and sober. Whatever he might think of Hrodmarr, the Vorund warrior's presence had improved the discipline of the men under Djuri's command. When the time for battle came, Djuri hoped they would remain loyal. He still suspected he'd been given this command so there was someone expendable in charge if things went wrong. He continued to inspect the camp before retiring to bed, his tent guarded by Ulf, who nodded in greeting as he approached. Djuri took heart that all was in order and everything was proceeding as he intended – that was all he could do. Hrodi and Radholf could worry about that spoiled brat, Alfarr.

***

Humli stirred in his bed, restlessly turning over and pushing away the covers – it was a hot, close night and the air felt like a thunderstorm was brewing. He lay still for a moment, listening to the slow, rhythmic breathing of Desta, Lina and their children. He smiled to himself, enjoying the fact that he was no longer an old man living on his own. It was good to have company in his cottage once again. He closed his eyes, thinking of his long-dead wife, a smile on his face.

***

*Come with me*, sent Joldir. In moments the world around me dissolved and reformed as the familiar surroundings of Joldir's farm. This time we were standing in the courtyard, enjoying the sunshine Joldir had conjured, as we looked at the mosaic of the dragon and chimera set into the stones. Once I thought it nothing more than artistry on Joldir's part. Now I understood its true significance.

"Djuri holds station and Desta remains safe with her father. Nuna seems elusive, though." Joldir rested his back against the wall, gazing fondly at his old house. I wondered what it really looked like now, after months of neglect.

I frowned, a nagging worry in the pit of my stomach. "It's like Nuna's vanished – there's no hint of her. I don't like it. Maybe you should try instead?"

Joldir shook his head. "Remember Nereth was once part of my Sight Fellowship. She's attuned to my gift like no other and can always sense if I'm the one seeking the Path. Unless we can find a way to end Nereth you must lead, while I remain your anchor."

"I know you're right ..."

Joldir put his hand on my shoulder, the gesture made possible by the world he had created. "I understand this is hard, but you've done well. Make sure you rest now you're safe and don't try to force things. Sometimes the more you grasp the harder it is to focus."

"It's not that. Something's changed. There's no hint of her presence. None at all. It's ... it's as if she's died." I swallowed the lump down in my throat.

Joldir stood up straighter and turned to look directly at me. "Listen to me. You've been living in the wilds for more than a week and you're still recovering from the attempt on your life. That can have all sorts of effects. If Nuna had died we would have received word of such an important event. Do you understand me?"

I sighed, trying to release some of the anxiety building up inside, a hand twisting my guts and gripping my heart, making it hard to breathe. "You're sure there's nothing to worry about? What about Ottama, what do we really know about her?"

"We'll solve this mystery in time, trust me. For now, just rest and recover your strength. We need you to be focussing on events in Romsdahl. Don't let things you can't influence distract you. Bandor's right, Gautarr can't be trusted and you need to keep your wits about you."

I nodded and embraced Joldir, trying to set aside my worries. We separated and I was unable to keep my eyes open, falling into a deep sleep in my chamber at Romsdahl Castle within moments of my return.

# CHAPTER 31

Dawn was creeping across the sky, a grey smudge on the horizon, as Randall, Kurt and their men reached the outskirts of their camp. When they first arrived at Romsdahl, Joarr and Randall ensured the camp was carefully organised, with an eye to defending themselves from a counter-attack as well as a charge by Gautarr from the city gates. A year on it was depressing to see how the camp had become a sprawling mess, many of the non-combatants supporting the war-effort scattered loosely across the countryside and beyond the palisade walls. Cooks, smiths, tanners, traders, families, whores and a good number of warriors too. Fear of disease had caused a significant number of men to move out of their fortified barracks and down into the canvas town. It probably *was* safer living there, unless the Landless Jarl's army arrived sooner than expected. Randall wondered how many more had succumbed to the bloody flux whilst he had been away.

Kurt cursed to himself. "Where are Joarr's scouts and watchmen? We should have been challenged long before – not when we reach the gates."

"Folk are getting lazy and bored," Randall replied as they drew nearer to the palisade. "Hello. Anyone there?" he called up.

"Who's asking?" came the reply.

Randall gave his name and watched as the gates were slowly opened. His heart sank when he saw it was Hasteinn, Joarr's second, who was guarding the gates with a number of his men.

"Coming back empty-handed?" Hasteinn asked with a grin.

"Our orders are to report to Sinarr, not you," Kurt answered sourly.

Hasteinn glanced at the glum faces of the men with Randall and smiled. "I'd say you're not bringing him good news. Go on then, make your way through."

"Want me to come with you?" Kurt asked as they trudged towards Sinarr's headquarters.

Randall smiled, appreciating the younger warrior's gesture as he shook his head. "Thanks, but this is something I need to do on my own. Take our crew and find them something hot to eat. I'll be along soon enough."

Kurt looked at him doubtfully but didn't argue, leaving Randall to continue the rest of the walk on his own. When he reached the farmhouse Sinarr's guards opened the door immediately. Clearly he was expected. Inside the foul smell of decay was worse than ever and Randall didn't even bother to hide the fact, taking a corner of his cloak and holding it over his nose and mouth as he walked into Sinarr's inner chamber.

"Randall. Ever the honest man, here to give an account of his failures," a familiar voice rasped in the darkness.

"We scoured that cliff face," Randall said, shuddering. "Looked hard, often the same place two or three times. We found tracks left on the top of the cliffs, so we came close, I know it, yet somehow they slipped by us. They made their way down the cliff face and we couldn't follow their trail further than a few feet on the stone, nor find anything on the beach. The tide would have washed everything away by then. Somehow, they got past us."

"Somehow."

Sinarr stepped into the light, and Randall saw that the jarl was dressed for battle in chainmail, with a two-handed sword strapped to his back. He neck creaked as he looked down on Randall, eyes unblinking.

"You failed me. It was almost as if they *knew* where you were and where you had sent your second. How can that be?"

Sinarr reached out, faster than Randall thought possible, striking his cloak away and gripping his jaw with his hand. He twisted Randall's face upwards, forcing him to stare into those clouded, bloodshot eyes. He gasped in fright and tried to pull away, but Sinarr's grip was too strong.

"Have I been blind? The Cripple has gifts that make him a threat to everything we are working towards. Has he been able to use them against you?" Sinarr tapped Randall's forehead with a thick finger. Cold was spreading from his jaw into his face, the pain making his teeth ache.

"Of course, it may not have been you. Any of your men could have been … vulnerable. I should have foreseen this, but without the witch's coven there is no way to be sure. No way to tell who the Cripple can reach. The Cripple blinded us in Norlhast and now he's in Romsdahl, whispering into the ears of our enemy."

Sinarr abruptly released Randall, who fell to the floor coughing and retching. His whole face felt like it was on fire, his tongue numb and lolling in his mouth like a dead eel. Randall attempted to stand and settled for crouching, limbs shaking and weak. When he tried to speak all he managed was to send a string of drool down his chin. He wiped it away with a trembling hand.

"What's done is done. When the Landless Jarl reaches Romsdahl Gautarr Falrufson will join the fight, I have seen it," Sinarr told Randall. "Ready your men for battle and send word to Joarr the Hammer to do the same. While the Cripple can see into the eyes of men, that doesn't blunt our swords or break our spears. We will crush the Reavesburg Clan here and shatter their spirit, once and for all."

Sinarr's eyes opened wide and he gave Randall a brown-toothed smile. Randall rose and fled from his commander without a word, running all the way.

***

My eyes flicked open and I woke with a start, heart hammering in my chest. It took me a few moments to realise I wasn't Randall and I was safe, for now. I rose and washed and dressed, trying to calm myself. Time and again the Sight awoke when I wasn't in control and it was always a frightening experience. However, I was beginning to think there was a pattern to this. Too often what I saw in such moments was significant and I reasoned that perhaps the stress experienced by those with the Sight opened their mind to me. I stared at my reflection in a glass mirror; clearly Sunian craftsmanship, the frame decorated with woven silver threads. I looked haggard and thin, hardly benefiting from a good night's sleep. I thought for a moment I saw a red handprint on my neck and jaw. When I blinked the image had disappeared.

I reached for my knife and shaved off the unkempt straggly beard that had sprouted on my face during the past week, improving my appearance to a degree. I sat down, rubbing more of Arissa's salve into the palm of my right hand, which was still red and tender to the touch, though it did seem to be healing. Now the scabs and dead skin were peeling off I could see an imprint, left by the hilt of my sword on my palm – another scar. I flexed my sore hand. If it came to fighting I doubted I'd be able to defend myself for long, not unless I mastered my blade with my left hand. With four days left until battle was joined, that was unlikely to happen.

***

I broke my fast with Ulfarr's crew down in the kitchens, noting Ekkill's absence. Tomas was furious when he found us and realised Ekkill had already gone, the air thick with his curses before he left.

"Let's hope their paths don't cross again too soon," Skari muttered through a mouthful of warm oatcakes and honey, washing it down with watered ale.

"Ekkill can look after himself," Ulfarr said. "Least Tomas isn't blaming us – so far. We'll have enough enemies on the battlefield soon enough, without having to worry about a dagger in the back."

"Or an accident during drills in the castle courtyard," added Patrick. I looked at him quizzically.

"Haki sent word to us this morning that we'll be joining his company," Ulfarr explained. "A crew of five might work well when it comes to scouting and hunting, but not for what's coming."

"And that's where you should be, out in the practice courts rather than cluttering up my kitchen," scolded on of the cooks, bustling past with a tray of freshly baked rolls. "Just because there's a war doesn't give you lot an excuse to get in my way. Out, all of you!"

Ulfarr gave a shrug that might have passed for a half-hearted apology. "Come on lads, let's go. Make sure you don't show me up this morning. Haki looked like he'd drawn the short straw when he gave me the news, so let's change his mind on that score."

Bandor looked back at me as they headed out but I waved him on. I had other business in Romsdahl this morning, as I filched two of the freshly baked loaves and slipped away before I was seen.

***

Thengill tore into the fresh bread, devouring it in moments before sitting back on his straw mattress with a satisfied air.

"Thanks. I've had nothing to eat since yesterday." He looked at me shrewdly. "What news? How did your audience with Gautarr go?"

After I finished my explanation Thengill gave me a half-hearted smile. "Good news. There's nothing more to do except wait and see what the outcome is on the field of battle." His face hardened. "I should be there."

"I know. I did try and argue for your release, but he wasn't in the mood to listen. I'm sorry."

"Don't be. I was in Asmarr's honour guard, with Dragmall, Hrodmarr and Sinarr. We were all groomed to become Asmarr's jarls one day, so our names were well-known in the south of Reavesburg. I should have thought how that would play out, even though Johan and Etta were both insistent I come with you."

Thengill's face twisted and he stood up, walking over to the wall of iron bars that separated us. There were other prisoners in the dungeons but Thengill had been put in a cell well apart from them, presumably for his own protection. He lowered his voice as he spoke to me.

"I'm no fool. Gautarr's only stayed my execution. Whatever Johan's position might be after the battle Gautarr's not going to let me live, so there's something I want you to do for me."

"Name it."

"I didn't leave things well with Arissa ..." Thengill paused, seeing the smile playing at the corner of my lips as I recalled the scene, and scowled. "Not my finest moment, I'm sure you'll agree. But I like the girl, Rothgar. I tried to tell her that day when we left and it came out ... badly. You've got a gift with words and you'll be able to put things much better than I could. Just tell her I'm sorry and ... Well, I want her to think well of me. I didn't expect things to end this way. The great stories don't often end with the hero swinging from a hangman's noose."

Awkwardly, I patted Thengill's hand. "You have my promise I'll speak to her once Johan has won and the Brotherhood is brought back together. You just have to be strong, Thengill. This isn't over."

Thengill shook the bars of the cell with his broad, strong hands, muscles bunching. "I should be out there, fighting for the Brotherhood. They need me and my axes. What happened to them?"

"Haki left them with Gautarr," I told him. "Although I don't think he'll fight with them – he favours a two-handed axe."

Thengill growled with frustration. "We need those weapons on the field, not locked up somewhere while our brothers are out there fighting the durath. Aside from Joldir's staff they're the most powerful runeblades we possess."

I frowned, remembering how Gautarr had inspected the

blade and Jora's pointed questions. "I think perhaps Gautarr understands more about the power of those weapons than he was letting on. Gautarr and Jora both recognised the symbol, I'm sure of it."

I left Thengill looking dejected behind the bars of his cell, wishing there was more I could do. I wondered if Etta or Johan had guessed what would happen when they sent Thengill into Gautarr's court. Had they been more concerned about the safety of those axes, knowing Thengill would never willingly surrender his weapons to them? My thoughts were dark as I returned to my chambers, cursing myself for not thinking ahead and taking better care of my friend.

# CHAPTER 32

The following day brought heavy rain and thundery showers, unpleasant enough in Romsdahl Castle and certainly not enjoyable for the Vorund army camped outside the walls. I wondered if it would delay Johan. A swift Sight message from Joldir assured me they continued to make good progress, now they had joined the main road leading to Romsdahl. I'd seen little of Ulfarr, Bandor and the rest of my companions since the previous morning. Haki had moved them from the guest chambers into the barracks with the rest of his men. This made good sense. They needed to be part of his company, which would not be helped if they received unequal treatment, even if Ulfarr grumbled it meant a hard bed for the rest of their stay.

A servant brought me breakfast in my chamber, probably having heard of my thievery in the kitchen from the cook. I ate alone and was beginning to wonder how to use the rest of my day when there was a knock at my door. Opening it I was surprised to see Freydja standing there, her brother Throm behind her.

"I wondered if you would walk with us," Freydja said as she absent-mindedly tucked a stray strand of black hair behind her ear. Throm folded his arms across his chest in a stance reminiscent of his uncle, leaving me with little choice other than to agree.

At first Freydja spoke of inconsequential things as we toured different parts of the castle; polite conversation about life at Romsdahl and how things had changed with the siege. She was a refined, cultured young noblewoman and I could see Jora's influence. They even moved in the same way, slow and graceful, never expending any unnecessary effort. After a time we found ourselves in the courtyard, the hot sun having burned off most traces of the morning storm. Freydja gestured for me to take a seat next to her under a broad oak tree, which cast its shadow across the bench.

"Your arrival ... it has ..." Freydja trailed off, her composure momentarily lost. I looked at her and waited for her to continue.

"There have been rumours and stories, this part year. After the Vorund Clan took Reavesburg, my uncle began mustering his forces in the south. At first, we hoped more help would come from further afield."

"Joarr attacked our walls at the beginning," Throm added. "We held them back and then their tactics changed, when it became clear this would be no easy victory. When Sinarr arrived just before winter and took command he gave the order to try and starve us out, seeking to take the city intact. We waited and the only news that reached us was grim. We heard that Ulfkell's Keep and Kalamar had been taken, the rest of Reavesburg under Adalrikr's rule. When we realised no help was coming we settled in for the winter, hoping it would weaken our enemies and give us a chance to drive them off come the spring. Uncle sent out Audwin Strongshield, seeking to muster more warriors, but by the time summer arrived we knew we didn't have the numbers."

"But there were these stories," Freydja interrupted. "Tales of an uprising in the west, led by a great warrior and his Company of Shadows, striking at our enemies and melting into the night. We heard Tullen was burned to the ground when the people there refused support his cause. There was news that the Vorund Clan had been driven out of Falsten and Delving. Then word reached us of something more, that the uprising had become an army – the Brotherhood of the Eagle." Freydja's eyes were bright.

"We've not been completely isolated. There are ways and means to communicate with the outside world, as you know," Throm told me. "It wasn't long before Uncle learned who led the Brotherhood." He grinned at the memory as Freydja tutted.

"Uncle has never seen eye to eye with Johan – you don't need me to tell you that. Still, most people took heart at the news, seeing the odds turning in their favour after more than a year."

Freydja nodded at Throm and he stepped away, remaining close by, although out of earshot.

"Is there something you can't discuss in front of your brother?" I asked in a low voice.

"It's just easier," Freydja said with a smile. "We don't have any secrets from each other. You know how it is with brothers and sisters, the bond there is between ... Oh, I'm so sorry, I didn't think. Saying such things when you lost your own brother just last year."

"There's no need to apologise. I know what you mean, how it was with Jorik and Nuna when we were growing up. I still think about it, try and hold on to those memories." Freydja's faltering smile returned at my words.

"You shared a lot of time with Bandor as well, didn't you? Growing up."

*So this is the reason I'm here.* "Yes, we were close. Still are."

"On the night of your sister's wedding Uncle pledged my hand to Johan's son and we spent time together, talking late into the night. I'd not seen him for years but that night, I was ... pleased. More than pleased, if I'm truthful."

"More pleased than when we were pledged, then?" I asked, startled at how her words stung. Freydja looked surprised.

"I didn't think you even wanted the match to go ahead. We were children, Rothgar, nothing more. Uncle told me for years he never truly intended to see us wed – I thought you knew that."

"Forgive me, I spoke in jest and it was a poor one. There's

been little time to reflect upon such things lately … I think I've spent too long with Ulfarr's crew." I squirmed at my weak words, grateful Freydja appeared satisfied with my explanation.

"I'd spent a year wondering if he'd been killed, with no answers to my questions. The first I knew that Bandor was still alive was when he walked into these halls, with you. I didn't know what to think at first, his appearance took me by surprise. Since our engagement has never been broken I was staring at my future husband. But Bandor didn't speak to me – and there's been no word from him since Haki took him into his company. I'm confused, Rothgar. Does he no longer consider us betrothed?"

I paused to gather my thoughts, Freydja's face becoming anxious. I realised we'd been careless in handling this, thinking only of Gautarr's views about Johan's weakened household now his lands and wealth had been taken from him. With this being a political marriage, it had never even occurred to me Freydja would have a say in the matter. Avoiding the subject altogether with Gautarr had seemed a sensible course of action, but on reflection we'd been foolish.

"Please don't look so worried," I began. "Haki has honoured Bandor and the rest of our company by including them in the warriors under his command. Their focus is to ready themselves for battle but please don't think for a moment that Bandor has forgotten you or the promise Johan made to your uncle. However, things have changed since that promise was made. In truth, Bandor is anxious about raising the subject."

"Why so?"

"Do you know what the Vorund Clan calls Johan? The Landless Jarl. Bandor is heir to nothing, his family's wealth lost, and we face a foe bent on destroying what little remains of his house."

Freydja drew herself up, her expression proud and her eyes fierce. "And what does that have to do with anything, may I ask?"

"If you're speaking of true love, then nothing at all," I replied calmly. "However, these matters will concern your uncle. He has made no mention of it since our arrival, treating Bandor as another member of Ulfarr's crew. If I am being frank with you, we expected Gautarr to break off the engagement and he would be within his rights to do so."

Freydja regarded me for a long moment, her face softening. "You speak plainly and honestly, so let me be frank with you. My uncle considers Romsdahl to be the centre of Amuran and would like nothing better than to see me married to one of his warriors – perhaps Audwin or Haki. However, the night we met, I saw many good qualities in Bandor, things I can admire and grow to love. I'm seventeen now, old enough to know my own mind. My uncle may have taken me in as his ward but Throm is older now and the true heir to our father's line and his wealth. The name Egill Falrufson still carries weight in the south, so I am far from helpless. However, I will not make my case to my uncle without first knowing Bandor's feelings. So please discreetly pass on the message to Bandor that I would still seek to be bound to him in marriage. I will await his answer." Freydja clasped my hands as she took her leave. "Although we were destined never to be wed, Rothgar, I think you will prove to be a loyal friend to my house. You have my thanks." She walked away, Throm lingering behind for a moment.

"I remember you fighting my uncle," he said. "You were truly skilful – even Ragnar was impressed, though he only said so to me privately. That day and what happened afterwards, they've preyed on my mind ever since."

"What do you mean?"

"Gautarr's ploy to ambush Jorik, it was … shameful. I can think of no other word. I owe my uncle a great deal, yet when Finnvidor Einarrson spoke to us – to me directly, in front of the elders of the clan, revealing how Uncle had sent our own warriors to try and kill your brother – I was ashamed. I knew my father would never have stooped to such tactics."

"Gautarr told me he did it for the good of the clan."

Throm raised his eyebrows. "And you believe him?"

"Does it matter? Jorik was his judge that day, and when he had defeated him in the circle he chose to seek your uncle's loyalty, rather than executing him. Was he wrong to do that?"

Throm took a deep breath. "You're no fool. We both know that when this is all over, if we're victorious, we face a decision about who will lead our clan. Gautarr will not bend the knee to Johan, so how will the commander of the Brotherhood win over the men of Romsdahl? You need support within our house. Freydja genuinely feels something for Bandor, which is why she's prepared to make those ties with Johan's house. When the time comes, you'll have the support of Egill's house, if you want it."

"Bold words," I told him. "You place a lot of trust in me by telling me all of this."

Throm smiled. "You have few friends in this castle. I don't think you'll be telling Gautarr, will you?"

I sighed and nodded reluctantly. "You have me there."

"Good, then let us know when you have Bandor's answer." Throm looked me up and down. "What Blackeyes did to you – breaking the body of a warrior like that. It was cruel. Unforgivable. He'll pay for it."

I stared after Throm as he walked away, arm in arm with Freydja. He was a few years older than me, which made him, what? Twenty? Twenty-one? He had always been in the shadow of his cousin, Ragnar, but now I saw politics were at play in Romsdahl. Out of necessity Throm was taking a risk confiding such things in me, a man he hardly knew. Soon battle would be joined, forcing people to act if they wanted to influence the aftermath and secure their position. I realised I had hugely under-estimated the ambitions of Freydja and her brother.

# CHAPTER 33

Bandor gawked when I finished telling him about my meeting with Freydja. He was dressed for battle in chainmail, sword hanging at his side, a shield slung over his back, face shining with sweat from sparring all morning with Haki's men. I'd called him aside as the drills finished and we were now sitting in my chamber, talking in hushed tones.

"And she wants my answer? Now?"

"Sooner would be better, I think."

Bandor sighed, shaking his head in disbelief. "Do you think Etta knew about this? About Freydja's feelings and Throm's ambitions?"

I shrugged. "I'm guessing Etta knew your arrival would cause a stir."

Bandor looked thoughtful, sitting back and running his hands through his red hair, wiping sweaty strands from his face. "This is important, Rothgar. In a way, I have no choice other than to agree, for the good of the clan and to help my father."

"That's not entirely true," I began before Bandor cut me off with a wave of his hand.

"It doesn't matter. I *like* her," he told me with a boyish grin. "She has spirit."

"And ambitions. You need to be careful and *think* about this."

"I know what you're saying, but you can pass on the answer that I intend to make good on my promise." Bandor's smile made his thin face more youthful and carefree. "This is no time to be cautious. All the pieces are in play and we have to try and win."

\*\*\*

"Where do you think you're going?" Haki asked me, hand resting easily on this hilt of his sword as he barred my path to the table at the barracks where the rest of his men were eating. Bandor frowned and Ulfarr nudged Skari, who was busy stuffing bread and black sausage into his mouth.

"I was planning on joining my friends," I told him.

Haki shook his head. "This is where the *warriors* eat and take their rest," he said, regarding my skinny frame with a sneer. "Clearly you don't belong here and you've no right to take *my* men away on your little errands without my permission. Understand?"

"Listen here –" Bandor started to say.

"Don't make things worse than they are, lad. It doesn't matter you're Johan's son. Here you belong to me. Who's your commander?"

"You are, Haki," Bandor said reluctantly.

"It's 'sir' here, son. Now, take a place on watch at the main gates with the rest of your crew and relieve the men there. If you can stay out of trouble you might earn back some rations this evening. Go."

"Great," muttered Skari, hastily eating the last of his sausage and pocketing the bread as he rose, glowering. I watched as Ulfarr's men filed out of the building with Bandor, many of Haki's warriors sniggering and pointing.

"Right, that's it. Stop gossiping like a bunch of women and get back to your food," barked Haki, before turning to speak to me in a quieter tone as the noise in the room died down. "You lot might have your special *bond* but they're my men now and they need to concentrate on the task in front of them. No one here gets special visitors or privileges and I don't want to find you snooping around. What are you doing here, anyway?"

"They're my friends," I replied, keeping my voice calm. "I didn't realise I wasn't welcome."

"Are you really that stupid?" hissed Haki. "I was there

when you and your brother humiliated my chief. I haven't forgotten that and neither have the men here. So yes, you're right – you're not welcome."

*** 

I sat alone in my chambers, opening my eyes after giving my report to Joldir. All seemed well in Johan's camp, with Ekkill already having returned to them earlier that night. The mood there was more confident now Gautarr was committing his men to the battle and it appeared Johan's gamble might just pay off.

I drew my sword, the grip uncomfortable where it nestled against the fresh scar on my palm, the flesh still tender. I carried out a few practice swings, wincing as I did so, and thought on Throm's words. My father never lived to see me become a warrior after I won respect and a name for myself in the battle of Noln. Tyrfingr Blackeyes took that away from me, breaking my body and making me less than a man in the eyes of people like Haki. I'd accomplished my mission and knew how important it was to our cause, yet now I felt unwanted, with no clear role to play in what was about to happen. I realised I'd grown used to being at the centre of events, working with Etta, counselling Johan, learning about magic from Joldir. There had been no opportunity to rest and take a breath until now, and I found I didn't know what to do with my free time – a strange feeling.

Someone had left food in my room; dried fruit, meats and fish and fresh bread, a small pat of butter and some red wine. I sat down and began to eat, not really tasting the food. I needed to find a way to get Bandor's message back to Freydja or Throm but I had no idea where their quarters were. As I sat there I became aware of something – an insistent tug at the back of my mind. Leif was calling me. It had been a while since I'd seen the world through Leif's eyes, as we were now more used to working together in our Fellowship. However, as I joined with him I realised there was something he wanted me to see. Leif was crouched down outside the canvas cover of a wagon. It took me a moment to recognise the voices inside as he strained to catch the words.

"... I don't agree with you on this, Etta."

"Since when, Joldir, has your opinion been the only thing in the world that matters? I say he doesn't need to know and he doesn't. That's final."

"So you say." Joldir sounded bitter.

"Listen to me. Things are going well according to Rothgar's latest report – better than we could have hoped. Even so, Romsdahl is a dangerous place. Rothgar needs his wits about him and he can't afford to be distracted."

"It's not as simple as that. When we're joined by the Sight he can sense things and he has tremendous natural ability. Rothgar can reach deep into people – you know this to be true. Please, don't put me in this position."

"Just bury your secrets deeper and use the skills *you* possess to hide them. You've evaded Nereth this long. I'm not saying we don't tell him, only wait a few days until things are more settled."

Joldir murmured something Leif was unable to catch. Quiet as a mouse, he crept around the wagon, listening to Joldir's footfalls inside to gauge where he was now standing.

"... not just one of your secrets, Etta, this is about the boy's family."

"He's no longer a boy, stop treating him as such."

Joldir paused for a moment before speaking. "I could fall in battle in a few days' time. Promise that if anything happens to me you'll tell him about Nuna."

"What is there to tell? We don't know anything for certain."

"Don't play word games with me," Joldir said, his voice rising, making Leif jump. "Alright, then, promise me you'll tell him of our suspicions."

"You have my word," Etta replied grudgingly.

The canvas at the back of the wagon was thrown back and Leif dived behind one of the wheels as Joldir stamped down the steps and strode off into the column of men milling on the road. Johan had obviously called a halt on their journey.

*What was that about?* I asked Leif.

The boy gave the mental equivalent of a shrug. *I don't know but I agreed with Joldir and thought you needed to hear what they were talking about.*

*But what did it mean?* I asked, perplexed.

*I'm not sure – Joldir thinks Nuna is in some kind of trouble, which is why you can't reach her with the Sight.*

***

I threw open the door, desperate for fresh air and a chance to gather my thoughts. I didn't see Tomas until the last moment, almost bowling straight into the young man. He staggered backwards and put a hand firmly on my chest as he righted himself.

"Where do you think you're going?"

"What?"

"You heard me, where are you going?"

I took a step back, eying the man carefully. "What business is it of yours?"

"Haki says you're not to go anywhere without me from now on. Think of me as your personal guard during your stay in Romsdahl."

*Gaoler more like.* "I see. Well, I'm not going anywhere."

Tomas frowned. "You seemed in a hurry to go somewhere just a moment ago."

I stepped back, reaching for the door handle. "I think you'll find you're mistaken," I told him, slamming the door in his face.

Inside, I breathed in deeply, trying to find the calm still centre necessary for me to walk the Path. I lay down on the bed and closed my eyes, reaching out, trying to find my sister. There was something there, faint but tangible, a single thread weaving through the clamour of voices I could sense on the edge of my perception. I carefully seized hold of the thread, trying not to break the connection.

I opened my eyes and blinked, taking a moment to register where I was. It was the courtyard of Ulfkell's Keep, a thick blanket of snow covering everything as more flakes drifted down from a heavy opalescent sky. The scent of wood smoke from the chimneys was familiar, as was the faint sound of gaming and songs from the barracks. I started as I saw Olfridor Halfhand walk past, instantly recognisable despite being huddled up in his cloak against the cold. My old weapons master raised his three-fingered hand to me in greeting and I nodded in return, breath catching in my throat for a moment. I was *home*.

I felt dizzy and glanced down, taking a moment to realise my body was different. Here I was whole, my arms and legs strong, back unbowed, muscles firm. Tears stung my eyes and some fell, freezing into small clear jewels of ice at my feet.

"Rothgar, you came," breathed a voice I knew instantly – Nuna.

She walked towards me, smiling, leaving a trail of footprints behind her in the snow. Blonde hair tied into two long plaits hung from her back, the cloak of her hood down despite the cold. I took a step towards her and then hesitated, unsure how this could be happening.

"Is this ... Are *you* doing all of this?" I asked.

Nuna smiled wider and laughed. "Of course."

My jaw dropped. I'd been mastering the Sight for more than a year and I still had no idea how to conjure up these alternate realities.

"But how ..." I trailed off as my sister reached me and drew me into an embrace.

"It's good to see you. I've missed you."

# CHAPTER 34

The fire in the Great Hall roared, meat slowly turning on a spit, fat crackling and a delicious smell wafting towards me. No sooner had my stomach started to rumble than a servant stepped forward and cut me three thick slices of meat, serving it on a trencher with bread and steaming gravy. The deer tasted every bit as good as it smelled and I savoured every mouthful as Nuna watched.

"How?" I gestured at this memory of our family home. "How have you done all this?"

Nuna grinned and took hold of my hand. "It's been incredible. Ottama opened my eyes."

I learned forward in my chair. "Nuna, this is … amazing, but even I'm not capable of magic such as this."

My sister smiled wider. "Ottama has taught me so much in such a short space of time. Did you know that there are many more like us in Amuran, including a small group in Norlhast? Ottama sensed I had the gift and because I'd shown her such kindness she trusted me, drawing me into her circle."

"You understand this is dangerous, don't you?" I explained my encounters with Nereth and how close she had come to capturing me. I suspected Ottama must be here, somewhere, listening to us talk. I chose my words carefully, not wanting to reveal the bond I shared with Joldir and Leif to a stranger.

"Of course, that's why Ottama told me it's safer working together with her as part of a Fellowship. Don't you understand what this means? We can talk to each other now. When I heard the story about how you disappeared from the city gates, I feared the worst. What made it harder was never knowing for certain what had happened to you. I don't really understand why, but when Valdimarr told me about the rebellion in Reavesburg I wondered if you were involved. I could sense you, I think that's the reason. All this time, you've been so close, if I could only have understood how to reach out to you."

I sighed, setting down my empty trencher, feeling satisfied even although I knew none of it was real. "What you see," I told her ruefully, gesturing at myself in my warrior's garb. "You've conjured how I used to appear. I'm not the man you remember."

"Still my brother, though. And you fashioned your own appearance when you came here. That had nothing to do with me." Nuna shook her head. "Part of me still thinks I'm dreaming about all of this, it just seems so incredible. Impossible."

"I've been told the gift runs in families, so perhaps this isn't so strange. We've so much to talk about."

Nuna was about to say something else when her eyes suddenly widened. "You need to go."

"What?"

"Someone's about to find you – I can sense them. You need to go, now."

***

My eyes opened as Tomas entered my room. He looked at me sitting upright on my bed, a frown creasing his forehead.

"So quiet in here, I began to think you must have jumped out the window."

"These are still my chambers. I would have expected you to knock before entering."

Tomas' frown deepened. "I did, three times, and there was no answer. What were you doing in here? Did I wake you?"

I shook my head and rose. "My thoughts were elsewhere, that's all. Why have you burst into my private quarters?"

Tomas looked unconvinced. "My apologies, but you've been asked to eat with Gautarr at his table today. Throm's waiting outside."

***

The small gathering in the feasting hall clapped politely as Karlin, Gautarr's resident bard, finished performing and bowed low to his audience. I had always enjoyed Darri's playing when I was growing up but Karlin was a different kind of entertainer. Darri's songs and music were legendary, whilst Karlin was a gifted storyteller, bringing to life a tale of the old times when men and dragons walked Amuran together alongside the avatars. This wasn't the first time I'd heard the story of the hunter Ennias and how, with Vellandir's counsel, he outwitted the mighty dragon Serathor. However, Karlin brought that vanished world to life with great skill, so I could picture in my mind the lost city of Ithis, where men and dragons once lived side by side, and the mountain caves that became Serathor's Tomb.

"Thank you, Karlin, that was wonderful," said Asta, Ragnar's wife. Their small children, Hroarr and Halla, shouted eagerly for more as their normally serious-minded father looked on indulgently.

Karlin beamed at her praise and he stood straight, sweeping his long brown hair back with a flick of his hand. "Would you like another tale, my lady? The legend of Kumil, perhaps?"

Ragnar shook his head. "Not in front of my children. That's a dark tale, to be told only when the fires have burned low and our young folk are safely abed."

His words were met with howls of protest from his children and I smiled as Asta tried to placate them, reminded of my late nephew. My eyes met those of Gautarr, who was watching me from the head of the table. Behind him I spied Thengill's crossed axes, newly mounted on the wall.

"Enough stories for now," boomed Gautarr. "Let's eat."

He snapped his fingers and servants emerged, carrying platters of food and drink to the table. Karlin was honoured with a seat beside Jora, who whispered something in his ear, the older woman's laughter carrying across the talk in the room. Tomas was sitting to my left, picking sparingly at the thick crust of a pigeon pie with his fingers, the rest of his food untouched. Freydja deliberately took her place on my right when she arrived and leaned across to speak to me in an undertone.

"Do I have an answer? I heard Haki had words with you after you spoke to Bandor."

"The answer is yes," I whispered, pleased to see Freydja smile.

Next to her Throm raised his cup in my direction, drinking deeply. I nodded back, though I felt a knot in my stomach as an image swam into my mind of Bandor pledging himself to Freydja, my part relegated to being nothing more than a wedding guest. Once they were wed a great deal would rest on the shoulders of Bandor and his new wife – they would be the future of our clan. I glanced at Ragnar and Asta, wondering whether they would agree with that sentiment.

"So, how go the preparations for war?" Gautarr asked his son.

"The men are ready to end this, once and for all. A year spent behind our walls makes them eager for battle against our old foe."

Gautarr looked in my direction. "I've no doubts about that. Has Audwin sent word?"

Ragnar nodded. "A raven arrived earlier this morning. They're ready to march as soon as we light our watchtower beacon. Two thousand men stand with him."

Gautarr seemed satisfied with Ragnar's answer, and glanced past me to where Tomas was sitting. "You're one of Haki's men, aren't you? Tomas, isn't it?"

"Aye," Tomas replied, meeting Gautarr's gaze briefly.

The big man chuckled, nudging Ragnar next to him. "Is he the one Haki was bawling out the other week? The one who missed every spear throw in the training circle and who let Domarr knock him on his arse three times with his practice sword?"

Ragnar made a show of trying to place the young man. "Ah, yes, I remember now. Not our most promising warrior, though Haki has obviously found some use for him."

Gautarr shook his head. "No good taking a beating from Domarr every time, is it? Young man like you should be faster; you need to apply yourself and show some steel, or you'll never get away from all the unpleasant jobs Haki dreams up for you. So, tell me, is our guest behaving himself? You kept him from getting under Haki's feet?" Tomas nodded, his beard failing to hide the scarlet blush creeping up his neck and across his cheeks.

Gautarr grunted and pointed at me with a thick finger. "Heard about your visit this morning from Haki. You might be my guest but I don't want you getting in the way of our warriors when they're preparing for battle. My niece and nephew can't spend every hour of the day entertaining you, either."

Karlin flashed me a smile, showing perfect white teeth as he swept his hair back away from his face. "I think our guest is a little bored now we've taken his friends away from him."

Ragnar laughed. "Yes, tell me, Rothgar, what part will you be playing in the coming battle?"

I took a long drink of ale from my mug, letting the buzz of conversation die down as I waited before setting it down on the table. "I'm here to make sure there's no question concerning your warriors' loyalty."

Throm snorted into his drink but otherwise there was a stunned silence in the feasting hall.

"Really?" sneered Ragnar. "What does the crippled son of Kolfinnar know of a warrior's heart? You're Johan's and Etta's lackey these days, from what I've heard, nothing more."

"I see," I replied mildly, though I felt the sting of Ragnar's words.

"And if we prove ... disloyal?" Gautarr asked in a quiet, dangerous voice.

"What fate do you think Hrodi Myndillson and his followers deserve?"

My question was met with deathly quiet, Jora's face white with barely suppressed rage. "How dare you! Our own guest ..." she spluttered to a halt.

Gautarr sat back in his chair, arms folded, glowering. "How can you sit there, eating my food, living under my protection and suggest my loyalty is in question? I'm sheltering you and your friends from the Vorund Clan."

"What gives you the right to judge such matters?" Ragnar muttered. "You'll be hiding safe behind these walls when we ride out to face Sinarr and Joarr."

Throm spoke up. "Rothgar was once considered worthy to be betrothed to my sister, so if you speak to him disrespectfully then you dishonour Freydja in turn."

"That match, as you know Cousin, was made in very different circumstances," Ragnar answered. "I meant no disrespect to you or your sister. What I'm finding difficult to stomach is sitting here with Johan's spy, listening as he tells us he's here to watch us and ensure we play our part."

I nodded. "Since we're all on the same side, I'm sure I'll have very little to do over the next few days. Much like in the coming battle, where there'll be little use for a cripple, as you've said. What I'm talking about it what happens afterwards, when the battle is won. In generations to come, what will the bards sing of? I hope those songs will tell the story of how the Reavesburg Clan united to reclaim their lands. If we turn upon ourselves, as Old Hrodi has done, then all is lost."

I could see everyone round the table pondering my words. I'd taken a gamble, but I wanted Gautarr and the rest of his house to really think about what would happen if we couldn't unite under one banner. Whilst it wasn't subtle diplomacy, when had Gautarr ever been subtle in his dealings with the clan?

Karlin raised his mug to me and leaned close to Jora. "I think we should be careful not to underestimate this one. I like him." His soft words broke the tension in the feasting hall, a murmur of relief rippling around the room, although I wasn't so foolish as to believe this matter was finished.

"So, you're the *worst* swordsman in Haki's company?" I whispered to Tomas as talk around the table began once more. "That's why you've been given the job of shadowing me?" I was being petty, but his constant presence was already starting to grate.

Tomas scowled. "Why else do you think I was on duty in the cellars the day you arrived? Ain't guarding them from the Vorund Clan, am I? There's no way they could find their way through the maze of tunnels under Romsdahl. It's to stop folk in the castle from thieving and making sure there's someone to open the gate when fresh supplies arrive."

Tomas folded his arms, staring at the remains of his pie. "Anyway, I can handle myself. It's Haki … he gets right under my skin … Things'll be better when Audwin's back in command." Tomas shot me a dark look. "Never had any problems when Audwin Strongshield was in charge."

"In that case we'll both be looking forward to his return," I replied, taking a bite from my pigeon pie.

# CHAPTER 35

"Who's your friend?" Thengill asked, sitting in the corner of his cell, his face hidden in shadows.

"Tomas, one of Haki's warriors. He's been assigned to … protect me whilst I'm staying at Romsdahl."

"I see." Thengill shifted and rose from the thin straw mattress and walked over to the bars. I offered him the food I'd saved from Gautarr's table.

"Are they feeding you? Treating you well?" I asked.

Thengill nodded. "Well enough, although pigeon pie is a welcome change. And you?"

"Gautarr treats me as an honoured guest," I answered loudly, before continuing in an undertone. "Although I've acquired a shadow."

Thengill raised an eyebrow, breaking off a piece of pie and taking a bite. A smile spread over his face as he chewed. "Funny how life's simple pleasures take on a whole new meaning when you're stuck inside a cell day and night. How go preparations for the battle?"

"Gautarr's calling his forces to him, with Audwin Strongshield on the march."

"Is it going to be enough?"

"The numbers are close."

Thengill sighed, taking another mouthful of pie with less enthusiasm this time. "It's hard to keep track of the days down here. I sleep more or less all the time, never sure whether it's day or night. Make sure you come and see me again, so I know what's happening."

I nodded. "Of course. In truth, there's been little for me to do since I arrived."

"Does that mean I'm the highlight of your day?" Thengill replied with a grin.

***

"Wouldn't have thought the pair of you would be friends," said Tomas as we climbed the stairs leading from the dungeons.

"Why not?"

"Well, he's a member of the Vorund Clan," Tomas explained. "Your own chief is sworn to fight them, so why does he keep one of his enemies by his side?"

"Thengill's proved his loyalty time and again. He's saved my life and I trust him without question. He might have fought for Vorund once, but he chose a different path years ago."

"And you think that washes away everything he did before then? He's shed Romsdahl blood, you know that, don't you? People here won't accept him and they'll demand Gautarr holds him to account for his past deeds."

"As would Sinarr, if Thengill fell into his hands."

"Making him clanless," muttered Tomas. "It's not a place I'd like to be."

"Be careful what you say. Thengill's part of Johan's Brotherhood, which in his eyes makes him a member of the Reavesburg Clan, whether Gautarr likes it or not."

***

In the privacy of my chambers I was able to reach out to Joldir, since Johan had called a halt for the evening. Our meeting place was beside the hearth in his former home in Lindos, winter winds sending hail battering against the shutters.

"Hardly seasonal," I told him.

"Indulge me. Life might be harder in wintertime but for those with the Sight a sense of isolation can be quite liberating. Something Arissa said brought the memory to mind and it wouldn't leave me alone, so I worked with it this evening."

I gave my report, listening to Joldir's news in turn as he explained that Johan would soon be dividing his forces. "Varinn and Eykr will lead a small force to protect those too

246

young or old to fight. Eykr's leg's still healing, so he wouldn't be much use in the coming battle. They'll be setting up tents to receive the injured – Varinn's skilful enough and he'll have Arissa to help him."

"Leaves them exposed, if Djuri decides to attack them rather than Johan."

"Petr will be leading a rearguard to try and protect both sides. The truth is we don't have the numbers we need. We'll be depending on Romsdahl's warriors to draw enough men away to give us the chance to strike at Sinarr."

Joldir's words finally registered. "You're leaving Varinn in charge of the healers? Where will you be?"

"At the battlefront," Joldir replied. "My runestaff is the only weapon powerful enough to destroy one of the Sundered. I'll have to leave the healing to others this time; we need to kill Sinarr and we may only get one chance."

Doubt nagged at me. "Joldir, some of the things I've seen. Sinarr is different from what we've fought before, and there's a darkness around him that leaves me truly afraid. Even his own warriors fear him."

"The Brotherhood will be with me. I don't pretend to fully understand what magic runs through Sinarr's veins. However, I do know it's magic born from the evil of the durath. A runeblade's power will work against anything from the shadow spirit world."

Although Joldir spoke confidently I saw the flicker of uncertainty in his eyes. Our plans were on a knife edge, built upon a series of chances, ifs and buts. I'd seen Joldir's skill in battle but I would have felt better knowing Thengill was at his side. Joldir must have seen some of this in my face, because he reached over and took my hand in his.

"There won't be much time to meet like this again. I've agreed to help forge more powerful runeblades for the Brotherhood ahead of the coming battle. We need every advantage when we face Sinarr."

"Anything else you want to tell me?" I asked.

Joldir frowned, perhaps wondering if there was something more than idle curiosity behind my question. "No, I don't think so. Just take care of yourself. The old rifts with Gautarr's house are still there, under the surface. If things don't go as we hope then make sure you have a means of escape. I know Throm has offered you friendship but be careful – you don't know how the game he's playing with his uncle will turn out. You may not be able to rely on him when the time comes."

I drew Joldir into an embrace. "Take care too. I'll see you soon."

***

Sleep would not come easily that night, as I felt guilty not mentioning Nuna's appearance to Joldir. I'd decided beforehand to see if he would share his concerns in the privacy of the Sight. However, it was clear Etta had won that particular argument and, since Joldir chose not to trust me with his fears for my sister, I held back on what I had discovered. While I enjoyed the small sense of power this gave me, Etta's training was so deeply ingrained I was starting to regret my petty triumph. Whatever else it might have been, my relationship with Joldir had always been honest. As dark thoughts and fears for the future clouded my mind, I gave in to temptation and cast my mind adrift.

***

Humli sat in his rocking chair, puffing at his pipe, the smell of tobacco wafting around him in the light breeze coming off the River Jelt. Desta sat next to him, a shawl wrapped around her shoulders. She swatted at an insect buzzing nearby and made an exasperated sound as it evaded her hand. Humli chuckled to himself – the annoying creatures never bothered him. Perhaps it was the smoke.

"Go inside if they're being a nuisance," he told her. "I'll be along in a moment."

Desta nodded but didn't move, drawing the shawl tighter and hugging herself, even though it was a warm evening. Humli watched his daughter stare into the dark fast-flow-

248

ing waters of the river.

"What is it, love?"

Desta looked at him. "What do you mean?"

"You've hardly said two words since you joined me out here. Is Finn alright? He's not sickening for something, is he?"

"No. No, nothing like that. I'm just worried about Haarl. He's been gone for so long and there's been no word."

"Probably a good thing," said Humli, trying to put on a brave face. "There'll be riders and ravens bringing news soon enough after battle's been joined. Means he's safe for now."

Desta looked unconvinced. "For now. I *know* Haarl's a warrior. That's the kind of man every young woman wants to marry, isn't it? And I knew the dangers, of course I did. At least, I thought I knew. But this is different."

Humli took another thoughtful puff and slowly blew out the smoke. "I'm sorry, child. I wish this trouble hadn't fallen on your shoulders. Hold on to the thought that it will be over soon."

Desta frowned. "That's just it. Haarl's gone to fight Johan's uprising – we're fighting our own clan. Gautarr Falrufson might not be a man I love, but I know he's on our side – one of us. If Haarl returns victorious what is there to celebrate? If Johan's army wins what happens next? If he drives the Vorund Clan from our homes, what then? What happens to those who sided with Tyrfingr Blackeyes? What happens to their wives and children?"

Humli reached across and put his arm around his daughter. "These are dark times, Desta. I can't promise our future will be easy but I'll be here for you, I promise."

He held her like that for a time, listening to her breathing, feeling her begin to relax. Humli was about to suggest they went inside when he heard the sound of horses on the road, causing him to start. It was late for travellers and they were far from the nearest inn. Humli rose from his seat and saw two men wearing travelling cloaks approaching them, riding side by side.

"Humli Freedman?" said one of the men. He was tall with a close-cropped beard and looked little more than twenty.

"Aye, who might want to know?"

"Forgive my manners. I'm Eidr and this is my friend, Kolsveinn." He gestured to a slightly smaller young man next to him, who acknowledged him with a nod.

"Greetings to you both," Humli replied. "What brings you to my home at such a late hour?" At this time most travellers still on the road would be making their way towards Reavesburg. However, these men had come from the opposite direction.

"We've been on the road for some days," Eidr explained. "We had business in Reavesburg and before then we were travelling through the western lands." His voice was smooth, well-mannered and confident. The accent marked him as being from Reavesburg rather than the Vorund Clan. Humli could see the tip of a scabbard poking out beneath his cloak.

Lina opened the door and stepped outside. "I heard voices. Has Haarl ..." her voice trailed off as she saw the men.

"Forgive us for disturbing you," said Kolsveinn. Even in the darkness Humli was struck by his sharp, piercing eyes, making it difficult to hold his stare for long.

Finn stirred and started to cry and the noise disturbed Lina's little boy, who also began to murmur. It was a sound Humli knew well – the boy needed comforting or he would soon be joining in with Finn's cries. Desta took an uncertain step towards the door but Lina didn't move, her hand still on the handle and her eyes fixed on the visitors.

"Ah, we've woken your children. I'm so sorry," Eidr said.

"Desta, if you could check on your boys I'll be along to help you shortly," Lina said, holding the door wide. Desta hesitated for a moment, then hurried inside and Humli heard her gather up Finn in her arms, whilst making shushing noises to calm Lina's child.

"You knew my name, sir, so I assume you being here's no accident?" Humli asked, hoping his face didn't betray his surprise at Lina's lie.

Kolsveinn smiled, though it didn't reach his eyes. "Indeed, your name was mentioned at the markets in Reavesburg. We understood your daughter was living with you and there was also mention of your other companion."

Humli was shaken. He'd done everything he could to keep Lina's presence a secret, but fishermen travelled up and down this river all the time. All it would have taken was for one of them to see Lina as they passed to set tongues wagging at the fish market. When he spoke he made every effort to keep his voice steady. "I like to keep my life private. Not sure I appreciate folk asking about my affairs in the markets and then arriving at my home, unannounced and late at night. What's your business here?"

Eidr spread his hands wide and gave an apologetic smile. "Forgive us, we didn't mean to alarm you. We have merely been searching for news of a friend of ours." He glanced at Lina. "Perhaps we've found her."

"And do I know you, sirs?" asked Lina. She closed the door firmly behind her and took a step towards Eidr and Kolsveinn, her face defiant.

"We might be distant kinsfolk. We're seeking news concerning our cousin, who we heard settled in Tullen recently, before it was destroyed."

Lina stared at Eidr, her arms folded across her chest. "I'm sorry to hear that. You must be worried about them. What was the name of this cousin of yours?"

Kolsveinn exchanged a look with Eidr, a smile playing on his lips. "Now I look at you I do wonder if we have met before. Your face seems very familiar. Perhaps, if you cast your mind back ..."

"Your cousin's name?"

"Lina," Eidr replied. "Her name was Lina."

"I've never heard of her," Lina answered. "I fear you've made a mistake and wasted your journey. I'm sorry."

Humli cleared his throat. "I wish I could offer you shelter, but as you can see there's little enough room in my cottage as it is. You won't find an inn for some miles, not since ... Well, after all the trouble this past year. You might be better to return to Reavesburg, if you want to sleep with a roof over your head."

"It's a warm night," Kolsveinn answered. "A night looking up at the stars will suit us just as well, though I thank you for the thought."

Humli could feel his heart pounding as the men politely said their goodbyes and left. He drew Lina close as they watched the pair head down the road, the sound of their horses fading as they were swallowed by the darkness. There was something about those men he didn't like.

"Do you want to tell me what that was all about?" he asked Lina.

She shook her head and broke away from Humli, hurrying inside. He followed, locking the door with shaking fingers.

"Lina. I need to know, who were those men? Are you in some sort of trouble? Why did you lie about the boy?"

Desta looked at them, her face worried as she nursed Finn back to sleep. Lina turned her back on Humli and picked up her son, holding him close, refusing to answer any of his questions.

# CHAPTER 36

Domarr the Oak grunted as Bandor turned his blunted practice sword, sidestepping his attack easily and countering with one of his own. His strikes were fast and precise, forcing Domarr onto the retreat as he backed away. There were murmurs of surprise and admiration from the warriors gathered in the courtyard surrounding the training circle. I'd managed to squirm my way to the front, standing next to Ulfarr, who was smiling as Bandor turned another half-hearted attack from Domarr.

"Lad's good, there's no denying it," Ulfarr said to Skari.

"He just needs to finish it," his second replied with a scowl. "Domarr's not as fast, but he's strong. Let him get too close and he'll finish you with one blow."

Throm had mentioned during Gautarr's feast that his cousin chose his warrior name, the Oak, to avoid reference to his father. Olfridor had acknowledged him as his natural son but Domarr rejected his father in favour of Gautarr. Domarr's chosen moniker was intended to reflect how he was strong and unyielding. Throm's assessment was less kind, remarking that the name suited him because Domarr was as thick as two short planks. I chuckled at the memory whilst applauding with Ulfarr, Skari and a good number of Haki's men as Bandor disarmed Domarr with a flurry of blows, sending his sword clattering across the cobbles. Domarr glowered, clutching his wrist as Bandor rested his sword against his neck.

"You lose," he told him, with a smirk.

Domarr shook his head and strode away to pick up his sword. "This time. Let's see who's grinning when the battle's over."

"Well fought," Haki acknowledged, patting Bandor on the back and waving at Myr to step into the ring. "Looks like Ulfarr's got at least one good sword in his crew. Now, let's see what you can do. Svafa, you're up next."

Myr rolled his neck and stretched his back before choosing his favoured practice sword. He acknowledged his opponent with a nod and launched himself into the attack, silent as always. Young Svafa charged forward with a roar and the men in the circle began shouting for their favourite.

"Is it true the fellow's a mute?" Karlin asked, making me start, as I hadn't heard him approach with the din.

"His tongue was cut out," I explained. "I don't know the full story. I'm not sure anyone in Ulfarr's crew does, if I'm honest."

"The poor fellow. It seems to have left him with some pent-up aggression," Karlin observed as Myr head-butted Svafa, sending him reeling backwards, blood spraying from his broken nose.

Myr took full advantage, kicking Svafa's legs from under him as the crowd cried out at the unfair move. Svafa crashed to the floor, writhing in pain, glaring as he noticed Myr's sword pointed at his chest.

"Good move. I taught him that," roared Skari, punching the air.

Ulfarr shook his head. "You can't *teach* someone to head-butt."

"There's more to it than you'd think," Skari answered, as several of Romsdahl's warriors started to boo and shout abuse. Myr was striding round the circle, waving his arms at the crowd, savouring the victory even if it wasn't a popular one.

"Stop that racket!" bellowed Haki, reaching down and helping a stunned Svafa to his feet. "He's taught you a useful lesson. Out there, there's no right way to win a fight – only thing that matters is who's still on his feet at the end of it, something you younger lads would do well to think on. Still, this is meant to be *weapons* training, not a brawling contest, so let's keep the next one clean ..."

I didn't know the next two men who began to spar, so I pushed my way out of the circle, trying to find Bandor so I could congratulate him. Throm called out to me and came running over.

"You've brought some good warriors with you. Everyone's talking about it. You don't often see Domarr bested so easily."

"They'd probably say they brought me along, rather than the other way around."

"I'm serious. A few more warriors like those and Sinarr's not got a chance."

"Thengill's a match for all of them," I told him. "You should speak to your uncle. You need him at your side, not in chains."

Throm shook his head. "I know you're being loyal to your crew, and I admire that, but putting Thengill into that fight is condemning him to death. Half of Haki's men would stick a knife in his back just for being there. How do you think the Vorund Clan's going to react when they see he's turned traitor? Honestly, I don't know what Johan was thinking when he decided to send him here."

I gripped Throm's arm. "Listen, you need every man. It goes far beyond house loyalties and clan rivalries. This is something bigger ..."

I lost the thread of the conversation as a horn sounded, every head turning towards the towers that stood either side of the main gate to the keep. The horn sounded again and I realised it was coming from the city walls, some way distant. I turned to Throm.

"Is that an attack?"

"No, three long blasts signal an attack. Two indicates someone is approaching."

Men were already hurrying towards the gates of the keep. Walking alongside Throm I joined them, heading out into the streets of Romsdahl and towards the main gates of the town. Soon the press swept me along, jostling and pushing me from side to side, an anxious murmur rippling through the throng as people tried to guess what was happening.

"This way," Throm told me, steering me towards a stairway leading up to the top of the outer defensive wall. Bandor fell into step behind me and we hurried upwards, keen to secure a good vantage point.

The climb left me panting with the exertion and I had to rest a hand on the battlements to steady myself. I glanced down towards the ground far below, where a cluster of warriors bearing a white parley flag were gathered just outside the range of a longbow. Another banner displayed the bear of the Vorund Clan. As I watched a single figure broke away and began to walk towards the wall. As he drew closer I saw he was wearing fine armour, polished plate over dark chainmail, a huge two-handed sword slung across his back. Several of the onlookers began hurling abuse at the Vorund messenger, whilst others raised their voices as they told them to be quiet. A few stones were thrown, falling far short of their intended target, drawing a furious response from Haki.

"Next man who throws something loses his hand. He's under a flag of parley and we'll hear him out. Now quieten down, all of you."

The crowd on the walls fell silent after a few grumbles and complaints. The messenger continued his approach, so close now I could faintly hear the scrape of his boots on the road. The man's head was uncovered, his helm under his arm. His long hair was dark but thinning, his scalp covered in bald patches. The wind blew it to one side, giving me a chance to see his face properly for the first time. His skin was pale, a web of purple welts and dark veins standing out starkly.

"Who *is* that?" muttered Bandor, peering out over the wall as far as he dared.

"It's Sinarr the Cold One," I told him.

"Gods," Throm breathed. "What's *happened* to him?"

Sinarr stopped still some way from the gates and drove

his white flag into the ground in front of him. He raised his head, scanning the battlements left and right, before speaking in a carrying tone, his voice harsh and cracked.

"Where's Gautarr?"

\*\*\*

Gautarr took his time responding to Sinarr's summons. When he finally arrived Ragnar was at his side, Jora just a step behind with Karlin, who had carried Sinarr's message back to the keep. Gautarr wore full battle armour, carrying his great axe as he climbed up the steps to the tower above the gates. He rested his weapon against the walls and leaned out over the stonework, hands placed on the battlements either side of him.

"So, Sinarr, this is a surprise. Last time you made this journey you didn't get the answer you wanted and these gates stayed closed. That was a year ago, and it doesn't look like time has been kind to you." Gautarr patted his broad belly, chainmail links clinking. "On short rations camped out there, are you? We're still eating well, even if you don't look so good. Has Adalrikr forgotten about you after all this time? We've seen you digging graves out to the west for your men and heard rumours of disease in your encampment. Looking at your face I could well believe it."

There was tension in the air, Gautarr's joke falling flat, the laughter of his people dying swiftly. Sinarr stared at Gautarr, saying nothing, before his gaze turned to my direction. His eyes looked straight into mine and I took a step back, knowing, without really being able to say why, that Sinarr recognised me.

"Gone deaf down there?" Gautarr called, when Sinarr still didn't answer. "Haven't you anything to say for yourself?"

Sinarr waited, allowing the half-hearted laugher to fade before he spoke. When he did so, he didn't address Gautarr. Instead he turned back towards the group of warriors standing a few hundred yards away.

"Bring him to me," he called, voice rasping and hoarse.

The crowd on the walls watched in silence as six men

broke away from the group, leading someone tied to their leader by a rope. His head was hooded and he stumbled as he walked, the rope jerking tight as it took his full weight for a moment until he found his feet. Sinarr bent over and placed his helm on the ground by his feet before drawing his sword from behind his back. Although clearly a two-handed weapon, he held the blade easily in one hand as he watched the men approach with their prisoner. My heart was pounding and I could tell Bandor was thinking the same thing as me. Had something happened to Johan's army on the road? Was Johan now Sinarr's prisoner?

Sinarr's warriors stopped when they reached him and one of them, who I recognised as Joarr, shoved the prisoner forwards onto his knees. I also saw Randall, the older man carrying a large sack over his shoulder, which he set onto the ground with a clank.

"Joarr the Hammer brought me a prize," Sinarr said with a smile. "Show them."

Randall untied and upended the sack, pouring out dozens of broken swords and axes with a rattling crash. Joarr pulled the hood back from their prisoner, revealing the bloodied face of Audwin Strongshield. Although I didn't know him well I still recognised him, mainly because of his black beard, which was tied into two long plaits down his chest.

"I saw Strongshield as he approached," Sinarr told the crowd as Audwin knelt before him, head bowed. "The dark waters of the scrying pool see everything – no one can hide from its gaze, so I saw the roads he was travelling, making it easy for Joarr to spring his trap. There will be no rescue for Romsdahl from the north now Strongshield's army has been defeated and scattered, not now your second has been delivered into my hands."

Sinarr walked over to Audwin and raised his sword, drawing horrified cries from the onlookers. "Audwin Strongshield, I condemn you as a traitor for defying Adalrikr Asmarrson, King of Laskar and the Northern Lands. You chose loyalty to the house of Gautarr Falrufson, knowing full well he was defying his rightful king. You chose the wrong path and must now accept the consequences."

"Adalrikr's no king to me," Audwin called out. "I'm sorry, Gautarr –"

Sinarr's blade swept down, cutting Audwin off mid-sentence as he struck his head from his body. He pitched forwards onto the ground, bright red blood gushing out and forming a spreading stain by Sinarr's feet.

"No," gasped Throm, staring down in horror, his cry mingling with many others up and down the wall.

Sinarr pointed his bloodied sword at the battlements, its tip aimed at Gautarr. "Know this. If you heed the counsel of Kolfinnar's cripple he will lead you to your deaths. Bend the knee to your king while you still can. I have been more than patient with you, Falrufson, and your time is almost up. You could have given this city over to me and saved your people from bloodshed. You still have that choice, even now, but understand this. If your gates are not opened to me before the Landless Jarl arrives with his meagre army then the time for mercy is over. You will watch me butcher his men outside these walls and then we will break down these gates and take this city. And after it is all over, I will kill every member of your family, whilst you look on."

# CHAPTER 37

The Great Hall in Gautarr's castle was in uproar. Most of Roms-dahl's warriors had crowded inside and were busy arguing about Sinarr's demands. Ragnar was shouting at Haki, Throm standing between the pair as he tried to intervene. Elsewhere I could see Domarr and Skari squaring up to one another, look-ing like they were about to come to blows. Gautarr strode to his customary place at the head of the table, picked up his axe and threw it down with a crash. The hall fell silent, everyone staring at the head of the war axe, now lying buried deep in the wooden table.

Gautarr glared at the men standing in front of him. "I'm still the jarl of Romsdahl, so rather than whimpering and snapping at each other like a pack of frightened hounds you'll all stand down and listen to me. Anyone got a problem with that?"

No one met Gautarr's eye, the silence lingering as he reached down and yanked his axe out of the table, freeing it in a shower of splinters. "I'm no fool, I know this is a bitter blow. Sinarr's counting on that display in front of our gates to weaken our spirits. The fight continues, so the first thing I need to do is name my new second and that's no easy task; Aud-win was a good man, someone I trusted with my life and who you all followed without question. There'll be time to mourn, I promise you, but now I need to find someone who's ready to step up and stand by my side in the coming battle."

Ragnar stepped forwards, falling to one knee with his hand on the hilt of his sword. "It would be my honour to serve you and lead your men in battle, Father."

Gautarr smiled but before he could speak Haki shouldered his way through the crowd and knelt before him. "I served under Audwin Strongshield and I've acted as your weapons master and second while he was away. I want to avenge my friend and serve you."

Haki was only in his middle twenties, making him a couple of years younger than Ragnar. However, his gesture roused a cheer amongst many of the warriors in the hall and I saw Gautarr take note of that as he surveyed the crowd and looked harder at Haki.

"You make me proud every day, Ragnar," Gautarr told his son. "However, Haki has been acting in this position during Audwin's absence and has earned the honour of leading our warriors into battle. Instead, Ragnar, when Johan arrives we'll ride out together and you'll be at my side as my shieldman and I yours, fighting as father and son. There's honour in that too."

"As your shieldman, then," Ragnar replied, rising as his father patted him on the shoulder. Most of the men cheered at Haki's appointment, though I noticed Tomas standing at the back of the room, shaking his head.

Gautarr raised his hands and the room quietened. "So, Haki, now I've named you my second what would your advice be?"

I could see a flush creeping up the blond man's neck as the attention of the room centred on him. Haki took a breath and stood straighter, never taking his eyes off Gautarr as he answered. "I know you'd want me to speak plainly, just as Audwin would've done. We've not just lost Strongshield, chief, we've lost two thousand swords. That makes this battle hard to win, if not impossible."

"So why fight it?" interjected Ragnar.

Gautarr raised an eyebrow at his son, who stared back defiantly. "I was asking for Haki's opinion, not yours."

"You're talking about riding out to battle," Ragnar said. "I'll fight with you, you know I will, only think about what you're saying. Without Audwin's warriors Sinarr outnumbers us almost two to one. Haki's right, this isn't a fight you can win."

"That doesn't make it one we shouldn't fight," Haki told Gautarr.

"Meaning?"

"We can stay behind these walls, watch as Johan's put to the sword and we'll live through that day, I don't doubt. We might survive for months afterwards, but where's this going to end? We've been under siege for more than a year and the people are frightened. We can bring in supplies through the tunnels, that's true, but it's not enough for the whole town. There's already hardship in the poorer areas and, sooner or later, the people's spirit is going to break. If that happens and we lose the outer wall we've lost the city, leaving us trapped in the castle."

"Which we can defend, and escape from if necessary through the tunnels," argued Ragnar.

Gautarr shook his head. "And where would that leave us? Landless fugitives, much like Jokellsward's become, fighting on until our luck runs out. Is that really what you're suggesting, Ragnar? Will Johan's journey take him to our walls, only to watch as our gates stay firmly shut when he was the one who came to our aid, when no one else did?"

Gautarr looked at his wife. "What do you think, Jora? How should I deal with this choice?"

Jora's face was taut as she sat at the table, Karlin next to her holding her hand. "Gautarr, Sinarr is never going to show mercy to our house. He means to kill us all – our children, our grandchildren. If we surrender we'll meet the same fate that befell Rothgar's house in Ulfkell's Keep."

Gautarr swallowed and his face softened. "It won't come to that."

Jora met his gaze. "It might, in which case it's better to have faced our enemy in battle than cowering here behind our walls. I don't want to lose you, my son or my nephews, but this is the choice Sinarr is forcing upon us."

"Your wife speaks wisely," added Haki. "Strongshield didn't deserve to die like that and I want to avenge him. We've still got a choice about how we face our enemies and I don't want to bow to Adalrikr as king. He's no king of mine and I don't plan on surrendering quietly."

There were more shouts and Gautarr nodded, patting Jora's hand before turning back to the crowd. "I've made my decision. When Johan's army reaches Romsdahl he won't face Sinarr alone. We'll fight by his side and see whether the Vorund Clan has the stomach for this war. And when we face them we'll be defending our homes, families and children. What are Sinarr's men fighting for? One man's ambition to wear a crown he doesn't deserve. I think we've more fire in our bellies, don't you?" The crowd roared louder at that, erupting into cheers as Gautarr ordered his servants to bring out ale and food.

"And what about you?" spat Domarr, grabbing hold of my sleeve as I moved to sit down. "Sinarr knew all about you and your mission here. How can that be?"

I shook off his hand. "How should I know? Do you really think I'm in league with him, after everything I've been through?"

"Truth is I don't know why you're here, other than to get us to fight your battles for you. My father seemed to think a lot of you. I don't see it."

"Is there a problem here?" asked Patrick, approaching me with Ulfarr and Tomas.

"Nothing that concerns you," Domarr replied, stepping back and pushing his way through the crowd.

"What was that all about?" asked Patrick, frowning at Domarr's retreating back.

"Don't worry about it. Let's just say being friends with Olfridor Halfhand isn't something Domarr looks on favourably."

"Just watch yourself," Tomas told me. "Domarr didn't like being bested in the circle by Bandor. If he can find a way to pay that back by making life difficult for you, he'll do it."

***

Leif stood before Johan under the shade of an old oak tree, nervously hopping from foot to foot, despite Joldir's reassuring presence. Johan looked down at him, his craggy face dappled by sunlight and shadow. At his side stood Petr, his fingers drumming idly on the hilt of his sword, the blade that killed Vandill back in Tullen. Damona sat under the tree, looking tired and drawn as the rest of Johan's army took the welcome chance to rest on their long journey southwards. A journey that was nearing its end. Nearby two of the Brotherhood, Gunnar and Yngvarr, were both keeping watch a discreet distance away.

"So close and now this," said Johan, his voice flat.

"At least Gautarr will not abandon us, which was our greatest fear," Joldir replied.

Petr sighed. "Our scouts found a handful of survivors from Audwin's army. Hundreds of bodies are scattered about the area, stripped of their armour and weapons and left to feed the crows. Those still breathing who joined us confirm Joldir's tale."

"Three score of men is hardly what we hoped for," muttered Johan.

"Three score of strangers now wandering through our camp, with no one to vouch for them. How do we know they can be trusted?" Damona asked, looking up at Johan anxiously.

"They all passed the test of the runestones before being admitted," Joldir told her.

"That didn't stop the attack on Rothgar that nearly killed my son," Damona replied with a withering look.

"No, it didn't …" Joldir began but he trailed off as Johan waved at him impatiently.

"Enough. I'm not discussing this again. They're three score men I can make good use of and they ride with us to Romsdahl. I'll not deny them their chance for vengeance when they could have fled to safety after Audwin's defeat." Johan turned to Petr. "It's time we were moving again. Send Yng-varr ahead with a small party to scout out the road ahead and have Faraldr do the same behind us. I want to know whether Sinarr's prepared any surprises and to make sure Djuri's still where he should be. We can't afford any mistakes, not now."

Petr nodded and moved away smartly to carry out Johan's commands, putting his arm around Yngvarr as he gave him his orders. Damona held out her hand and Johan helped her rise. She looked tired, although *everyone* was tired after days of marching and riding. Leif could barely keep his eyes open after long nights working in Joldir's forge, watching as he wove more magic into the runeblades of the Brotherhood. Damona drew her husband into an embrace and Johan's face became kinder as he smiled and turned to Leif.

"And how are you, young man? Joldir tells me you have been helping him as his apprentice artificer."

Leif gulped, his mouth dry. "I'm apprenticed to Curruck the smith, if that's what you mean, my lord. Curruck's agreed I can spend time with Joldir too when my chores are done, so I've been learning from him too."

Damona laughed. "A bright young boy, clearly. You're friends with Egill, Ingirith's son, aren't you?"

Leif nodded, unable to think of anything else to say. In truth, he wasn't entirely sure why Joldir had asked him to come and see Johan in the first place.

"I need to ask you a favour," Joldir began, leaning heavily on his runestaff, which was disguised as an ordinary piece of wood. Leif stared hard at it, and thought he saw the air around the staff shimmer. For a moment there were patterns swirling within the grain of the wood, chimera entwined with dragon, claws and fangs bared, eyes gleaming. Then the image was gone and all that remained was the oak staff, worn smooth in one place by Joldir's hand.

Johan smiled. "If it's something within my power, I'll see if I can help you. What is it you seek?"

"Etta and I have long suspected the durath have some

interest in the boy. His imprisonment at Tullen was for a purpose, I am sure of it. The power of the Sight running through him is strong and he has a natural aptitude in the fine work necessary to be an artificer. These are qualities we do not want to fall into the hands of our enemies."

"Commendable qualities, I agree. Why are you telling me this?"

"Because when the battle comes I'll not be able to keep him safe."

Johan looked thoughtful as Damona wrapped her arm around his waist, drawing him close once more. "You know I can't make promises, nor release you from the part you must play in the coming fight. I need you by my side to defeat Sinarr. I need the wielder of the runestaff who's already destroyed one of the Sundered Souls."

"I'm not asking for you to spare me from battle," Joldir replied. "The boy is also important to Rothgar's growing skills. There's a bond between them that needs to be protected and I have … I can put it no other way. I have a *feeling* Leif represents the future and he has an important role to play in all of this."

Leif looked at Joldir in puzzlement, not instantly recognising the description of himself, although he supposed it *was* true. After all, he had done those things …

Johan nodded. "Varinn has command of the small force I'm leaving to defend our camp when we finally march out to fight Sinarr's men. The hospital will be positioned there to receive the injured – it'll be as safe as anywhere will be when the fighting starts. Djuri may be many things, but I don't think he would be so dishonourable as to attack women, children and the old."

"The man turned his cloak," said Damona. "Who knows what he will do?"

Johan spread out his hands, looking apologetically at Joldir. "Such are the times we live in, my friend. What I can do is ask Varinn to keep an eye out for Leif, although in battle much can happen and he may be needed elsewhere." Johan turned to Leif. "If that happens, Leif, you must look after your-self if Varinn and Arissa are not there to help you. The best thing you can do if the camp is attacked is run – and if it's not safe to do that, then hide."

Leif frowned, remembering the day Vorund raiders burned his village and his sisters were murdered. His father had hidden and run too, never coming to the aid of Halma and Gisla. He felt his lip tremble as he swallowed down the feelings and said nothing. Johan Jokellsward was a warrior, the jarl of Kalamar and leader of the Brotherhood of the Eagle. It didn't do to argue with someone like that.

Johan seemed to sense something of Leif's thoughts, be-cause he crouched down and put a hand on his shoulder. "It's not glamorous or the stuff of legend, but the tale can't carry on if you're not there to live it. Do you understand? Stay safe for me, can you promise you'll do that?"

Leif nodded, feeling his face redden. Joldir smiled and shook Johan's hand as he stood up. "Thank you, I'll rest easier knowing Varinn is there for Leif and Arissa."

"Just work your magic and make our blades strong," Johan told him. "I plan to cut off the head of the snake, and I need your runeblades to do that."

"Come on Leif," said Joldir, placing his hand on his shoulder again and steering him away from Johan and Damona. "We have work to do."

# CHAPTER 38

My body was strong and whole, my posture upright as I rode through the streets of Reavesburg, feeling the muscular power of my courser as his hooves clattered over the cobbles of the main street leading to Ulfkell's Keep. Nuna rode next to me, her golden hair tied back in a simple ponytail that rippled behind her in the wind like a ribbon of spun gold.

"Go on."

"What?" I asked her.

"Go on. Tell me."

"Tell you ...?"

"That you're impressed, of course!"

"Oh. Well, yes, I'm impressed."

"You're very quiet for someone who's so impressed," Nuna said, looking at me with a playful sidelong glance, making me laugh.

"I ... No, never mind, it's nothing."

Nuna leaned over and punched me lightly on the arm. "No it's not, I can tell. What's the matter? I thought you'd be pleased." A small frown creased her forehead.

"I am. All this, everything you've created it's wonderful. It's just ..."

"Just what?" The frown deepened.

I took a deep breath. "I don't want to appear ungrateful but this is ... It's difficult for me to say. What you've done is amazing but ... It leaves me cold."

Nuna reined in her horse, stopping in the street and forcing me to do the same so we could continue our conversation. "Rothgar, this is our home."

"No, that's just it, it's not. This is a memory of our home.

268

I'm not the same and neither are you. This ... looking backwards, it's not good for either of us. I don't think it's wise to use your gift to dwell on the past and create memories that aren't real."

Nuna stared at me for a while. "I see. Is there anything else you want to tell me?"

Despite seeing she was upset, a knot of anger tightened in my belly – the words were out my mouth before I could stop them. "I don't want to see people I've lost, like Olfridor and Jorik. They're gone and it feels like we're insulting their memory to bring them back like ... Well, you're treating them as your playthings."

Nuna sat there in silence, head upright, chin pointed forwards. "I thought you'd be pleased. I thought you'd like coming here, back to a place that's special for both of us."

I shook my head and spoke more softly. "I like seeing you, of course I do. What's important to me is understanding what's happening now. Seeing events unfolding in Norlhast through your eyes, knowing you're safe and being so proud at how you've grown into the Lady of Norlhast Keep. Seeing my sister flourish, even in difficult times, that's what matters to me."

Nuna's frown took on an ugly aspect and she looked away for a moment. "It's not as if you've let me into *your* life. Your walls are shut tight to me, while you watched my life from the shadows, hidden as you *spied* on me. How do you think that makes me feel, knowing you've been doing this for, what was it? More than a year? You say what I've done is wrong and dare to judge me when you've invaded not just my life but my thoughts and feelings. They're private – not something you can just meddle with when the mood takes you. I feel ... violated. So forgive me if I tried to create something that meant we could meet as equals, when it's obvious all you want is for this to be on your terms."

My heart lurched at her words, ice coiling in my guts as I realised how angry Nuna was. "I'm sorry," I told her. "I didn't know you felt that way. That wasn't how it was, I promise you. Even now, I don't have full control over the Sight and there were times when I was drawn to you, before I even realised it was happening. Joldir's still teaching me, so you have to understand I'm bound to make mistakes."

"Joldir? Who's *Joldir*? Some complete stranger I've never met who you've been sharing my innermost thoughts with for more than a year? Gods, Rothgar, listen to yourself!"

Nuna gave her horse a gentle kick and began to ride away. I watched her head off, hesitating for a moment before I followed. The stonework of Ulfkell's Keep drew near but as we approached I noticed those on the streets were hurrying away, darting into their homes and closing the doors behind them. People reached out and pulled closed the shutters to their windows, while there were no warriors patrolling the battlements of the keep. A dog barked somewhere in the distance for a time, then fell silent, so that the only sound was our horses' hooves echoing off the cobbles.

"Do you know what my favourite memory of Ulfkell's Keep is?" I ventured, my voice falling flat in this silent world. Nuna shrugged, staring straight ahead. "It was after our father's funeral, when the snows had come and Reavesburg was cut off from the rest of the world for the winter. We sneaked off into the kitchens together and Cook treated us to our favourite dish, the one we used to have when we were children. Can you remember?"

"No, I don't think I do."

I sighed, wishing I could have put things better. Even in the dream world of the Sight life could be complicated. "I'm sorry, Nuna, I didn't mean to offend you. I was just trying to explain how I was feeling and coming here ... It's painful for me. I know you didn't mean it that way, but that's how I feel."

Nuna sighed. "I'm sorry too, I should have thought how this would affect you, when you're so far away from home. So, who is this Joldir? He sounds like he's been important in guiding you, much as Ottama has helped me. I'd like to meet him one day, when all of this is over."

"Perhaps one day you will," I said, relieved to put our argument behind us. "I owe him my life. I wouldn't have survived Blackeyes' torture were it not for him."

Nuna gave me a hesitant smile and I thought I heard the sound, far away, of gulls calling to each other down by the quayside. "Perhaps, after the battle, we could all meet together on your terms at a place of this Joldir's choosing. We all have a gift and we should be able to use it together."

I reached down, patting my horse's neck. I could feel every hair, the warmth of the animal's body, the heat of her blood and the strength of her muscle. There was no doubt the Sight ran strong in my family.

"Yes, that would be good. I don't know what the future will bring but if we defeat Sinarr then, yes, I'd like that very much. Just not here, that's all."

"In that case indulge me in one thing," Nuna told me, reaching into her riding cloak and pulling out a small leather drawstring purse. When she passed it over to me I was surprised at its weight.

"What is it?" I asked, beginning to untie the string.

"Don't open it yet," Nuna said. "Think of this as a promise and a sign of my faith in you. Bring it with you when we meet again."

I took the purse and put it into my pocket. "I promise."

Nuna beamed, a smile that brought back memories so powerful I felt a catch in my throat. "I'll be thinking of you so, please, take care of yourself. I couldn't bear to lose you a second time."

***

I awoke from the trance state of the Sight with a start, blinking back tears. I rose unsteadily from my bed and walked to the window of my chamber, opening the shutters and breathing in the fresh air. It was mid-afternoon, and as I looked out over the castle courtyard Haki was drilling his men once more. I could see Bandor practising his shield work with Svafa, as

Haki looked on. Elsewhere Ulfarr, Skari, Patrick and Myr were paired with other Romsdahl warriors, while nearby Ragnar and Throm were sparring. I was surprised at how evenly matched the two of them were, Throm showing skill combined with the restraint and cunning that was often lacking in a young warrior. Ragnar repelled another attack and replied with one of his own, which Throm deflected with his shield, pushing his cousin backwards as he tried to gain the initiative.

Romsdahl's warriors were clearly skilled. They had defended our southern borders for generations against the Vorund Clan and never been defeated. Yet whilst we would not be outmatched in any test of swordsmanship, there was no denying we were outnumbered. I closed my eyes, feeling fearful for my friends and also guilty I couldn't play a part in defending Romsdahl. I ran my hand idly over the scar on the palm of my hand, feeling the ridges in my flesh. I had finished Arissa's salve and I flexed my hand, which was still stiff but less sore than before. Arissa knew her craft and I'd have to thank her, assuming I ever saw her again.

Closing the window I walked around my room, feeling restless, listening to Tomas pacing in the corridor outside. I frowned as I noticed a weight in the pocket of my cloak and reached inside, my stomach turning over as my fingers closed around a small leather pouch. Hands trembling, I drew it out, noticing as I did the heavy weight despite the small size of the brown leather purse. Sitting down on my bed I fumbled with the knots as I began to untie the string, thinking, *telling* myself, this was something I'd taken when I left Johan's camp. The bottle of ataraxia Joldir had given to me perhaps. No. I could feel the weight of the stoppered glass bottle resting in another pocket of my cloak. At last the strings were untied and I pulled the bag open and peered inside. Whatever it contained it was small and the light in my chamber was dim, so I upended the bag, watching as a small glass object dropped onto the covers of my bed with an audible thump.

I reached down and picked it up, turning it over in my

hand to inspect it from every angle. It was glasswork of exquisite detail, beyond anything I had ever seen before. The craftsmen of Sunis would have been hard-pressed to match something of this quality. It was a glass sculpture of an eagle, wings outstretched, mirroring the symbol of the Reavesburg Clan. I walked back over to the window, opening the shutters once more to give me better light to appreciate Nuna's gift, my broken promise forgotten as I stared at it. The glass was crystal clear, the light shining through it casting a thousand tiny rainbows onto the wall opposite. The body of the eagle was etched to bring out every feather, the curl of the creature's talons, the hook of its beak, the glint of its eye. It was probably worth more than all the wealth Gautarr Falrufson possessed.

"Nuna," I said to myself as I marvelled at her gift. "I declare that I am ... Impressed."

Still hardly able to believe what I was seeing, this tangible proof that the Realm of Dream and the world of the Real could touch each other, I returned the eagle to the drawstring purse, tied it tightly and put it back in my cloak.

# CHAPTER 39

The following morning I was woken by a commotion outside my room. I could hear shouts and people running past, sounding both excited and anxious. I pulled the door open to find Tomas standing guard as usual.

"What's happening?"

Tomas shrugged. "Not sure, but everyone's heading down to the walls."

"Has Johan arrived?"

Tomas shrugged again. "Not that I've heard ... Hey, Svafa," he called to the young warrior approaching us down the corridor. "What's happening? Where's everyone going?"

Svafa paused, glaring briefly at me, his nose still swollen and bruised. "There's another messenger from the Vorund camp outside the gates. Gautarr's gone down to see what he has to say."

Tomas glanced at me and I nodded. "Come on, let's go."

***

I found a vantage point on the walls not far from where I had seen Sinarr execute Audwin. Gautarr had ordered that his body be recovered and Audwin Strongshield now rested in the crypt beneath Romsdahl Castle. However, I could still clearly see the dark stain marking the spot where he had died. Standing a few paces away was Joarr the Hammer, easily recognisable amongst the score of warriors guarding him with his thick blond hair and beard, which flowed down his armoured chest and reached as far as his belt. His hand rested on the handle of his warhammer, the huge metal head etched with runes.

"What's going on?" Tomas asked a man nearby.

"We're still waiting for Gautarr to show up. Joarr's demanded an audience with our chief."

"Getting to be a bit of a habit, this," observed Tomas.

"Something tells me this won't be good news," I said, peering over the wall. Audwin's death yesterday had hit the people hard. Today would be worse. Again, I thought anxiously of Johan and began to wonder if my worst fears were about to be realised.

I heard a series of shouts behind me and turned to look down the main street leading to the city gates. I could see Haki at the front of a group of warriors, all of them dressed for battle, who were forcing their way through the gathering crowd. Gautarr was riding his war horse through the gap Haki was creating, Ragnar and Throm either side of him, Domarr bringing up the rear.

"Where is he?" Gautarr bellowed as he reached the gates and dismounted. He hurried up the steps to the gatehouse two at a time, pushing people out of the way.

"Here he is, at last," Joarr called out as Gautarr came into view. "Did my summons wake you, old man?"

Gautarr spat out over the battlements. "You came here under the flag of parley, so say what it is you have to say and be quick about it."

Joarr shook his head. "I'm here to give you one last chance to end this."

"Really? You think I'll listen to anything you say, the man who murdered my brother?"

Gautarr's remarks caused a series of shouts and curses to be thrown at Joarr, who stood there calmly, waiting for the din to subside, before he answered. "Your brother was a great man, worthy to lead your house. He saved the lives of his men that day and fought with honour. Don't you remember? It was Egill who challenged me to fight as Asmarr's champion that day outside Viskanir. I shattered him with *Foebreaker* here," Joarr said, patting his warhammer. "I etched his name into the iron when it was over, one fight I'll never forget."

"Is that what this is about?" asked Gautarr. "You want to

fight for Romsdahl this time? To try and add my name to that cursed hammer?"

"No," hissed Throm. "If we're talking about a champions' duel then it should be me, to avenge my father. I can beat him, Uncle, I know it."

Joarr shook his head. "It may come to that, but not before Sinarr's dealt with Johan Landless' doomed uprising. No, today I'm here to offer you terms. One final chance to open your gates, so you can avoid the death of your people and those closest to you. Time is short, so think carefully before you give your answer."

"You've sat outside my walls for more than a year," Gautarr shouted. "What makes you think today will be any different? You talk of how my brother fought with honour – did Sinarr treat Audwin Strongshield with respect or mercy, killing a warrior when he was on his knees with his hands bound behind his back? Now you've shown us what the Vorund Clan's idea of honour is, don't think we'll make this easy for you. If you want to end this then come and take this city from me, if you think you can. And when that day comes just remember I'll be seeking you out, Joarr. I'll look forward to that day, because I know how it ends."

Joarr raised *Foebreaker* above his head, held the huge weapon there for a time and then let it drop to the ground once more. "So be it, old man."

A few people began to point and I squinted, my eyes drawn to movement by the Vorund Clan's defensive palisade. Gates swung open in the palisade walls and men began to swarm through it, spreading out along its length as a drum began to beat out a steady rhythm.

"This is on you, Falrufson," Joarr shouted as he cast away the white flag and motioned to his men. They turned their backs on Romsdahl and began to walk away, trampling the white cloth into the mud as they left.

The drum continued to beat, the sound carrying across the distance to Romsdahl. I could see ladders being raised now and placed against the wooden walls. Shouts and jeers drifted over to us, Vorund's guards hurling abuse, clashing swords and axes against their shields.

Tomas glanced at me, looking confused. "What are they doing?"

A sick feeling was spreading through my guts as I watched ropes drop over the walls and saw men being dragged forwards by Vorund's warriors, holding down those who struggled as they were tied to the ropes and then hoisted up.

"They're executing their prisoners," I told Tomas. "Audwin wasn't the only one to be captured. They're showing Romsdahl the fate that awaits them if they don't surrender."

A collective shudder passed through those gathered on Romsdahl's walls as they began to understand what they were seeing. At first I thought Sinarr was hanging his prisoners as they jerked and struggled on the ropes. Looking more closely, I could see that they were tied under their arms. Other men scaled the ladders either side of the prisoners, pulled out hammers and began nailing the men to the palisade.

"No," gasped Tomas as their screams reached us. "No!"

Gautarr stood straight and tall, staring unflinchingly as Audwin's men were crucified two at a time, in a line that stretched the full length of the palisade. I counted eighty men by the time it was over. The crowd on the main street had fallen silent, their eyes wide with shock, faces white with fear. Somewhere a woman started sobbing, the sound carrying and filling the space, mingling with the anguished cries from the prisoners. One in particular was screaming "Help me! Help me, please," over and over, his voice already hoarse.

Ragnar swallowed, looking like he wanted to say something but failing to find the words. Gautarr turned stiffly, looking out over the crowd and his warriors.

"Someone shut that woman up," snarled Domarr, looking in the direction of the weeping woman. I saw Freydja gently escort her away, the sound fading as they walked down the road.

"So, now you know," Gautarr announced to the crowd. "That's the true nature of our foe, men who no longer hold to the warrior's codes, the laws of Reave or the rules that governed the founders of the clans when Laskar was first settled. The words of Sinarr the Cold One and Joarr the Hammer are worth nothing, so don't be fooled by their offers of mercy. You've seen the fate of those they've captured. Don't be tricked into thinking we'll fare any better if we surrender to them. Judge them by their actions and judge me by mine. We've defied them for the past year and a half, so I need every man and woman here to remain strong for a little longer. When the time comes, when I ride out with my warriors to break Sinarr and his followers, I need every one of you on this wall. Everyone who's able to fight needs to stand where I am now and hold them back if they try and reach our gates. We're fighting for our families, homes and livelihoods – we're fighting for each other. Stand together with me and we can carry the day, and by nightfall it'll be Sinarr and Joarr's heads that'll adorn our city walls."

Gautarr put his arms round Ragnar and Throm. "Adalrikr rose to power by spilling the blood of his kin. Well, that's no king I can serve. Let's send him a message from the folk of Romsdahl. Let him hear it loud and clear, when we kill his jarls and scatter his army, when we burn his camp and torch his ships. Adalrikr might call himself King of the North but he doesn't rule here and he never will. Not now, not ever!"

"Gautarr!" Haki shouted, clashing his sword against his shield. "Gautarr. Gautarr. Gautarr."

The warriors took up his lead, adding their voices to his and beating out a defiant rhythm on their shields, Tomas bellowing out loudly next to me. Gautarr took hold of Throm and Ragnar's hands, raising them up with his in a victory salute, as if the battle was already won, provoking a cheer from the crowd. Haki continued to lead the chant with his warriors, until Romsdahl reverberated with a defiant roar, drowning out the desperate voices of the men outside, slowly dying on the palisade.

# CHAPTER 40

As the sun set some men lit braziers in the castle courtyard, getting ready to ward off the night's chill as they swapped stories and told jokes while eating and drinking together. Ulfarr had gathered his crew and I walked over to join them as they sat around one of the fires, although Tomas hung back, looking uncertain.

"What are you standing there for?" Ulfarr asked him, waving him forward.

"Wasn't sure I'd be welcome, after I helped lock up your friend," Tomas answered, looking at Skari, who hawked and spat into the flames.

"That was Gautarr's decision, not yours," Ulfarr told him. "We're all part of the same clan and we'll be fighting side by side come the morning. There's space round this fire if you want to join us."

"Something to drink would be welcome," Tomas answered, stepping forwards. I reached over and handed him the skin of wine Patrick had just passed to me. Tomas took a long draft and passed it to Myr, who accepted it with a nod.

"Haki's not been making you practise today?" I asked.

Bandor shook his head. "No. He's been busy making final preparations for the defence of the wall and main gate, making sure there's an ample supply of arrows, spears, rocks and anything else we can throw at our enemies."

"This Johan had better show up on time," muttered Tomas. "I don't want to be waiting another few days, wondering what Sinarr's going to do next."

"He'll be here," Bandor answered tersely.

"No offence meant," said Tomas, holding up his hand. "I

was just saying I've had enough of waiting around. This has been the longest year I've ever known."

"Sinarr doesn't want to delay Johan," I added. "He wants this done with and to fight the Brotherhood within sight of Romsdahl's walls, so the people see his victory."

Ulfarr sighed. "A few thousand warriors behind these walls will have something to say about that."

"And what about your plans, Princeling?" asked Skari. He took the wine from Myr, gulped down a long swig and passed it to Ulfarr. "What'll you be doing tomorrow, while the rest of us fight?"

I met Skari's gaze and held it. "I'll be taking part in defending the walls, should it come to that."

Skari looked surprised. "Hmm. Thought you'd take the chance to stay safe inside the castle."

"Well, you thought wrong," Bandor said, clapping me on the shoulder.

Skari looked ready to take things further but Haki approached, Domarr and a few other warriors just behind him.

"Evening lads. How're we all doing?"

"I can't complain," Ulfarr replied. "Just spending some time with my friends before tomorrow comes."

"It'll come round soon enough," Haki answered. "Make sure you don't drink so much you're no use to me when it does." Domarr laughed humourlessly.

"Guess we've all got our ways of passing the time before a battle," Ulfarr said with a smile. "Some folk can't sit still, others like me can't sleep and need to while away the small hours somehow. Come the morning, we'll be ready, you can count on that."

"I wasn't asking for your *opinion*, Ulfarr," Haki replied as his eyes fixed on Tomas and narrowed.

"Haki," Tomas said by way of greeting as he stared into the fire.

"Still shadowing our noble guest, I see. You won't get out of things that easily tomorrow. He can look after himself

– I need all the warriors with me when we charge the Vorund lines. I'll be watching out for you, so don't think you can slink away. I've a special place for you, right at the front."

Tomas' head jerked up. "I want to fight, you know that. I'll be there." I felt a pang of pity for the young man as his voice quavered.

"What's this about?" asked Patrick, rising to his feet.

"You're new here, so let me fill you in," said Domarr with a cruel grin. "Tomas' father was a coward. Everyone knows it."

Haki laughed. "Yes, and everyone's wondering if coward's blood runs in Tomas' veins. I guess we'll see tomorrow, won't we?"

Patrick frowned. "You're Gautarr's second, so you should know it's your job to get the men ready to fight. Calling your warriors cowards isn't the way to go about things."

"I don't need lessons in war from some Berian mercenary with delusions he was once a knight, *Sir* Patrick Wild. The way I understand it a knighthood is something your folk purchase with a bag of gold or pass down from father to son. In Laskar a warrior has to prove his worth by shedding the blood of his enemies. If you're a knight and a so-called leader of men what are you doing following him?" Haki jabbed a finger at Ulfarr, who merely raised an eyebrow at the comment and took a sip from the wineskin.

"Guess I'm just more approachable than you, Haki." Ulfarr said finally. "I've always been a good listener, so people are drawn to me."

Bandor was the only one who laughed. Domarr took a step forwards, fists clenched, tendons taut on his arms. Ulfarr took another sip of wine and then gave the skin to Patrick, who was still standing and staring at Haki and his men. After a long pause Patrick took his place in the circle around the fire.

"Are we done here, or do you have any more words to give my men heart before the battle?" Ulfarr asked.

Haki's lip curled. "You've all done well in the training circle but we'll see the true worth of you and your men soon enough. As for him," he said, jerking his head at Tomas, "I already know I'll be disappointed. Not every man has the qualities necessary to be a warrior, and with his father there was never any chance."

"We'll be watching you, Tomas," Domarr added. "If you even think of running, I'll cut you down myself."

"That's enough," said Bandor. "This stops now."

"The Landless Jarl's son has spoken," Haki said with a smirk. "You'd think differently, I'm sure, if it was one of your friends who'd died because of his father's cowardice. Now you know the kind of man you're defending. If I were you, I'd make sure it isn't Tomas who's guarding your back when battle is joined." Haki turned on his heel and his men fell into step behind him, sniggering as they vanished into the deepening darkness.

"That wasn't what happened," Tomas muttered, hugging himself and staring into the fire.

"Does it matter?" asked Ulfarr. "The deeds of your father aren't yours, are they?"

"It matters to Haki, and whether it's the truth or not he won't let it drop. That story follows me round everywhere I go. Audwin put a stop to it when he was in charge. After Haki became weapons master he encouraged all that talk about my father once more. Folk who before would just have whispered something behind my back began to insult me to my face." Tomas cut a dejected figure, staring into the fire and shaking his head when Patrick offered him some wine.

"Ulfarr's right, you don't have to listen to him," Patrick told him.

"The men do, though."

"Then you'll have to prove them wrong tomorrow," Ulfarr said. "Give them a different story by proving yourself in battle." Tomas nodded, looking unconvinced, glancing up nervously in the direction of Haki and Domarr, who were now busy talking to another group of warriors, all of them laughing and joking.

"We need to watch our backs with Haki," Skari said, looking in the same direction. "He's no Petr Hamarrson, that's for sure. I don't know what Gautarr was thinking making him his second. Did you see Ragnar's face? He was convinced he'd be named."

"It's because of the plan for the battle," I explained. "Gautarr knows the men on foot in the first charge will be in the most danger. He wants Ragnar by his side in the cavalry, in relative safety, while Haki leads the attack."

Patrick looked thoughtful. "Comforting words, Rothgar – I'm glad you joined us tonight. I think you're right – we might not have to worry about Haki after tomorrow in that case."

"Don't be so sure," muttered Skari, shaking his head. "He'll come through this whole thing unscathed, mark my words. That sort always do. It's us I'm more worried about. We need to stay tight and look out for each other. That goes for you too, Ulfarr – you need to take care, because I don't think being a member of Johan's Brotherhood is something that counts in our favour round here."

Ulfarr, who had been drafted into the ranks of Gautarr's archers, sighed, nodding in agreement. "Just take care of yourselves and don't worry about me. This time tomorrow we'll be sat where we are now telling tales of how the Brotherhood carried the day."

"Don't forget the old saying, though, when we were living in the hill country of Kalamar," Skari said with a grin, the firelight distorting his one-eyed face into something demonic.

"What saying?"

"If we start losing, run away."

*\*\**

Soon enough the wine was drunk, the fire in the brazier was burning low and our stock of stories had been told. The summer days were drawing shorter, the nights longer and colder than a few weeks ago. I wrapped my cloak around me, reflecting that the season would soon be turning.

"Take care of yourself," I told Bandor, clasping his arm as

I said goodbye.

"You too," he replied. "Freydja asked her uncle to assign me to a different place in the battle tomorrow, did you know that? I said no, of course. She did it from the best of motives, but word would have gotten around soon enough. Ulfarr's right, the Brotherhood isn't well-regarded in Romsdahl. This is our chance to change things, and show Falrufson's men we can fight alongside them, stand our ground and win their respect. That could be important, afterwards."

I grimaced. "Only if you're still alive. Gautarr openly protected his own son – Freydja was well within her rights to ask a similar favour for her betrothed. You could have ridden as one of Gautarr's shieldmen and still gained honour."

"I know, Freydja said the same. It didn't seem right, though, to abandon my crew and the decision's made now. There's no undoing it."

I drew Bandor into a firm embrace, patting him on the back. "I wish I could be there with you. I'm sorry I can't."

"Just take care of yourself, alright? If things don't go our way Romsdahl's walls might not be the safest place either."

# CHAPTER 41

From my vantage point on the wall above the main gates of Romsdahl I watched the sun rise, edging the clouds blood red. Jora was in command of the defence of the town, standing with Karlin, Freydja and Asta, all of them armoured. Archers stood ready, buckets full of arrows at their feet, piles of stones nearby for when those ran out. The dawn light revealed Johan's army in the distance, out beyond the palisade wall. None of Romsdahl's defenders spoke, all of us knowing Johan's arrival meant battle was about to be joined.

I shuddered as an image flashed before my eyes – Sinarr, crouched over the scrying pool within a circle of blood, chanting words of power with his dead lips.

"I see you, Cripple. When this is over and Romsdahl falls I shall find you, bind you and take you to Adalrikr as my tribute. You cannot hide from me."

I squeezed my eyes tight shut, swaying on my feet. I gripped the stonework with both hands, trying to shake the vision from my mind. Sinarr's scrying made it impossible to hide from him and when I opened my eyes all I could see was the abandoned farmhouse and the dark waters of the pool. Flames sprang up around the circle, which burned blue and cold, never touching the hoarfrost in the room, which glittered like a thousand sapphires in the sinister light.

"By the sacrifice of blood I call upon Arkon, avatar of war. Grant me victory. I call upon Rathlin, avatar of the dead. What Adalrikr stole from you when he bound my spirit I will repay hundredfold. I call upon Morvanos, avatar of chaos. Know that your loyal servants are returning. Adalrikr is gathering the Sundered to him and, one by one, they are heeding his call. Together, we shall accomplish the victory denied you by the Creator, I swear it."

Sinarr stared into the dark waters of the scrying pool, where my face shimmered and swam into focus. "I see you clearly, now. You will watch as I slay your friends. Then I will come for you."

Gasping, I leant over the edge of the walls and retched.

***

"What's the matter with him?" A voice I recognised. Freydja.

"Rothgar? Are you alright? Can you hear me, young man?" asked Karlin.

Someone took my arms, helping me to sit up. My head was splitting, Freydja and Karlin's faces peering at me through a strange fog of swirling colours and bright after-images. I could still see the blue flames of Sinarr's circle, burned on the back of my eyes.

"Someone should take him back to Romsdahl Castle," said Asta.

I shook my head, instantly regretting it as the pain momentarily blinded me. "No," I gasped. "I'm needed here – I have to do my part."

"You'll be of little use to us like this," Karlin replied.

I shrugged off his grip and rose, unsteadily, to my feet. Karlin suddenly seemed taller, broader. A huge man with a warrior's build, bare-chested with a tattoo of a black bear on his torso. A handsome face framed with long dark hair, dark rivers of blood running from both of his eyes. I blinked and Karlin's softer features looked back at me, face curious.

"*Are* you alright?" he asked.

"I think so. I'm fine," I lied.

Freydja looked unconvinced. "Alright. Well, stay with me until you're feeling better. At least that way I can keep an eye on you."

***

The wagons, carts and wayns of Johan's caravan of followers had been drawn into a tight defensive circle on top of a small rise overlooking Sinarr's army, the walls of Romsdahl visible in the distance. Tents had been erected last night under Joldir's direction to give them space to tend the wounded once the fighting started. Leif could hear Varinn shouting orders as the final hurried works were carried out to secure their defences. Eykr limped along next to him, his broken leg not yet healed enough for him to ride out with Johan, and he was one of the few young warriors Varinn had under his command to protect the camp. Most of those nervously standing there were grey-beards or boys just into their teens. Leif was too young to fight but as a smith's apprentice he had been busy all night; helping with final repairs to the men's armour, fixing buckles, edging blades. Despite the heat of the forge, Leif felt cold and a chill had set itself in his bones. Was it fear? He'd been afraid before but this was different, somehow.

Arissa gave Joldir a tearful farewell before he went to take his place with the rest of the mounted warriors surrounding Johan Jokellsward. Leif could see Svan, Yngvarr and Ragni waiting for him, alongside the Flint cousins and Jolinn Hrodidottir, the fierce shieldmaiden from Olt, with her second, Lars.

Joldir drew Leif into a hug. "Take care, both of you. Look out for each other, and if the tide of the battle turns make sure you stay together. Promise me?"

Leif nodded, taking Arissa's hands, which were shaking. He thought Joldir looked ill, his face pale and waxen, the colour drained from him. Leif didn't feel too good himself – perhaps this was what all people looked like and felt before a battle.

"Joldir, I don't think I can ..." Arissa's voice trailed off, and she cast an anxious look at the spiked palisade walls.

"Yes, you can. I've taught you all you need to know to run the hospital. Ingirith and Maeva know how to bind a wound and set bones – they're warrior's wives, after all. You'll all be able to help each other – you don't have to do this on your own."

Arissa nodded, holding Joldir tightly with one arm as

her hand squeezed Leif's. "They're warrior's *widows*, you mean. I'm sorry, I don't know why I said that. Joldir ... Please take care."

"I have to go," he told her, gently pushing her away. "I'll see you soon, I promise."

Leif had never seen Joldir in armour before, dark chain-mail rings covering his body and a sword, etched with runes that Leif had help craft, hanging from his side. Across his back was slung his runestaff, the polished wood shimmering with hidden power. Looking at Joldir now, the man who had given him a home and taught him about the mysteries of the Sight was gone.

"You've been a good father to me," Arissa told Joldir, tears running down her face.

He turned back, a thin smile on his face. "And you've been a good daughter. Take care and I'll see you later."

As Joldir ran through the small gap left in the entrance to the circle Varinn closed it behind him, pushing a series of sharpened stakes into place. Ingirith came over and put her arm around Arissa.

"It'll be alright, my love. Now I need you to come with me and help get everything ready in the hospital tent. Maeva's fretting in there and I need a calm head and a steady hand or, so help me, it won't just be Johan's warriors that'll need stitching back together."

"What about Leif?"

"Etta's calling for him," Ingirith replied. "Leif, can you run along to her and either stay with her or else find Dalla at the back of the camp? She's looking after the other children, including my little Egill and Kitta. Do you know where I mean?"

Leif nodded and ran off towards Joldir's wagon, where Etta was staying. She was sitting on the seat at the front of the wagon, wrapped in a thick travelling cloak, hood up, face half in shadow, though her one good eye glittered with excitement. It was the first time in months that Leif had seen her out of bed. Next to her stood Ekkill, dressed for war in black leather armour, his bow slung over his shoulder, quiver stuffed full of white-fletched arrows. He saw Leif approach and nodded at him, a smirk playing on his lips. Etta's toothless grin was warmer and she held out her thin withered hand towards him.

"Leif, my boy, there you are. Come here."

When Leif reached the wagon Etta reached down and took hold of Leif's chin, inspecting him with her good eye, tutting as she did so.

"He's ice cold. And look at those rings under his eyes, he looks exhausted."

"I was working in the smithy all night," Leif said defensively. Etta continued to peer at him, her stare making him feel uncomfortable. Finally she released her grip and waved him to climb up onto the wagon.

In front of them Johan's army began to divide. Petr Hamarrson broke off from the main body of men, leading a small force westwards to block Djuri's approach. They included Old Gunnar and Sigolf Amundson, the elder of Falsten's huge frame almost crushing his horse. Leif could clearly see the banners of Olt and Vorund flying high above Djuri's warriors, who must have numbered well in excess of a thousand swords. Petr had less than three hundred men under his command. Johan shouted to the remainder of his force, giving his horse the spurs and cantering down towards Romsdahl.

"This isn't going to take long," muttered Ekkill, shaking his head.

"Then why aren't you out there fighting, to help give Johan a chance?" asked Leif.

Ekkill shrugged. "I don't think I'd make much of a difference, lad. And someone's got to defend the camp if the fighting comes this way."

Leif scowled, and sat down next to Etta. "Why did you call me over here?" he asked.

Etta turned and put her frail hand on top of his. "I just wanted to keep an eye on you."

***

Djuri stretched on his horse, arching his back as he tried to ease the aching muscles from so many days' riding. Next to him, Hrodmarr lent forwards, hands resting on the pommel of his saddle, peering at the small force spreading itself out along the road to bar their approach to the camp and the rest of Johan's army.

"I'll admit, I'm slightly disappointed," he rasped. "Thought the Landless Jarl would give us more sport."

"We'll sweep them aside in moments," Alfarr agreed with a high, nervous, laugh. In the past few days Old Hrodi's grandson had dogged Hrodmarr's every move, a constant shadow as he sought to curry favour.

Djuri ground his teeth, a knot in his stomach, and turned away, leading his horse along the lines of warriors. Ulf rode next to him. Djuri spied Haarl in the crowd, sitting astride his own warhorse, and nodded to him. The young warrior looked pale, the scar across his forehead from the battle at Noln standing out clearly.

"You alright?" Djuri asked.

Haarl shook his head. "Don't feel right," he said in an undertone. "We're fighting our own kin here."

"It was always going to come to this," Ulf told him.

"I guess so. I just thought that, somehow, Johan would find another way to decide things. I don't know, trial by combat ..." Haarl's voice trailed off and he stared into the distance, swallowing hard.

"Sinarr the Cold One was never going to agree to terms like those, not while he has superior numbers," Ulf explained.

"I suppose you're right," Haarl said quietly.

Djuri tried to smile, grimacing as a sudden shiver ran all the way down his spine. *Gods*, he felt cold this morning. "Way I see things this is a chance for peace. I admire Johan – I've always looked up to him and I don't mind admitting that. But he's fighting a lost cause and this day gives us the chance to bring an end to the bloodshed."

Haarl nodded, looking unconvinced, as did a number of those amongst the ranks of Reavesburg warriors from Ulfkell's Keep. Djuri glanced behind them, to where Hrodi's army from Olt were standing, the majority of them armed with bows or spears. Led by their elder they seemed more confident; Hrodi watching over proceedings from his fine black destrier, his son Radholf talking to him, pointing out the lay of the land and how Johan was deploying his men. He heard hooves behind him and turned to see Bjorr riding up towards them.

"Time to get the men into position," Djuri told the Vorund warrior. "As soon as Johan Jokellsward's men are committed to attacking Sinarr's defences we ride down the men he's left behind, then take the camp. We don't want to leave Johan anywhere to retreat once the battle turns against him."

"The men are ready, Turncloak," Bjorr replied with a grin, nodding towards the hill. "This fight's been a long time coming and I think it's going to be worth it. They're there for the taking."

Djuri nodded to Ulf and Haarl. "Come on, let's get this over with."

# CHAPTER 42

My hands shook and I clamped them under my arms, wrapped in my cloak, resting against the stone wall forming part of the defences above the gatehouse. Many of Jora's warriors looked down on me with disgust, mistaking my condition for nerves and thinking I was a coward. I lacked the energy to care, my hand searching out the bottle of ataraxia in the pocket of my cloak. Something had happened as a result of Sinarr's blood magic. I could feel the presence of *everyone*, their thoughts worming their way into my skull; whispered snatches of half-formed unspoken words, waves of emotions and an overriding, palpable sense of fear. I blinked, trying to clear my mind and close it to the weight of those now pressing down upon me. I felt as if I was drowning, losing all sense of who I was.

"Rothgar?" Freydja was crouching down next to me, holding my hand, drawing disapproving glances from Jora and Asta. I tried to focus on her face, her long raven-black hair blowing in the wind, the colour reminiscent of her brother and cousin. The clamour faded slightly.

"Something's wrong," I told her, tongue thick and numb in my mouth. "Sinarr's using magic to try and … I don't know what he's doing, but …" I couldn't find the words to explain my mounting sense of dread. Somewhere far off I could hear a man crying.

Freydja's expression was grim. "What does he need magic for? He already has the men he needs to win this battle."

"That's enough!" Jora's reprimand turned several people's heads in our direction. Like all the women in Gautarr's household she was wearing silver banded armour, polished to a glittering sheen. "There will be no more talk like that in front of me, young lady, do you understand? Your uncle is going to carry this day."

Freydja bowed her head. "Of course, Aunt Jora. I meant no offence," she replied, before whispering to me "So what does this mean? How do you know this?"

"There isn't time to explain how I know. I think it has something to do with Johan and Sinarr is going to use magic against him."

"What can any of us do against that, even if it's true?" Freydja asked, her face uncertain, still trying to decide if she was listening to the ravings of a madman.

"Honestly, I don't know."

For a moment I was alone on the battlements, the sky an overcast grey, and the warrior crying blood stood before me. Then the scene was gone, replaced by the bustle of activity as people waited for Romsdahl's army, Freydja by my side. I saw Asta pointing towards the keep, Karlin turning and raising his arm. A wave of excitement washed over me, the shared hopes of hundreds of defenders on the walls becoming one with mine, my identity lost for a moment. I closed my eyes. *I am Rothgar Kolfinnarson, brother of the last chief of the Reavesburg Clan and part of a dynasty going back to the time of Marl. I am Rothgar Kolfinnarson, the cripple who has sworn fealty to Johan Jokellsward. I am Rothgar Kolfinnarson, a member of the Brotherhood of the Eagle, avowed to destroy Adalrikr Asmarrson and bring an end to the durath.*

I wanted to reach out to my Fellowship and draw strength and protection from them. I resisted the temptation, knowing the last thing I could afford to do was distract Joldir as he rode with Johan. Instead, I thought of the bottle of ataraxia in my cloak. One draught should be enough to close my mind and rebuild the walls that protected me. I reached inside, fingers brushing the glass, seeking out the stopper only for the scene to change again. Once more I was alone on the walls with the crying warrior, who slowly shook his head. He opened his mouth to speak –

"Gautarr Falrufson, Jarl of Romsdahl, approaches," Karlin's voice resounded across the battlements, snatching me from the vision and bringing me back to the present. Huge cheers went up and I hauled myself onto my knees so I could peer over the wall into the main street below. I could hear them now, the tramping of booted feet and horses' hooves as a column comprising archers, infantry and mounted warriors processed down the street, stretching all the way back to Romsdahl Castle.

Gautarr was at the head of his army, Throm riding on his left and Ragnar to his right. I caught a glimpse of Bandor, his red hair standing out as always, towards the front of the men on foot under Haki's command, Skari, Myr and Patrick with him. As they reached the gates and halted their march I saw him reach down and pull on his helmet, looking pale. Gautarr's armoured warhorse snorted and stamped his feet, impatient to be on his way.

"The time has come," Gautarr called out. He was carrying a heavy shield and an axe, his great two-handed battle axe strapped to his back. "Johan Jokellsward has heeded the call of his clan and come to our aid and now he needs us. I'll not hide behind these walls as a craven and watch him bleed for me. Honour demands that we fight with our kin and protect our clan, so let's get to it and if any of those Vorund dogs get in our way we'll send them straight to Navan's Halls."

Gautarr raised his axe into the air and a great shout went up, people cheering his name and, to my surprise, Johan's as well. The gates swung open and the army of Romsdahl began to move out onto the battlefield, amid the cheers and clamour of those watching from the walls.

\*\*\*

Randall looked out from the wall of the palisade across the open ground, watching as Gautarr's army spread out in front of Romsdahl's gates. The palisade had been constructed in two concentric arcs, hemming Romsdahl in from all sides until it reached the cliffs, beyond which the fleet on the waters of the

Redfars Sea acted as a blockade. The inner circle was designed to repel a counter-attack such as the one now unfolding before them, whilst the outer circle defended them from any force trying to break the siege and reach Romsdahl. Randall turned the other way, squinting to try and clearly see Johan's advancing forces.

Joarr was standing next to him, hand on the handle of his warhammer, fingers unconsciously tapping a short tattoo. "So, it's finally happening."

"Looks that way. Seems they'll be testing both sides of our defences before the day is out."

"Going to be a short day if this is all they've got to send against us. I thought you said Sinarr was obsessed with this Landless Jarl and saw him as a real threat?"

Randall shrugged. "It's what he represents. Sinarr sees Johan as a symbol of Reavesburg's resistance, someone who has to be crushed and made an example of."

Joarr barked with laughter. "Well, he's going to get his wish."

Below them on the outside of the wall one of the crucified prisoners shouted out abuse at the pair of them. Joarr scowled and his second, Hasteinn, approached, spear in hand.

"You got something to say?" he bellowed, jabbing the butt of his spear down into the shoulder of the man.

"Gautarr's ... coming for ... you ..." the dying man hissed through cracked lips, his head lolling on his neck. His hands and fingers were black. Further down the line a number of men had died in the night and the crows were already feasting upon their remains. Randall tried to suppress a shudder.

Hasteinn raised the spear again, but Joarr stayed his hand. "Enough. Don't let the insults of those we've already defeated rile you. Let him see what happens to his chief when he fights the Vorund Clan – after that you can do what you like with him."

"I've got to go," Randall said. "Sinarr wants to face Johan on the open ground, not behind the walls of the palisade. Your orders are to hold against Gautarr and to capture him if you can. When Johan's forces are defeated Sinarr's men will join with yours and together we'll break Romsdahl."

Joarr took in a deep breath, broad chest swelling and his nostrils flared above his thick blond beard. "Time was when one jarl would speak to another about tactics, not just pass on their messages through one of their men. And why is he facing Johan on open ground? He's giving up the advantage of a perfectly good defendable position. What's he playing at?"

Randall shook his head. "You want me to tell Sinarr how you feel when I report back?"

"No, I don't think so," Joarr replied with a grimace. "Though I can tell from your face you feel the same way. Good luck. May Dinuvillan smile on you."

"Aye, and on you, Joarr. Crack some skulls for me, so we can finally finish this."

Joarr hefted *Foehammer* into the air with a grin. "You can count on it."

***

Yngvarr's courser whinnied as he watched while the rest of Johan's warriors were deployed. He could see the archers, led by his friend Faraldr, fanning out as they took their positions. Yngvarr wished he was there with him – he'd always been more comfortable with a bow than a sword. But Johan had gathered most of the remaining members of the Brotherhood together as his guard for the coming battle, and Yngvarr had been honoured to act as Johan's shieldman. They'd been together ever since they'd been forced to flee for their lives from Ulfkell's Keep. A year and a half spent on the road, fighting and surviving, watching as one by one the men of Kalamar died. He glanced around, catching Ragni's eye. The amiable man was one of the few companions left alive from that terrible day. Svan was the only other Kalamar warrior in their company, a hungry grin on his face as he held his axe, leaning in the saddle to whisper something to Johan, who nodded.

The rest of the Brotherhood had joined them along their

journey; Geirmarr and Geirmundi Flint, leading their men from Delving, Jolinn and the men from Olt who'd stayed loyal to their clan, young Lars riding alongside her. Then there was Joldir, whose inclusion in their company had raised eyebrows from those who only knew him as their artificer and healer. Yngvarr thought differently; he hadn't been in the fight at Tullen but he remembered the stories Petr had told afterwards. How Joldir had fought with his runestaff, defending Johan and his company against the durath. Eight felt like a good number for Johan's honour guard: nine members of the Brotherhood riding out to face Sinarr. It sounded like a lucky number – the sort of thing you heard in stories. In the distance a horn sounded, five times in short succession, and Yngvarr felt his heart beating in his chest, his mouth dry.

"Romsdahl sends forth their warriors," Svan observed.

"And Sinarr's men come to meet us," added Joldir, pointing towards the palisade where the gates were swinging open. In moments warriors began to swarm onto the battlefield, their ranks moving forwards with discipline, marching to the beat of a drum. The standard of the black bear within a white circle fluttered in the light breeze; Sinarr the Cold One's banner.

"What are they doing?" asked Geirmarr. "Surely they should be holding the palisade wall, forcing us to attack them?"

"Sinarr wants to fight us in person," Johan replied, a dark look on his face as the number of warriors marching towards them continued to swell. "He means to show that he doesn't fear us."

Svan let out a loud war cry, clashing his axe against his shield, a cry that was taken up amongst the ranks of Reavesburg's warriors. "Then we'll prove him wrong. Come on, Johan, give the order. It's time."

Yngvarr narrowed his eyes, watching as the Vorund Clan's warriors continued to disgorge from the gate, black shapes moving inexorably forwards to the solemn beat of the drum. Hundreds of them, row after row advancing towards their position.

Next to him Ragni breathed out slowly. "That doesn't look good."

"What's the matter?" Jolinn remarked, nodding in the direction of the approaching army. "Scared of a fight?"

Ragni looked offended. "I've been in enough in my time, but I can count and they outnumber us, that's clear to see."

Jolinn gave a wicked grin. "You're forgetting, you've got me fighting on your side."

Lars laughed. "Aye. They've got no chance."

"By my reckoning that's two thousand men, so they out-number us two to one," Joldir said, his voice calm. "The only way we can win this is to cut off the head of the snake."

Yngvarr glanced behind them, to where Petr's men were moving into position to block Djuri's advance. There was no retreat for the Brotherhood. He gripped his sword firmly and took a deep breath. The only way was forwards, into the heart of the enemy.

"Sounds like a good plan to me," he said. "Svan's right. Let's get on with it."

"Isn't he making this rather easy?" Joldir asked, nodding towards the advancing army. "His standard there at the very front, marking him out. Why do that? Why take the risk?"

Johan shook his head. "I don't know. What I do know is if we wait here then the time Petr buys us will be for nothing. We have to strike now."

Johan rose up in his saddle, lifting his sword high into the air – a new weapon etched with six runes, which Joldir had forged to enable him to fight the durath on horseback. Yngvarr was relieved to see that none of them glowed blue, though if he felt safe now it was only for a moment. Sinarr's army advanced upon them remorselessly.

"Men of Reavesburg. Men of the Brotherhood. Our time has come. Carve me a path to Sinarr the Cold One, so we can end this. Fight with me now, to show Adalrikr that he has no claim to call himself King of the North, for we defy him. We will not be ruled by the Vorund Clan, not now and not ever!"

A roar erupted from the mass of warriors surrounding Johan and Yngvarr joined them, enjoying the feeling of release as he gave vent to his battle cry. Pride swelled in his chest as he looked at Johan, remembering everything they had been through to reach this point. This was their moment, he could feel it.

"This day will live long in Reavesburg's history," he told himself. "The bards will sing about the Battle of Romsdahl for years to come, and I'm a part of it."

He gave his courser the spurs and as one Johan's army began to advance towards Sinarr's warriors.

# CHAPTER 43

Svafa was breathing hard. Even at walking pace it was tiring crossing the ground separating their lines from the Vorund Clan whilst wearing full armour, carrying a shield in one hand and holding a siege ladder in the other, despite sharing the load with his fellow warriors. His nose ached where that bald bastard, Myr, had broken it in the training circle a couple of days ago. He grimaced, spying the warrior just to his left, loping towards the palisade with a hungry grin on his face, holding the two-handed sword he carried with confidence. He was flanked by Skari and the rest of Ulfarr's crew. Svafa didn't trust them and hadn't forgotten how Myr had embarrassed him in front of all his friends. Well, there'd be a reckoning soon enough. He'd get even with Myr and the rest of them, assuming they lived through this.

The air thrummed and Svafa ducked instinctively but when he glanced upwards he saw the flight of the arrows were heading towards Vorund's warriors. Sigdan's archers were trying to protect them, attacking the enemy and giving Haki's men a little more time to reach the palisade. There were shouts from the wooden walls and a few arrows let fly in return, their aim wayward.

"Come on!" bellowed Haki from a few rows behind. "Keep moving."

The ground was pitted and uneven and Svafa caught his foot in a tussock of grass, half stumbling forwards, shield knocking into the man next to him, who snarled and shoved him back. Gasping, Svafa caught himself before he pitched over onto his face, avoiding being trampled by the press of warriors as they picked up their pace and the wooden walls drew nearer.

By the age of eighteen Svafa had already fought the Vorund Clan during two raids, one led by Audwin Strongshield and the second by Haki. He thought he had the measure of their enemy until the day the blockade appeared on the Redfars Sea a year and a half ago. The size of Joarr's army had been a shock, that feeling turning to despair following Sinarr the Cold One's arrival last year when it dawned on people there would be no swift end to the siege. Svafa hated the watching and waiting as their enemy remained camped outside their walls for month after month. Worse than that, he'd been afraid; unable to imagine how they could defeat such a large host. Johan Jokellsward's men had given them hope and a chance to end this, one way or the other. He gripped his shield and jogged onwards, the fear of waiting replaced with a sense of release and purpose as the palisade wall drew nearer.

Another rush of arrows overhead, a dark cloud that cleared the wall and fell within the defensive circle. Svafa heard screams, not just from the Vorund Clan but also from the walls themselves. He realised with a jolt that some of Audwin's captured men were still alive as they hung from the walls, yelling incoherently. As he watched another wave of arrows hit, some striking the crucified prisoners, at least one of those men suddenly sagging, falling limp and silent as the shaft pierced his chest. Svafa felt a cold rage settling in his stomach and he began yelling his own battle cry.

*\*\**

"Third line, let fly," cried Sigdan, a large man with a distinctive bushy moustache that extended an inch beyond his ears.

Ulfarr picked another arrow from his quiver as the air thrummed around him and a cloud of deadly feathered shafts flew into the air. Already the men in the first row were drawing back their bows, taking aim.

"First row, let fly."

The two hundred archers in Sigdan's company were divided into three rows, each one drawing, aiming and then releasing their arrows in turn. The tactics ensured the Vorund Clan came under sustained attack, disrupting them from their defence of the wall as Haki's men rushed to towards it.

"Second row, let fly."

Ulfarr released his bow, watching the arrow sail high into the air with the others, quickly becoming indiscernible from the rest as they arched over Haki's company. There was a creak of bowstrings as the third row behind him prepared to shoot again. Ulfarr watched in dismay as a couple of their shafts dropped short of the intended target, landing amongst Haki's men. He drew in a sharp breath through his teeth and picked another arrow, fingers running through the fletching.

"Keep your aim true," bellowed Sigdan, moustache bristling. "Make every arrow count or you'll be answering to me when this is over. Third row, now."

Ulfarr drew back on his bow, muscles already aching, and took aim.

***

Djuri watched as Petr Hamarrson deployed his small force efficiently across the road, blocking their approach to the camp beyond on the hill, where the assortment of carts and wagons had been drawn into a large defensive circle. A unit of archers, perhaps a hundred in total, broke off to take to slightly higher ground to the west of the road. Djuri raised his arm towards Radholf, who nodded and began barking orders. Archers from Olt began to take up their own positions.

Djuri had met Petr once in Ulfkell's Keep four years ago, when he had accompanied Johan and Rugga on one of their visits from Kalamar to see Kolfinnar. He'd heard about Petr's rise since then to become Johan's second in the Brotherhood. It didn't surprise Djuri at all; despite his youth Petr was intelligent, knew his craft and commanded the respect of his men. Djuri had to admire his opponents. There was no panic in their ranks as they faced his larger force, each man taking up his position and staring straight at them, waiting silently for battle. Distant cries drifted up from Romsdahl, where Gautarr's warriors were mounting their attack against the palisade. Djuri watched as Johan's army continued to advance towards the wave of men spilling from the outer palisade walls, Sinarr at their head.

"Come on," hissed Haarl through gritted teeth. "Give the order."

Djuri shook his head. "Not yet. We wait until Johan and Sinarr are engaged. Last thing we want are for the Brotherhood to turn around and come back at us before we're finished here."

\*\*\*

The rain of arrows from Sigdan's men continued to fall relentlessly on Vorund's defenders but they had now managed to organise themselves. Archers were taking up positions at slits in the walls and had begun loosing arrows into Haki's men. One thudded into Svafa's shield, jarring his arm. He offered up a prayer of thanks to Dinuvillan and kept on running towards the palisade. They were nearly there now, just the ditch to negotiate.

"Bridge that gap," shouted Haki, and Svafa watched as a group of men burst into the lead, shields raised in one arm and carrying long planks of timber between them with the other.

He recognised Tomas among the group and shouted his encouragement as they continued their advance, more arrows finding their mark in their ranks. The men tasked with bridging the ditch raised their planks into the air while others tried to protect them with a wall of shields. The arrows of the defenders switched their focus, now concentrating on that shield wall. Domarr was leading the advance party and roared at his men, who dropped the first plank across the ditch with a crash. A second and then a third plank were raised, during which one of the men was knocked forwards, dropping with a short-lived scream onto the sharpened wooden stakes at the bottom of the ditch.

"Drop those timbers, come on!" Domarr called out, watching as both upraised planks crashed into place and were pressed together. Three more timbers were raised as the hail of arrows intensified, men in the shield wall dropping to the ground one by one.

Another cloud of arrows passed overhead from Sigdan's archers and Svafa knew that was the last wave. They were too close to the palisade now to avoid being hit by their own side. The three final planks dropped to the ground to a ragged cheer – the makeshift bridge was now complete. Domarr led the survivors of his advance party over to the other side, arrows skittering from shields and sending several more men over the edge of the bridge and onto the stakes below.

"That looks awful narrow," Skari shouted to Bandor.

"Best not think about it," Bandor replied.

"Doesn't look much better on the other side."

"Don't think about that, either."

"Ladders," Haki called, and Svafa moved forwards, ready to play his part as he surged towards the bridge with his fellows, hurrying to bring the ladders up to the walls.

Skari's words stayed with him as the bridge drew closer, narrowing all the time. He took a breath, felt another arrow slam into his shield, although this one skittered off harmlessly. On his other side the warrior next to him gasped as an arrow sprouted from this throat, buried right up to the fletching. He fell away and the reminder of the group swayed under the weight of the ladder just as they reached the bridge. Svafa's eyes opened wide as they careered towards the edge, the wooden bridge already pitted with arrows and littered with bodies. Pulling with all his might, together with his fellows, they hauled themselves back into the centre.

*Over halfway – nearly there* Svafa thought as he stumbled over another body. Ahead he could see Domarr's warriors, shields raised above their heads, shouting encouragement. An arrowhead burst out of the back of the man directly in front of Svafa, showering him in blood. He was too surprised to think about what he had just seen, hurdling his late companion as his feet touched the packed earth on the other side of the ditch.

Men were screaming on all sides and the ground was already stained with blood.

Domarr's crew parted, allowing Svafa and his companions to rush up to the wall, struggling to raise the heavy wooden ladder up. In the corner his eye he could see other ladders being hauled across the bridge, men starting to raise those too. There was a thundering sound, interspersed with screams and shouts of pain, as Haki's warriors began to surge over the makeshift bridge.

Everything centred upon taking the gate – Svafa watched his ladder slam into place against the palisade wall, knowing that being at the front of this attack was not the best place to be. He took a breath to steady his nerves and found himself next to Tomas, who turned to him with a wild gleam in his eyes, face already specked with blood.

"I'm with you, let's go," he cried, before clambering up the first steps on the ladder. Svafa took another deep breath and followed him.

*** 

Ulfarr watched as the final wave of arrows was loosed and arced over the walls. Haki's men were too close now and he lowered his bow, back and arms aching.

"Hold," Sigdan called out. "Stow your gear and let's move out. We need to help protect the chief's horsemen when it's time for them to join the attack."

Ulfarr glanced towards the bridge and gate beyond in the palisade wall, watching as Haki's men swarmed across, ladders being raised and falling into place. He could hear the sounds of battle clearly and wondered how Skari and the rest of his crew were faring. *No sense in worrying about it now,* he told himself. *Just need to play your part and let them do theirs and we'll see where everything stands when all this is over.*

Shouts within their ranks stirred him from his thoughts. A couple of men stumbled and fell as arrows landed amongst them. Ulfarr had already strapped on his shield before they began to move and raised it now, hearing arrows clang against it.

Sigdan looked outraged as they came under attack. "Bastards! Keep moving, we still need to get into position."

Ulfarr didn't like it; running *towards* the enemy and not having the chance to fight back. He was more for skirmishing than full on war, he decided. Bit late, of course, to realise that particular fact – he knew what he had signed up for when he first joined Johan's Brotherhood. Still –

Sigdan staggered, an arrow protruding from his chest, blood sprouting from the wound. His wide eyes met with Ulfarr's and he opened his mouth but no words came out, just a hoarse bubbling wheeze, before he fell flat on his face, blood spreading out thickly below his corpse. A shocked groan rippled out amongst his company as people realised what had just happened and their advance stuttered to a halt.

"Sigdan's fallen," cried one of the archers nearby, dropping to his knees and turning his commander over. Sigdan's eyes were fixed, staring lifelessly back at him as more arrows found their mark up and down the ranks of his company, bringing more men down, injured or dying.

Ulfarr could see the panic growing in the men's eyes as they looked at each other, their resolve wavering. *Myshall's bane, this lot are about to break.*

He raised his voice and called out to them, pointing towards the palisade. "We can't just stand stock still while they pick us off. Moving target's harder to hit, so stop gaping and follow your orders. We're here to fight for your home, so let's get on with it. Everyone, with me."

The men turned to look in his direction. *But which way are they going to go?* To his surprise they followed his lead, falling into line once more and heading on, crouching low to evade more arrows as they ran towards the Vorund Clan's defences.

*Nicely done, Ulfarr. You could have been retreated towards the safety of Romsdahl's walls just then but no, you found a way to make sure you kept marching towards the enemy. I can hear*

*Skari's voice already …*

# CHAPTER 44

I blinked, squinting in the early morning sun as I stared across the distance from Romsdahl to the palisade. My hands clutched at the stonework, bent into white-knuckled claws, and it was an effort to release my grip. Around me I could hear people discussing in anxious tones how the battle was going as they watched Haki's men press forwards and swarm around the gates. Down below Sigdan's – no – *Ulfarr's* company of archers was also advancing while the five hundred mounted warriors led by Gautarr watched proceedings from just outside the walls.

"They're climbing the palisade," Asta said, hands clasped tightly under her arms as she hugged herself.

"This is it," added Karlin. "They have to take the gate and quickly. If they're repelled then we won't have a chance of joining with Johan's forces."

Jora tutted. "My eyes aren't what they used to be. What's happening on the other side? Has Johan reached the outer wall yet?"

Karlin leaned over the battlements, peering into the distance. "It's hard to say, my lady. There seems to be a huge force beyond the outer palisade, much larger than we were led to believe. Perhaps Johan has been able to call more warriors to his banner during his journey south."

I grimaced. "You're looking at two armies facing each other. Sinarr has chosen to face Johan on the field."

"What nonsense," Jora snapped. "The Vorund Clan have hidden behind those walls for eighteen months. They're not likely to come out from them now – look at how Haki's men are having to fight to prise the gate open."

"No, he's right," Freydja corrected her. "Look closely. There are two separate forces beyond the wall, moving in opposite directions towards each other."

Karlin frowned. "He *is* right. That's not what I expected at all. They should just have allowed Johan's army to attack and break his strength against their walls."

"Hmm." Jora pursed her lips, giving me a sideways glance as she leant in closer to Karlin. "Well, they've made their first mistake and Johan will punish them for their arrogance."

The noise around me faded, Freydja becoming translucent before she vanished in front of my eyes. The weeping warrior stood with me, the two of us alone upon the battlements.

"What's happening? Who *are* you?" I asked, staggering slightly, disorientated with the change of scene.

The warrior stared at me, unmoving though the faint sound of crying reached me, from far off, from another place and time. With the sun behind him, his eyes were dark shadows, from which poured a stream of blood down each cheek. He was tall and strong, the tattoo of the black bear standing out on his bare chest. He gestured to the marking.

"I was so proud when I earned this. I was just eighteen when Asmarr honoured me and I became one of his bodyguards. I was younger even than your friend Thengill, receiving the honour a year before he was chosen, a fact which always riled him." The warrior chuckled, though it was a flat, humourless sound. "So long ago. So far away."

"Who are you?" I pressed.

The man summoned a cloak of shadow and wrapped himself in it, shards of dark coalescing around him until he was dressed for battle in black chainmail. "I suppose I've changed, though not for the better. Magic draws the worlds close and Sinarr the Cold One uses it to gain power in order to destroy your friends. What he doesn't understand is he's opened the door to me as well. I can help you."

I reached down to my sword and drew it, runes glimmering blue, flickering then fading away. I frowned, wondering what that could mean, then levelled the blade at the cloaked stranger.

"I won't ask you again. Tell me your name and who you are. Then I'll decide if I want help from you."

"My name was stolen, along with my life."

"What kind of an answer is that?" I stared at the face, fighting against my natural revulsion, trying to look past the blood. His face was familiar – I *had* seen it somewhere before.

"You asked who I am. I am a shade, trapped between the world of the living and the dead, unable to journey on to Navan's Halls until Adalrikr's treachery is avenged, though in truth the young man is as much the victim as I was. I should use Adalrikr's true name; Vashtas, Flayer of Souls, leader of the durath during the War of the Avatars, the first of the Sundered who swore service to Morvanos. Vashtas took everything I was and destroyed it, consuming me utterly, using me to get close to Adalrikr before he shed my skin and took possession of him.

"Yet afterwards some vestige of the man I once was remained. Bound to Vashtas forever, the fading remnant of his previous host. Even as a mere shadow of Vashtas this creature was a powerful servant. Adalrikr raised him up to become one of his jarls as he began to forge a new kingdom."

My sword felt heavy, forcing me to lower it slightly and relax my aching arm. "You're *Sinarr*?" I asked, slowly comprehending what the shade was telling me.

The warrior nodded. "My name was stolen, along with my life. Now I am the Weeping Warrior. I seek to redress the balance, if you'll help me."

\*\*\*

Randall held Sinarr the Cold One's banner aloft as Vorund's warriors advanced. That part of this plan bothered him as they drew closer to Johan's army, a mixture of archers, mounted warriors and infantry who were all looking fixedly in his direction. Sinarr was at the head of his army, walking on foot rather than accepting the use of a mount, though Randall suspected no animal would tolerate being near him. Even his own men were keeping their distance, spread out around their leader in a semi-circle, several steps behind. He couldn't blame them. For one thing, Sinarr was radiating cold, his footsteps leaving a trail of frost on the ground with every step. Worse still, in the dawn light Sinarr's deathly, diseased pallor had caused several of his men to baulk at the sight of him. The stench of death hung in the air, clinging to the standard Randall carried, his knees and back protesting at its weight.

*I'm getting too old for this,* thought Randall. *But I don't think Sinarr has any intention of letting me go and find a quiet farmstead somewhere far away from here for the remainder of my years. Not until Johan and the rest of the Brotherhood following the Landless Jarl are put in their graves, and maybe not even then. How have I landed myself here?* What *have I landed myself in?*

Sinarr held up his hand and the drummer ceased his beat, the thousands of warriors at his back stopping their march a moment later. Randall glanced up and saw crows circling overhead, cawing to one another. *They know what's coming.*

Sinarr turned to him. "Plant your standard here. This is where we make our stand."

Randall did as he was told, glad to be rid of the thing. He unslung his shield and drew his sword, both more comfortable, familiar weights that his body was well used to carrying. Sinarr stepped forwards, addressing himself to Johan's men in a voice so loud Randall wouldn't have been surprised if it had carried all the way back to Romsdahl itself.

"Welcome, Johan Jokellsward. You have vexed my king for many months and he has ordered me to destroy you and all your followers. I intend to carry out those orders with honour, fighting you in the field rather than behind the miserable walls that have been my home for so long. You have refused to be bowed, even when your chief was killed and his jarls scattered, choosing to fight on even though the cause was hopeless. You did not give up your fight even after I shattered your stronghold and killed the people of Kalamar. Many would have bent the knee after that and there would have been no shame in it. Not you. Even when you became the Landless Jarl you fought on, never wavering in your resolve as you led your uprising and brought your people here.

"You have done well, come much further than many would have predicted. I have been watching you and knew it would always end here. So determined were you to see this through, to have your day and exact your vengeance that you have led everyone you love here to die. And die they will, because you refused to see reason and accept the offer of friendship that King Adalrikr extended to you. Your people died at Kalamar. Your Brotherhood will end its days at Romsdahl."

Sinarr reached behind his shoulder and drew his sword, raising it into the air, where it glinted in the light of the sun. Randall saw frost spreading along its length from the hilt.

"I am waiting."

***

"This is a trap," Joldir announced calmly. Yngvarr was inclined to agree as he stared down at Sinarr, waiting for them – isolated and alone, separated from his host as he invited them to advance on him. It was either a trap or Sinarr the Cold One was insane – Yngvarr reflected that both possibilities could be correct.

"And now we're here what do you suggest?" Johan replied, his eyes fixed on Sinarr.

"Not walking into the trap?"

Johan laughed, shaking his head. "It's wise counsel, Joldir, but we're faced with a set of poor choices. Retreat isn't an option and, outnumbered as we are, I'd rather we charged the enemy than wait until they attack us."

"Johan's right," added Svan. "I'm done with him goading us. The plan was to take off his head, right? I'm not seeing or hearing anything to persuade me that's not still the right plan. We've got a perfect chance to strike at Sinarr, so let's not squander it."

Jolinn blew out long and hard, Lars sitting on his horse next to her looking pale as he took in the size of the army they were facing. She rested her hand on the well-worn pommel of her sword. "I can't say what it is, but something's wrong. I'm more worried about that than I am about the fact we're outnumbered. He wants you to attack him, Johan, and that makes this dangerous."

Johan looked at her. "I asked you to be my shieldmaiden. Are you saying that you're no longer with me?"

Jolinn's bright blue eyes flashed and her face darkened for a moment. "I've given up everything to follow you, like most of the people here. I'm just telling you what I think – that there's something wrong here. Really wrong, and I don't like it. Tell me you don't feel the same way."

Johan shook his head. "You're right, but we're trapped. If I'm going to face death it'll be on my own terms, leading the attack right at Sinarr. We have magic of our own that will thwart his plans."

"Give the order, chief," Svan said, his horse picking up on his enthusiasm and skittering excitedly. He hefted his axe into his hand and looked at Johan expectantly.

Johan looked around at his company, meeting everyone's eye in turn. "Are you with me?" he asked eventually.

"Aye," Yngvarr found himself saying. "Aye, chief. It's time. No more running."

The others all gave similar responses, each with more conviction than the last. Jolinn looked at Lars, who shrugged. "You're right, Jolinn, but this plan of ours is still our best chance. We have to try."

"Not a ringing endorsement, perhaps," Jolinn said to Johan with a smile, a rare sight that softened her features. "Still, he's right. Let's give Sinarr what he wants and maybe he'll get more than he bargained for."

Johan raised his sword, meeting Sinarr's challenge. "Then let's ride. Charge!"

# CHAPTER 45

Svafa fought back-to-back with Tomas, grunting as he blocked another attack with his shield, stabbing with his sword, trying to find an opening. His opponent anticipated the move, returning it with interest, forcing him back, his feet slipping on the blood-stained ground beside the palisade wall. There was a blur and the head of the warrior he was fighting snapped to one side, neck broken, and he slumped to the floor in a boneless heap. Skari gave a roar, raising his warhammer high in the air, using the momentum of his attack to strike at another Vorund warrior, driving him backwards into the wall, where he buried the hammer in his throat.

Svafa was glad they were fighting on the same side – he'd seen Skari account for six men already and he suspected the true number was twice that. Tomas gutted the man he was fighting with a cry and Svafa took the chance to catch his breath, glancing around him. They were fighting on the other side of the wall, within the Vorund Clan's defensive enclosure, with more warriors climbing over the palisade every moment using the ladders. Svafa saw Patrick leading a group of men as they pounded at a number of the stakes making up the wall, several already lying uprooted on the floor, widening the gap and allowing more of Haki's men to burst through. Nearby, next to the larger defensive structure surrounding the gates, which included two watchtowers, Haki himself was fighting with Domarr, trying to force the main gate open.

"With me," Tomas shouted, charging towards Haki and Domarr. The young man seemed to be possessed with a rage as he fought that amazed Svafa, who could see nothing of the coward Haki liked to mention at every opportunity.

He took a step to follow Tomas, only to find his path was blocked by two more Vorund warriors – a skinny young man with a few wisps of beard on his chin and an older warrior with a white scar on his cheek and half an ear. The skinny man jabbed at Svafa with a spear, pressing him back and Half-Ear stepped in closer, striking hard with his axe, the blows raining down on his shield in quick succession. Svafa gripped the strap with all his might, his arm numbed by the jarring impact. He struggled to move into freer space but the skinny man hemmed him in, forcing him to parry those attacks with his sword. He blinked, breath catching in his chest, limbs tiring, then his shield was gone, hooked away by the half-eared axeman, leaving him clutching the useless brown leather strap.

"Yes!" roared Domarr nearby as the gates swung open, men pulling them back to allow a surging tide of screaming warriors through to join the fray.

Half-Ear turned at the noise and Svafa punched him in the side of the head, his hand still holding the strap. The man grunted and went down on one knee but then the skinny man was back, driving his spear at Svafa, the point narrowly missing his ribs. Svafa stepped in close as the man's strike carried him forwards and head-butted him squarely in the face, dropping him to the ground as he clutched at his broken nose. Seeing stars, Svafa shook his head, took hold of his sword with both hands and drove it down through the skinny man's throat, killing him in a shower of blood. Svafa gasped, tugging at the blade, unable to free it from the man's corpse as Half-Ear got back on his feet, eyes narrowed, the scar rippling across his face. Svafa's hands were slick with blood as he reached for his knife, cursing as he fumbled it and watched it tumble away to land at his feet.

Half-Ear grinned, stepped forwards and raised his axe above his head. There was a crunch and Svafa gasped as his face was sprayed with bloody gore, the tip of a sword point bursting from Half-Ear's chest. The axe fell from nerveless fingers and Half-Ear collapsed. Behind him stood Myr the Silent, holding his bloody two-handed sword. He nodded to the skinny warrior with a grin and tapped his bald head with a leather-gloved finger.

"With us, lad," said Bandor next to him. "Don't get separated again or you won't last long."

Svafa frowned as he retrieved his knife and pulled his sword free. He was older than Bandor, but the jarl's son was so confident, looking comfortable and relaxed in the midst of the battle, which was now turning in their favour, more and more Romsdahl warriors arriving and pressing back their foes, buying Svafa a moment's respite.

"Thank you," he gasped, glancing around for Tomas. There was no sign of him in the throng.

***

Arrows flew through the air from either side, thudding into the ground, hitting shields or striking flesh. Djuri watched as the company of archers led by the greybeard took cover in a field behind a stone wall as another wave of arrows from Olt's bowmen flew at them to little effect. Petr had chosen the ground for this battle well, the road rising up at this point where his band of warriors stood waiting for the attack, calm as you like.

The greybeard's men rose up from behind the wall and loosed more arrows, a thick cloud striking into the heart of their cavalry this time. Horses screamed when they were struck, bucking and pitching their riders from their saddles, well-ordered lines bending and breaking. Haarl swore, steadying his own mount with a whisper and a pat on her neck.

In the distance Johan's army finally began their charge towards Sinarr. Djuri smiled and signalled the advance. "It's time. Ride them down," he shouted, spurring his own horse forwards.

***

Yngvarr bent low in the saddle, following Johan's lead as their horsemen charged towards the circle where Sinarr was waiting. He could hear the battle cries of the warriors on foot run-

317

ning behind them. Overhead, Faraldr's archers loosed the first volley of arrows at their foes, landing amongst Sinarr's lines, several men dropping to the muddy earth. He gritted his teeth, clutched his sword tightly in one hand, keeping his shield up with the other. In front of him Sinarr the Cold One stood, arms outstretched, sword in hand, oblivious to the arrows raining down all around him.

*** 

Randall swallowed as he watched the huge wedge of horse-flesh, armour and blades break from the main ranks of Johan's army and pound towards his position. He thought he could see long flowing red hair streaming out behind their leader – Johan Jokellsward himself. The horsemen were aiming straight for Sinarr.

An arrow thudded into the ground, right next to him. Randall shifted slightly to one side, watching with alarm as a second arrow struck where his foot had been moments before. With a curse he raised his shield, crouching down to make himself as small a target as possible. *Standing by the bloody standard probably isn't the wisest move you've ever made.*

Sinarr looked around at the circle of warriors behind him as Johan's charge bore down. "To me."

Several men stepped forwards at those words, dropping their shields and weapons as they did so. Randall frowned, completely confused, as he watched a dozen now unarmed warriors fan out in front of Sinarr, forming a loose defensive arc as they hunkered down, all staring straight ahead at the galloping horses now little more than a hundred yards away. No one else from Sinarr's ranks moved or made any effort to close the gap and protect their leader, instead standing there transfixed. Randall knew what he should do. Sinarr was Adalrikr's jarl and he'd been under his command for years. He took a step but Sinarr turned and looked right at him with those clouded eyes, shaking his head.

"Hold the rest of them back and let Johan come to me. It's time."

\*\*\*

"What's that sound?" asked Skari, grinning evilly as he approached the rest of his crew and patted Myr on the shoulder. Svafa cocked his head, straining to listen amongst the din.

"Horses," said Patrick, craning his neck to see more clearly.

"We're being charged," Haki shouted, waving his arms and pointing in the direction of the sound, which Svafa could hear clearly now. A rhythmic beat of hooves on the earth, sending a tremor through the ground that he could feel through his boots.

"Form up," called Domarr. "Spears to the front, form a line, three men deep. Hurry up."

"Come on, they're almost –" Haki's words were cut off by a wet squelch and where his blond head had been just a moment ago there was now a large blood splattered rock, which tottered between his shoulders briefly before rolling onto the ground. Haki's body stood on its feet a moment longer before dropping with a crash. His men fell silent and only the drumming of hooves could be heard.

Svafa glanced up, seeing a man raising another rock to hurl into the packed throng of warriors pressed together as they continued to squeeze through the gates. An arrow struck him from behind and he tottered back, still clutching the rock, before vanishing from sight with a cry.

"Hold steady," shouted Domarr. "Get in line."

Men hurried forwards, struggling to get into position as they pointed their spears at a large group of mounted warriors, led by a blond bearded man wielding a warhammer, who were now charging them at full speed.

"Take them down," cried their attacker as the warhorses broke upon the still forming spear wall with a noise like a thunderclap. Some of the beasts were skewered, brought down shrieking and flailing, riders tumbling in all directions as the charge broke through, Vorund's cavalry trampling men underfoot as they drove into the middle of the Romsdahl advance.

Their chief laid about with his warhammer, breaking bones and crushing skulls in a frenzy before his men closed ranks around him. In the corner of his eye Svafa saw movement as Tomas ran straight at the circle of horsemen, aiming for the blond man with the warhammer.

"It's Joarr the Hammer," he shouted, barging past other Romsdahl warriors as he pressed forwards. "Kill him. Bring down Adalrikr's jarl."

"Better help him out," said Skari, hefting his own warhammer in his hand and setting off after him. After a moment's hesitation Svafa followed.

***

Ulfarr smiled with satisfaction as his arrow dropped the warrior hiding in the watchtower and a few of the men now under his commanded muttered their appreciation. The gates were open and most of Haki's warriors were through. Ulfarr glanced behind him and saw that Gautarr's mounted force had broken into a swift trot as they approached the palisade.

"This way," Ulfarr called, leading his men over the bridge, which was down to four long planks, the others having dropped into the ditch. Bodies were piled high on either side, arrows sticking out from some, others impaled on the wicked sharpened stakes below, a few unfortunates writhing in agony as they bled to death.

He glanced up at the prisoners nailed to the walls, seeing with dismay that those nearby were all dead, stuck through with arrows that he guessed had been loosed by his own company. He looked down at his feet, making sure he didn't lose his footing on the bridge, which swayed with each step. *They were dead anyway. They just hadn't stopped breathing – you did them a mercy, that's all.*

Head down, he hurried through the gap in the palisade wall with the rest of his company, the noise of battle rising up to greet him as he stepped inside.

# CHAPTER 46

Svan was the first to reach the thin line of warriors protecting Sinarr. Either side of them, the rest of Johan's cavalry smashed into Sinarr's lines, either forcing them back or ending their days on the point of a spear or a pike. Yngvarr knew he couldn't help them until the task in front of him was done. He raised his sword, noticing for the first time that the three runes Joldir had etched into it were glowing bright blue.

There was no time to shout a warning. The nearest warrior sprang at Svan with a snarl, wrapping his arms around his horse's neck, biting at the animal and bearing it to the ground. Yngvarr had no time to watch, focusing on the warrior nearest him, who uttered a keening wail and leapt feet into the air, teeth bared. Yngvarr swung his sword and cut through the man in mid-air, separating his head from his shoulders. A shower of ice rather than blood hailed down on him, causing his horse to rear. Momentarily blinded, Yngvarr struggled to stay upright, gasping as he heard more shrieks from the durath surrounding him.

There was a crash as the rest of Johan's shieldmen ploughed into the battle, which Yngvarr heard and felt rather than saw. He shook his head, blinking to clear his sight, just in time to smash one of the durath in the face with his shield as he attacked. Nearby Johan took one of the warriors down with a flick of his sword, a rune dimming on the blade as the shadow spirit disintegrated into a shower of ice shards. Jolinn and Lars guarded his flank, Joldir the rear, all fighting fiercely and Yngvarr rode to their side, cursing as one of the durath danced away from his sword swing, cackling and running away on all fours. Ragni went down, his throat bitten out by a young

321

man whose handsome features were twisted into a feral snarl, blood running down his chin. Moments later Geirmundi, the youngest of the Flint cousins, drove his sword into the creature's throat, leaving it thrashing on the ground as its lifeblood bled out, transforming into water ice before its body froze and shattered.

Sinarr the Cold One stepped forwards, striking at Geirmarr Flint with his huge sword, which Delving's elder just managed to parry. The durath sprang upon him from all sides, dragging him from his horse, biting at him, sending his sword spinning from his grasp. Johan spurred his horse forwards, drawing the rest of the Brotherhood with him as they sped to Geirmarr's aid, his cousin screaming as he cut down another of the durath blocking their path. Sinarr reached down, taking hold of Geirmarr's neck in a mottled fist, lifting him high into the air as the durath began to devour his terrified horse. Geirmarr beat feebly at his foe as Sinarr opened him up, his blade spilling his guts out onto the ground before he threw him straight at his attackers. Geirmarr's limp body took both Johan and Lars from their saddles, forcing Jolinn to turn her own mount to try and protect them as the durath swarmed forwards.

Yngvarr pressed on towards Sinarr but Geirmundi reached him first, swinging his sword left and right in a savage fury. Sinarr's blade whistled round and would have taken Geirmundi's head except Joldir was there, his own sword blocking the blow, runes blazing blue-white. Seconds later Joldir's sword shattered with a deafening ring, some of the shards burying themselves in Sinarr's face. He bellowed, slamming his fist into the skull of Joldir's horse, killing the animal outright and bringing Joldir down with a cry.

Yngvarr rounded Sinarr and struck at his back, his sword sparking off the jarl's dark armour. He swung again and then Sinarr's sword swept round, cutting his horse's legs out from under him, sending him slamming into the ground and half-spilling him from the saddle. He fought to free one of his feet from the stirrups as his dying steed shrieked and writhed underneath him.

Geirmundi struck again while Sinarr's back was turned, thrusting his sword through a gap in the warrior's armour, causing him to cry out. The last of the runes on his weapon blazed and went dull as Geirmundi forced his blade further, pushing it into Sinarr's heart. The huge warrior turned with such speed it ripped the sword from Geirmundi's grasp. He stared wide-eyed as Sinarr swung his great sword, splitting him in two at the waist. His horse panicked, galloping off with his legs still firmly set in the saddle as the rest of his body fell to the ground in a great gout of blood. Sinarr turned and looked straight at Yngvarr, whose horse had already died, leaving him pinned with one foot still entangled in a stirrup.

*Not so like the legends, then.* Yngvarr frantically strained against the weight, trying to push the horse's corpse away without success as Sinarr strode towards him. Joldir was nearest, now on his feet with his runestaff in both hands, but he was busy fighting two of the durath and they were pressing him back.

Jolinn's sword struck Sinarr's hip, the momentum from her mounted charge bowling him clean over. The speed of her horse carried her away from the fight as she rode in a wide circle, cutting down a shadow spirit that dived at her, the last of the runes on her blade dimming as it died, falling away in a cascade of tinkling crystals. Her horse slowed and she looked on from the edge of the circle, unsure what to do now the power of her runeblade was exhausted.

No blood flowed from the wounds to Sinarr's side and chest, where Geirmundi's sword was still buried. Regaining his feet he reached behind him and, with a grunt, pulled out the blade from his back and tossed it away. In front of him Johan and Lars approached warily on foot, swords held out in front of them, runes glowing. Johan had now drawn his two-handed sword, its six runes blazing so brightly Yngvarr could hardly look at them. Again he pushed with all his might, trying to roll away his horse far enough to free his stubbornly trapped foot.

"So, this is what it feels to be alive," rasped Sinarr, leering at Johan and Lars.

He reached out and pulled one of the shards of Joldir's broken blade from his face, letting it fly with a flick of his wrist. The piece of metal struck deep into Lars' thigh and he gasped in pain, clutching the wound. There was a scream nearby as Joldir shattered the last of the durath, runestaff quivering in his hands with the force of the blow. He began to sprint towards Sinarr and at the same moment Jolinn charged again, this time with Ragni's sword in her hands. Sinarr crouched low, parrying Jolinn's swing and shoulder-charging her mount, knocking down her horse with a bone-crunching noise. Johan was on him then, sword whirling in his hands, drawing a series of parries and counter-attacks from Sinarr as he fended both him and Joldir off. Jolinn regained her feet only for Sinarr to catch her on the temple with the hilt of his sword, leaving her sprawled on the ground. Lars shouted out her name as he limped into the fight.

Yngvarr heard footsteps and turned to see the white-haired standard bearer walking calmly towards him, shield up and sword drawn. Yngvarr tried to twist on the ground and raise his sword but the older man knocked it from his grasp with a swift kick, breaking at least two of his fingers.

"Sorry, lad."

Yngvarr closed his eyes moments before the older man brought his sword down on his neck.

\*\*\*

Ulfarr's company loosed arrow after arrow into the flanks of the enemy as they tried to encircle Haki's men, although there was no sign of Gautarr's second. Domarr the Oak now seemed to be giving the orders. Although they had got through the gate, more and more of Vorund's warriors were arriving at the scene of the battle and they were hemming the Romsdahl men in. Ulfarr let another arrow fly, taking down a mounted warrior, the shaft protruding from his throat. He drew another from his quiver. *Four left. Better make them count, and then its blade work.* He glanced around and saw the space around his bowmen being encroached upon, only their remaining arrows slowing down their attackers and not by much even then.

"Where are our horsemen?" shouted one of his men next to him.

"Stuck outside because they can't get through the gate," growled Ulfarr, killing another man, his arrow protruding from his chest. *Three left now,* he thought, running his hand over the feathers on the next shaft he drew out and nocked to his bow. He let fly, bringing down another warrior, leaving him flailing on the ground with an arrow in his belly.

"There's too many of them – we're trapped," said the man next to him, his shoulders dropping as he lowered his bow.

"Shut up and keep sticking them with arrows as long as you can," snarled Ulfarr, watching as his next arrow missed the target. He cursed and pulled out his last.

***

Svafa had managed to pick up another shield and crouched behind it, fighting closely with Myr and Bandor on one side, Skari and Patrick on the other.

"Have to find a way to push out. Get Gautarr's men into the fight," called Bandor.

Svafa knew it was impossible, as the weight of numbers against them increased all the time. Joarr the Hammer, who had led the initial charge on horseback, had fallen back as more men on foot swarmed forwards but he continued to shout out orders. Svafa could also see a row of archers forming about fifty yards away.

"Look out," he yelled as the first volley hit, striking men all around them, including several of the Vorund Clan. The man Svafa had been fighting dropped to his knees, an arrow in the small of his back. Svafa smashed his sword into his face and pushed him away.

"They're killing their own men," Patrick cried, looking

horrified.

Svafa glanced at their own bowmen, who were drawing their swords as they were charged by Vorund's warriors.

"Fall back," growled Skari. "We can't win this."

Myr grunted as an arrow struck him in the shoulder, knocking him to the floor. Their attackers had re-grouped and surged forwards once more, Tomas stepping in front to protect Myr. Svafa joined him, working together to close the gap as the Vorund Clan pressed them on all sides.

"If we fall back I can't help my father," Bandor argued, bringing down another opponent with a perfectly executed combination of moves.

"You can't help him if you're dead," Skari replied as he shattered the skull of another man, his warhammer caked in blood and matted hair.

Patrick was helping Myr retreat when the arrow punched through his breastplate, taking him right above the heart. He stared down, looking completely surprised as blood began to well up from the wound. The second arrow struck him in the throat and he fell to the ground. Myr gave an inarticulate cry and dived forwards once more, swinging his sword even with the arrow still buried deep in his shoulder. Tomas took off the arm of one warrior who got too close and Svafa stabbed another, who dropped back wounded, only to be replaced by more of his fellows.

"Myr. Get back. All of you. Fall back, now," Skari shouted.

Reluctantly, Svafa began to retreat. He stepped over the still body of Patrick Wild and watched as he disappeared under the boots of the Vorund Clan, who advanced on them mercilessly as arrows continued to rain down from the sky.

# CHAPTER 47

Sinarr turned as Randall approached, his face ragged where the broken sword had torn through his flesh. There was no blood on his face or from the wound where one of Johan's warriors had driven his sword through Sinarr's back. Once, that would have struck Randall as odd. Within the circle the sounds of the battle were dim, muffled shouts; men and horses screaming, the clash of metal. Randall knew well war enough to understand something different was happening here. He shivered, feeling a chill on his skin. Quickly he looked around, gauging the number of remaining opponents now he'd dispatched the poor young warrior trapped under his horse. There were just three still on their feet. Randall recognised Johan Jokellsward with his flowing red hair, crouched low, his two-handed sword held out in front of him, breathing deeply. Next to him were two more warriors, one holding a staff that pulsed with magic, bright colours flowing up and down the length of its shaft. The other man was bleeding heavily from a wound in his thigh, favouring his uninjured leg as he turned towards Randall, sword and shield raised.

Randall looked over at the battle lines, where the fighting was fierce; each warrior engaged in their own savage contest, fighting for their lives. Johan's army was to hard-pressed and unable to come to the defence of their jarl. Randall took another step forward, noticing he was the only Vorund warrior coming to Sinarr's aid. Mind you, looking at the carnage around him, it didn't look like Sinarr needed much assistance.

"Randall," Sinarr's voice rasped, the dead sound falling flat in the circle.

No one moved, the only sound Johan's laboured breathing, his companions looking at Randall and Sinarr in turn, weighing each of them up, working out how to tackle this new opponent.

"Sinarr. Thought I'd lend you a hand."

Sinarr blinked, bloodshot eyes staring sightlessly at him. "Strange. You're the only one to approach. It takes a rare kind of courage to cross the circle when you have not been summoned."

"Well, I'm your standard bearer, after all. Didn't seem right, somehow, to fly the flag of the bear but leave my jarl to fight unaided."

Sinarr smiled, the gestured opening up the bloodless wounds on his ruined face, a sight from Randall's worst nightmares. "Why else?"

The question struck Randall hard, a blow he felt in his chest, the sensation settling in his guts, ice cold. "Why? Because ... I have to know. I *need* to know what's happening here, what this is all about. I need to know who you are."

"You already know who I am. You're just afraid to say it."

Randall licked his lips. "You're dead, though you still walk among the living in Amuran. How is that possible?"

"I'll take him," hissed the younger warrior with the injured leg, peeling off from Johan's side and moving towards Randall, the runes on his sword glowing bright blue. The warrior with the staff also began to move out wide, trying to get an angle to attack Sinarr's flank as Johan continued to face him.

Sinarr's horrific smile widened, revealing broken brown teeth in the side of his head. "The world is changing, Randall. Adalrikr serves a higher power as he unites the north, a power that draws on the old magic, from the Age of Glory. All things are possible."

"Not if you die at my hand," growled Johan, moving slowly, circling his opponent.

Sinarr turned to him. "How can you kill that which is already dead? Why do you think I drew you to me today? I mean to end the Brotherhood of the Eagle here on this battle-field. I mean to end your life, Jokellsward."

"We'll see who's right," cried Johan, stepping forwards and striking at Sinarr with a series of blows, steel moving in a bright blue arc that forced Sinarr backwards as he parried each attack. There was no time for Randall to watch any more as the limping warrior reached him.

"I'll have your head, old man," he said, sword striking out, swift and precise.

Randall blocked the blade, kept his shield high and set his shoulder behind it as he moved quickly forwards, using his weight to try and force the man off balance. The young warrior read the move, stepping aside though Randall saw him wince as he did so. He moved in again, offering his opponent no respite, sword strokes flowing without thinking as he executed the familiar moves he knew so well from years spent on the practice courts. There were plenty of young Vorund warriors who thought they could best Randall. They'd learned you didn't get to be a grey-bearded warrior without knowing your craft.

Randall could see the young man was tiring – blood flowing freely down his leg as he was forced to move left and then right to try and defend himself. Might be the lad would bleed out in time but that didn't stop him being deadly now, so Randall focussed on finishing the fight, trying to sweep his enemy's feet out from under him. The young man sprang back and staggered, gasping in pain, almost losing his footing. It was all the opportunity Randall needed as he struck out with his shield, forcing wide the shield of his foe and leaving his side unguarded. Randall's sword snaked forwards, the warrior half-parrying the attack just a fraction too late. Randall felt his blade scrape across the breastplate of the man before plunging into the yielding flesh of his throat. Hot blood pulsed from the wound and Randall whipped his sword away, dropping back and crouching behind his shield, still wary of the counter-attack.

The young warrior gasped, a choking bubbling sound, sinking to his knees, eyes wide. His sword dropped from his fingers and he pitched over onto his face, unmoving, blood spreading out over the frosted grass. Randall looked up to see Johan was continuing his attack, Sinarr's greatsword held lazily in one hand, fending off him off with little effort, the range of the weapon making it difficult for Johan to approach too closely. On the other side the warrior wielding the staff stepped in, trying to get close enough to land a telling blow. Sinarr swayed first one way then the other, evading the attack before his left hand stretched out, catching the staff as the warrior brought it down once more.

There was a flash of bright light, as if Sinarr's fist had closed around a bright star, the staff pulsing and vibrating in the Reavesburg warrior's hands. Sinarr's sword parried Johan's blade, pushing him backwards and sending him rolling away on the ground. Sinarr turned to the staff-wielding warrior, who was still struggling to free his weapon, flames dancing around his own hands.

"You thought *this* would be enough to end me?" mocked Sinarr, leering at his foe.

The colour drained from the man's face as Sinarr planted his sword in the ground and took hold of the staff with both hands. Even from a distance, Randall could feel heat emanating from the staff, saw flames licking up around Sinarr's fists as they gripped the wood. Sinarr yanked the staff free of the warrior's hands and, with a roar, broke the weapon in two across his knee.

There was a noise like a thunderclap, followed by a rushing wind and the Reavesburg warrior was blasted off his feet and thrown fifty feet through the air, landing with a sickening crash. Johan staggered and Randall also lost his footing, hiding his face behind his shield as he felt a hot wind whip around him. As the noise died down Randall dared to peer out from around the rim. Johan was back on his feet, sword held out in front of him in a two-handed grip, his face defiant. Randall had to admire that, after what he'd just seen. Sinarr advanced towards Johan unarmed, his sword left planted in the earth behind him. Johan swung his sword, a powerful two-handed stroke that buried itself deep in Sinarr's shoulder. The remaining runes on the blade flickered and went dark as Sinarr was pitched over onto his side, slamming into the ground with a crash, tearing Johan's sword from his grasp.

Randall began to move forwards again although he was too slow to reach Johan as he took up the sword dropped by the shieldmaiden, who lay sprawled out, unmoving, next to her horse. He raised the blade with a shaking hand as Sinarr pushed himself up onto his feet, his huge fist pulling out Johan's sword from his shoulder and tossing it aside as if it were a wooden toy. He looked straight at Johan and began to laugh.

***

I blinked as I found myself back on Romsdahl's wall, alone except for the Weeping Warrior. I could barely stand, the alternating visions of friend and foe on the battlefield leaving me giddy and disorientated.

"Your friend's courage is not enough," the shade told me. "We have little time whilst the three worlds are close. I can aid you but I need your help if we are to turn the tide."

The image of Johan, staring defiantly as Sinarr bore down on him was impossible to shake from my mind. "What do I have to do?"

"Follow me."

Mist hung in the air and I watched as it coalesced into the forms of the people around me. I could see Karlin, staring out anxiously over the walls, watching events unfold. Next to him Jora was holding his hand tightly, her knuckles white. Freydja and Asta were side by side, faces pinched and drawn with worry. All of them were standing motionless. I glanced up and saw a bird in the sky, frozen in mid-flight, wings outstretched, silhouetted against the morning sun.

"What have you done?" I asked.

The Weeping Warrior set off down the steps that led to the main gate without a backwards glance. "Follow me and touch nothing on the way."

I hastened down the steps and almost slipped, my legs weak and shaky. The shade didn't wait for me and I had to run to catch up with him, breath already rasping in my chest, as he walked through the gates and out into the open ground, towards the palisade. As we approached I could see Gautarr's mounted warriors massed in front of the bridge Haki's men had erected. The way was still barred by his warriors fighting on foot, hemmed in at the gates by Joarr's larger force. I could see Ragnar, motionless like those on the walls at Romsdahl, frustration clear on his face as he stood in his stirrups, trying to see a way through.

The Weeping Warrior led me through the melee to the other side of the palisade wall, where each man stood frozen in the act of battle. I saw Ulfarr drawing his sword, his mouth opened wide in an unending silent scream. Nearby was Skari and the rest of his crew, making their desperate retreat. I could see blood, sweat and spittle suspended in droplets in the air together with arrows hanging in mid-flight. My stomach lurched when I saw one of them a few inches from Bandor's head and, without thinking, I reached out, intending to pluck it from the air.

"Stop," the Weeping Warrior said, his hand firm around my wrist. "Perhaps the arrow will find your friend, perhaps it will miss. It is not for you to decide who lives and who dies on the field – we're here for Sinarr alone. Touch nothing else and follow me."

"He's my friend – do you expect me to do nothing?" I protested, though a chill ran down my spine at his words.

Up close, I could see Sinarr's eyes were blind, even as they bored into me. "And his life counts for more than any other? Who are you, to choose who lives and who dies? I didn't bring you here to meddle and satisfy your petty desires. Your sole purpose is to destroy Sinarr the Cold One and we cannot afford to waste any more time."

"I still don't understand what you mean. How have you done this?" I asked, chastened and filled with a sense of dread as I looked at Bandor, still as a statue, his fate hanging in the balance.

"We have stepped outside time. Navan's river still flows but we are between the worlds of life and death, reality and dream. We act in a single moment and all turns on upon it, as Sinarr the Cold One foresaw. You must not distract yourself over the fate of your friends. You can only help them and give the Brotherhood a chance of victory if you defeat the undead."

"Me? I thought you were ..." I trailed off, realising the Weeping Warrior hadn't told me anything of his intentions. *Why am I here? What can I do?*

The shade stared at me, his face a mask of blood. "My spirit has been broken – all I can do is show you the way. Why do you think Sinarr is so desperate to find you? Why does he use magic to watch you? Because he knows you hold the power to destroy him and his kind."

"But how? How can I do this?"

The Weeping Warrior looked at me with the dark shadows of his sightless eyes. "All I can do is show you the way. Follow me."

# CHAPTER 48

Leif watched with mounting horror as Petr's men were forced backwards towards their camp, Djuri Turncloak's superior numbers gradually overwhelming them. The Brotherhood's warriors were clustered protectively around Petr, Sigolf on horseback, swinging his axe left and right at the front of the battle with his shieldmen from Falsten at his side. A separate group had broken away from Djuri's forces, charging the archers led by Old Gunnar, who was ordering his men to regroup. Leif gasped as he saw Gunnar cry out and fall, a spear protruding from his chest. He blinked, remembering another time when his village had burned, its defenders cut down by the Vorund Clan as they showed no mercy. He squeezed his eyes shut, willing himself not to cry.

"Won't be long now," hissed Ekkill, bow held loosely in his hand, an arrow ready in the other. "What do you want to do?"

Etta peered into the distance, where Johan's army was now fully engaged fighting Sinarr's men. She looked down at Leif. "How does it go?" she asked him.

Leif stared at her, unsure whether to admit how much of Rothgar's visions he was sharing these days. There were times when it was hard to remember who *he* was.

Ekkill made an exasperated sound. "Why are you asking the boy? You can see they're never going to be able to help us in time. If we're to leave, it needs to be now."

"Leif?"

Leif swallowed. "Wait," he said finally. "Something's about to happen and … I need to be here."

Etta took his hand and gave it a squeeze. "Then we wait,

boy. We wait."

Ekkill shook his head, saying nothing more.

*** 

"Sinarr's magic is most powerful within the circle," the Weeping Warrior told me as we drew near. "However, while the three realms are close, bound by The Cold One's blood magic, your powers are also at their height."

I was breathless from my forced march across the frozen battlefield, legs and back aching while my head spun. I paused just outside the circle, taking in deep breaths as I tried to clear my thoughts.

"It's time," said the Weeping Warrior, inviting me to cross the circle where Johan faced Sinarr.

"I don't know what to do," I gasped, panic rising. "You've brought me here and I've no idea how to defeat Sinarr. The runeblades don't work."

The Weeping Warrior hung his head, reached out behind him and drew out a two-handed sword from across his back. I recognised the weapon as the same one Sinarr the Cold One was wielding in this battle, although the shade's blade was dull and spotted from long disuse.

"I wish I could help. There was a time when I would have thought nothing of facing any man in battle. Now, I can barely remember how to hold this sword. So much has been taken from me ... So much I once knew, lost and forgotten. In this world my sword and skills are nothing more than a fading memory ..."

I took another breath, trying to stay calm. "I know ... I understand what you've lost, but you need to help me. Tell me what to do."

The Weeping Warrior's blind eyes stared at me. "You must draw him into *your* world using the Sight, where you can face him on your terms. And your blade must be inscribed with the runes of power necessary to break the undead, rather than one of the durath."

I stared back, uncomprehending. "What?"

"I can give you the knowledge you need once you draw him into your world. Quickly, you must act now."

I remembered how Nuna had conjured up Ulfkell's Keep and invited to me walk with her in our former home. I thought of Nereth, exploring the memories of her own childhood and how Joldir had created a safe place for us to meet when using the Sight. I had never used the Sight in this way myself and Joldir was not here to guide me, his dead or unconscious body sprawled on the battlefield, the broken runestaff smouldering at Sinarr's feet.

I closed my eyes. *Leif, are you there? I need you to help me now and lend me your strength.* Without waiting for an answer I stepped into the circle, the air around me shimmering as I did so. It was cold, frost making the tussocks of grass underfoot crisp and brittle. The wider battle became distant, like I was witnessing events through a mist, whilst at the same time the scene where Johan and Sinarr fought came into sharp relief. I had seen events as they unfolded before me through Yngvarr and Randall's eyes but it was still a shock to see the bodies of Johan's warriors lying motionless as he waited, sword drawn, for Sinarr to attack. I could see Joldir some distance away, but in this frozen moment of time it was impossible to tell if he was still alive. The top half of Geirmundi's body lay at my feet in a pool of blood and I thought back to the day when we had travelled together to meet Old Hrodi outside Olt. He was someone I'd warmed to, a man I might have become friends with in time. A dull ache settled in my heart as I looked around and saw the lives of so many of the Brotherhood ended. My eyes turned to Randall, the old Vorund greybeard, standing over the body of Lars. I put my hand on the hilt of my sword, thinking how easy it would be to cut down Randall as he stood there, defenceless. I took half a step towards him before realising I was losing focus on what I was here to do. I had no idea how long the Weeping Warrior would be able to maintain this moment outside time – I had to find a way to defeat Sinarr.

I set aside my pain, worries and fears as I reached out

and found the Path, drawing the threads of magic around me. The shade was right – within the circle there were powerful currents of magic. The Path stood before me, shining bright and clear in a way I had never experienced before. This time, rather than simply follow it, I tried to imagine where it led – to *create* the destination, fashioning that place with my mind. I chose a clear memory, working with that as I tried to reach out and find Sinarr. At first I felt nothing. I could see him before me in the Real but with the Sight Sinarr was more of an absence than a presence. An echo of the spirit who now possessed Adalrikr, far away in Vorund Fastness. A feeling of panic began to well up in me again as I realised I had no idea what to do next.

*You can't find him with the Sight, Rothgar. He doesn't have the gift.* Leif was joining with me, lending me his strength. The new world I was conjuring with the Sight began to solidify, the battleground around me fading as I felt stone in place of mud and grass underfoot.

*You can't call him with the Sight,* Leif told me. *You need to bring him with you.*

I frowned, trying to understand what Leif meant even as I built the world around me, shaping dreams into reality, directing the magic flowing around and through me with my force of will. With nothing to lose I reached out, weaving Sinarr's physical form into the world I was creating and in that intuitive leap I knew Leif was right. There was something different about Sinarr – he wasn't an object or an approximation of something I was creating. For an instant the three worlds touched – the world of Death, Dream and the Real – and I felt Sinarr the Cold One cross the divide.

Sinarr stood in front of me in the fighting circle at Ulfkell's Keep. It was raining hard, water making the cobbles of the courtyard slick and treacherous, just like the day I challenged Gautarr Falrufson after the clan moot. Remembering how losing my footing cost me that particular battle I frowned and watched as the rain vanished, the sky becoming grey and overcast, whilst the rainclouds swiftly rolled away.

Sinarr moved fractionally, his sword standing buried in the cobbles next to him. His fingers twitched and he reached out for the blade, thick fingers wrapping themselves around the hilt. I held my own sword out, palm smooth, no hint of the scars left when my hand had been burned. I stretched my back, felt it resist and then stretched again, feeling the flesh and muscles move the way they used to, before Tyrfingr shattered me in the Great Hall of Ulfkell's Keep. I moved forward, revelling in the strength of my restored body, appreciating properly how Olfridor Halfhand had spent all those years training me, making me strong enough to wield a sword with skill and power. Slowly Sinarr raised his head, looking about at his new surroundings. It took several moments before he looked in my direction and truly saw me.

"This I did not foresee. Crippled no longer, Rothgar Kolfinnarson. I always thought the worlds conjured by the Sight could only be shared with the living who possessed the gift. I see I was wrong."

"Your blood magic has given me the power to reach the undead. I brought you here, so you can finally be destroyed."

Sinarr's lacerated features rippled in surprise. "So I see. Do you really think by slaying me in the world of Dream that will defeat me in the Real?"

The sword Bandor gifted to me felt light in my hand as I raised it, runes glittering along its length. The blue runes of the dragon and chimera flickered alongside red images of a coiled serpent, a green glow of locked castle gates and a dull orange of crossed spears. The Weeping Warrior had given me a vision of these new runes of power and I'd woven them into the steel of my sword as my version of Ulfkell's Keep took shape. Sinarr's eyes lingered on the blade before fixing on something behind me. I turned, seeing the Weeping Warrior standing just beyond the circle, arms folded across his chest as he watched silently.

"My *own shade* aids you. That is … fitting, I suppose. So,

you know four of the seven runes of power. It will not aid you. I have fought greater warriors than you and always triumphed. Whatever knowledge you have gained will be lost when I slay you."

I broke into a run as Sinarr gripped hold of his sword, muscles straining as he tried to pull it from the ground. The evil grin spread across his ruined face faltered as the weapon remained stuck fast in the stone cobbles. His dull eyes, clouded and bloodshot, widened and he strained again to wrench his sword free. I was almost upon him when he understood.

"Stop! There's no honour in ending things this way. Who are you? What have you done?" he roared, instinctively raising his armoured arm above his head as I took my short sword in two hands and swung it down in a powerful over-head stroke. The runes blazed as the edge bit through armour and flesh, cutting Sinarr's arm off just below the elbow. He screamed, dropping to his knees as he clutched at the bloodless wound.

"No one said this was going to be a fair contest," I re-plied, feeling giddy as magic coursed through me and I drove the blade home, straight through his heart.

Sinarr stared at me in surprise, mouth open, as his dying breath clouded in front of us, ice-cold. Crystals of ice began to spread up his neck, frost covering his blue lips, creep-ing over his nose and eyes. The death rattle in his chest sounded like crushed hailstones. I put my foot on his chest and pulled out my sword, the runes dark, their energy spent. There was a cracking sound and Sinarr the Cold One fell apart before my eyes, pieces splitting and falling away like icebergs calving from a glacier in spring. Within moments Sinarr was gone, leaving nothing more than a jumble of frozen meat and broken armour at my feet.

I laughed out loud, flushed with triumph, hardly able to believe how I'd been able to channel the Sight to defeat such a foe. Then without warning my world shattered, a rushing wind tearing at my clothes, forcing me to my knees. I felt Leif's presence vanish and a dark void opened up beneath my feet and swallowed me.

# CHAPTER 49

I rose on shaking legs, dizzy and disorientated. The circular chamber I was standing in was lit by a few flickering torches set into a damp stone wall. I was underground, the air around me cold and stale and I could feel the immense weight of rock, worked stone and earth pressing down from above. I held out my sword, sensing I was not alone. It felt real enough in my grip and I saw the new runes etched along its length were still there. All of them blazed back into life, although the rainbow of colours did little to penetrate the gloom. I could feel the ridges on my palm were back, my body no longer whole and strong; this was real.

"Welcome to Vorund Fastness," said an echoing voice from the other side of the chamber.

I peered in that direction, noticing there was a pool of deeper shadow in the middle of the room. It was moving, undulating ripples of twisting night and shade, weaving together into a vortex that sank into the depths in the centre of the chamber. I tore my eyes away with an effort, concentrating on the voice.

"Who are you?" I called out.

The light on the far side of the chamber became brighter, the torch flames burning higher, revealing a man standing on his own on the other side of the swirling pool of darkness. He was dressed in polished plate armour, in the style of a Berian knight, though he wasn't wearing a helm. I was looking at a young man, not much older than twenty, long blond hair pulled back from his face by a silver circlet set with a bright clear jewel that rested in the centre of his forehead. His hand caressed the hilt of the sword at his side and a smirk played on his lips.

"Who are you?" I asked again, glancing left and right as I began to edge around the chamber, looking for a means of escape. As far as I could tell, the two of us were alone.

"I am Adalrikr Asmarrson, King of Laskar. It is customary to kneel before your king, rather than raise a sword against him, Rothgar Kolfinnarson." His voice was cultured, a rich tone that carried across the space between us. I did not lower my weapon, though my arms felt weak at the mere mention of his name.

Adalrikr smiled with no trace of warmth touching his handsome face. "Yes, you should be afraid. You know me by other names, don't you? Adalrikr Kinslayer, Vashtas the Flayer of Souls, Baltus, First of the Sundered. I can see why Etta has been at such pains to protect you – you're more gifted than you realised. Surviving an attack by one of the Sundered, destroying my last host, they're impressive feats for a cripple. And you're much more than that, aren't you? You're able to use the Sight like few others can. A pity that you're young, inexperienced and careless, meddling with powers you barely understand. Whilst the three worlds intersect I was able to use the power of the Shadow Realm to bring you to me."

"You brought me here?" I felt slow and stupid, fear clouding my mind and driving out any ideas for escape. It was all I could do to keep my sword pointing at Adalrikr.

He shook his head, disappointed at my ignorance. "You've heard of the Calling, I am sure. There is power here, at Vorund Fastness. I have opened a gate to the Realm of Shadows, where Vellandir cruelly banished my kind. What kind of capricious god does such a thing? They called Balvarran the whisperer of lies yet none told untruths as great as those spoken by Vellandir. As the first servants of Morvanos, we were the rightful rulers of Amuran, only to have that stolen away. When I finally learned of this place I knew the Fates were calling me to restore my stolen birthright. Here was the opportunity for the rest of the durath to return to Amuran, where they could be reunited with the Sundered and serve us once more."

"I've seen such a gate before, in Tullen," I told him, seizing hold of one of the few things I could fully understand in Adalrikr's monologue.

Adalrikr sneered. "Yes. You did me a great service, crushing that little rebellion within my own ranks. Sandar Tindirson was unworthy to serve me, turning traitor and trying to call the banished to him, rather than their true master. I might have rewarded you, if you hadn't had a hand in the destruction of one of my ancient brothers. Just eight Sundered Souls left loyal to me now, all those centuries on from when we first pledged our allegiance to Morvanos. The Sundered are all making the journey here, to join me and build my new kingdom. You might have killed one of my dearest brethren but you're already too late to stop the Calling and the gathering of the Sundered. Doomed as it is, your hopeless defiance cannot go unpunished, you must understand that."

"I understand well enough, Adalrikr."

"I. Am. Your. King!" screamed Adalrikr, his features contorted with rage, only to be swept away the next instant by a radiant smile. "You ignorant fool."

"You ordered the death of my brother and his family. You persecuted our people, driving them from their homes. You're no king of mine. You're right, I know you by your various names, but Kinslayer fits you the best. Because that's what you are, a murderer and a madman." It probably wasn't the wisest thing to say – Adalrikr's nostrils flared and his face darkened. His eyes glittered and I thought I saw a flash of red, though it might have been a trick of the flickering torchlight.

"I grow bored – I don't need to justify myself to a worm. Throw down your sword and come to me."

I felt a great weight pressing between my shoulder blades and I took two hesitant steps forwards before forcing myself to a halt. My hand shook, the runes blazing brighter than ever along the length of my sword.

Adalrikr raised an eyebrow. "There are other ways. I could use you as a tribute, although I doubt any shadow spirit would willingly possess a broken shell of a man like you. You have to *want* to possess and consume your host, otherwise the battle is already lost. There's precious little meat on you either. Perhaps that's all you're fit for – stringy meagre flesh for the durath to ... well, it is hardly the right word ... feast upon. I understand Sandar's followers acquired quite a taste for human meat before the end."

Adalrikr began to walk towards me, and as he moved I saw a stairway lay directly behind him, half-hidden in the gloom. I began to move in the opposite direction, circling around the whirling vortex of shadows.

"Stop." It was a voice of command and my steps faltered. I turned to see Adalrikr closing the distance between us, smiling all the while.

My feet were lead weights, each step a mammoth effort. Sweat broke out on my brow and across my back. Gasping I turned to face the First of the Sundered, raising my sword into the position Olfridor had taught me all those years ago.

"Shall we have some sport first, before I end this?" Adalrikr laughed, drawing his own blade in a quick, fluid motion. Adalrikr was only a dozen strides from me when he stopped, a shocked expression on his face. I turned to see the Weeping Warrior step out from the shadows, his own sword raised, as he interposed himself between us.

Adalrikr recovered quickly. "Sinarr. Not quite the same as I remember you, though. You look ... terrible."

"I remember you well enough," the shade replied, looking around the chamber. "I remember when this place ran with the blood of those I swore an oath to protect. Here, I finally remember how to wield my blade once more. I remember *everything*."

Adalrikr laughed and shook his head dismissively. "No mere shade can harm me."

"Tell that to Sinarr the Cold One," the Weeping Warrior shouted, springing forwards and swinging his greatsword down at Adalrikr.

Adalrikr met the strike with a two-handed parry with his shorter sword, turning away the blow in a shower of sparks. The Weeping Warrior stepped forwards using a combination of moves that put Adalrikr onto the defensive and I saw surprise creeping across his face. The clash of steel on steel sounded real enough as it reverberated around the chamber. The shade lunged forwards, Adalrikr sweeping the tip of his sword aside so it glanced off his breastplate just above his heart. There was a scrape of metal and as Sinarr moved away I could see a long scratch left on the polished steel. Adalrikr roared in fury, his blade a blur as he went on the attack, screaming in frustration as the Weeping Warrior defended himself easily and replied with a stroke that knocked Adalrikr backwards as he desperately parried it away.

"I could have my vengeance on you now," hissed the Weeping Warrior, sounding calm and composed even as Adalrikr sucked in a great lungful of air, sweat running down his face. "But your dark spirit would just slip away, take another form and cause more misery. That is not enough for me."

The Weeping Warrior's sword darted out, the tip catching Adalrikr below his right eye. He screamed in pain and fury, sinking to his knees as he put his hand to the wound, which ran freely with blood.

"What have you done to me?" he screamed, his face in his hands.

"Something to remember me and the rest of Asmarr's loyal guards by," replied the shade, before he turned and walked over to me. "The Cold One's magic is broken. The worlds move apart once more, so I must depart soon from the world of the Real and return to my existence as a shade. Come swiftly or I will be unable to help you return to Romsdahl."

I nodded, trying to tear my eyes away from the scene of Adalrikr writhing on the ground, clutching his face and calling out for help. I looked down at my sword, runes glowing. "You might not be able to kill him, but I can," I told the shade. "My blade has been forged to destroy the durath."

Sinarr shook his head. "No. Your blade now carries knowledge you will need to create the weapons that will end *all* of the Sundered. This is my gift to you – do not throw it away by dying here. Remember how Joldir's staff broke whilst your blade ended the Cold One? It will require weapons specially crafted to slay the First of the Sundered and his most powerful followers, using the runes laid out before you on your blade." As he spoke the Weeping Warrior began to fade before solidifying once more. "Time is short. Come with me now or stay here and die."

I glanced back at Adalrikr who was now back on his feet, the right side of his face sheeting blood. Underneath the wound I could see a spider's web of black lines working their way through his skin. He picked up his sword and began to run at me, screaming, as warriors came charging down the stairs and swarmed into the chamber.

"Now," I cried. "Do it, now."

The world lurched and the chamber vanished. In moments I was back on the frozen battlefield outside Romsdahl, Sinarr the Cold One kneeling before me, my sword driven deep into his heart, my hand wrapped around the hilt.

The Weeping Warrior stood in front of me, his final words little more than a whisper. "You are the instrument of my vengeance, Rothgar, do not fail me. Take advice from one who now inhabits the shadowy realms between life and death and remember your purpose. When the time comes, you will know what to do."

Moments later the sounds of battle assaulted my ears as Sinarr the Cold One shattered into a thousand pieces at my feet. When I looked up the Weeping Warrior was gone and Johan was standing in front of me, an astonished expression on his face.

# CHAPTER 50

Randall blinked, unsure what he had just seen. When Johan raised the shieldmaiden's sword Sinarr's form flickered, solid flesh becoming shadowy and translucent. Randall felt his skin crawl, knowing something was wrong. He took a hesitant step forwards, drawing in a sharp breath as Sinarr vanished altogether – Johan's bewildered face staring at the space where he had been moments before. Randall took another step, Johan noticing him for the first time, eyes narrowing as he turned to face his new enemy. The air was heavy, the noise of battle muffled and distant within the magic circle. Randall heard a buzzing noise, the air humming as the droning grew louder and then Sinarr reappeared once more. Randall had a second to register Rothgar the Cripple standing in front of Sinarr, short sword plunged into his heart. Randall gasped, willing himself to move forward. He watched helplessly as Sinarr broke apart before his astonished eyes, a blast of cold air howling around the circle as the noise of battle suddenly assaulted him on all sides.

***

"Someone bring down that fat bastard on the horse before he kills any more of my men," Hrodmarr yelled. "He's so big I can't believe they keep missing him. Archers, take –"

The ground shook beneath Djuri, powerful enough that he could feel it even on horseback. He glanced around him, looking at Haarl and Ulf's confused faces. His horse, bred for battle and calm in the face of the fiercest fighting, whickered nervously. He pulled at the reins as she reared, concentrating on keeping in the saddle as he brought his sword down, cutting off a gasping hand trying to drag him from his mount.

There was a crash like a thunderclap and everyone turned towards the noise, their individual fights momentarily forgotten. Djuri frowned, ignoring Hrodmarr's shouts as he peered towards the battle lines where Sinarr and Johan's forces were engaged. His eyes widened as he saw a whirling vortex, the tail of a tornado spiralling down from the sky and touching the ground. Moments later there was a bright flash and amid distant shouts of terror Djuri felt another tremor pass through the ground as the tornado tore itself into shreds, blasting outwards. Wind ripped across the ground, pressing the grass flat under dark clouds that were billowing out across the sky and moving at frightening speed, men running away in all directions as they tried to escape.

"Gods, what is that?" gasped Haarl next to him.

"I don't know," Djuri began but he never got the chance to finish his thought as the blast wave reached them.

The wind howled like a savage beast, driving blinding hail at them. Djuri bent his head, hailstones rattling off his helm, the noise ringing in his ears. His horse panicked as the stinging hail struck her bare flesh, rearing and throwing Djuri to the ground. He hit someone as he landed, unsure whether it was friend of foe as he tumbled onto his back. The wind roared, the noise drowning out everything else. Someone stepped on him, bruising his ribs and Djuri cried out, his voice lost as the hail thundered down, larger now. Hailstones as big as marbles fell from the sky and drove men to their knees, those with enough presence of mind raising their shields above their heads to protect themselves. Djuri copied them, gasping as he found his feet, ribs aching. The ice bounced off his shield with a deafening clatter and it felt like Djuri's teeth would be shaken from his head. There was another thunderclap and the hail abruptly stopped. Djuri shook his ringing head, trying to clear it as his men began running away from Petr's warriors, who were still recovering from the storm. Djuri frowned. He could see Hrodmarr shouting at him but he couldn't make out the words. Then his eyes followed the direction in which Hrodmarr was pointing and he saw Bjorr running forwards, yelling at his men. A wall of shields was advancing down the road towards them. Shields emblazoned with the symbol of the eagle, the warriors carrying them chanting something, over and over.

"Vengeance for Strongshield. Vengeance for the fallen."

Djuri swore, watching as the shield wall bore down on the ranks of Olt's warriors, still disorientated from the storm. Radholf was on his horse, calling for his father as Old Hrodi knelt on the ground, winded and staring in disbelief as the advancing army. Djuri did a quick headcount as he called his own men to him, ignoring the battle cry of Petr's warriors at his back. Old Hrodi had brought six hundred men from Olt but this force was larger – at least a thousand swords and spears bearing down on them. Reavesburg's warriors began to charge and, glancing behind him, he saw Petr's forces also mounting a renewed attack, the enormous warrior on the armoured warhorse taking off the head of one of Djuri's men with a swing of his axe.

"Move, now!" It was Ulf, also unhorsed, who dragged him forwards, towards the lines Hrodmarr was organising.

Djuri ran, slipping on the muddy ground, mind racing. He'd thought Audwin's forces had been broken – clearly he was mistaken. Johan had forced their hand with his dawn attack, so they hadn't had time to fully sweep the area with their scouts before Sinarr had marched out to battle. He gritted his teeth, watching as the mass of warriors broke into two halves, one racing towards Hrodi's men, the rest charging their rear, where the battle lines were still forming – too slowly.

Olt's warriors fell under their charge first, Radholf dropping from his horse with a spear in his chest. Old Hrodi vanished, trampled by the horde of Reavesburg warriors as they fell upon Olt's men with a concussive crack; swords, axes and spears bringing down their ill-prepared foes as the charge drove deep into Olt's ranks. There was no more time to think as the remainder of Audwin's forces clashed with Djuri's men, bearing down on them with a roar as they cut down anyone in their path.

"With me," Djuri shouted to Ulf. "Haarl, organise some men to hold off Petr or they'll cut us down from behind."

Haarl, who was still mounted, nodded. He fell back, standing tall in his saddle as he called warriors to him – drawing them together so they formed a wall of shields to face Petr's advancing men, who had taken heart at the arrival of their new allies. Djuri tightened his grip on the handle of his shield as he set about him, bringing down two Reavesburg warriors who found themselves isolated from the rest of their men after their initial charge, Ulf snarling at his side, defending him from more attackers. His wedge of warriors began slowly cutting a bloody path towards Hrodmarr, a circle of Vorund clansmen surrounding him to protect him from Audwin's forces.

There was another sound now – somewhere people were cheering. Djuri risked a glance back and saw men running away from the defensive palisade; hundreds of them, scattering as archers picked them off, one by one. Ice poured into Djuri's heart as he saw the banner of the bear topple and fall to the ground to more cheers, other Vorund banners up and down the battle field also falling. Johan Jokellsward's name was being chanted now, louder and louder. Others heard it too – the march of Djuri's warriors faltering as people began to understand what was happening elsewhere on the battlefield. Hrodmarr's heard turned, a scowl on his face before it vanished in a shower of blood and teeth as a throwing axe found its target. His defensive circle wavered for a moment before being swallowed by the press of Reavesburg men on all sides, the Vorund Clan warriors vanishing like a rock pool swallowed by the onrush of high tide.

Elsewhere men were breaking away as the first of the fleeing warriors from Sinarr's army rushed past them as if Morvanos himself were on their tails. Audwin's warriors screamed all the louder, driving at Djuri's men, cutting anyone down whose resolve wavered, spreading panic through their ranks. Djuri glanced behind him and saw Johan's army pursing Sinarr's fleeing men, close enough that he could make out their faces and even recognise some of them. Petr was ordering his warriors forwards, charging towards Haarl's position as Johan's warriors also joined the fray.

"It's over," Ulf shouted, pulling at Djuri's arm. "We need to fall back now or we're dead."

The world seemed to slow down, Djuri aware of his beating heart and ragged breathing, a ringing sensation filling his ears. Perhaps it was fitting for it to end here – he'd chosen his side and chosen wrong. Petr Hamarrson was just fifty feet away – a worthy opponent and perhaps the chance to salvage some honour from this horrible mess. He took a step towards Johan's second before thinking of the men from Ulfkell's Keep who had followed him here. Djuri hesitated for another few heartbeats before shouting the order to retreat, falling back with the rest of his warriors, Ulf at his side.

***

Leif watched in amazement as Sinarr's army scattered before Reavesburg's warriors. Djuri's men ceased their advance towards the camp, joining those fleeing for their lives as their spirit broke.

"That's remarkable timing," Ekkill observed, relief in his voice.

Etta shook her head disbelievingly. "Audwin's men were always loyal and they would never let his death go unavenged. Even so, I would like to know who it was that rallied such a force to him and had the wherewithal to bring them to this fight at this moment. It turned the battle. Johan owes them a great debt – we all do."

"Sinarr the Cold One is dead," Leif told them. He'd seen it with his own eyes … sort of, and he thought it was important they knew what was happening.

"So Johan carried the day and turned the tide." Etta sounded livelier than Leif had seen her for months. She gave his hand another uncharacteristic squeeze.

"Look, there. Smoke coming from the inner palisade," said Ekkill.

Leif gasped as one of the watchtowers, already blazing brightly, crashed to the ground in a cloud of black smoke. The sound reached them a few seconds later, a rumbling roar mingled with cheers and cries of fear. Leif thought about what had just happened and what he had seen, trying to make sense of it. Rothgar had fought Sinarr the Cold One with runes of power, helped by Sinarr's own *spirit*? He didn't really pretend to understand it all and then Adalrikr had appeared and tried to kill Rothgar. Leif hadn't felt so afraid since his mother had changed in Tullen. Nearby Varinn was shouting orders, telling people to make ready for the wounded to arrive, although most people in the camp were cheering, watching as the Vorund Clan fled before the Brotherhood of the Eagle.

"It's alright, Leif," Etta told him, her wrinkled face full of joy. "We've won. The siege of Romsdahl is broken."

It was only then that Leif realised he was crying.

# CHAPTER 51

Hundreds of crows descended to feast upon the flesh of the dead, the cries of dying men and horses mingling with their incessant cawing. I shuddered, my mind drawn back to the crows' cage in Ulfkell's Keep. Tyrfingr Blackeyes' face swam before my eyes and I squeezed them shut, stumbling over a corpse on unsteady feet. Jolinn caught my arm, holding me upright.

"You alright?" she asked. Her short blonde hair was matted with blood, a dark swollen bruise on one side of her head, blackening her eye and running down her jaw and cheek-bone.

I nodded. "Thanks. It's just these damn birds and the noise …" I trailed off, fighting the urge to retch as the wind changed, filling my nose with the cloying scent of blood and death.

Jolinn's face softened, her blue eyes looking at me kindly. "I heard what Blackeyes did to you. Are you sure you want to do this? We could just head to the camp."

"No, I need to see this for myself. I want to know what happened."

We walked on, Jolinn still supporting my arm and I didn't argue. Every muscle in my body ached and I felt drained, pain stabbing through my eyes into my skull. Slowly we drew closer to the area where Petr and Djuri had been fighting. A number of warriors were still milling around, checking the wounded, killing any of the Vorund Clan who were still alive and stripping the bodies of anything useful. I saw Petr among them and he recognised me, raising his arm in greeting as he walked in our direction.

"Brother," he said, drawing me into a tight embrace. "We won the day." He looked exhausted but his eyes sparkled with the thrill of victory.

"Petr, I'm so glad to see you," said Jolinn as she hugged him too.

"Is it true? Sinarr the Cold One is dead, killed by Johan himself?"

Jolinn nodded. "It's true. The durath were waiting for us ..." Her voice shook and she broke off, looking away. Nearby two crows squabbled, although there was no need – they would all eat their fill before night fell.

"Where's Lars?" Petr asked Jolinn.

"He fell," she replied, swallowing hard. "We also lost the Flints, Ragni and Yngvarr. Svan was unhorsed but he's alright. Joldir hasn't woken yet."

The three of us stood together, quiet for a time. "Old Gunnar died in the battle too," Petr told us, breaking the silence. "More of our friends gone and so few of Kalamar's warriors left. We have to remember they died freeing Romsdahl. As for Joldir, he's strong, and I know he'll come through this. He'll be awake in no time, telling the healers how they've stitched him up all wrong."

I laughed with little humour. I was so tired; all I wanted to do was go back to the camp but I had to finish this first, so we took our leave of Petr and continued our search. It didn't take long to find the jumbled remains of the shield wall that had been broken by Petr's final charge. Haarl was lying there next to his dead horse, limbs twisted at an odd angle, his eyes wide and staring sightlessly up at the sky, where the birds circled overhead. His face was pale, lips blue and his chainmail armour was rent and torn, his chest and stomach bloody from numerous wounds. I squatted down and gently closed his eyes, his flesh soft and smooth but already cold.

"He dead?" asked one of Petr's men nearby.

"He's gone," I replied. "I recognise him – he's one of our warriors. Make sure he's brought to the pyre rather than left for the crows."

The warrior called to one of his fellows for help. I watched as they took Haarl's body and left it with the gathering number of fallen warriors who had fought for the Brotherhood, waiting for dusk when Johan would light their pyre and speed them on to Navan's Halls. I looked around and found Jolinn had moved further up the hill. When I reached her, she was looking down at the body of her half-brother, Radholf, lying pinned to the ground, the broken shaft of a spear protruding from his chest. His face was contorted in shock and pain, blood congealing in the corner of his mouth.

"I'm sorry," I told her.

Jolinn looked up sharply. "What for? I never thought much of any of them and the feeling was mutual. Radholf was never going to favour the bastard daughter his father sired with a whore, was he?"

A man moaned nearby and as we approached I recognised Old Hrodi, his long white hair and whiskers streaked with blood. His hands were clasped around his belly, blood welling up between his arthritic fingers. He turned towards us, eyelids fluttering.

"Jolinn, my daughter. Is that really you? And Rothgar. Come to gloat at my downfall, have you?" His voice was weak, his life fading.

Jolinn stared down at her father, eyes blazing and her lips pursed, saying nothing. I knelt down next to him, watching as he struggled to breathe.

"You betrayed me twice," I said quietly.

"I had nothing against you, Rothgar. I liked your father, respected him when he was chief. But ... You must understand, a leader must protect his people. I did what I did to ... protect the people of Olt."

Jolinn took in a sharp breath. "How *dare* you say that. Protect your people? Because you sided with the Vorund Clan, Karl and Lars are dead and you've lost your last son. Look around you, Father. This is the price we've all paid for you breaking your oath as Gautarr's bannerman."

Hrodi Whitebeard's head turned towards the body of his son, lying amongst a pile of Olt's warriors. "You think ... I don't know that, child? I was trying to ensure ... Radholf would have something to be elder of when his time finally came. Instead, I've outlived all four of my sons ..."

"You still have a daughter," I told him.

"Pah. One who led my own people in an uprising against me, dividing the folk of Olt forever. Radholf was a dullard ... but at least he was loyal and understood why we did what we did. What we *had* to do. Do you think your victory here matters? All you've done ..." Hrodi was wracked by a fit of coughing, wincing in pain as he struggled to continue. "All you've done ... is set us on the path for slaughter when Adalrikr takes his vengeance. You can't hope to defeat him – why can't you see this?" Hrodi coughed again, gasping in pain as he clutched at his stomach. Fresh blood mingled with the dried blood covering his lips, trickling down his white beard.

I looked up at Jolinn. "He's dying. If you want to make your peace with him you need to do it quickly."

Jolinn stared back at me, blue eyes hard as diamonds. "Make my peace? It's too late for that." She turned her back and stalked off, leaving me kneeling beside Hrodi. The old man choked and whimpered in pain. I looked up and saw Jolinn was talking to Petr and two of his men, pointing in our direction.

"I'm thirsty," whispered Hrodi, touching my sleeve with blood-stained fingers.

I looked down at him, taking hold of his hand. "I often wondered what I would have done that day in the Great Hall, had I been in your position. Tyrfingr Blackeyes wouldn't have let anyone leave Ulfkell's Keep alive if they hadn't sworn loyalty to him. He killed Brunn Fourwinds in front of you all and then tortured me with fire and iron for an afternoon. Would I have had the courage to intervene or defy him? I'm not sure I would."

Old Hrodi's eyelids fluttered, his breathing shallow. "I

remember. Not a day goes by when I don't think of it. At least now I'll never have to relive that day again. My father always said you should ... never live your life with regrets. What's done ... in the past ... cannot be changed. Can't be undone. You have to live life looking forwards ... do your best ... Never look back."

Another fit of coughing took him, wracking him harder than ever, and Hrodi writhed in pain. He gripped my hand tighter as his other hand slid from his belly, resting by his side, allowing his wounds to bleed freely. "All good advice, though I couldn't live by it ... after the fall of Ulfkell's Keep. Not a day goes by when I don't think on it ... Not a day." His voice was little more than a whisper and he pulled me close. "I was a coward ... but if I'd tried to help you, I would have died. My son ... would have been killed, my grandson left fatherless. So, you're right – I sat ... I watched ... I bent the knee to Adalrikr. I made my choice ... You asked if you would have done anything different. You're wise for someone so young. Who can say? I thought I'd made the right choice and regretted it ever since ... I'll be remembered as an oath breaker, which is a poor legacy after serving your household since I was a boy. I tried to keep my people safe ... Look at where it's led us ..."

I held Hrodi's hand in both of mine, wondering what to say. Perhaps I didn't need to say anything and just being with him was enough as he passed into Navan's Halls. Hrodi's breathing slowed, he coughed one final time and became still. I placed his hand on his chest and stood as I heard booted feet approaching me.

"Jolinn tells me you've found Hrodi Myndillson," said Petr.

"He's dead. Passed away in front of my eyes," I replied as Jolinn crossed her arms and scowled.

"Justice of some sorts," Petr commented, giving Jolinn a sidelong glance.

"He made his choice," she said, arms folded as she stared at his body.

I wiped my hands clean on the corner of another fallen warrior's cloak and began to trudge towards Johan's camp, wrapped up in my own thoughts. Without a word, Jolinn fell into step alongside me, still hugging herself as we walked together in silence. I looked down at my hands, noticed blood under my nails and absently began picking at them.

"What did he say to you?" Jolinn asked.

I shrugged. "He told me he had regrets. For what it's worth, I believed him."

We approached Johan's camp, Varinn calling out to us in greeting. A steady stream of people were walking, limping or being carried by their friends towards the hospital tent, the gates to the camp now opened wide. I caught a glimpse of Arissa at the entrance, talking to some of the other womenfolk, her apron splattered dark with blood. Ekkill jumped down from one of the wagons and sauntered over.

"Johan's been asking for you. He wants to see you, now."

I turned to Jolinn. "You should get that cut on your head seen to."

"It's nothing – I'd rather hear what Johan has to say."

Ekkill raised an eyebrow and smirked. "He wasn't asking for you. Just Rothgar."

"Go," I told her. "I'll speak to you later and check you're alright."

Jolinn didn't look happy as she left us and headed over to the hospital tent. I followed Ekkill, who led me towards the wagon where Etta and Leif had watched the battle unfold. My aged tutor was still sitting huddled up in her cloak on her seat. Johan was standing in front of the wagon, Eykr and Faraldr at his side.

"Walk with me," he said, gesturing for Ekkill and his men to wait.

Etta looked up at that. "There was a time when we shared counsel with you, Johan."

Johan turned, his face gaunt, tiredness etched on his features. "Whilst I trust your counsel, this concerns me and

Rothgar and I would speak to him in private."

Etta blinked and adjusted her cloak, wrapping it tighter around her skinny frame. "As you wish."

I fell into step with Johan as we walked together, watching as more people poured into the camp each minute. Audwin's men were setting up their own camp just beyond the ring of wagons and carts, which I thought was interesting, since they were Gautarr's bannermen.

"Who commands them following Audwin's death?" I asked.

"A fellow called Adakan. I've never met him before today but now consider him one of my closest friends. Without his intervention our camp would already have been destroyed."

"And Djuri and his men?"

"Turncloak and his warriors are fleeing for their lives. Some of Adakan's men are tracking them and I don't think they'll be coming back. There's time for all of this later. I wanted to speak to you before Gautarr demands an audience. I saw what happened on the battlefield, though I don't pretend to understand it. You owe me an explanation."

"The way I heard it, you were the one to kill Sinarr the Cold One. What is there to explain?" My voice betrayed more bitterness than I intended, my words less guarded in my exhaustion and pain.

Johan glared at me and I was struck by how similar his blue eyes were to those of Jolinn. As he held my gaze I saw something else – fatigue, worry, fear, the weight of the responsibilities of command, as men lived or died with each decision he made. "That was uncalled for," he said at length, his voice calm. "Those stories were circulating before I even knew it. People had seen me fighting Sinarr and the next moment he was dead. Few were close enough to see you make your ... appearance, so they drew their own conclusions. Before I decide whether or not to deny their tales I would have your explanation for what took place. I'd like to know how you managed to travel on foot from Romsdahl Castle and across two separate battle lines to be there. How you managed to kill – no, that's not even the right word. Destroy. How you managed to destroy Sinarr the Cold One utterly, while he killed the rest of the Brotherhood at will. Killed good men, some of whom had travelled with me and been loyal to me since the beginning. I'm no fool – I realise you saved my life and you have my thanks for that but I still deserve an explanation."

I cleared my throat, rubbing my aching forehead. "I'll explain what I can, although I think some of these mysteries may need to be unlocked by Joldir and Etta."

"Talk to me first," Johan said, his face serious.

I drew my sword, the runes dark now but their design and appearance clearly different from before. "It begins with how magic touched the world of the Real to create this."

# CHAPTER 52

Ulfarr passed me the wineskin as we sat around the fire, the smell of the fresh fish cooking for our midday meal filling the air. "Let's drink to Patrick's memory."

"For Patrick. I'll miss him."

My stomach rumbled as I took a long swig. The wine was warm and slightly sour but I didn't mind as I wiped my mouth and passed the skin on to Skari. Myr sat across from me, his arm and shoulder bandaged, his face as inscrutable as always. If he felt any pain and discomfort he gave no sign, nodding his agreement at Ulfarr's words. Jolinn was also sitting with us, whilst around another fire nearby were several of Olt's warriors who had followed her into battle.

"Patrick. Lars. Karl. Old Gunnar and Ragni. Yngvarr. Geirmundi. Geirmarr. For all those the Brotherhood has lost," Jolinn recited, before taking a drink from the skin.

"Tried to rob him, you know," Ulfarr said, drawing a chuckle from Skari.

"Rob who?" I asked.

"Patrick. That's how we met. He was travelling alone on the northern border between Reavesburg and Norlhast when we spotted him. There were eight of us then and we set about him, trying to take what we could. I thought we'd be able to intimidate him, only he wouldn't back down, drew his sword and defended himself. After keeping us at bay for a time I called a halt, realising he had more skill than the rest of my crew. Told him we could use a man like him, that we could help each other."

"Hah. He must have been desperate to join the band that tried to kill him," Skari said with a grin, shaking his head.

Ulfarr nodded. "He was being pragmatic. Afterwards, when I thought back on it, he was ready to die that day and I spared him, gave him a choice. A man has more chance of surviving as part of a crew than on his own. He taught me a fair few things about how to wield a blade these last couple of years. He was a good man."

"You were thieves?" Jolinn asked as Ulfarr's words sank in.

"Aye, lass, before we joined the Brotherhood, that's what we were," Skari replied. "What of it?"

Jolinn shook her head. "Nothing. I just didn't know."

"Did you really believe his story? That he was once a Berian knight?" Skari asked.

Ulfarr shrugged and took the wineskin as it came back to him, scowling as he realised it was empty.

"There's another one where that came from," said Skari, reaching behind him and tossing Ulfarr a fresh skin. "Reckon we've all earned it."

Ulfarr pulled out the stopper and took a long draught. "I think it was true, for what it's worth," he said in answer to Skari's question. "As for what happened in Beria, what led him to be travelling alone in the wilds of Laskar, he never spoke of it. That's a story that's gone with him to the grave."

I thought about saying more, remembering my conversation with Patrick on the way to Romsdahl. I hesitated, wondering why he'd chosen to confide in me and not share the story with his closest companions. Before I could say anything further I heard the sound of horses' hooves, travelling at some speed, and looked up to see a score of riders approaching from the direction of Romsdahl, one of them holding the banner of the eagle in his hand. They passed the pyre Johan had lit the previous day, built from the remains of the wooden palisade. It still smouldered, the heat rising from its centre causing the air to shimmer. Nearby the carrion birds continued to feast on the stripped bodies of the Vorund Clan and their fallen allies. Honour for the victors, while the vanquished lay where they fell. I took another drink and waited for the delegation from Romsdahl to arrive.

Johan must have been told of their approach, because he emerged from his tent and began to walk towards them, accompanied by the surviving warriors of Kalamar. Bandor was on his right, Petr his left and behind them came Svan, Eykr, Faraldr and Varinn. Just seven of them now. Falsten's elder, Sigolf Admundson, was also in attendance, the huge man puffing as he walked, looking completely different from the ferocious warrior who'd fought alongside Petr. Ulfarr motioned to his crew and we rose to join them, Jolinn's men from Olt also accompanying us. At the head of the riders was Ragnar and I saw Tomas and Throm amongst the men with him, together with Ekkill.

Ragnar dismounted when he reached our camp and strode over to Johan. "My father, Gautarr Falrufson, Jarl of Romsdahl sends you greetings and offers his heartfelt thanks for your aid in the battle."

"If he's so grateful, why isn't he here himself?" chided Sigolf. A number of men in the camp murmured in agreement.

Ragnar looked irritated at the interruption, though he masked it quickly. With Audwin and Haki both dead Ragnar finally had his wish to act as his father's second. I wondered if he was enjoying the experience.

"No insult is intended, I assure you."

"Really? So why did we have to send a messenger to Gautarr before you made this approach?" pressed Sigolf, nodding in Ekkill's direction. "We're not fools. Everyone can see your father is already acting as if he's the new chief. I don't recall being invited to a clan moot to settle that issue."

"And I don't recall it being agreed you speak for the western men. That honour was accorded to the elder of Lake Tull." Ragnar's dark eyes flashed dangerously as he spoke. He hadn't seen Sigolf fight and no doubt mistook him for nothing more than an overweight farmer.

"Enough, friend," Johan told Sigolf. "Apologies, Ragnar.

We are not here to bicker or take insult at the merest slight after our greatest victory. As you know, Sandar Tindirson and Tullen are no more and with Geirmarr Flint's death on the battlefield I believe Sigolf has earned the right to speak on behalf of the western lands."

"And you consider such favours are yours to give?" Ragnar replied, eyes narrowed.

"It is my opinion, of course. All such matters should be determined at a clan moot, which is why my messenger requested the same," Johan told him in an even voice.

Ragnar turned in my direction. "There are other matters to attend to as well. The prisoner in our dungeons, Thengill, is a warrior of the Vorund Clan and our sworn enemy. You offered great insult to your host by welcoming this man into your ranks."

"Thengill has proved his loyalty time and again," Johan replied. "The clan moot must decide his fate. However, the Brotherhood was created to fight against evil and we face dangers extending far beyond the loyalties of houses and clans. Be in no doubt, I will be pleading Thengill's case before the moot."

"You're entitled to your opinion," said Ragnar, looking unconvinced. "We would like to understand more about this Brotherhood you have gathered about yourself, Johan Jokellsward. The clan moot will be held in Romsdahl Castle tomorrow evening, after my father has hosted a feast to celebrate our victory. He would be honoured by your attendance."

"And I would be honoured to accept," Johan replied with a short bow. "There is also the matter of my son's betrothal to your cousin to conclude."

"Tomorrow evening, then," Ragnar said as he mounted his horse. "I shall look forward to it."

Romsdahl's warriors rode away, Ekkill remaining behind. "Is that a wineskin?" he said with a smile as he slid out of his saddle. Myr passed it to him with a curt nod.

"I don't like this and I don't trust him or Gautarr," Bandor told his father. "You shouldn't have accepted meeting in

Romsdahl Castle. It should have been on neutral ground."

Johan shook his head. "The laws governing a clan moot are sacred. Even Gautarr wouldn't be so bold as to break them and, in truth, he needs us. Provoking a war within the Reavesburg Clan is not his aim, I'm sure."

"But controlling it is. What if he won't follow you? What then?" asked Sigolf.

"That will be a decision for the clan moot," Johan replied. "Whatever the outcome, war is coming. Adalrikr will not allow our rebellion to go unchallenged, so we need to find a way to stand together. It's time they learned the truth and for the Romsdahl house to join the Brotherhood."

"Will they want to join us, if they know the truth?" Sigolf muttered, watching Ragnar's retreating back.

Johan grimaced, his gaunt features strained. "We have to try."

*** 

The following morning I went to the hospital tent to pay Joldir a visit. Arissa emerged as I arrived, clutching a pile of stained bandages. She looked dead on her feet.

"Have you been working all night?" I asked. Arissa nodded, dropping the dirty bandages into a fire pit, where they began to smoulder. I drew her into a hug. "You need to take some rest."

Arissa pursed her lips. "I'll rest when the work is finished. I'm glad you're here, though. Joldir's been asking for you."

The smell inside the tent was horrendous – a combination of blood, sweat and excrement that made my eyes water. I stood at the entrance for a moment, blinking my eyes until they cleared and I became used to the odour. I could see Ingirith working with the healers as they moved amongst their patients. A few were groaning in pain but most seemed to be asleep. I guessed it was calmer now that it had been yesterday. Most wounds had been stitched and injuries treated. Now whether these men lived or died would come down to how strong they were and their desire for life.

Maeva approached me, looking haggard. "Rothgar, are you here to see Joldir?"

I nodded. "Is he awake yet?"

"He's very tired. Please don't spend too long with him."

Maeva showed me to the bed where Joldir was lying. His eyes were wide open, staring at the roof of the tent. He turned as I approached and gave me a thin smile. Leif was sitting by his side.

"Shouldn't you be helping Curruck at the forge?" I asked him with a grin. Leif shrugged in response.

"He asked to stay," Joldir explained. "The smith can do without his apprentice for one day."

I sat on the floor by his thin straw mattress, looking at the bandages covering both of his hands. Joldir saw me staring. "Before you ask, I don't know how bad it is but I know it's bad enough. It's what Arissa hasn't said that's got me worried. An artificer and healer who can't use his hands – that's not going to be much use to Johan, is it?" He chuckled weakly.

"It's still good to see you again. I thought, when I saw ..." I trailed off as I saw Joldir's face harden.

"I've heard all sorts of rumours," Joldir told me. "Some people are saying Johan killed Sinarr in single combat. However, there's also another story circulating. That tale says you were on the walls of Romsdahl one moment, safe and sound, then in the fighting circle alongside Johan the next. In that version of the story your sword shattered Sinarr the Cold One. Show me your blade."

I drew out my sword, attracting glances from a number of people inside the hospital tent. Joldir stared intently at the interlocking patterns of four runes, cut into the polished metal surface in exquisite detail.

"It's a work of art. I know my own handiwork and this isn't it, so do you want to tell me how you came by such a weapon?"

I was as honest with Joldir as I had been with Johan, explaining how the closeness of the realms, brought together by Sinarr's blood magic, had increased my powers with the Sight and how the Weeping Warrior came to my aid. Joldir knew my abilities with the craft too well, however, and a frown creased his forehead as he listened to my tale.

"World building, then drawing Sinarr into that world from the Real. That takes a great deal of skill and control. And you did this for the *first time* during the battle? Forgive me if I sound sceptical, but it's not that easy."

"I'm not sure I could do it again. I was able to work with Leif, which helped me to control the power I was using. I've never experienced the Sight like that before – it was closer, somehow, easier to reach out with and mould. I also think I gained some insight recently into how it worked." I hesitated as I wondered whether to say anything further.

"There's something you're not telling me," Joldir pressed. "What is it?"

I reached into my cloak and drew out the small glass sculpture of the eagle Nuna gifted to me last time we met through the Sight. "I should have been honest with you earlier, Joldir. Nuna's power with the Sight has increased and we've been using it to communicate privately. We've –"

Joldir's eyes widened and he recoiled in fright. "Rothgar, what have you done?"

I glanced around me and gasped as I realised the three of us were no longer sitting in the hospital tent.

# CHAPTER 53

There was an empty feeling in the pit of my stomach as I drew my blade. Joldir stood on shaking legs, holding on to Leif with his bandaged hands. The three of us were high up in a mountain range, a cold wind tugging at our clothes. We were standing above a slope covered in a jumble of jagged grey stones and scree that dropped away sharply. Behind us, on the other side of a narrow path, great slabs of smooth rock rose up, stretching towards the peaks of the mountain high above. It was a desolate place, with no vegetation of any kind to break up the monotonous harsh landscape.

"What's happening?" Leif asked, looking scared.

"The eagle," growled Joldir, pointing at the glass sculpture I was still holding.

I looked down at the object. "What do you mean?"

Joldir took a deep breath, his voice more measured as he explained. "It's a trap. I've seen such things before, during my studies with the Chapter in Seroch. Tell me again, where did you get this?"

"Nuna gave it to me. It was a gift."

"*When* did she give this?"

I was confused in the face of Joldir's cold fury. I couldn't understand how this had happened, racking my brain as I answered. "We met in a shared world Nuna created through the Sight, a few days before the battle. When I returned to Romsdahl Castle it was there with me. Seeing how my sister was able to work the Sight in that way gave me some understanding of how to defeat Sinarr."

"It's an anchor," Joldir explained. "They're normally used by a Fellowship if they need to travel to a safe place in an instant using the Sight, without having the find the Path. This has been made by someone who's attuned to our Fellowship. When we were all together for the first time the magic activated."

"Trapping us," I finished, feeling stupid and sick with worry and fear.

Joldir groaned and shook his head. "I knew I should have told you sooner. Etta made me promise not to mention anything because she didn't want you worrying about Nuna when you had so much else to deal with. I didn't agree. Her absence felt wrong and I was fearful for her. I'm sorry Rothgar, there's no way Nuna could have made that eagle."

I tried to compose myself and control how my body was reacting. Breathing deeply, I took in our surroundings more closely. We were in another world created using the Sight. The question was whose world was this? I stared down at the eagle, noticing tiny flaws in its structure for the first time. I held the glass up to the light, seeing tiny black specks inside. I swallowed, my mouth dry, as I realised they were moving. Liquid shadow drifting through the glasswork, growing larger even as I watched.

"What is it?" Joldir asked, peering over my shoulder.

"We need to get out of here," Leif said, his voice shrill with fear.

"The anchor's holding us here," Joldir told us, gesturing towards the object with his bandaged hands. "We need to find a way to destroy it."

I took a tight hold of the eagle and threw it at the cliff face as hard as I could. It struck the stone with a chiming ring and the rock rippled as if a stone had been dropped into a pool. The eagle glittered in the sun as it spun away, landing with a soft thud on the path. I reached out with shaking fingers, picking up the object. The glass was unmarked and the sculpture remained completely unharmed, although the whirling black shadows were larger, moving in an odd, random way, veering off at jagged angles.

"That's no way to treat my gift," Nuna remarked.

I sprang backwards, almost losing my footing and slipping down the mountainside. Nuna tossed back her head and laughed, blonde locks glittering in the sunlight. The sound jarred in my ears.

"Nuna," I said, heart pounding in my chest.

"That's not Nuna," Joldir muttered.

"Indeed," Nuna replied, looking at him. "Finally the Crow Man is unmasked, eh, Gildas? I feel so foolish – I should have known it was you."

"Gildas?" I repeated, looking at Joldir.

"The name I went by years ago, when I was a student at Seroch, before I returned to the north," he explained.

Nuna smirked, shaking her head. "He's not told you, has he? He was so ashamed of his northern origins back then. The name Joldir was forgotten and Gildas was born as he tried to woo the noble ladies of Seroch. You've lost the accent of your birthplace, I see. Even so, despite all your affectations you never really belonged in Seroch, did you?" She laughed again, mocking him.

Joldir stood up straighter, looking defiantly at Nuna. "I was a young man and foolish, my head turned by having too much too soon. My mistakes are nothing compared to the ones you've made, Nereth. What have you done?"

As I stared at the woman her features became indistinct, shifting like melting wax before reforming into Nereth's beautiful proud face. Her gold hair rippled and as she shook her head the blonde plaits unravelled, a long swathe of jet-black hair falling down her back. Nereth was dressed like a shield-maiden in silver banded armour and a smile played on her lips as she turned to me.

"That's better. You had no idea, did you? I've watched your sister very closely, for a long time, waiting for the moment when I was ready to take her form. Even when I made the odd mistake you just saw what you wanted to see. You're a fool, Rothgar."

"And you're a traitor. You betrayed your Chapter and your friends," cried Joldir. "You were my apprentice and after I'd taught you so much you turned on me."

Nereth looked at him scornfully. "I chose to survive."

"You murdered Ramill."

"And you failed him. The difference is I have no regrets, unlike you."

"Enough of this," I shouted, levelling my sword at Nereth and advancing towards her. "You will let us go or, I swear, this time I will kill you. Where's my sister? What have you done with her?"

"I don't fear you," Nereth sneered. "In this world you're a cripple, not a warrior. Only the Sight makes you interesting but you have no idea how to control your power. The Crow Man can't rescue you this time. You're all bound to me, until this is over."

I glanced at the glass eagle in my hand, which was now black, a dark cloud of boiling shadow swirling within the object. I set the eagle on the ground, raised my sword and brought it down on the sculpture. The glass rang and my sword shook with the impact. I stared in dismay as the eagle remained intact, though the blackness within seemed to shift and twist, as if angry at my intervention.

"I think you'll enjoy this," Nereth told me.

The glass eagle tremored on the path at my feet, rattling and jumping on the stones all by itself. I backed away with Joldir and Leif. There was a cracking sound and the glass split apart, shards sent spinning away as a storm of crows burst out of the object, cawing madly, wings flapping in a deafening din. There was a dull clang as my sword fell from my fingers, landing at my feet as I screamed. The air was thick with the birds, flying in all directions, their beaks and claws raking my flesh as they attacked us. My cry was cut short as I fell to the ground beneath the black cloud, my breath knocked from me. I began to slide down the scree slope, feet and bloodied hands trying to find some purchase as the rocks rolled past me.

"Joldir. Leif. I'm sorry," I called out as the crows continued to harry me.

I looked up to see Leif running forwards, his hands above his head to ward off the birds. My slide came to a halt, leaving me stranded on the scree-covered slope. The crows formed a dark wedge, angling towards Leif. I watched as he stooped, picked up a rock, and ran straight at Nereth.

I opened my mouth to shout out a warning, to tell the boy to stop. As I watched the flat stone morphed into a long, thin dagger. Nereth snarled in surprise, reaching to her side, drawing out a sword. Leif was on her before the blade was halfway out of the scabbard. He drove the knife into her ribs, forcing her back. He struck again and again, the stone dagger scraping off Nereth's armour, the ferocity of his attack stunning her, dropping her onto one knee, arms raised as she warded him off.

The crows faded and the world shimmered before snapping back into focus. Leif's next strike was blocked when Nereth grabbed his wrist, bending back his arm as she struggled to stand. Desperately, I began to try and crawl my way up the scree slope, making little progress as the stones rattled past me. The crows vanished as Leif and Nereth fought on the narrow path. Joldir glanced down at his bandaged hands, clumsily picked up a large rock and ran forwards as Leif kicked out at Nereth, catching her knee and causing her to cry out in pain.

"How have you done this?" she gasped, pinning his wrists with one hand as she tried to draw her sword with the other.

"Does it matter?" Joldir said, swinging the rock and catching her on the side of the head with a sickening thud. Nereth dropped to the ground, unconscious, and Joldir grabbed Leif and looked directly at me.

"Time to go, while we still can."

The light changed, becoming dim, the air warm and full of the smells from the hospital. I gasped, looking down at my hand where the glass eagle was no more, fine sand trickling between my fingers onto the covers on Joldir's bed, a dry patter as it fell on the cloth. I looked up but no one nearby seemed to have noticed anything was amiss, even though sweat poured from me and Joldir sat heavily on his mattress, face pale.

"Myshall's bane, that was close," he muttered.

"I'm so sorry," I replied, my face red with shame. "Leif, you saved our lives back there."

Leif was staring at me, a blank look on his face, as if we wasn't seeing us properly.

"You managed to shape Nereth's world," Joldir explained, taking hold of the boy's hand. "How did you to do that?"

Leif shrugged as he looked at us in turn. "I don't know, exactly. I was with Rothgar when he formed his world using the Sight to fight Sinarr. I just ... did the same thing, when I realised we couldn't escape. I worked with Nereth's world, rather than fight against it. Are we safe now?"

Joldir nodded. "For now. We must build up the walls that shield our minds. Do you remember how I taught you to do this?"

I glanced at Joldir. "Gildas? Why did Nereth call you that?"

Joldir smiled weakly. "I didn't want to be Joldir the clansman when I arrived at Seroch. I was young and proud and the people there, well, let's just say they were different. Everyone in Mirtan aspires to join one of the three Chapters, so Seroch was full of ambitious people, all of them refined and cultured. And there I was, from the windswept north, having grown up in a turf-covered hovel. I decided to become Gildas, invented a past more in keeping with my new company and set Joldir aside, for a time. As I said, I'm not proud of it now but back then I was desperate to be accepted. I *needed* to be accepted, in order to continue my studies."

*There's more to this* I thought, as I blinked sweat out of my eyes, struggling to stay with Joldir before a wave of visions overwhelmed me.

# CHAPTER 54

Nuna's eyes fluttered open.

*Where am I?*

She felt weak and thirsty, her head spinning. Slowly she looked around, trying to make sense of the room she was in.

*My chambers. What am I doing here?*

Light streamed in through the windows, the shutters pulled back wide to let in the sea air. Outside, gulls were calling to each other.

*Norlhast. I'm in Norlhast. I'm the Lady of Norlhast Keep.*

Someone was knocking on the door to her chamber and calling out. Nuna carefully levered herself with her elbows into a sitting position, though the effort made her feel dizzy and sick. Her throat was scratchy, her tongue and mouth dry. She tried unsuccessfully to speak, her voice a hoarse rasping sound. Peering over the side of the bed she could see a wooden chair lying on its side and a young servant girl on the floor. Nuna felt sure she had gone to a great deal of trouble to get to know this woman and now she couldn't even remember her name.

The knocking grew louder. "Nuna? Ottama? Is everything alright?"

It was Brosa, her bodyguard, no doubt keeping watch outside her room. Slowly his words clicked into place. It was her maid Ottama slumped on the floor. She stirred.

"What's all this noise?" Kalfr's voice.

"I heard a crash inside Nuna's chambers and when I called out there was no answer."

"Why are you standing here, then?"

"The door's locked."

Kalfr swore and there was an enormous crash. The door juddered on its hinges, dust floating down, but it stayed firmly shut. There was a groan on the other side of the door.

"Like I said, it's locked."

"Then who else has a key? Get my brother, this instant." Nuna heard the sound of running feet retreating down the corridor.

"My lady? Ottama? Are you both alright?" Kalfr called through the door. "Help's on its way."

Nuna stared at the door and saw the key in the lock. Even if they found the spare they would never get the door open whilst that was there. Gingerly, Nuna swung herself round, lowering her feet onto the carpeted floor. She swayed as she tried to stand and Nuna was forced to sit back down, waiting for the sensation to pass.

"Kalfr," she croaked, the words scratching her throat as she looked towards the door.

Ottama was on her feet, glowering at Nuna. Her maid's normally placid, pleasant features were contorted into a feral snarl. Nuna screamed in fright, provoking more shouting and pounding from the other side of the door. Nuna struggled to stand as Ottama unsteadily advanced towards her. She was limping, her hand clasped to her side and when she moved it away her palm was covered in blood.

"Ottama, what's wrong with you?"

"It's you that should be worried, child."

At first Nuna thought it was the dizziness as Ottama's features swam before her eyes, changing into something – *someone* quite different. She pulled away her bonnet, shaking out her brown hair from the tight bun in which it was usually styled. Long, silky, dark hair flowed out and Nuna stared in horror as her old enemy, Nereth, looked at her with black eyes full of malevolence.

"What are you doing here? Where's Ottama?" Nuna shrieked, scrambling back across the bed to get away from Nereth.

"Gods, it's been *boring*, watching you every single day in this dreary, damp keep. At least when I had Karas bewitched I could have some sport with my sisters. Waiting on you, though, that's been another matter entirely. *'You will attend my chambers again tomorrow morning and instruct Katla exactly how to arrange my hair in this fashion,'*" mimicked Nereth, a wicked smile curling her lips.

Nuna could tell Nereth was hurt. She favoured her left side and was holding her ribs, blood oozing out between her fingers. That didn't stop her being dangerous. Her eyes flicked to the door, where someone was trying the key. Nereth saw it too. Nuna sprang from the bed and reached the door first, colliding with it in her haste, fingers scrabbling and missing the key in the lock as she slid to the floor. Nereth was on top of her in an instant, drawing out a dagger from her belt. Nuna screamed and lashed out, striking Nereth in her wounded side. The woman gasped, dropping the dagger, her fingers slick with blood. The point of the blade buried itself deep into the floor, an inch from Nuna's hand. Nereth dived for the dagger but Nuna shoved her back, knocking her over. She reached up behind her to try and turn the key in the lock, cursing as she realised her position was all wrong and it wouldn't move.

Nereth rose to her feet, clawing her way up the post of the bed, her chest heaving as she drew in ragged breaths. "I told your brother I'd kill you to avenge my sisters. Although he escaped that doesn't stop me finishing you."

Nuna's fingers continued to twist the key, willing it to turn. She could hear Brosa, Kalfr and Sigurd behind the door, shouting her name. Unless she opened the door from the inside there was nothing they could do.

Nuna looked down and seized the dagger on the floor. "You're welcome to try."

Nereth's eyes narrowed and as she hesitated Nuna tried to stand, wincing as she felt pain blossom in her hip and shoulder where she'd slammed into the door. Nuna raised the dagger, pointing it at Nereth as she used her free hand to try and turn the key.

*Why doesn't she use her magic?* Nuna looked more closely at Nereth, seeing how much pain she was in. *Perhaps she can't. Maybe something went wrong when the spell disguising her as Ottama broke.*

Nuna gripped the dagger more tightly and planted her feet. The key finally turned with a loud satisfying click and Nuna stepped to one side as the door burst open. Sigurd entered first and stopped short when he saw Nereth standing in front of him, her teeth bared in fury.

"You," he cried, drawing his sword, the ring of steel filling Nuna's chambers as Brosa and Kalfr also drew their blades.

"Get her out of here," shouted Sigurd, pointing at Nuna.

Nereth backed away towards the open window, a sheen of sweat breaking out on her forehead. The air became dense and heavy, the hairs on Nuna's arms standing on end as Brosa's strong hand started to steer her through the doorway.

"Take care, Brother," Kalfr said in alarm, also sensing the change in the room.

Sigurd stepped forwards and raised his sword as Nereth turned and dived for the window. Sigurd's blade caught Nereth across her back as she disappeared through the gap, falling towards the ground below with a scream.

"Let. Me. Go," hissed Nuna, shaking herself free of Brosa and pushing past Kalfr.

"No," said Sigurd, staring down at the base of the tower.

"Let me see," Nuna told him, shoving him to one side and peering down. There was nothing there. Sigurd was staring at his bloodied blade and the fine spray of blood around the whitewashed window frame and ceiling is disbelief.

"She can't have disappeared," Nuna cried, feeling dizzy as she looked at the long drop to the ground.

"That's twice she's evaded me," Sigurd said, glowering. "It won't happen again."

\*\*\*

Nuna soon wearied of telling the same tale over and over to

Sigurd, Brosa, Albrikt and her husband. Somehow they managed to keep the story from Valdimarr, although Nuna was sure it was only a matter of time before news of the incident reached him. They were all worried about her, of course, but that didn't stop her being tired, hungry and hurt. She was grateful when Katla insisted she retire for the rest of the afternoon, bringing up a jug of watered wine and some food to her freshly cleaned chambers a short while later.

"You're an angel, Katla. Have I ever told you that?"

Katla blushed, shaking her head. "I'm pleased to be of service."

"You got me out of that room, away from all those old men with their endless questions."

"My lady, one of those old men is your husband," Katla answered, with a shy grin.

Nuna smiled and the next moment she was sobbing, tears streaming down her face. Katla stared at her in shock for a moment before, hesitantly, sitting on the side of the bed and drawing her mistress into a hug.

"My lady, you mustn't cry," Katla said in soothing tones, stroking Nuna's long blonde hair. "It's over now and you're safe."

Nuna shuddered. According to Albrikt she'd been in some sort of endless slumber for the past few weeks. Ottama had tricked her, offering to show her more of this strange gift – the Sight. Nuna had no idea how real any of it was any more. Had it had all been some trick to allow Ottama – no, *Nereth*, close enough to work some kind of magic on her? She still couldn't remember all the details, her confused story baffling her listeners as much as it did herself.

Sigurd ordered his men to search Norlhast Keep high and low for any sign of Nereth, becoming enraged when Vrand reported there was no trace of her. Nuna went to Ottama's chambers herself. She picked up her maid's hairbrush, looking at the wisps of brown hair caught in the bristles. Nuna thought of the time when she first made friends with Ottama as she dressed her hair. Nereth's mocking words came back to her and Nuna gripped the handle of the brush tightly. *Even then, it wasn't really her. I've been at Norlhast Keep for over a year and Nereth has been at my side, keeping watch on me all this time.*

She felt stupid at being deceived for so long. Sigurd tried to be kind, telling her Ottama had been in his service for years before she became her maid, and he had never noticed any difference. Nuna knew he meant well, but it wasn't the same thing at all. She sobbed all the harder, Katla making shushing noises as she hugged her close.

"She was my friend," Nuna told her, clutching Katla's hand. "I thought she was my friend."

"She wasn't my lady, not really," Katla replied, squeezing her hand in return. "Does it really matter? You must know you're not short of friends here. The people here love you. You're the Lady of Norlhast Keep and that's down to you, no one else."

Nuna blinked away her tears and dried her face, sniffing in a very unladylike way. She looked closer at Katla, seeing her properly for the first time. The young woman had stayed with her, even after her close friend Amma was killed by Blackeyes' men. Katla had accompanied her without complaint when they sailed for Norlhast to start a new life there, leaving behind her family and everyone she knew in Reavesburg. Nuna felt a pang of guilt as she realised how much she had favoured Ottama over Katla, telling herself it was important she ingratiated herself with the locals. Without meaning to she'd ignored Katla and left her in the shadows, while she'd been tricked by a woman she thought was a friend.

Nuna smiled, tears pricking the corners of her eyes as she drew Katla into a tight embrace. "I'm glad you're here with me."

# CHAPTER 55

"You were gone from us for quite some time today," Etta scolded. "Whatever happened to your defensive walls? Where's your control? It's a wonder Nereth hasn't been the end of you months ago."

"My sister was in danger," I snapped. "You wouldn't understand."

"Wouldn't I?"

I folded my arms as I sat on the stool by Etta's bed in her tent, refusing to meet her gaze.

"So," Etta said after a time. "We now have an answer to one of the questions that always bothered me."

"Which is?"

"Who opened the postern gate and let Tyrfingr Black-eyes into Ulfkell's Keep on the night Jorik was killed."

"Ottama," I whispered, remembering walking past her that night on my way back from Desta's chambers.

"Nereth," corrected Etta. "She must have been there from the beginning, after you unmasked her at Karas' court and she made her escape from Sigurd's dungeons. She never fled Norlhast at all – just took on a disguise and bided her time. We invited our enemy right into our midst during your sister's wedding and we never suspected a thing."

"She plays her parts so well. I thought …" My voice broke and it took me a moment to be able to continue. "I really thought it was Nuna."

Etta sighed. "You saw what you wanted to see, I understand that. I keep forgetting you're only eighteen. We've raised you to take on responsibilities that far outstrip your years and you bear them well. The odd lapse of judgement is no great surprise. In my experience we learn most from our mistakes. If I'm hard on you it's only because in the world we're living in any mistake could be your last – you see that, don't you?"

I nodded. "Of course I do."

Etta raised an eyebrow. "I'm sure you do. And Nereth made mistakes too, despite all her cunning plans."

"Like Leif?"

"Like Leif, yes. The way he took charge in her world, forcing it to change according to his will." Etta chuckled. "I bet she didn't see *that* coming. It makes it all the more important we protect him and the rest of your Fellowship. You must apply yourself, Rothgar, so there's no gap in your defences. After everything that's happened in the last few days using ataraxia would be advisable. Give your mind time to rest and recover."

I rubbed the sides of my head, a residual ache there, just behind my eyes. "What kind of a world do we live in, Etta, where the realms of the living and the dead collide with those of the Real and Dream?"

"I can make an educated guess. I think you could too, if you applied your mind to the question."

I thought about that for a time, reflecting on what I had seen and learned. Pieces of the puzzle began to fall into place, as if I had known this all along and yet somehow forgotten. "The Calling is Adalrikr's attempt to restore the lesser durath to Amuran, and in doing so the other realms are affected too, making magic more potent and Amuran less stable as a result, like in the war. When Sinarr's blood magic made him powerful it also established a link with the Realm of the Dead, bringing his shade into this world."

"My thoughts exactly," Etta replied with a smile, looking at me proudly. "Although I wouldn't say Adalrikr is *attempting* to bring back the durath from the Shadow Realm – the magic of the Calling has already succeeded. Sandar was able to work much the same thing in Tullen and we know the fate of the tributes brought to Vorund is to become hosts for the durath. That is the only limitation. Durath summoned from the Shadow Realm must find a host if they are to survive the transition to the Real. Adalrikr has been in power at Vorund for more than four years, growing the numbers of durath in his service all that time. And I think you're right – the other realms are all affected. How else could Sinarr the Cold One exist as one of the undead, years after Adalrikr cast him aside as his host?"

I shivered, my skin crawling at the thought. "When we talk of such things, our task seems hopeless."

"I don't think so. Though I will admit that it's more difficult than even I'd first imagined. Joldir's staff took years to create, imbued with magic and power and fashioned with one purpose – to destroy the Sundered Souls. Now it lies shattered on the battlefield, its magic spent and the only weapon we have left of equal power are Thengill's axes."

"The runeblades didn't work because Sinarr was one of the undead."

"And who's to say there aren't more creatures like Sinarr the Cold One? The Weeping Warrior gave you that blade and the knowledge of those runes for a purpose. This is something I need to dwell on for a time."

I drew my blade, staring at the new runes that now ran along its length, Joldir's craftsmanship intertwined with a gift of knowledge and power from beyond the grave. Whilst the new runes were black the dragon and chimera runes glowed blue, illuminating the soft light within Etta's tent with an un-earthly quality.

"At least we're not surrounded by the undead," I ob-served with forced levity, gazing at the sword for a time before sheathing it again. Even now the durath were in our camp, somewhere nearby.

"The runestones can never be fully effective," Etta re-minded me. "We saw that when the durath attacked your Fellowship in the camp. These are dangerous times, and in all of this we have seen Nereth is bent on vengeance against you.

Her powers were weakened by her fight with Leif, especially when she was forced to use the last of her magic to escape from Sigurd. But she will recover her strength, I'm sure of it. She may be Adalrikr's servant but her agenda against you is personal. You must be careful. Promise me you will be, Rothgar."

I held up my hands in mock surrender. "I promise. I really do."

"Hmm. We'll see, won't we?"

"It was good to see you outside the other day," I said, more to change the subject than anything else. "I thought you might never leave your bed again."

"Hah. I just wanted to find out if I still could, and the excuse of seeing the battle unfold was too good to miss. Looks like I became overexcited."

I reached over and put my hand on top of Etta's thin arm. "Then rest while you can. We still need you."

Etta grinned, patting my hand. "Oh, of course you do. Don't worry, I don't intend on going anywhere until this is all over."

***

The air outside Etta's tent was fresher, less oppressive, and I breathed deeply, trying to relax as my headache eased a little more. There was no one nearby. The durath may have infiltrated our camp but they were not showing their hand – not yet. I wended my way through the protective runestones, making for Johan's tent where the rest of the Brotherhood were gathered. It was late afternoon and I wanted something to eat and drink, a chance to recover from recent events and do something normal with my friends. Later today the clan moot would take place at Romsdahl Castle – when all the politicking would start once more and the leadership of Reavesburg Clan would be decided. I thought of Desta, far away in Reavesburg, waiting for news of the war in the south, unaware Finn was now fatherless. What kind of a war were we fighting, where the people I cared about suffered, even when we're victorious? I sighed and continued walking towards the feasting tent, arranging a convincing smile on my face as I passed the guards and stepped inside.

# CHAPTER 56

Johan Jokellsward and his followers arrived at Romsdahl Castle that evening dressed in all their finery, their travel-stained garb stowed away for this grand occasion. Johan was accompanied by Damona, resplendent in a long white gown, with Ingirith and Maeva accorded the honour of acting as her maids. Bandor sat next to his father wearing a fine blue cloak trimmed with white fox fur, his armour polished and gleaming and Freydja, as his betrothed, took a seat at his left. That drew some comments from people in the hall. Freydja remained calm and serene, ignoring it all as she spoke to Bandor, whose eyes never strayed from her for long.

The surviving warriors of Kalamar, proudly led by Petr, took their places on Johan's side of the table as his honour guard, with Svan walking to his seat at the table arm in arm with Dalla. Sigolf Admundson and Jolinn Hrodidottir, representing the warriors of Falsten, Delving and Olt took their places next. Then it was my turn to enter the hall, Ulfarr at my side with Skari, Myr and Ekkill, as we walked the length of the hall and joined the assembly. Gautarr Falrufson sat at the head of the table, the rest of his family and Romsdahl's warriors and nobles sitting opposite us. Our host clapped his hands and music began to play while his servants entered carrying platters of food and jugs of ale and wine. A boar was being roasted above the fire and the smells of pheasant and goose being served at the table made my mouth water.

Two more tables had been set in the hall for the rest of Romsdahl's warriors and they were still walking in when Gautarr stood, raising a huge mug of foaming ale into the air. "The Vorund Clan has been vanquished. Romsdahl is free!" There were plenty of roars at that. "Let's eat and drink with our friends and allies, because this day will go down in the history of our clan as the day when Adalrikr discovered he doesn't rule the north."

The crowd roared louder still, stamping their feet, clapping their hands, banging mugs and the hilts of their daggers on the tables as they cheered in approval. The music started up again and the feast began.

Ekkill tapped me on the shoulder and pointed across the room. "Someone doesn't look too happy."

I glanced over to the table by the wall, where Domarr was sitting with a group of warriors, looking sullen and disinterested in his food and what was going on around him. The rest of his family was sitting on the central table; Ragnar with his wife and children, Throm next to them. Also eating with us were Svafa and Tomas, who had both earned honour for their part in the battle. Adakan, a man in his mid-twenties with brown hair and a neat beard, sat closer to Gautarr, in recognition of the number of men under his command and the role he'd played in helping to turn the tide and break the Vorund Clan. He watched proceedings warily with dark, brooding eyes.

Ulfarr spoke to me in an undertone. "Gautarr was furious with Domarr when he learned Joarr the Hammer had escaped. I think he was being harsh, because when that storm struck it caused mayhem. Brought down half the palisade and enabled Gautarr's cavalry to break through and rout Joarr's forces. But when Joarr managed to slip away Gautarr wasn't going to take the blame for that one, was he?"

I shook my head, looking away as Domarr saw me watching and stared back at me darkly. "Perhaps we should talk about something else."

There was no shortage of food and drink but as the evening wore on the celebratory atmosphere faded, the mood turning more fractious once had Karlin opened the formal clan moot. The first question was determining who had the right to speak and vote on the matters facing the clan. Hereditary titles were no longer a guarantee of such rights, not now the Reavesburg Clan was so divided, as Karlin explained to those crowded inside the hall.

"For many years the leaders of six houses governed the affairs of the Reavesburg Clan. Times have changed. Reavesburg itself is now ruled by Tyrfingr Blackeyes, while Noln's elder, Lundvarr, has sworn fealty to Adalrikr. Olt's warriors were divided in the recent battle but it is a fact that Alfarr, Hrodi Myndillson's grandson, has pledged his cause and the men still under his command to fight for the Vorund Clan. Tullen by Lake Tull, for years the foremost house of the western lands, has been destroyed, whilst Kalamar's warriors have been vanquished."

"Have a care," growled Svan, as Dalla patted his hand and restrained him from getting up from his seat.

Karlin gave Svan an apologetic look. "I did not intend to cause offence – these are simply the facts. It will not be forgotten that Johan and the house of Kalamar came to our aid, with the warriors of Olt, Delving and Falsten. However, Gautarr Falrufson and his house at Romsdahl has weathered this storm and survived with his fortress and his warriors. Clearly, his right to speak and vote in this moot is beyond question."

"Now there's a surprise," muttered Ekkill under his breath.

The debate began, with people putting forward their cases to represent what remained of the Reavesburg Clan. When it was clear she had their support it was quickly agreed that Jolinn should speak for the warriors of Olt and she named an older warrior, Beinir, as her new second to replace Lars. This was no great surprise, as the ties between Olt and Romsdahl were strong and Gautarr obviously wanted to reward Jolinn's loyalty. Adakan was also granted the right to speak, reflecting the fact he commanded the second largest single group of warriors after Gautarr himself. I felt unsure if this was wise. I didn't know the young warrior and clearly we owed him a great debt but, until today, he had been one of Gautarr's northern bannermen. I wondered if Gautarr saw him as someone he could easily sway to his cause. Despite my misgivings, Johan spoke eloquently on Adakan's behalf and supported the decision.

After more debate it was agreed Sigolf would speak for the western men, comprising the surviving warriors of Delving and Falsten. This prompted a great cheer from the people of Falsten crowded into the hall, who had never seen their small town attract such significance before. There was also wholehearted support from the Delving folk, still mourning the deaths of their leaders, amongst whom Sigolf was a popular figure. As the noise died down Karlin looked around the room and asked if there were any more nominations.

"You jest with us, surely?" Svan said, his voice low and dangerous. "You know that Johan commands the Brotherhood, that he gathered together the army that marched to your aid and liberated your home. If anyone has the right to speak it's him. Speak and, more importantly, lead. I say Johan Jokellsward is the rightful chief of the Reavesburg Clan."

The hall erupted, people standing and gesticulating as they shouted at each other. Some tried to shout Svan down, while others on our side of the table began chanting Johan's name. Eventually, the clamour died down and Gautarr rose to speak.

"Johan, I see you've gathered men loyal to you and your cause. What you've achieved is remarkable, truly, and we are in your debt, of that there's no doubt. But the name the Vorund Clan gave you, the Landless Jarl ... No. No, wait, hear me out." Gautarr paused, placating hands outstretched, until the objections from half the crowd fell back to a low rumble of discontent. "The truth is, you lead this army but you no longer speak for a people or a house. Kalamar is gone. The right to speak at a clan moot is granted by the people. Where are the people of Kalamar?"

"What if we say he speaks for us?" Sigolf shouted.

"And us," added Jolinn. "He's our leader and our chief, whatever reason you might try and find to remove him from your council."

"And that's who he should be," Throm announced, speaking up for the first time. All eyes turned on him.

"And what do you mean by that, cousin?" Ragnar asked, glowering.

"These are not normal times," Throm replied. "The Romsdahl house commands the most warriors, no question. However, that's not enough. This was a battle where magic played its part. Indeed, the outcome turned on breaking the magic of Sinarr and his allies. The account given of the battle between Sinarr and Johan was illuminating. How Sinarr was able to withstand a series of killing blows until he was torn asunder by a magical blade, wielded by Rothgar Kolfinnarson, one of Johan's closest followers." His eyes flicked in my direction before he turned back to his uncle. "How he came to be there has yet to be explained but there's no denying the effectiveness of his handiwork. The circle of ice where Sinarr fell remains, reminding us all this was no figment of our imagination."

I glanced in Adakan's direction and saw the man staring right at me with those dark eyes. I turned away. Several people were cheering my name, although I noted a good number were not and Romsdahl's warriors looked at me suspiciously.

"He's good. I like this one," Ekkill whispered to me, a wolfish grin on his face as he listened to Throm continue his speech.

"Johan and his followers understand the use of magic. They understand the nature of our foes and how to destroy them, something I hope they intend to share with us if we can find a way to work together. And we must, for Adalrikr will not take this defeat lightly. He will return, seeking vengeance, and we will need to be at our strongest to survive. The warriors of Romsdahl alone cannot defeat Adalrikr – we need the rest of the Reavesburg Clan at our side. Johan Jokellsward was born to lead us in this struggle. Whilst his house is no more, he speaks for than just a people – he speaks for a movement, a movement that has grown into an uprising against Adalrikr."

Freydja was smiling at her brother's words. However, Jora's eyes were narrowed slits as she spoke to Throm. "How could you? We have given you shelter, brought you up from when you were a boy and this is how you repay us? Your uncle's time to be chief is now and you, of all people – our own kin – you *dare* to speak against him?"

Throm turned to Jora, his face open and sincere. I admired his calm demeanour as he met her flinty stare. I wondered how much he resembled his late father, Egill, at this moment. "Aunt Jora, I love both you and my uncle. As you said, you have given me a home, raised me alongside Ragnar, making us closer to brothers than cousins. I mean no insult, but a clan moot is a place for honesty so that the right decisions are made. The future of our clan hangs in the balance, and that is more important than loyalty to one house or another."

"And what would your decision be?" asked Gautarr with a sneer. "What does my nephew think is the right course of action? Speaking honestly."

Throm smiled, maintaining his composure. "You have granted Sigolf and Jolinn the right to speak for their houses at the moot, and their views on who they will follow are very clear. If we are to avoid a split within our clan a way forward must be found that we can all accept. I say that those appointed as the elders and leaders of their houses remain as such and, during this time of war, we set the matter of clan chief to one side. As I've said, no one knows our foes better than Johan Jokellsward. I say we appoint him as our battle chief, with full rights to speak at the clan moot and to lead us into this war with the Vorund Clan. All of our houses should be pledged to the Brotherhood of the Eagle, with Johan leading us in this war."

Gautarr was clearly surprised by Throm's answer and I watched as he thought on what his nephew had said, brows furrowed. He turned to Adakan, his bannerman and now a leader with full rights at the clan moot. "And what do you think of this suggestion, Adakan?"

The warrior looked self-conscious as he stood, aware all eyes were looking at him. "You've been head of our house since I was a boy and I'm loyal to you still, Gautarr, you know that. But I can see wisdom in Throm's words as well. The House of Romsdahl cannot win this fight unaided, and the Brotherhood follows Johan. This proposal to appoint a battle chief is a sensible compromise, which means no one is dishonoured."

Johan stood and nodded to Gautarr. "What you said before is true. My lands have been taken, my people scattered or dead. All I have now is my family," he smiled, lines creasing about his eyes, as he looked at Damona and Bandor. "And I have more than that. The Brotherhood has given me purpose, one I can fulfil through leading our warriors in this war. I would be willing to serve all of Reavesburg as battle chief, if that is the will of this meeting."

Our side of the table roared in approval and I was pleased to see Tomas and Svafa nodding with more muted support. Gautarr and Jora exchanged a look and the pair whispered together before Gautarr stood and spoke to Johan, his voice loud so all could hear.

"And afterwards? I don't doubt your battle skills, Johan. You would serve us all well in this war, I'm sure, but what happens when we're victorious? What then, when the question of who is clan chief must be decided, once and for all?"

Johan took his time before replying, a distant look on his face. "Kalamar is gone forever, both town and castle destroyed. To represent the people in a clan moot I must speak for a house, so I would like to stake my claim to establish a new one, founded upon Reavesburg itself with Ulfkell's Keep as my new home. Then the question of whether the seat of power for the Reavesburg Clan is found at Ulfkell's Keep or Romsdahl Castle can finally be settled."

I stared at Johan, hardly able to believe what I had heard.

I wasn't the only one to be taken aback. Svan and Dalla were busy speaking to each other, Bandor looked shocked and his mother leaned in close to Johan, whispering urgently to her husband.

Gautarr grinned and nodded. "I don't like the idea of Tyrfingr Blackeyes sitting on Reave's Chair any more than you do, but Ulfkell's Keep is a strong fortress – it could take years to recapture it. If you don't succeed, there will be no seat for you to hold. And once the war is over and the Reavesburg Clan lands have been freed there will be no need for you to be our battle chief. I can live with these terms, but can you? Honestly?"

Johan nodded, turning to Damona. "I can. In truth, all that matters to me is conquering the Vorund Clan. Kalamar lies in the past."

"In that case, Johan Jokellsward, I agree to the suggestion of my nephew and drink to your health. To Johan Jokellsward, Battle Chief of the Reavesburg Clan." Gautarr raised his mug and everyone in the hall drank a toast to Johan, Domarr the Oak a notable exception, scowling as he watched proceedings, his drink untouched. Throm sat back in his chair, looking drained and relieved. Ragnar and Asta were deep in conversation next to him and everyone began talking at once, noise filling the hall.

Ekkill leaned across and whispered into my ear. "That was well-played. Throm has revealed himself to be accomplished in the arts of politicking." I frowned, unable to form a reply, Johan's words concerning Ulfkell's Keep swirling in my mind.

Karlin stood once more, raising his hands and asking for quiet. When the hall was still he spoke, his voice loud and clear as it filled the chamber. "The speakers are appointed. Let the clan moot begin."

# CHAPTER 57

"Now the speakers have been appointed, there is one matter I insist we attend to without delay," Gautarr told his audience, turning in my direction. "Johan might lead us into battle but this is still my house and I am still jarl of Romsdahl. Have Thengill brought here, now."

The hall filled with a low murmur as we waited for Thengill to be fetched from the dungeons. Thengill walked with a straight back as he entered the hall surrounded by guards, despite his bound hands and travel-stained clothes. The Romsdahl warriors began to hurl abuse, while Johan's men tried to shout them down. Gautarr was forced to pound the handle of his axe on the table, sending plates and cups jumping, to quieten the uproar.

Freydja stood and raised her hands before Gautarr could address the moot. "Uncle, please. I would speak to you concerning this."

Gautarr stared at her in surprise before his face softened. "Freydja, the ancient rites have been followed to appoint the speakers at this clan moot. I don't recall you being named as one of them."

Freydja smiled. "I know, but there is something I must say, before we proceed any further." She drew herself up with poise and refinement, making the most of her height and drawing the eyes of every man in the room.

"I will grant you this indulgence, Niece, since it is so important to you."

Bandor rose from his seat, his hand entwined with Freydja's as he swallowed and met Gautarr's gaze. "I have been betrothed to Freydja for more than a year. Dinuvillan has smiled upon our fortunes and brought us together again, against all the odds. When I went to battle I knew there was a chance I wouldn't return. Some of my friends died, as did many warriors of Romsdahl, including my own commander, Haki. If we're set on this path to war then I know I'll probably lose more friends. I want to enjoy the time I have left, whether my life is long or short, and I know Freydja thinks the same."

A shy grin spread over Freydja's face. "What he's saying, Uncle, is that we would like to be wed, today, with everyone in this castle as our witnesses. I want this too and, more than anything, I want your blessing on our marriage. You've raised me as your own daughter and kept me safe all these years but is anyone really safe any longer?"

Gautarr turned to Johan and Damona. "And this is what you both want as well? Do you support this union?"

"I want what will make my son happy," Damona replied.

"If the son of the Landless Jarl is considered a worthy match," added Johan.

Gautarr's gaze lingered on his niece and Bandor, watching them intently. "You're young, Freydja. This is a big decision, one that will affect the rest of your life."

"I want this. We want this. Do we have your blessing?"

Gautarr laughed. "Aye, how could I deny you after you've asked such a question in front of all of Romsdahl? Yes, you have my support and I would not be the one to deny you happiness. And Bandor is no longer the son of the Landless Jarl but the son of Reavesburg's battle chief. There is honour in that, no question."

Bandor bowed his head. "I will treat your niece well, I promise you. You have my thanks."

"And no doubt you will want to discuss the terms of her dowry?" Gautarr said to Johan.

"If I may," Bandor interjected. "I have one more favour to ask of you, concerning that subject."

"And what might that be?"

Bandor bowed his head. "I will not seek a dowry for

your niece's hand in marriage. I would ask instead for a weregild."

Gautarr's eyes narrowed. "That's ... unconventional. A blood price, then?"

"In a way," Bandor explained. "The price I seek is Thengill's freedom and acceptance –"

The hall erupted once more, the Romsdahl warriors vocalising their displeasure at the idea. Thengill stood there impassively, Ulfarr, Myr and Skari all looking on anxiously. Slowly the noise quietened.

"Under our laws I may name my price, can I not?" Bandor asked. "It is a bargain that we strike between us. What use is gold to me, when we march to war? I consider Thengill to be a brother – we have been through so much together and he has made the choice to fight with us, rather than for Adalrikr. That must count for something in these times. We need every warrior willing to side with us if Adalrikr is to be defeated and he is a member of the Brotherhood, sworn to see the Kinslayer brought down. I ask for you to show leniency and look beyond his clan and the deeds of the past and consider where his loyalties lie today."

"I have no question concerning Thengill's allegiance," Johan told the warriors packed into the hall. "We face a foe the like of which we have never seen before. Please, if our houses are to be joined through marriage then I would ask you not to darken that day by passing judgement on a man who is no more a member of the Vorund Clan than I am."

Gautarr sat there for a time, deep in thought. "Gods, are you actually considering this?" hissed Ragnar.

"A weregild dowry. Strange times indeed," Gautarr answered. "And yes, my son, I'm considering this boon my future son-in-law has asked of me. You've heard Bandor and Johan speak in Thengill's defence. If this is the marriage price, so be it. I'll seal this pact between our families with Thengill's freedom, if that's truly what you want, Freydja."

Freydja beamed at Bandor, hand still clasped tightly in

his. "It is, Uncle. It is."

Domarr the Oak rose with a few of his fellow warriors and stalked from the hall. Jora looked as if she was about to say something but Gautarr put his hand on hers and watched in silence as his nephew pushed open the doors and walked outside.

Gautarr turned to Karlin. "It would appear you have a marriage ceremony to perform."

***

I watched Freydja dancing with Bandor, the tables pushed to the sides of the hall to give everyone space as Karlin's players filled the room with energetic music. Freydja looked delighted, dark hair flying out across her shoulders as Bandor spun her around, his face bright red and shining with sweat. Johan and Damona danced beside them and even Gautarr and Jora took to the floor. Once more the unwelcome thought intruded that it could have been me, had things turned out differently. I drank deeply from my cup, savouring the taste of sweet red wine – a fine vintage Gautarr had brought up from his cellars especially for this occasion. It took some of the edge off my mood, or so I told myself.

On the other side of the hall Thengill raised his mug to me in greeting, observing from the sidelines with his friends around him; Myr and Skari's faces were alert and ready for trouble, Ulfarr watching everyone carefully, drinking far less than he would normally. Svafa was busy talking to them, making a show of friendship and the young man went up in my estimation. I knew that gesture would cost him but he had fought side by side with Ulfarr's crew and I could tell there was a bond between them now – sword brothers, united against a common foe. Throm walked up to me, Tomas at his side. He smiled, sweeping his sweaty dark hair out of his eyes and blew out his cheeks.

"The heat in this hall is unbearable," he announced. "I think it was more comfortable fighting the Vorund Clan than dancing in here. Certainly less tiring."

I smiled in return. "Tomas. I hear people are no longer foolish enough to call you a coward after your deeds."

"Aye. I think I've proved myself to those doubters," he answered, his face sporting numerous cuts and scratches. "Just a pity Haki isn't around to see this day. It would have been satisfying to see the look on his face. Feels like I've shaken something off – stepped out of my father's shadow."

"You did well," Throm told him, slapping a hand down on his shoulder. Tomas grinned and left us to find more food.

"You did too," I said to Throm. "You gave me your word and you stuck to it."

"You don't look so happy. We won, man, and you defeated Sinarr the Cold One. Now you're standing here scowling as if that's the last thing you wanted."

"I might have slain Sinarr but I don't see the celebrations centring around me," I replied, taking another sip of wine and feeling light-headed in the heat of the hall. "In fact, it's scarcely been mentioned since I returned to Romsdahl Castle."

"Is that really such a surprise?" Throm asked, leaning close to me and speaking in a lower tone. "There are all manner of rumours circulating – tales of magical swords, how the men fighting Johan's warriors were more like animals, turning to *ice* when they died. A magical fighting circle no one was able to cross. How one moment you were seen cowering on the walls of Romsdahl and the next Sinarr is no more, a jumble of frozen flesh and bone lying at your feet. People are suspicious of you, Rothgar, and with good reason. Perhaps if you told me how you managed such a feat I could quell the rumours and tell people the true story."

"I might tell you one day, when the time is right. Your chief needs to speak with Johan first. Let's just say for now that I've learned Amuran is a stranger place than I ever thought possible."

Throm looked like he was about to argue with me, then he shrugged and took a drink from his cup, wiping his mouth with the back of his hand. "Fair enough, let's leave such matters for the jarls and battle chiefs to sort out between them."

"I thought you played your hand well. You kept your word while remaining loyal to Gautarr. You didn't dispute his claim to be chief and your suggestion allowed Johan to be recognised and treated with honour. Sooner or later, though, you'll have to choose a side when the time comes to settle who rules the Reavesburg Clan."

"Nothing is certain in war – much could change before then," Throm replied, looking thoughtful.

"Rothgar," Bandor was shouting at me as he approached, weaving drunkenly, a grin splitting his youthful face. Freydja was talking to Ragnar and Asta, laughing with them, although I thought Ragnar's smile looked forced. I drew Bandor into a hug and patted his back.

"Are you alright?" he asked. "You've hardly moved from that spot all evening."

"I'm fine. Just tired, that's all."

"Listen, what my father said about Reavesburg and Ulfkell's Keep. I just wanted you to know he never mentioned that to me before tonight. It's still your home too and we want you there beside us, when all this is over."

The smile on my face became fixed. "Just the small matter of Tyrfingr Blackeyes sitting on Reave's Chair."

"He has to die," Bandor told me, a dark look on his face for a fleeting moment. "He took my sister's life. I won't rest until he's dead and the Reavesburg Clan has taken back everything that belongs to us."

"Except Kalamar."

Bandor stared at me. "Kalamar's gone. There's a difference. When those ancient walls were shattered, I couldn't believe my eyes. My childhood home, utterly destroyed and gone forever."

"So, Ulfkell's Keep calls to your household, does it?" I took another sip of wine, my hand trembling a little.

Bandor frowned. "It does, which is only right. I know this must be difficult for you but someone must claim the ancestral seat of power. You swore an oath to serve my father and his house and he has the right to stake that claim and every reason too – to see justice is done, to drive away the Vorund Clan once and for all."

"It's *my* ancestral home, Bandor," I replied, my voice rising more than I'd intended.

Bandor sucked in a breath, letting it out slowly. "No one has forgotten that." He made an impatient sound and began to head back towards Freydja. I cursed myself for not handling things better.

"Bandor," I called out. He paused and turned back to me.

"I'm sorry, that was the drink talking, nothing more. Congratulations to both of you," I told him. "You'll be happy with Freydja, I know you will. I wish you both well, truly."

Bandor sighed and smiled. "I know you do. I'll see you later."

***

"You alright?"

I turned to see Jolinn striding towards me across the courtyard, where I was leaning against the broad trunk of the oak tree that gave its shade to this space. The sun had set and it was cool out here, pleasant after the stifling heat of the hall. Jolinn's face was still bruised, a purple welt mirroring the hilt of Sinarr's sword, and one of her eyes was blood red. She gave no outward sign of being in pain, though I was sure it must still hurt. There was a crooked smile on her lips as she approached.

"Hiding out here, are you?"

"Not exactly, just getting some air."

"Hmm. Dancing's not really my thing, if I'm honest," she told me, dropping down on to her haunches with her back against the tree. I saw a brief grimace pass over her face before she smiled again, running her hand over her close-cropped blonde hair.

"I saw that look on your face, when Johan made his claim to Ulfkell's Keep."

"It's fine."

Jolinn raised an eyebrow. "Really?"

"Of course. I swore an oath of service to Johan's house, so any claim I might have had is in the past. Times have moved on, or so everyone keeps telling me."

Jolinn leant her head back, resting it on the smooth bark of the tree. I noticed a few people had carved their names into the trunk and idly wondered who they were and what had happened to them.

"I wasn't able to forget who my father was," said Jolinn after a time. "Everyone in Olt knew Hrodi Whitebeard and he didn't object to me using the name Hrodidottir, so he legitimised me to an extent, I suppose. But I was never treated as one of the family – more of an embarrassment, really, especially when I began to get noticed on the practice courts, besting some of his warriors with a blade. And why not? I figured if I was going to make my way in the world it would be on my own terms, and there's nothing more self-sufficient than a warrior.

"As I grew older, though, I began to realise how all the wealth and power of Olt was going to pass to my half-brother Radholf and, eventually, to that idiot son of his, Alfarr. I never received an extra penny from my father or his family, even though I was living in their home. Just the coin I was due as one of their warriors. It was enough, although it began to rankle after a time."

"Why are you telling me all this?" I asked.

"I guess I'm saying life isn't fair. That doesn't stop us making the best of what we have, though, does it? From what I understand, your interests are served by Johan taking Ulfkell's Keep. You might not be the ruling family any more, but does it really matter? Do you even want to rule the clan, if you could?"

I thought about that for a while. "I was brought up as the second son, so ruling the clan was never really something I seriously considered. Jorik was groomed to succeed my father and I just imagined that one day I'd be one of his jarls, helping him govern Reavesburg."

"How differently things have turned out," Jolinn said.

"But you're still close to the seat of power – you have considerable influence for one so young. You've achieved a great deal, just not in the way you were expecting."

I smiled. "I know you're right. It was just, when Johan spoke those words, it made it real, somehow, even though nothing's really changed. The realisation hit me and I understood that part of my life is over. Like I said, it's something I've always known, but hearing Ulfkell's Keep and Reave's Chair spoken about like that before the leaders of the whole clan, it ..."

"Forced you to swallow your pride?" Jolinn finished for me.

"Yes, something like that."

Jolinn laughed. "At least you're bright enough to understand that – not many men your age would. Come on, you can't stay here for the rest of the night or people will think you've taken umbrage."

I sighed and stood up, brushing the dirt from the seat of my breeches and offered Jolinn my arm. She took it as I helped her to stand, a strong warrior grip.

"I'll go back inside, but I'm not dancing," I told her.

Jolinn laughed. "Neither am I, though I could manage some more of that red wine Gautarr's opened. That slips down very well and I think we've both earned a drink, don't you?"

We must have looked like an odd couple as we walked back through the gates, the tall lithe shieldmaiden of Olt arm in arm with Johan's crippled young counsellor. Jolinn found me a cup of wine, passing it to me with a sly grin. I took a sip, thinking it tasted less refined than the stuff I'd been drinking earlier, although I didn't really care. Jolinn was right, of course: life wasn't always fair. As I glanced around the festivities in the hall I took a moment to reflect on what we had achieved, against the odds.

*Sinarr the Cold One is dead and the Brotherhood grows stronger.* I imagined the reactions of Adalrikr Kinslayer and Tyrfingr Blackeyes when they received reports of events in

Romsdahl. We posed a real threat to their ambitions and my vengeance for what took place in Ulfkell's Keep was one step closer. I sipped my wine and smiled.

# EPILOGUE

"My lady, it grows dark. Perhaps we should return in the morning?" said Katla.

"No. I'll not sleep for a moment unless I see what they've found. Come with me, I need you by my side."

Nuna rose from her chair, muscles stiff and sore from numerous aches and pains caused by her fight with Nereth. She pushed them from her mind as she leaned on her maid's arm and together they walked over to the door Brosa held open for them. Her bodyguard fell into step behind them as they followed Styrman. The old servant led them through the gates of Norlhast Keep, more guards accompanying them as they walked through Norlhast's streets. Nuna already knew where they were heading – after all, she was the one who told them to look there in the first place. Kalfr met them outside the mean house with its turf roof. Rothgar had shown her the house when they had stayed in Norlhast together – Karas' old dwelling, when he had been in thrall to the coven.

"You were right, my lady," Kalfr told her as they approached. "You don't have to go inside if you don't want to. I'm not sure if –"

"Kalfr, please lead the way," Nuna said, abruptly cutting him off. "I am no feeble creature in need of your protection. Show me what you've found."

Kalfr nodded and opened the door, leading them inside the dark dwelling. It was cold and smelled dank – no one had lived here in some time. Nuna shivered, drawing her cloak tight as her eyes became accustomed to the gloom, the only light provided by a few lamps scattered around the room as the fire pit was dark. Most of the lamps were gathered in one corner. Sigurd was standing there with his father and both of them turned as Kalfr led them inside.

"My lady, it's just as you said," Sigurd told her. "Are you sure you want to see this?"

Nuna didn't answer as she stepped forwards, peering into the hole that had been dug in the corner by Albrikt's sons, the only people she was willing to trust with this. They had uncovered a shallow grave, the skeleton crammed into the space, despite its small stature. The clothing was stained and already rotting but it was unmistakably the outfit worn by a maid. Styrman looked closer and gave a sigh, bending down on old knees to reach into the grave, delicately picking up the pendant of a small silver necklace between his finger and thumb.

"It's Ottama," he said, his voice little more than a whisper. "This was her mother's – she never took it off. Oh, Ottama …"

"The poor girl's been dead for a year, perhaps longer," Albrikt told her, his face looking older and more careworn in the lantern light. "Dinuvillan, protect us." He made a sign to ward off evil.

Sigurd looked closely at Nuna. "How did you know?"

Nuna wondered what to say. Although she trusted the men in this room with her life she wasn't even sure she understood the truth herself.

"Something Nereth said, before she fled," she told them, uncomfortable with the lie that came to her lips. That story would serve for now.

"I half-expected it to be a trap," Sigurd said. "Yet here she is, just as you said."

Nuna put her hand on Styrman's shoulder. "No one must know of this, particularly Valdimarr and his cronies. We must move quickly and bury her properly, including the pendant. It's only right she keeps it."

Styrman nodded, letting the silver necklace drop from his fingers with a soft thud. Nuna squeezed his shoulder.

"I'm sorry."

Styrman sniffed. "Nothing to be sorry about, my lady. It's you that's given the young girl peace, and you have my thanks for that."

Nuna was crying when she left the house, Katla and Brosa at her side. She'd lost a friend and grieved for Ottama, even though she'd never truly known the girl. Her emotions left her confused, angry and weary. She reached out and took Katla's arm, holding her tight.

"Shall we return to the keep?" Katla asked.

Nuna nodded and they set off, feeling cold even though it was a summer night. She glanced back once towards the house, where weak yellow light leaked out into the streets around the door frame. Standing there was a young woman, her brown hair tied back in a tight bun. She smiled shyly, nodding in thanks to Nuna before she raised the hood of her cloak and melted into the night. Nuna knew she would never see the young woman again.

"She can rest in peace now," Nuna said, wiping the tears from her eyes as they walked back to the keep.

# CHARACTER LIST

Square brackets around a [name] denotes that this character has already passed into Navan's Halls at the start of Sundered Souls.

## The Reavesburg Clan

The Brotherhood of the Eagle – an uprising of Reavesburg's warriors fighting occupation by the Vorund Clan

**Johan Jokellsward** – leader of the Brotherhood of the Eagle and jarl of Kalamar. His stronghold of Kalamar Castle on the northern border with Norlhast was sacked by Sinarr the Cold One. Also known as **Johan Landless** or the **Landless Jarl**
**Damona Johanswyfe** – wife of Johan and mother of Bandor and Reesha
    **[Reesha Jorikswyfe]** – Johan Jokellsward's daughter and Jorik Kolfinnarson's wife. Reesha, Jorik and their son, Kolfinnar the Younger were killed in the fall of Ulfkell's Keep, murdered by Tyrfingr Blackeyes
    **Bandor Johanson** – Johan's only son, engaged to Freyjda Egilldottir

Survivors of Kalamar and founding members of the Brotherhood

**Ingirith Ruggaswyfe** – widow of Rugga and confidante of Damona
    **Egill Ruggason** – Ingirith's son
    **Kitta Ruggadottir** – Ingirith's daughter

**Petr Hamarrson** – a warrior of Kalamar, Johan's second
**Svan** – a warrior of Kalamar, married to Dalla
**Dalla Svanswyfe** – wife of Svan
**Brandr** – a warrior of Kalamar, married to Maeva
**Maeva Brandrswyfe** – wife of Brandr
**Eykr** – a warrior of Kalamar
**Faraldr** – a warrior of Kalamar
**Gunnarr** – a warrior of Kalamar, known as **Old Gunnarr**
**Harvald** – a warrior of Kalamar
**Ragni** – a warrior of Kalamar
**Varinn** – a warrior of Kalamar
**Yngvarr** – a warrior of Kalamar

Other warriors of the Brotherhood

**Ulfarr** – the former leader of a band of outlaws, now a follower
of Johan Jokellsward
**Skari One Eye** – the longest serving member of Ulfarr's crew
**Myr the Silent** – one of Ulfarr's crew
**Sir Patrick Wild** – one of Ulfarr's crew, a fallen Berian knight
from Brighthorn Keep
**Ekkill** – one of Etta's spies, now acting as a scout in Ulfarr's
crew
**Thengill** – an exiled warrior from Vorund, loyal to their former
chief Asmarr, now serving in Ulfarr's crew. He is immune to
the powers of the Sight and cannot be possessed by the durath
**Sigolf Admundson** – elder of Falsten, the first Reavesburg
town to answer Johan's call to arms
**Geirmarr Flint** – elder of the mining town of Delving in the
Baros Mountains, who joined to Johan's call to arms
**Geirmundi Flint** – cousin of Geirmarr Flint

Camp followers and Johan's advisors

**Rothgar Kolfinnarson** – second son of Kolfinnar Marlson, late
chief of the Reavesburg Clan. Brother of Nuna Karaswyfe. Pos-

sesses the gift of the Sight and, together with Joldir and Leif, he has formed a powerful Sight Fellowship combining their abilities to serve the Brotherhood

**Etta the Crone** – aged former counsellor and spymaster for Reavesburg's clan chiefs until their fall to the Vorund Clan. Now acting as Johan's advisor

**Joldir** – a mage and advisor to Johan as well as one of Etta's agents. A gifted healer and the Brotherhood's artificer as well as a Sightwielder, he has trained Rothgar and Leif in the use of this skill

**Arissa** – a former bard and adoptive daughter of Joldir, now serving as a healer in Johan's army

**Leif Andersson** – a boy rescued by the Brotherhood when they defeated the durath in Tullen. Possesses the Sight and part of Rothgar's Fellowship. His mother, Lina, has been possessed by the durath. The rest of Leif's family were killed during the occupation by Vorund

**Sefa** – a young woman left destitute after the fall of Kalamar. Now a prostitute working for Ekkill and one of Etta's spies

**Curruck** – a blacksmith serving the Brotherhood

<u>Fallen warriors of the Brotherhood</u>

**[Rugga, the Rock of Kalamar]** – a good friend of Johan, killed in battle with the durath at Tullen

**[Kimbi]** – Kalamar warrior killed in battle with the durath at Tullen

**[Ham]** – Kalamar warrior killed in battle with the durath at Tullen

**[Olaf]** – one of Ulfarr's crew, killed in battle with the durath at Tullen

The household of Gautarr Falrufson at his stronghold of Romsdahl Castle on the southern border with Vorund – currently besieged by the Vorund Clan

**Gautarr Falrufson** – jarl of Romsdahl, father of Ragnar and uncle of Throm and Freydja

**Jora Gautarrswfye** – the wife of Gautarr Falrufson

> **[Hroarr Gautarrson]** – the late eldest son of Gautarr Falrufson, he drowned at sea during a storm

> **[Svena Gautarrdottir]** – the late daughter of Gautarr Falrufson, died of a pox in childhood

> **Ragnar Gautarrson** – younger son of Gautarr Falrufson and his sole surviving child

> **Asta Ragnarswfe** – called **Asta the Fair**, the wife of Ragnar Gautarrson

>> **Hroarr Ragnarson** – son of Ragnar Gautarrson

>> **Halla Ragnardottir** – daughter of Ragnar Gautarrson

**[Egill Falrufson]** – the eldest brother of Gautarr Falrufson and the leader of the Romsdahl household until his death at the hand of Joarr the Hammer. Father of Throm and Freydja

**[Tora Egillswyfe]** – the wife of Egill Falrufson. After her death her children were fostered by Gautarr Falrufson

> **Throm Egillson** – Egill's son and Gautarr's nephew, raised by him since being orphaned

> **Freydja Egilldottir** – Egill's daughter and Gautarr's niece, raised by him since being orphaned. Betrothed to Bandor Johanson

**Audwin Strongshield** – a warrior of Romsdahl, Gautarr's second

**Adakan** – a warrior of Romsdahl, part of Audwin's company

**Haki** – a warrior of Romsdahl, acting as Gautarr's second in Audwin Strongshield's absence

**Domarr the Oak** – the bastard son of Olfridor Falrufson, a mighty warrior, loyal to Gautarr

**Sigdan** – commander of Gautarr's archers

**Svafa** – a warrior of Romsdahl

**Tomas** – a warrior of Romsdahl
**Karlin** – the resident bard at Romsdahl
**[Falruf]** – the father of Gautarr, Olfridor and Egill

The town of Reavesburg, capital of the Reavesburg Clan and site of their stronghold of Ulfkell's Keep, now occupied by the Vorund Clan and ruled by Tyrfingr Blackeyes

**Djuri** – a warrior of Ulfkell's Keep
**Ulf** – a warrior of Ulfkell's Keep
**Haarl** – a warrior of Ulfkell's Keep and childhood friend of Rothgar. Married to Desta
**Desta Haarlswyfe** – servant at Ulfkell's Keep and Rothgar's secret lover before the fall of Ulfkell's Keep. Now married to Haarl

> **Finnvidor Haarlson** – the son of Haarl and Desta, known as **Finn**

**Humli** – Desta's father, a widowed fisherman living on the River Jelt
**Lina Anderswyfe** – Leif's mother, now possessed by the durath and taking shelter with Humli after the Brotherhood destroyed her home in Tullen
**Darri** – the resident bard at Ulfkell's Keep
**Lundvarr** – town elder of the neighbouring merchant port of Noln
**Eidr** – a traveller in Reavesburg
**Kolsveinn** – a traveller in Reavesburg

The household of Hrodi Myndillson in Olt, occupied by the Vorund Clan

**Hrodi Myndillson** – town elder of Olt also known as **Old Hrodi** or **Hrodi Whitebeard**

> **Radholf Hrodison** – eldest and only surviving son of Hrodi Myndillson

>> **Alfarr Radholfson** – eldest son of Radholf and grand-

son of Hrodi
**Jolinn Hrodidottir** – a warrior of Olt and the illegitimate daughter of Old Hrodi
**Arnfast** – a warrior of Olt
**Karl** – a warrior of Olt and Jolinn's lover
**Lars** – a warrior of Olt, Jolinn's second
**Beinir** – a warrior of Olt
**Birna** – healer at the town of Olt

The fallen household of Jorik Kolfinnarson, ninth Reavesburg clan chief, murdered by the Vorund Clan

**[Jorik Kolfinnarson]** – ninth Reavesburg clan chief
**[Reesha Jorikswyfe]** – Jorik Kolfinnarson's wife and Johan Jo-kellsward's daughter
**[Kolfinnar the Younger]** – Jorik Kolfinnarson's son
**Rothgar Kolfinnarson** – Jorik's younger brother, a survivor of the fall of Ulfkell's Keep and now a counsellor to Johan Jo-kellsward
**Nuna Karaswyfe** – Jorik's sister, a survivor of the fall of Ulf-kell's Keep. Married to Karas Greystorm of the Norlhast Clan
**[Finnvidor Einarrson]** – jarl of Ulfkell's Keep
**[Olfridor Halfhand]** – Jorik's weapons master. Brother of Gau-tarr and Egill Falrufson
**[Brunn Fourwinds]** – a warrior of Ulfkell's Keep and captain of Kolfinnar's warship, *Marl's Pride*
**[Amma]** – Nuna's maid at Ulfkell's Keep

Former Clan Chiefs of Reavesburg

**[Reave]** – first clan chief and founder of the Reavesburg Clan
**[Sigborn Reaveson]** – Reave's son and second clan chief, also known as **Sigborn Dragonslayer**
**[Ulfkell Sigbornson]** – Sigborn's son and third clan chief, the last of Reave's line
**[Pengill Svennson]** – fourth clan chief of Reavesburg

**[Oli Pengillson]** – fifth clan chief of Reavesburg

**[Hroar Helstromson]** – sixth clan chief of Reavesburg, Kolfinnar Marlson's grandfather

**[Marl Hroarson]** – Kolfinnar Marlson's father and seventh clan chief

**[Kolfinnar Marlson]** – eighth Reavesburg clan chief and father to Jorik, Rothgar and Nuna

**[Alaine Kolfinnarswyfe]** – Kolfinnar's late wife, mother of Jorik, Rothgar and Nuna

**[Jorik Kolfinnarson]** – Kolfinnar's eldest son and ninth clan chief

Other fallen members of the Reavesburg Clan

**[Anders]** – Leif's father, a farmer from Brindling, killed by the durath

    **[Halma]** – Leif's elder sister, murdered by the Vorund Clan

    **[Gisla]** – Leif's younger sister, murdered by the Vorund Clan

**The Vorund Clan**

**Adalrikr Asmarrson** – Vorund clan chief, Adalrikr took the title from his own father, Asmarr, after murdering him and his three elder brothers. Also known as **Adalrikr Kinslayer** and now styling himself as the **King of Laskar** or the **King of the North**. Adalrikr is a durath and one of the original Sundered Souls created by Morvanos, known during the time of the War of the Avatars as **Baltus, First of the Sundered** and also **Vash-tas, Flayer of Souls**

**Tyrfingr Blackeyes** – Adalrikr's jarl, ruling the territory of Reavesburg from Ulfkell's Keep

**Galin Ironfist** – a warrior in Tyrfingr's service, Blackeyes' second

**Bjorr** – a warrior in Galin Ironfist's company

**Sinarr the Cold One** – Adalrikr's jarl, in command of the siege of Romsdahl

**Randall Vorstson** – a warrior and Sinarr's second

**Kurt** – a warrior in Sinarr the Cold One's company

**Joarr the Hammer** – Adalrikr's jarl, now besieging Romsdahl. Joarr killed Egill Falrufson, the brother of Gautarr Falrufson, in single combat

**Hasteinn** – a warrior and Joarr's second

**Hrodmarr Hroarson** – a warrior of Vorund, leader of Adalrikr's forces in Olt

**Valdimarr** – a noble in Adalrikr's service, his emissary in Norlhast

**Dromundr** – a warrior in Valdimarr's service in Norlhast

**Geilir Goldentooth** – a warrior in Adalrikr's service, conqueror of the Riltbalt Clan

**[Asmarr]** – former chief of the Vorund Clan and Adalrikr's father

**[Dragmall]** – a warrior in Asmarr's service, friend of Thengill

## The Durath

**Adalrikr Kinslayer** – the first of the Sundered Souls (see above under Vorund Clan)

**Lina Anderswyfe** – Leif's mother, now possessed by the durath and taking shelter with Humli after the Brotherhood destroyed her home in Tullen

**Gerrick** – a durath spy, captured in Johan's camp

**[Sandar Tindirson]** – town elder of Tullen on the shores of Lake Tull, secretly one of the durath and slain by the Brotherhood

**[Vandill]** – a fisherman living at Lake Tull, secretly one of the durath and slain by the Brotherhood

## The Norlhast Clan

**Karas Greystorm** – Norlhast's former clan chief, now jarl of Norlhast under Vorund rule

[**Katrin Karaswyfe**] – the late first wife of Karas Greystorm she died in childbirth, her son stillborn

[**Thora Karaswyfe**] – the late second wife of Karas Greystorm, she died of the blood plague.

> [**Gretta Karasdottir**] – the late eldest daughter of Karas Greystorm, she died in childhood of the blood plague
>
> [**Katrin Karasdottir**] – the late youngest daughter of Karas Greystorm, she died in childhood of the blood plague

**Nuna Karaswyfe** – the third wife of Karas Greystorm, daughter of Kolfinnar Marlson of the Reavesburg Clan and sister of Rothgar Kolfinnarson. The marriage of Nuna and Karas was the foundation for an ill-fated alliance between the Reavesburg and Norlhast Clans

**Sigurd Albriktson** – former jarl of Norlhast Keep

**Kalfr Albriktson** – younger brother of Sigurd and warrior of the Norlhast Clan

**Luta Kalfrswyfe** – the wife of Kalfr Albriktson

> **Thyra** – Kalfr's eldest daughter
>
> **Tassi** – Kalfr's eldest son
>
> **Gilla** – Kalfr's youngest daughter
>
> **Varinn** – Kalfr's youngest son

**Nereth** – the leader of a trio of mages, known as the coven, who acted as advisors to Karas Greystorm and tried to prevent his marriage to Nuna. Nereth was imprisoned after she attempted to murder Rothgar and Nuna. Nereth subsequently escaped, her whereabouts unknown

[**Lysa**] – a member of Nereth's coven, killed when she attempted to murder Rothgar and Nuna

[**Shula**] – a member of Nereth's coven, killed when she attempted to murder Rothgar and Nuna

**Albrikt the Wise** – chief counsellor to Karas Greystorm, reinstated to his position after the fall of the coven. Father of Sigurd and Kalfr

**Vrand** – a warrior of the Norlhast Clan

**Brosa** – a warrior of the Norlhast Clan and Nuna's personal

bodyguard
**Katla** – Nuna's maid, previously in her service at Ulfkell's Keep
**Ottama** – Nuna's maid
**Styrman** – a servant at Norlhast Keep
**[Bekan Bekansson]** – the previous Norlhast clan chief, who was killed in single combat by Karas Greystorm
**[Norl]** – founder of the Norlhast Clan

## The Helsburg Clan

**Bothvatr Dalkrson** – chief of the Helsburg Clan

## The Vittag Clan

**Ingioy the White Widow** – chief of the Vittag Clan
**Valka** – daughter of Ingioy and one of her jarls

## The Riltbalt Clan

**Gunnsteinn Haddison** – chief of the Riltbalt Clan

## The Jorvind Clan

**Onundr Arisson** – chief of the Jorvind Clan

## The Kingdom of Mirtan

**Serena** – Grand Mage of the Three Chapters and ruler of Mirtan
**[Ramill]** – mage of Mirtan and the tutor of Joldir and Nereth

## The Gods

**The Creator** – the god who, through his servants the avatars, created the world of Amuran

## The Avatars

**Altandu** – avatar of light
**Arkon** – avatar of war
**Balvarran** – avatar of greed, lust and envy, whisperer of lies in the courts of kings during the Age of Glory
**Bruar** – avatar of fire
**Ceren** – avatar of darkness
**Culdaff** – avatar of the air and winds
**Dinas** – avatar of time
**Dinuvillan** – avatar of good fortune
**Garradon** – avatar of defensive battle, general of Vellandir's forces opposed to Morvanos
**Ilanasa** – avatar of healing
**Lamornna** – avatar of nature and creation
**Meras** – avatar of love
**Morvanos** – avatar of chaos, leader of the rebellion that began the War of the Avatars
**Myshall** – avatar of misfortune
**Nanquido** – avatar of the waters and the seas
**Navan** – avatar who guards the Halls of the Dead in the afterlife
**Rannoch** – avatar of the earth
**Rathlin** – avatar of death
**Vellandir** – avatar of law and justice, leader of the avatars who opposed Morvanos

# ACKNOWLEDGEMENTS

Thanks are due to my wife, Liz, my daughter, Emma and my good friend Laurence Keighley. All of them contributed by reading early versions of Sundered Souls. As a writer it's essential to receive honest, unbiased feedback to help you spot those problems you can't see for yourself because you're too close to the text. This small group played a key role in shaping this book, finding typing errors, pointing out plot holes and giving their thoughts on the realism (or otherwise) of the characters. In other words, they had to wade through a whole lot of stuff, ranging from the mediocre through to the downright terrible, so you didn't have to. You owe them a debt of gratitude, as do I.

My agent, John Jarrold, has been an invaluable source of guidance and encouragement over the years we've worked together. An author's life is one that comes with incredible highs and some pretty awful lows. John's refreshing realism, combined with an infectiously positive attitude to life, has kept my feet on the ground and helped pick me up when I've been struggling. I'm really glad to have him in my corner.

The cover was created by US artist Anne Zedwick. Every time I look at this I'm struck at how the artwork reflects the story perfectly, giving my amateur ramblings a much-needed veneer of professionalism. Once again, she's done a cracking job.

Finally, thank you to all my readers. Nothing gives me greater pleasure than knowing the novel I've written is something you read and enjoyed. It's brilliant reading your reviews and seeing how my writing has connected with you, drawing us into a shared world, even when we live on other sides of the real one. I'm especially grateful if you were one of those kind souls who took the time and trouble to share the word with your family and friends. Personal recommendations and word of mouth are crucial when it comes to finding your audience. For all those people who have gone the extra mile and helped in this way, a special thank you.

Finally, if you want to learn more about me and my writing you can find me at:
Twitter – @TimHardieAuthor
Facebook – @Tim.Hardie.Author.Public
Website – www.timhardieauthor.co.uk

Printed in Great Britain
by Amazon